Paul Thomas is the author of seven novels and a collection of stories, *Sex Crimes*. His second novel, *Inside Dope*, won the Crime Writers' Association of Australia's inaugural Ned Kelly award for crime novel of the year. His fiction has been widely published internationally, and translated into several languages. He has also written several books on sport, and lives in Wellington.

work in progress

paul thomas

BLACK SWAN

To Susan
And in loving memory of my father

This novel was written with the assistance of Creative New Zealand

National Library of New Zealand Cataloguing-in-Publication Data
Thomas, Paul, 1951-
Work in progress / by Paul Thomas.
ISBN-13: 978-1-86941-825-0
ISBN-10: 1-86941-825-5
I. Title
NZ823.2—dc 22

A BLACK SWAN BOOK
published by
Random House New Zealand
18 Poland Road, Glenfield, Auckland, New Zealand
www.randomhouse.co.nz

First published 2006

© 2006 Paul Thomas

The moral rights of the author have been asserted

ISBN-13 978 1 86941 825 0
ISBN-10 86941 825 5

Design: Elin Bruhn Termannsen
Cover design and illustration: Katy Yiakmis
Cover photograph: Photolibrary
Printed in Australia by Griffin Press

Dressed to die, the sensual strut begun,
With my red veins full of money,
in the final direction of the elementary town
I advance for as long as forever is.

Dylan Thomas, *Twenty-four Years*

*To Anna,
with many thanks
for your support.
All best,
Paul.*

part one

one

It begins, as momentous days do, like any other.

I wake up with a headache like distant thunder and inflammatory bladder pressure. You have to be deeply, congenitally lazy to abide this mushrooming discomfort, which can only be relieved — unless you've really let yourself go or have an ultra-docile domestic — by getting out of bed. I stick it out for fifteen minutes. As I stand over the bowl urinating like a buffalo, I probe my ear canals with a cotton bud, an activity that has given me a certain curious pleasure for over forty years.

The thunder gets louder. It's the fallout from another small failure of will — those few extra drinks that separate civilised self-indulgence from decadence. For a couple of decades I've been thinking about — to the point of visualisation — cutting down or even giving up, and during that time my consumption has galloped over the horizon like a runaway horse. But what's done is done and I'm all too well aware of the futility of pious waking-hour resolutions.

I shower and dress in baggy shorts, an extra-large T-shirt

and jandals. A silly get-up for a man of my age, you may think, but I am, after all, a bohemian. I leave the flat, coins clinking in my pocket and a paperback under my arm. On Ponsonby Road the traffic is at a standstill; motorists and passengers do their makeup or babble into cellphones as they wait for the system to unclog. It's high summer. Ahead of me, the harbour is a swathe of chemical blue, shimmering temptingly like an exotic cocktail. Away to the right, the Skytower looms freakishly above the skyline, a monument to the art of the deal. The juxtaposition says all there is to say about this careless conglomeration: nature did its best but it wasn't enough.

The only free table at the café is right down the back where you can hear the toilet flush and the smokers dredge up their two-toned phlegm. A girl with a stud in her upper lip and milky puppy fat sagging over her belt takes my breakfast order: orange juice, pain au chocolat, double espresso. She serves me most mornings but I don't know her name.

'Hey, how are you today?' she drones.

'Fine,' I reply. 'And you?'

My cold smile/grimace forestalls further interaction. She's inert, uninteresting, undesirable and I haven't had my coffee yet. I would happily interact with the manager, a svelte Brazilian whom I once saw at the beach, a fluorescent yellow thong trapped between her caramel cheeks, but she's nowhere to be seen.

The salesman at the next table departs in a sweet-sour miasma of aftershave and hair gel. I take his place, putting another metre between me and the lavatorial noises off, and claim his abandoned newspaper with a mock-regretful little smile at another regular who doesn't possess my scavenging speed off the mark. These days I don't take much interest in what's going on in the world or, indeed, my own back yard; catching up with the news is like shaving — something one does every few days. I do, however, feel obliged to stay abreast of celebrity culture, if only to keep up my side of the conversation.

I'm beginning to feel better. The thunder is faint now, like the bass from the flat next door after I've thumped on the wall for the third time. This, I tell myself, is the benefit of having a routine. The surge of optimism that accompanies a fading hangover is a dangerous thing, a form of hubris. It will encourage me to have a second double espresso, which can't be good for me. How much caffeine concentrate can an overloaded system absorb before the fuses start to blow? It will send me back into the fray at lunch, which in turn will cause me to help myself to someone's cigarettes and what could be more hubristic than smoking? Sometimes late at night and the worse for wear, I have the sense that everything I've ever ingested which is bad for me is still in my system, stacked up like unsold books in a publisher's warehouse, and I'm running out of room.

I pass the paper on to the other regular and turn to my paperback, a 1972 edition of *Goldfinger* that I picked up in a second-hand bookshop, drawn by the cover, a still-life with camera, putter and iron, nail polish and applicator, binoculars, golf ball, semi-automatic pistol, silver tankard, cigarette and lighter, martini glass, speargun spear and, mysteriously, lump of Swiss cheese. By 1972, *Goldfinger* was into its 22nd printing and, according to the blurb, 26 million Bond books had been sold by Pan alone. These numbers would give any writer pause for thought, however lofty their aspirations, however indifferent to commercial success they profess to be.

There's a risk attached to reading in public. The dungareed and ponytailed young man at the next table cranes his neck to see the cover, undergraduate mischief stirring in his watery eyes.

'James Bond?' He retracts his neck and lounges as if he

owns the place. 'Titty titty bang bang.'

I flash my repellent smile/grimace. 'In a nutshell.'

His gaze slides over me like a damp cloth. 'I've seen you around somewhere,' he says, nodding sagely. 'You don't work at varsity, do you?'

If I ignore him he'll bother someone else, but vanity gets the better of me, as it usually does. 'No, but I give the odd lecture.'

'What on?'

'Writing — it's what I do.' I hold up the paperback. 'You could call this professional curiosity.'

'Are you rich and famous?'

'No.'

'Poor and obscure?'

'Somewhere in between.'

'Maybe I've heard of you.'

I put the book down. 'Do you read?'

'Not much.' He bares yellowing teeth. 'Porn, mainly.'

That's inconvenient but I've never had a problem lying to strangers. 'Can't say I've tried my hand at it.'

'You should. Think about it: you'd never run out of wanking material.'

'You have that problem, do you?'

'Well, there's nothing worse than trying to squeeze one last wank out of something that doesn't really do it for you any more. As I always say, there's nothing worse than a bad wank.'

I stand up. I resent being driven out of my café by this maniac but there's no telling what he's leading up to. 'If you'll excuse me . . .'

'Off for a wank, eh?' He consults his plastic digital watch. 'Aren't we the early bird? Personally I try to hold out till morning tea.'

'Happy wanking.'

'Cheers, mate.'

I set off briskly. He calls out that he didn't catch my name but I don't look back.

My flat is on the ground floor of a squat concrete structure that was already an eyesore before some prankster decided to paint it shocking pink. It consists of a kitchen/laundry, a living/dining room, a study/guest bedroom, a bathroom/toilet and a defiantly sole-purpose main bedroom. By now normal, responsible, acquisitive citizens are at work, but I'm not a morning person. I don't mean that I'm a little slow and fuzzy first thing and seldom hit top gear before lunch; I mean that it takes me a good few hours of procrastination to get in the mood for work. I take comfort from Raymond Chandler's dictum that a writer is working when he or she is looking out the window. I seem to have spent half my life staring out windows. You could say it's got me where I am today.

Today will be a write-off in more ways than one. I've got a three- or four-bottle lunch, after which I won't be an afternoon person either. My career is littered with lost afternoons but I don't beat myself up about it. If you can work drunk, there's no reason for restraint, no fail-safe.

It's not as if I'm neglecting a potential masterpiece. I'm between projects, as they say; have been for a couple of months. The older I get, the more time I spend between projects. Given that the projects take progressively longer, my productivity, which wasn't spectacular to start with, is declining to the extent that I wonder how many more books I've got in me. When I was young and fanciful, I saw myself pegging out at the desk in liver-spotted old age, having filled several bookshelves. That expectation has gone the way of all the others.

Not content with running out of steam, I'm also trending downmarket. My first novel, *The Ghost in the Cathedral*, was a searing indictment of the British class system as experienced by a New Zealand war hero at Oxford in the late 1940s. Perhaps not surprisingly, it was more favourably received in the colonies than in Britain. The second, *Forsaking All Others*, chronicled a doomed love affair between an aristocratic young Frenchwoman and a New Zealand painter starving for his art in a Parisian garret. It, too, went down better in the new world than the old. This turbulent Kiwi has since popped up in various parts of the world in various guises — hippie backpacker, revolutionary volunteer, diplomat. His most recent manifestation was as a private detective tracking down a runaway on Sydney's mean streets. True to form, *When All Else Fails* failed to storm the Australian bestseller list.

My flamboyant handwriting covers some thirty pages of my current notebook but there's no progress here and no momentum. There are plenty of 'ideas': woolly premises cocooned in a few woolly sentences. They remind me of the writer who was convinced that his dreams were a motherlode of sensational material. He would often wake up in the night, his chest tight with excitement, in awe of the creativity of his resting mind. Come morning, though, these seeds that would have brought forth great work had dispersed, and no amount of feverish mental effort could bring them back. The solution was to keep a pen and paper on the bedside table; even the sleepiest, sketchiest note would be enough to jog his memory in the morning. Next morning and every morning thereafter he lunged for the pad to find the words: 'Boy meets girl.'

The other day my search engine salvaged an article by Ian Fleming explaining his modus operandi. There was only one recipe for a bestseller, he insisted — the reader simply *has* to turn the page. No doubt he's right but in my heart of hearts I fear that I lack the peculiar talent — or indeed the will — to pull off this trick. I disagree with Fleming's view that most people have sufficiently vivid imaginations to come up with a blockbuster storyline if they'd just put their minds to it. He was ahead of his time: Dr No, Sir Hugo Drax, Ernst Stavro Blofeld and those other foaming arch-villains were flush with weapons of mass destruction. Besides, if you're going to tackle big-picture terrorism, you've got to top not only September 11 but all the doomsday scenarios subsequently aired in op-ed page think pieces: anthrax, nerve gas, dirty bombs, cruise missiles, container ships stuffed with nukes. In other words, you need a livelier imagination than some furrow-browed bore from the University of Manitoba.

I put in a bridge-building call to the books page editor of our daily newspaper. She used to bombard me with review copies until the Saturday morning I went to savour my spiky little piece only to find that some illiterate had tampered with it. I'd written: 'Sad to report, this — the tenth instalment in a series that began in 1984 — doesn't live up to its predecessors.' What appeared under my name was, 'Sad to report this, but the tenth instalment in a series which began in 1984 doesn't live up to its predecessors.' Spot the difference you might say, in which case don't bother sending me a postcard from Disneyland.

The point is, some comic-reading clerk had decided that that's what I really meant to write or — and it was this possibility that caused me to splutter like a thermal pool — had taken it upon himself to improve what I'd written. There are some areas of activity on which I'm prepared to take advice from the man in the street — how to get from A to B, for instance — but writing isn't one of them. So I rang my pal the books page editor and suggested, in the sort of casually brutal way I thought she'd expect from a bohemian, that she should keep her fuckwit staff on a tighter leash. The fuckwit in question was, of course, the lady herself.

She's sent me one book since, a slab of highfalutin pornography written by an attractive young woman, as this crap usually is. I couldn't be bothered with it but when I heard on the grapevine that it was selling like hotcakes and being hailed as dazzling, ground-breaking art, I set about a review with murderous zeal. Having delayed firing off this incendiary device to give it a final, killing polish, I ran into the author at a party. The cover photo was flattering — as they invariably are — but not outrageously so. She was familiar with my work and enthused about it with a shiny-eyed admiration I hadn't encountered for years. I claimed I'd bought her book (breaking my rule about never buying first novels) and was impatiently waiting for a couple of clear days to revel in it at leisure. As her date farewelled the hostess, she slipped me her card (when did writers start having business cards?) and told me, huskily and with a fiery stare, to give her a ring.

More on Tania in due course.

The books page editor greets me with frigid silence.

'Haven't forgiven me, eh?'

'Sorry?'

'Last time we spoke I was a bit rough on your editing. It obviously still rankles.'

'I'd forgotten all about it, to tell the truth,' she says, clumsily emphasising the lie. 'God, if I took it personally every time someone kicked up a fuss over their copy being changed, I'd be in therapy.'

'So you're not expecting an apology?'

'I'm a journalist,' she says. 'I have low expectations.'

'No hard feelings?'

'There never were.'

'So how come you don't send me books any more?'

'You sent the last one back.'

'As I said in the covering note,' I say, 'I had a conflict of interest.'

'Do you still have it?'

'You mean the same one?'

'Well, yeah.'

'Yes, I do.'

'Oh.'

'What do you mean, "Oh"?'

'I'd heard you and Tania had a fling,' she says, 'but there's obviously more to it?'

'As I say, nothing's changed.'

'Well, anyway,' she says, 'I haven't got anything much at the moment but I'll keep you in mind.'

'What about the new Dellasandro?'

'I sent that out yesterday — to Tania, as a matter of fact. She put up her hand weeks ago.'

Lunch is with a couple of female friends. It's all above board: their husbands are old buddies of mine and while I've done many silly and reprehensible things involving women in my time, I wouldn't seriously contemplate being silly and reprehensible with Sally Hampton or Brigit Cole. It has some appeal but no percentage. Although there's something to be said for the two-decade age difference between me and Tania, the late thirties/early forties is the demographic where I really feel at home. Which is where Sally and Brigit come in. They are, to all intents and purposes, ladies of leisure: they can stay in shape and steer clear of the stress that ravages the faces of overstretched mothers and working stiffs in hock to the bank. Sally's a cute little handful; at parties, men queue up to talk to her or eye her covetously from across the room. Brigit could make a bundle doing TV ads. She has the teeth for toothpaste, the skin for anti-ageing cosmetics, the healthy sheen for cereals and mineral water and the aura of suburban prosperity for European stationwagons and high-end investment products.

Every now and again they take me out to lunch. This is

not because I'm a breath of fresh air or a source of enlightenment — they've known me too long to take me seriously and their husbands are more plugged into the Zeitgeist than I am. Their husbands work in advertising and direct marketing: they always wear black, they never wear ties, they listen to Eminem. No, Sally and Brigit pick up the tab because they can afford to. They subsidise me in other little ways as well; you could say I'm their pet charity.

Today is not quite a free lunch: they want the inside story on Tania. They've both read *Submission*; it was their coffee-cum-reading group's book of the month and it seems the ladies didn't quite know what to make of it. But as Sally and Brigit waded through one swampy episode after another they had the comfort of knowing that, wearing my writer's hat, I could tell them whether there was merit that they, being mere wives and mothers, had failed to discern and, wearing my lover's hat, whether *Submission*'s ravening protagonist was a self-portrait.

We lunch at the Viaduct Basin, which is not where I would choose. You can eat well enough here, and if you're into escapism, the sight of a billionaire's mini-liner complete with helicopter and uniformed servants will soon have you imagining yourself in someone else's shoes. But this is a boom village where everyone is on the make. There's no ethic here, only blunt ambition. Be rich, be cool, be envied.

The waiter's pre-programmed familiarity doesn't seem to bother my companions. They order a $75 bottle of chardonnay; I ask for a German beer with the proviso that it's served ice-cold; if not, I don't want it. The waiter seems to think this is eccentricity on a dysfunctional scale but Sally sends him on his way with a burst of frothy charm. The interrogation begins. I report that Tania is twenty-nine, lives alone in Point Chevalier, doesn't drive, works at least ten hours a day and is well into her second novel, which promises to be more of the same. My beer arrives; it's acceptable.

'Is she anything like Louise?' asks Sally.

Louise, *Submission*'s narrator/protagonist, spends the majority of its 396 pages hysterically embroiled in sexual or para-sexual activity.

'Let's see,' I tease. 'They're both lapsed Catholics, they both went to boarding school, they both did arts degrees and hitchhiked around Europe, they both . . .'

'Sex-wise,' blurts Sally, loudly enough to be heard at the next table.

'Well, put it this way,' I say. 'Tania insisted that I read the book before we got into a relationship so I'd know what I was letting myself in for.'

'That seems fairly conclusive,' says Brigit. 'So when she asked what you thought of it, what did you say?'

'I lied — I said it was good.'

'Why did you lie?' asks Brigit.

Sally answers for me. 'Why do you think?'

'That must've been a bit tricky,' says Brigit. 'The lying, I mean.'

'It was,' I say. 'Like most writers, she never tires of discussing her work so I've had to do lots of it.'

I finish the beer and pour myself a glass of chardonnay. Sally waves the near-empty bottle at the waiter.

'I suppose it's your bedtime reading,' says Brigit, turning imaginary pages. '"Now then, darling, which bit shall we do tonight?"'

I smile at her, remembering the maniac in the cafe. 'A Kama Sutra for our troubled times.'

Brigit smiles back, raising her eyebrows laconically.

'All right, spill the beans,' demands Sally. 'Which bits have you done?'

'Well, we've tossed each other off at the movies and in the back of a cab. Useful tip: don't leave home without a packet of tissues. We've done it in the bathroom while our dinner guests talked among themselves. We've tied each other up . . .'

'You're mad,' says Sally. 'You could get arrested for that. I mean, what did the taxi driver do?'

'It was after midnight on a Saturday night,' I say. 'We didn't throw up or piss on the floor or try to bash his head in — and we tipped. I dare say he wishes there were more people like us.'

'Okay, what else?'

'She wouldn't let me wash for a week.'

'Oh my God,' says Sally with genuine queasiness.

Brigit, on the other hand, seems determined to see the funny side. 'Did she return the favour?'

'She was keen to,' I say, 'but I resisted.'

'That wasn't very daring of you,' says Brigit.

'Call me old-fashioned,' I say, 'but I've never felt that sex should require physical courage.'

'And that disgusting thing Louise did to the Maori construction worker,' says Sally. 'Has she done that to you?'

I shrug.

'She has, hasn't she?' shrieks Sally. 'You're sick!'

'I couldn't stop her,' I say. 'I was tied up at the time.'

'How does it feel,' asks Brigit, 'to be in a relationship with a sex bomb young enough to be your daughter?'

'Is that a trick question?'

'Not at all,' says Brigit. 'If Louise and Tania are basically one and the same, then she's not easily satisfied. Rampant as I'm sure you are, Max, the fact is you peaked sexually thirty-odd years ago.'

Brigit has a point. Tania is sex-crazed, although I'm not sure if it comes entirely naturally. She has an image to live up to and, I suspect, is enjoying the scandalised attention too much to let on that it's mostly in her head. Oh, she's got the gear — the garter belts and fishnet stockings and crotchless panties — and the moves, such as offering a taste of her fingers after she's touched herself up under the table, but there's a theatrical self-consciousness about it all. I doubt true wantons make such a drama of it. Why should they? Tomorrow's another day and the show must go on. Tania has the vamp look down pat, but when the costumes come off she's angular and a little awkward — touchingly so. When we fall into each other, I don't make soft landings on succulent flesh; *au contraire*, I risk snagging myself on bony outcrops sheathed in coarse skin. Still, all things considered, I think most forty-nine-year-old men would trade places with me. Certainly the married ones.

'I do what I can,' I say. 'After that, she's on her own.' These two consider me worldly so I don't add that I was a little taken aback the first time Tania slid out from under me and finished herself off. I'd watched women masturbate before, of course, but always with the sense that it was more for my benefit than theirs.

'Louise admits she's incapable of being faithful,' says Brigit. 'Even when she's in love.'

'The issue hasn't come up,' I say.

'You must've thought about it,' says Sally.

Of course I have. Tania works all day and we're together four or five nights a week, which doesn't leave much time for gallivanting. She claims she catches up on her sleep on our nights off and I have no particular reason to disbelieve her. Apart from the mania permeating her book.

'Not really,' I say. 'I don't want to get ahead of myself.'

Our entrées arrive. Sally and Brigit eat without visible enjoyment, like carbo-loading marathoners. I get the feeling that Tania's commitment to sex has triggered a vague sense of deprivation. However, there's an unspoken agreement that while my sex life is always on the table, as it were, theirs are off limits. They know me better than to think I'd snitch if they let slip some tasty revelations or expressed dissatisfaction with their lot, and well enough to know that I wouldn't forget in a hurry.

I ask what they thought of *Submission*. Sally thinks it's over the top: women don't behave like that. Brigit observes that Tania does.

'Women in the real world.'

'You mean women like you and me?' says Brigit. 'I don't think you can make blanket statements about what people do and don't get up to. When all's said and done, you and I lead pretty narrow lives.'

Sally asks her, 'Did it turn you on?'

Brigit shrugs. 'Once or twice.'

'Which bits?'

Brigit transfers her gaze to a point exactly halfway between me and Sally. 'I think my husband should be the first to know that, don't you?'

two

Lunch is winding down. Not before time: we're out of wine and the one-track conversation is starting to drag. Sally, though, is wired. Her eyes glow and her party-girl laughter jars like a car alarm. And she knows I can't resist one for the road.

She squeezes my arm for perhaps the tenth time. 'Attaboy, Maxie.'

As Sally scans the wine-list, Brigit's eyes lock onto mine. These two have different appetites. Brigit's from the school of always leaving something on the plate and in the bottom of the glass. She also runs by the clock so now she's thinking about her children finishing school and her husband getting home from work and what's expected of her. Sally's always one of the last to leave and sees days like these as mental health days. The Hamptons will be having dial-a-pizza tonight and if Rick wants some attention after a shitty day, he'll have to make do with the dog. Sally will be blobbed out in front of TV, radiating do-not-disturb vibes.

So Brigit's look doesn't come as a surprise. I'd expect it to convey the mild, indulgent contempt we can't quite suppress when someone we're fond of but deep down feel superior to behaves in a manner that validates our sense of superiority. And I'd expect it to take in me and my notorious inability to know when I've had enough. But it's not that sort of look. Nor is it a look of irritation or resignation at Sally getting her own way again. It's a look of concern.

The waiter brings a half-bottle of Rose de Provence, a good choice. Sally raises her glass. 'Well, here's to the happy couple.'

'Who said anything about happiness?' I say.

'Okay, here's to the horny couple.' Sally lets rip with her giddy laugh; Brigit seems to be counting the bubbles in her mineral water. 'So when are we going to meet Tania?'

'You want to meet her, do you?'

'You better believe it,' says Sally. 'I want to see this wild woman in the flesh.'

'Once the novelty wears off,' says Brigit, 'she'll probably turn out to be quite normal.'

'What's normal?' asks Sally.

'Fitting right in at our dinner parties,' says Brigit. 'Which involves arguing at cross-purposes and getting drunk and maudlin listening to Pink Floyd.'

'You should get out more, Bridgie,' says Sally.

Brigit smiles. 'I'm not complaining; I like normality.'

'I wouldn't count on it,' I say. 'For a start, Tania hates rock music, especially the old stuff, and she doesn't drink.'

'Well, no wonder you spend so much time in bed,' says Brigit.

When Sally's laugh peters out she puts a hand on my knee. 'Don't take any notice of us, Max — we're just jealous.'

And Brigit gives me the look again.

As we leave the restaurant, Brigit invites me back to her place for a swim. To my mind, a swim is the most effective anti-hangover measure there is, both curative and preventive. I keep a pair of swimming trunks at the Coles and have pitched up there hangdog on many a foul morning after. Sally would like to tag along but decides it's not practical, a conclusion Brigit is quick to endorse. She's had enough of Sally for one day.

We share a cab. Sally sits up front and gives directions to the driver, a stoic Samoan, like a viceroy's wife telling a houseboy how the master likes his tea. When we get to her place she gives us a slack, heavy-lidded grin over her shoulder. 'Okay, you two: keep your cossies on and don't do anything I wouldn't do.'

As we drive away, Brigit throws her head back. Her sigh goes on and on.

'That's our Sally,' I say.

'She's getting worse.'

'You think so?'

'Don't you get sick of the groping? God, it was embarrassing — she couldn't keep her hands off you.'

I shrug. 'Par for the course; we both know it doesn't mean anything.'

'Do we?'

'Well, don't we?'

Brigit looks straight ahead. 'I used to. Now I'm not so sure.'

I shift position, not wanting to miss anything that happens on her face. 'Why not?'

She shifts too so we're facing each other. 'I've just got this feeling she's gearing up for an affair. You're not the only man she can't keep her hands off. I'm talking about guys she doesn't know, guys she's just met. I mean, what are they meant to think?'

'Which guys?'

'We went to a gallery opening the other day . . . I don't

know who they were and I don't think she did either. That's the point though — it didn't matter.'

I say slowly, 'If I was you, I'd be careful who I shared this theory with.'

'What do you take me for? I'm only telling you because forewarned is forearmed.'

I make out I don't know what she's on about.

'Come on, Max, you know how it works: people don't have affairs with strangers; nine times out of ten it's someone they know or work with. Well, Sally doesn't work so that narrows the field down even further. You're not married, which removes one complication, and I think we've just established — not that I thought we needed to — that you have an active interest in sex. From her point of view, you're an obvious choice. For most of that lunch I felt like I was sitting in on a job interview.'

'You put in your sixpence worth.'

'It was either that or sit there like a stuffed dummy.'

That's not quite how I saw it but never mind. 'Well, thanks for the warning. If the minx makes a grab for me, I'll be ready.'

Brigit smiles patiently. 'I'm not being a prude here, by the way. If there weren't other people involved, I wouldn't give a damn what the pair of you got up to.'

We arrive. I stare into the middle distance as Brigit pays. As we walk up the path I say, 'I know what you're saying but shouldn't you take it up with her?'

She puts the key in the lock. 'As I said, I'm thinking about the repercussions — for all of us. If Sally wants to have a fling with someone outside our little circle, that's her business.'

Brigit hands me a towel and tells me to go ahead. It doesn't look as if she'll be joining me which is disappointing; Brigit in swimwear is always a sight worth seeing.

'You're not coming in?'

She doesn't reply right away, which makes me wonder if she's got a pretty good idea what's going through my mind. 'We'll see,' she says eventually. 'Right now I've got to collect Sophie.'

Sophie is their ten-year-old. The school is only five minutes' walk away and this is a neighbourhood of immaculate avenues and strict if unofficial homogeneity. But around here mothers collect their kids from school for the same reason people do all sorts of things — because they can.

Within a minute of taking the plunge, the pressure behind my eyes eases. I thrash up and down the pool a few times, towel off and flop onto a recliner. Brigit has left me a bottle of Becks which is, of course, ice cold. The torrid blast of the noonday sun has toned down to balmy warmth. Leaves flutter, bumblebees hover spoilt for choice by the teeming rose gardens and every now and again an expensive car passes by with a well-bred murmur. There's no machine noise, no insidious rhythms, no DJ rant, no howling domestics. I could easily doze off but there's much to think about. Is Brigit on to something? Is Sally on the brink of going extra-marital? The circumstantial evidence accumulates: wandering hands, pointed eye contact and monomania — there's no conversation she can't hijack and re-route to the Republic of Sex. I haven't dwelt on it for the same reason as Brigit: the potential for upheaval. I like the status quo. I like being treated to extravagant lunches and lounging poolside in this agreeable neck of the woods. I know which side my bread's buttered on.

And yet . . . Brigit's style is thoughtful understatement so I can take it that she believes Sally's past the point of no return — an affair is inevitable, it's just a matter of with whom. Until now I've never entertained the notion that Sally might cast me as the male lead in the private screenings in her head. Something stirs in the damp, matted south. Imagine that:

mother and daughter return to find a tent pitched beside their pool. But these after-school collections aren't the brisk logistical operations they'd be if the dads were on the job. For the mums it's a chance to compare notes, daughters, clothes, cars, jawlines, backsides ... If they use the time well, they'll come away knowing exactly where they stand.

Question: why am I lying here with a swell in my trunks toying with the idea of having sex with a good friend's wife when I've just finished telling her and Brigit, in near-pornographic detail, about my new lover? Because romping with Tania isn't as sensational as I made it sound, and I'm sillier and more reprehensible than I like to think. Which raises another question, one I bobbed and weaved to avoid answering at lunch: how serious is it with Tania? It has one big thing going for it, which is that we don't live in each other's pockets. Tania works all day every day, and when she knocks off she either goes to bed with a book or we make a night of it. She's dedicated, all right; she's also a relentless self-promoter and, I suspect, totally calculating in her choice of material. I suppose most successful writers are. A careers adviser would tell me I'm in the wrong job but what else is there? I was fifteen when I decided I wanted to be a writer; by the time I was twenty-five I was, and have been ever since. Writers don't change jobs. They don't reinvent themselves or resign to 'pursue other interests'. They soldier on, even if no one cares.

Mother and daughter get home. I'm seemly, having got off the subject of a dangerous liaison and onto the deflationary double-header of my relationship with Tania and our respective career trajectories. I rarely go gooey over children but Sophie's irresistible. She sweet-talks me back into the pool and puts me through the hoops like Percy the performing porpoise until Brigit, leggy and lissom in her one-piece, comes to the rescue.

We stretch out on the recliners. Brigit has brought me another beer. Such a thoughtful woman. And attractive. She has one leg extended, the other bent at the knee, one arm on the arm-rest, the other draped over her inner thigh. I'm casually propped on one elbow, hoping she can't sense my swarming awareness. When Sophie demands an audience for her solo aquatics, Brigit obliges, which allows my gaze the run of her body. It pans hurriedly — for this offer can't last — from top to toe. Would she expect this furtive inspection? Do women wearily take it for granted that men just can't help themselves?

Even though I find Brigit significantly more attractive than Sally, nothing stirs in the damp and matted south. That erotic charge was generated by tangibility: if Sally has pencilled me in for her forthcoming trip off the rails, we're no longer in the realm of fantasy. She could make her move at any moment and then it will be up to me... I suppose the illicitness factor contributes to the excitement, although dancing on the edge of the cliff isn't as much of a thrill as it used to be. And if it was the other way around — if Sally had suggested that Brigit had her eye on me — I wouldn't be taking it seriously. Brigit's too sensible, too controlled, too content with what she's got, which is why she has a less overt sexual presence than Sally. I'm sure Brigit and Alan have a robust sex life — I've certainly never heard him join the chorus of the deprived — but her sexuality, like the daring lingerie he no doubt gives her every birthday, only comes out at night, behind their bedroom door.

Halfway through Sophie's sixth underwater handstand, Brigit decides she's done her duty. I wrench my eyes away and fixate on an unremarkable rhododendron. I know she's watching me, waiting for me to look at her, but I'm not wearing sunglasses and, as we know, the eyes are windows to the soul.

She murmurs, 'I guess it's now or never,' swings her legs off the recliner and goes to the edge of the pool, hooking a casual finger under her swimsuit to adjust the fit. Without bending at the knees, she reaches down to test the water.

'Come on, Mum,' cries Sophie. 'It's really warm.'

Brigit poises on tiptoe, then disappears in a fluid, streamlined movement. When she surfaces at the far end of the pool Sophie says, 'Whoa! Awesome dive, Mum.'

Brigit insists that I stick around until Alan gets home — 'He'll blame me if you don't' — so I use the PC in the games room to email Tania: 'What's happening? I'll be here for another hour or so. If I don't hear back, I'll call you after 7.'

At 5.30 twelve-year-old Luke appears, flushed from cricket practice. To put off doing his homework he challenges me to pool: best of three. When I win the decider with a fluky ricochet he shakes hands and thanks me for not letting him win; it bugs him when his father does that. I check the email but there's no reply.

And here's Alan, contemporary as ever in baggy cream linen trousers, a black silk T-shirt and black loafers without socks. He punches me lightly on the shoulder and kisses his wife with gusto. Alan reminds me of those European actors who slum it for the money playing terrorists and criminal freaks in Hollywood blow-'em-ups but really belong in wordy little arthouse films about mad love. He's slightly taller and slightly younger than me, with longish, expensively cut greying hair and a thin, interestingly lined face. Within two minutes of walking in the door he's telling us about his new best friend, a B-list director from LA who's shooting his latest ad. As he talks, he gets two bottles of Becks out of the fridge, flips off the tops and hands one to me. I'm ready to move on — one's always served quality wine in this house, no matter how mundane the circumstances — but Alan is the sort of host who thinks for his guests. Now he's decided I'll stay for a barbecue. Brigit suggests I've probably got a better offer.

'Oh yeah,' he says. 'The lady writer. A hottie in more ways than one, I hear. You don't have to comment on that, mate — Bridgie can fill me in when you've gone.'

She shakes her head. 'My lips are sealed.'

'Yeah, right. So what are you up to tonight, Max?'

'I don't know,' I say. 'I haven't connected with Tania yet.'

'Give her a call and get her over. She's not a vego, is she?'

'Not quite.'

'Food's the least of your worries,' says Brigit, who's taking it easy in jeans and a white T-shirt and showing off her painted toenails. 'Tania doesn't like dated rock music and she doesn't drink.'

'She smoke dope?' Alan asks me.

'Yeah.'

He shrugs. 'Well, that's a couple of things we've got in common.'

I'm interested in Brigit's reaction to this but she avoids my eye.

Still nothing from Tania. I wonder if she was thrown by the name on my email — colefamily@ . . . — and deleted it unread, suspecting a virus or a saliva-flecked denunciation from some sunken-eyed morals campaigner: 'You'll have to answer to God for this filth and I pray that in this instance He is not merciful.'

Out in the courtyard I explain that when Tania's on a roll, she doesn't take email breaks. Brigit asks what sort of hours I'm putting in these days; less than Tania, I say. Alan has changed into shorts and a 'Free Tibet' T-shirt. Why here, I wonder, why now? There's nothing I can do about it. He asks why I don't just ring Tania. If she's on a roll, I say, she won't thank me for it.

'Mate,' he says, 'you sound a bit pussy-whipped.'

'One way of putting it,' says Brigit.

Alan fetches a bottle of pinot noir from a celebrated boutique vineyard. For what it cost, I'd get four bottles of the Aussie quaffer I live on. He starts the barbecue to cook burgers for the kids. When Brigit goes inside he tells me he's almost finished *Submission*.

I wait.

'Pretty out there.'

'Yeah,' I say, 'but is it any good?'

'The critics seem to think so.'

'What do you think?'

'Well, you know, it's edgy stuff. Makes you think.'

'What about?'

'How liberated we really are.' He deftly flips the burgers. 'How we let other people's concepts of what's normal fuck us up. How couples keep sexual secrets from each other.'

'I'm pretty sure it's been done before.'

'Everything's been done before,' he says. 'The trick is to package it so the market thinks it's brand new.'

'Trick being the operative word.'

He shrugs, dismissing my quibble as other-worldly. 'That's real life in the big city, Max. So what's she like?'

'Well, you know how you should always distinguish between the writer and the work?'

'Uh-huh.'

'In her case, you can make an exception.'

Alan looks up from the burgers, eyebrows arched. 'Way to go, Max. I thought you'd lost a bit of weight.'

At 7.05 I ring Tania but get the answerphone. Ditto at 7.25, 7.45 and 8. We don't often go two nights in a row without getting together but this wouldn't be a first. Perhaps she's soaking in an aromatic bubble-bath with the new Dellasandro novel, a 900-page behemoth that has trampled over several reviewers who took it on without adequate firepower.

I finally accept the invitation to dinner, which is a far cry from the traditional barbecue fare of blood and charcoal. Alan grills marinated chicken breasts to go with Brigit's risotto; more fine wine is produced, which he and I swill while Brigit sips like a kitten. We talk about politics and world affairs — or rather, Alan does. He has the full set of liberal opinions buttressed by hours of selective downloading and, like most know-it-alls with a point of view, tends to take it personally when others aren't swayed by his arguments. Over the years I've discovered that the best way of dealing with white liberal guilt in full flood is to nod thoughtfully and help myself to the wine.

When I first met Alan almost thirty years ago he was a conservative of the instinctive, private-school variety. When I remind him of this his counter-punch is to accuse me of turning into a reactionary. I'm certainly more mainstream nowadays but it's all relative. When I was twenty I was, as Alan would say, 'out there'.

If I had one wish it would be for more talent, so I envy hardly anyone who isn't a writer. But I envy Alan. Life has worked out well for him. He's highly paid to do what he enjoys doing. You may wonder what a man of the left is doing working in such a quintessentially capitalist industry as advertising but Alan and his ilk differentiate between creative small c capitalism — in which everyone has a good time and no one gets hurt — and exploitative big C Capitalism, which scours the globe leaving scorched earth and broken lives in its wake. I'm not sure where this leaves ultra-liberals whose superannuation funds invest in big C Capitalist companies.

You may question whether advertising is a worthy profession for someone who considers himself an idealist, given that it cynically panders to our vanities and exploits our weaknesses, but Alan doesn't, which in itself is enviable. He can enthuse about an advertising slogan as if it was the purest poetry ever written, thus 'Oh, what a feeling' rates up there with 'Of one whose hand, like the base Indian, threw a pearl away, richer than all his tribe'. He can find a television ad for instant coffee as magical as *Fellini Satyricon*. How I envy him his conviction that everything he does is brilliant, his incapacity for dispassionate comparison. In this respect he reminds me of Tania.

Speaking of whom . . . I excuse myself to try again.

'This is Tania. I'm either too busy or having too good a time to answer the phone so leave a message . . .'

She'll be in bed now, Dellasandro bookmarked, toys stowed away, sleeping the quicksand sleep into which happy toilers sink.

Things have also worked out well for Alan in the procreation department. Some of the children I encounter are, frankly, monsters. I look at the parents — mild-mannered, reasonable people in the main and not particularly unsightly — and wonder where the fuck did these surly goblins spring from? Occasionally it works the other way round and a couple of turnips bewilderingly produce a charmer just to buck the trend. Sophie and Luke, however, are everything a parent could wish for — bright, lively, attractive, loving. I don't advertise this but I've witnessed scenes in this house that brought a lump to my throat and made me realise what I've missed out on. However, I walked away from the whole idea of family many years ago and it's too late to turn back now.

Most of all I envy him Brigit. In all the time I've known them, I've never seen her berate him or put him down. I've never heard her be disloyal. I've never seen her light up for another man, and a few have tried to find the switch. She gives the impression that she wouldn't swap places with any woman.

At 10.10 Alan puts on The Doors. At 10.15 Brigit begins clearing the table. I struggle to my feet.

'Relax, Max,' she says. 'You'll do yourself an injury.'

Alan remains seated, rolling a joint. He doesn't do much around the house but that's the deal.

When the dishes are done, Brigit comes in to say goodnight. Alan gives vague undertakings about what he and I will and won't do and for how long, which she breezily disregards: 'Just spare me the self-pity when the alarm goes off.'

She blows me a kiss from the doorway and is gone and suddenly I feel tired, sated and ready to be alone. An hour or so later Alan deposits me in one of the plush cabs his firm uses and sends me across town to my empty flat.

three

The limo driver has an immigrant pallor and his sixty-year-old hair has turned a colour I can't name. Thankfully he's not a talker but every so often I catch his eye in the rear-view mirror, prompting a baleful mock-smile. He doesn't know me but he doesn't like me: why is that? What does it take to be disliked at first sight? Has it got something to do with the state I'm in and the fumes wafting off me? Perhaps he's an AA zealot who has hauled himself out of the gutter and now despises anyone who takes a drink. But if that was it, his face would be squeezed into a killjoy frown and he'd struggle to hold his tongue. This fake smile brims with informed contempt. It's the sort of smile you give an enemy when you're sure you've got the upper hand.

He pulls up outside my place. 'Here we are then, Mr Napier. It's all taken care of.'

The accent is prole English. Our eyes meet again and there's a chink in the booze haze. Our paths have crossed before, deep in the past. He made the connection the moment I slumped onto his back seat — having the passenger's name would have helped — and has been waiting for me to catch up.

The smile lingers. 'You don't remember, do you?'

'I know it was a long time ago.'

'Yeah, but I never forget a face,' he says. 'Even when the years have taken their toll.'

Cheeky cunt. 'Well, we've all been through some changes. For instance, I don't imagine your hair's always been that colour.'

'No, it was red — like my politics. They haven't changed. Can't say the same for you, though. I heard you on the radio a while ago: you're a proper little Tory these days, aren't you?'

Now it all comes back. Like many of the pointless episodes and embarrassments that clutter my memory, it dates from the seventies. In my capacity as student activist I took part in a futile attempt to build bridges between the new left — the sons and daughters of the middle class who'd been radicalised by the Vietnam War — and the uppity wing of the trade union movement. The lack of such an alliance had scuppered the May 1968 student uprising in Paris — or so the theory went — and we were determined not to make the same mistake.

A few meetings were held in scruffy, smoky union offices in Karangahape Road. The delegations didn't have much in common: they had blunt faces and alarming accents — Jock, Geordie, Scouse, Brummie; we had soft hands and hair down to our shoulders. For us, peace and nuclear disarmament was the big picture but their involvement in those causes was strictly tactical. Their hearts belonged to Moscow, and the USSR wasn't in the Cold War to make up the numbers. On the home front, that meant undermining the economy even though it was the closest thing to socialism this side of Cuba. Their leader was a union secretary called Willie Smaile who wore National Health spectacles and never raised his voice but could silence that tumult of strangled vowels by clearing his throat. Even then it was easy to picture Willie, come the revolution, signing off on lists of enemies of the people and anti-social elements. And if I'd thought about it, it wouldn't have been hard to imagine my driver, a union apparatchik then, ensconced in the bowels of the state security apparatus where the lists were drawn up. Our group, a raucous debating society of idealists, anarchists and dilettantes, would have been among the first intake at the re-education camps — if we were lucky.

'So I'm not big on political correctness,' I say. 'So shoot me. Anyway, what's an old Bolshevik doing driving a limo?'

'Basic rule of warfare, Mr Napier: know your enemy.'

'I thought the war was over and your lot lost. Consigned to the dustbin of history and all that.'

'Well, that's where your lot and my lot differ,' he says. 'We understand the difference between fashion and history.'

'Speaking of history, what's Willie up to these days? Running a blackjack table at the casino, perhaps?'

'Willie's retired. I hear he plays a lot of bowls.'

I get out of the car. He winds down the window, his secret policeman's smile on full beam. 'As they say, Mr Napier: we know where you live.'

This blast from the past has brought me back to life. When you start drinking at noon, the day tends to disintegrate, and half an hour ago I was a mess with a three-bottle flush; now I'm thinking it's only midnight when all's said and done. Midnight is late to some people but I'm not one of them, not when there's half a bottle of Spanish brandy in a kitchen cupboard and, if I'm not mistaken, a scattering of refugee cigarettes lying low in the study.

I have emails from Tania and my agent in London. Tania's was sent mid-afternoon, before mine to her. It says, 'Can't make it tonight but we need to talk. I'll be in touch. T.'

We need to talk, do we? Maybe she's hit the wall with the Dellasandro book and wants to offload it. Not very likely. I can't imagine Tania admitting to anyone, least of all another writer, that she doesn't have the intellectual grunt to take on the big boys. Maybe she's scored one of those writers' residencies or fellowships they dish out and wants to know how I'd feel about her A) Getting it instead of me, and B) Taking off to Europe or the States for a year. The answers are A) Pissed off, and B) Pissed off.

I open the message from Shelley, my agent, with a tremor of wishful anticipation. Even after all these years I haven't quite stopped believing in fairytales — I don't think anyone in this game ever does — so I still dare to hope it might be the big break. Something like: 'Darling, Hope you've got a bottle of bubbly in the fridge because I've got fab news. You know how I've been banging on to our people in New York for ages now to get your stuff in front of one of the heavy hitters? Well, they've finally delivered — in the form of Lorna Duff at Goldman, no less. AND SHE LOVES IT!!!! To cut to the chase, she's preparing an offer for US rights to the entire oeuvre. She hasn't indicated a figure yet but as one of our guys put it, "Lorna only deals in telephone numbers."'

Or: 'My dear, Do you have a current passport? The reason I ask is that Jeff Dravitz at Shining Path Pictures wants you to get your arse up to LA ASAP to talk about your screenplay. You'd probably given up on it — it must be three or four years, yeah? — but as I've always told you, nothing happens quickly in that industry. Six years from first draft to screen isn't unusual. What's especially brill about this is that Dravitz is a player: if he gets on board a project, it flies. We haven't talked money yet but SPP's going rate for a first-time screenplay is in the mid six figures.'

Or even: 'Max, old thing, deep in the forest something finally stirred! *In the Midst of Life* has been shortlisted for the

Haile Selassie Award, which I'm reliably informed is the Horn of Africa's richest and most prestigious literary prize. Meanwhile your French publishers — remember them? — have been in touch to say they plan to bring out a new quality-format edition of your earlier stuff with some real marketing muscle — and euros — behind it. I always said you were going to be big in France, *non*? It's taken a little longer than I expected but better late than never.'

This is what Shelley has to say:

> Max, After a great deal of thought and much soul-searching, I've come reluctantly but firmly to the view that it's time for us to go our separate ways. The stark fact of the matter is that the relationship isn't working for either of us: I can no longer get fired up at the prospect of handling your work and you're not getting the kind of outcomes in terms of advances, TLC and marketing push that you're obviously looking for. You need an agent who believes in you, who's passionate about your work and will go out and fight for it. I'm no longer that agent.
> If you're thinking that this comes as a complete bolt from the blue, let me gently remind you that I've expressed reservations about various aspects of your recent books and indeed questioned the whole idea of *When All Else Fails,* which never made sense to me on artistic or commercial grounds. If you're thinking you had no idea my concerns were ever more than peripheral, I'd have to say that's because you don't listen too well. While we're on that subject, the fact is that you invariably react negatively to any comment or criticism, however constructive, from any source.

The reason you've been less than well served by your editors over the years is that they get fed up with you carrying on as if the slightest alteration amounts to desecration and eventually cease to care. And if you're now thinking that this amounts to kicking a man when he's down, then I'm forced to say that's entirely in character: your propensity for self-pity and elaborate self-justification in the face of setbacks has always stopped you from learning from them.

I'm sorry if it seems as if I've been storing all this up to dump it on you in one go but it's not about that. In the first place, I owe you a full explanation; secondly, I sincerely believe the best thing I can do for you now is to be absolutely, brutally frank. So here's the bottom line: I think you've lost your way. I think you've lost the vision and voice and original take of your early work and have fallen into the trap of trying different genres and formulae in the hope that one of them will pay off, rather like someone playing a slot machine. The reality is, Max, that most successful genre writers believe in what they're doing. Regardless of what you or I or the critics might think of their stuff, they're as passionate about it and as convinced of its merit as any 'serious' writer. Writers who come at genre cynically, thinking it's just hack-work which anyone can do, will fail and deserve to fail. So if I could offer you one piece of advice it would be this: if you're not passionate about it, don't do it. And if that means you've reached the end of the road, then so be it. You'd be in pretty good company: we both know writers who've lost the drive and run out of things to say. True, some of them still make a good living by repeating themselves with the names changed but I doubt that that's good for the soul.

That's really all I've got say, Max. I hope you don't think too badly of me but I can live with it if you do because I'm sure this is the right step for both of us. I wish you luck, happiness and success in whatever you decide to do, especially if that means proving me wrong.

Best

Shelley

PS My PA will be in touch to formalise the contractual issues. Needless to say, we herewith renounce any claim over the work we've handled in the past.

I read it three times, mumbling the usual slurs, slosh more brandy into my glass and retrieve the cigarettes from under some old photographs in the bottom drawer. The idea is out of sight, out of mind; by definition you can't hide objects from yourself. And why would I want to? There are some things you should never be without in this life and brandy and cigarettes are two of them.

My hand shakes as I light up. This is obviously bad; the question is how bad? Shelley has been my agent for nineteen years. She's not in the super league but then, if she was, she wouldn't have taken me on in the first place. She's a pro and knows a lot of people and her agency has affiliates here, there and everywhere. True, over the years I've sent her many a waspish fax or email and in private I've often cursed her for an idle, feckless bitch. 'Jesus Christ,' begins this windy soliloquy, 'do I have to do everything myself? I've done the hard part; I've written the fucking book.' Periodically, I've sought out other agents and dropped hints that I wasn't 'wedded' to Shelley but no luncheon invitations were forthcoming so I settled for her, for better or for worse. And now she's sacked me. When you've been a writer as long as I have, getting the sack from your agent is a very ugly, very ominous development. It means she thinks you're all washed up and she's not the only one.

I can approach another agent here or in Sydney with a story about the distance and the time difference and the lack of face time but they probably won't buy it; in the global village, everyone lives just around the corner. They'll assume Shelley and I had a bust-up and it won't take them long to work out who dumped whom.

The intercom buzzer startles me. These days I don't often have visitors at half past midnight. I think of the limo driver with hair by Madame Tussaud — 'we know where you live.' Wasn't it about this time of night the KGB made house calls?

I make my way to the kitchen on creaky legs. 'Who is it?'

'Tania.'

A timely reminder: the lower your expectations, the better the news; I was expecting pest activity or a drunk jabbing the wrong button. Tania and I haven't tried tenderness yet but there was a lot to get through and tonight I'll sleep easier for being in her arms. I could buzz her in but I'd rather go to meet her.

From the foyer I have a rear view of Tania through the glass doors. She's talking to someone, which I don't like the look of. She spins around as I yank open the door. She's wearing calf-length boots, a thigh-length skirt and an abbreviated white T-shirt over a black push-up bra. I've mentioned that she can be a little awkward but now she's awkwardness personified. A forced smile comes and goes and she shifts from foot to foot, like a wallflower press-ganged onto the dance floor.

'Hi there. I was in the neighbourhood and saw your lights were on.' Her gaze tilts down. 'You're smoking. I mean, what the fuck, Max?'

This is the paradox of Tania: when it comes to sex, she practises what she preaches which is if it feels good, do it. When it comes to consumption, however, she preaches, and practises restraint. And when it comes to tobacco, she lines up with the prohibitionists, with their shoot-from-the-hip statistics and punitive reflexes. I've rationalised this as a positive in that it forces me to keep a lid on my dirty little secret.

I discard the cigarette. 'Oh, someone left them. I just felt like one for some reason.'

Befuddled and disoriented as I am, I'm aware that something's not quite right and that we're not alone. On the footpath a young man slouches against a snazzy little convertible with its top down. With his painstakingly unkempt hair and clothes and delinquent pout he could be a male model, or just someone who spends a lot of time in front of the mirror.

'Who's he?' I ask.

Tania resists the urge to look over her shoulder. 'Marcus. Look, did you get my email?'

I nod.

'Well, like I said, we need to talk and now's as good a time as any.'

'Does that include Marcus? Does he need to talk too?'

She rolls her eyes, then turns to him. 'Call me tomorrow, okay?'

He pushes off the car, hands thrust deep into his pockets. 'You going to be all right?'

'I'll be fine,' she says.

He flicks me a cold-eyed glance. 'How'll you get home?'

'I'll get a cab.' She stretches out to squeeze his forearm. 'Don't worry about it.'

He nods. 'Okay.'

As Tania turns away, Marcus takes a couple of quick, light steps and assumes the doggy position. One hand sneaks over her exposed midriff and under the waistband of her skirt while the other helps itself to her breasts. Her eyes widen and she bites down on her lower lip. Marcus bows his head to dip his tongue in her ear. She chuckles — a low, drawn-out sound full of pleasure and regret.

'Marcus, behave,' she says, wriggling free.

He backs away, grinning. 'I'll call you.'

'Do that.'

He turns and saunters to his car. Head down, Tania swerves around me and goes inside, leaving me and Marcus to wrap things up.

He opens the glovebox and brings out a g-string that looks familiar. 'Don't take it too hard, Pops,' he says, twirling his trophy. 'Time waits for no man.'

Marcus starts his car as rowdily as one would expect, saving me the trouble of a reply. I stand there sucking down night air and petrol fumes until my nausea settles.

Tania, who's in the kitchen getting a glass of water, doesn't bother to look up as I come in.

'You didn't tell me you had a son,' I say.

'Oh, tres amusant.'

As she brushes past, I flip up the hem of her skirt, which scarcely adds to the sum of human knowledge. She spins around, flame-eyed, with half a mind to slap my face.

I stick my chin out. 'Go on. Just bear in mind: whatever you can do, I can do better.'

She retreats to the other side of the table. 'Understand this, Max,' she says, slitting her eyes, 'if you lay a finger on me, I'm going straight to the cops. That wouldn't be a good look, would it?'

'It worked for Mailer.' I advance and we circle the table

like cyclists in the pursuit. 'You know what this reminds me of? That scene where Louise deliberately makes her lover jealous to provoke him into dishing out some rough stuff. As I remember, he knocks her around a bit, ties her up and sodomises her — sans KY — and she loves every second of it.'

'This isn't a game,' she snaps. I change direction and the pursuit continues counter-clockwise. 'I came here to tell you that our relationship's over.'

'Well, you would say that, wouldn't you? It's not the same if you come right out and say you want to be beaten up and buttfucked.'

She stops. Seeing I haven't planned for the eventuality of getting my hands on her, I stop too. Her upper lip peels back. 'Listen to him. If that was what I wanted, I'd be shit out of luck, wouldn't I? You're pissed, Max, and we both know what that means.'

Yes, we both know what that means.

'I'm getting a second wind,' I say. Or should that be third or even fourth? It's been such a long, liquid day I've lost track. 'I might surprise you.'

She strikes a pose, hands on hips, all apprehension gone. 'Well, I suppose there's always a first time.'

No suitable riposte comes to mind — perhaps there isn't one. What do come to mind are brandy and cigarettes. When I return from the study, Tania is on the sofa, arms folded, legs crossed.

I light a cigarette. She shakes her head, her mouth pulled down. 'Well, if I needed another reason . . .'

'Yeah, let's talk about reasons.'

She stares past me, mentally rehearsing her speech one last time. 'I guess it's partly my fault — I was naïve. I thought we'd be soulmates but we're not and we never will be. The gap's too big. I'm not just talking about the age difference; I'm talking about attitude, lifestyle, taste, where we're at and where we're going . . . What it boils down to is I can't afford to lose my edge.'

'What the fuck are you talking about?'

Now she stares at me, hard. 'How many hours' work did you do today? Or, to put it another way, how many hours' drinking did you do today? You're going nowhere, Max . . . Actually, it's worse than that: you're going backwards. I know where I want to go and I need people around me who'll help me get there, not drag me down.'

'And where does Marcus fit into this masterplan?'

She can't help smiling. 'Marcus is quite simply a stunning fuck. He doesn't have to be anything else.'

'So where exactly do you want to go?'

'All the way. I'm going to be big. Really big.'

I shake my head. 'No you're not.'

'Why not?'

'Because, as the man said, you can't fool all of the people all of the time. Luck and gimmickry and self-promotion will only get you so far, Tania. After that, it comes down to talent.'

She smiles again, the serene smile of the mastermind who's always one step ahead. 'You're so transparent, Max. We both know you were blown away by *Submission*. Look, I can understand that this is hard for you, and feel free to hate me if that'll help, but please, don't compromise your intellectual and artistic integrity. Say what you like about me as a person but this is about the work. You can't have forgotten what that means.'

I pull up a chair and plant myself in front of her. 'Let me tell you something, Tania: I've fucked more women writers than you've had hot baths. There's a very simple formula — a few words of insincere praise and you can pick your hole. You want to know what I really thought of it?'

Tania shakes her head slowly, sadly, even sympathetically, as if she derives no pleasure from seeing me hit rock-bottom.

I go into the study and retrieve the hard copy of my review from the locked drawer of my filing cabinet. I'd forgotten just how extreme it is. It begins by asking how hard it can be to write designer porn. It goes on to say that *Submission* reads like the secret scribblings of a dangerously frustrated librarian dashed off in a hot flush after attending a two-day creative writing course run by the Happy Hooker. And that it does for chick-lit what O.J. Simpson did for interracial marriage. And so forth. And so on. I don't just pound *Submission* into submission, I thrash it to a pulp, then pulverise it into particles of anti-matter. It is, by some distance, the cruellest, most damaging review I've ever written and there are a few authors out there I wouldn't care to meet down a dark alley.

I hesitate. Should I do this? Right now, Tania's in that state of blissful unreality induced by the dramatic success of one's first novel. There's nothing like it for turning heads. Quite why the critics were so insistent that *Submission* was what it manifestly wasn't I'm not sure, but reviewers can be pack animals: sometimes the lead dog goes the wrong way and the rest of the pack follows. And of course there are critics who simply can't tell the difference: give them *Lolita* and some dismal slice of 'real life' and they'd struggle to arrange them in order of merit.

Do I really want to burst her bubble? That will happen soon enough. It's odds-on that the pack will savage her next book. They'll review the content rather than the hype, the penny will drop and they'll be all the more rabid for having been taken in last time. Why not let her enjoy it while it lasts? Sure, she turned out to be a tramp, but why should I have expected otherwise? A few hours ago I was telling Alan — admittedly for effect — that to all intents and purposes Louise *was* Tania. I wasn't born yesterday; I knew all too well that the novel's shallowness and opportunism were no accident. The truth is, I sniffed adventure and found it heady. I liked the thought of squiring around this hot item. I even calculated that it would boost my dwindling profile. No fool like an old fool.

Tania's still on the sofa, insouciantly swinging one booted foot. She doesn't seem surprised that I've returned empty-handed. 'Well?'

'Can't find it.'

'I knew it,' she crows, clapping her hands. 'There never was a review, was there? Trish told me why you pulled out. Fuck, Max, you are so behind the times — that conflict-of-interest stuff went out with the electric typewriter. You don't let the fact you're sleeping with the author stop you from handing in a rave review, especially when the work speaks for itself.'

I shrug. 'I suppose not.'

'Come on, admit it: it blew you away.'

Her face is ablaze with triumph and I'm massively tempted to bellow the truth, even resort to low-level violence to jerk her out of her cocoon of conceit. But I've made my decision and I'll stick to it. 'Yeah, it's something else, all right.'

She nods, satisfied. 'I knew you still had your integrity.' She considers me thoughtfully. 'Sorry about Marcus. It was a spur-of-the-moment thing — I saw your lights on and thought let's do it. You know me.'

'What the hell?' I say. 'He got a kick out of it.'

'He's a very naughty boy . . .'

'But a stunning fuck.'

She smiles dreamily. 'Oh yeah.'

'Worth cutting a little slack?'

'Definitely.'

She sinks back into the sofa, uncrossing her legs. It's been a long, excessive, traumatic day and I'm obviously not seeing straight because it looks to me as if she's parting her thighs. And not just a tantalising fraction either — I could get my head in there. No, it's definitely not me. There it is, in all its neatly barbered glory, glistening at me. Hello there, had a busy night, have we?

What the fuck is this woman on?

I look up. She's watching me with a loose, slightly unhinged grin, not unlike Sally's in the taxi. 'Enjoying the view?'

'Well, familiarity's supposed to breed contempt but . . .'

'Not in this case, right?' She hitches her skirt higher. 'So are you just going to sit there twiddling your thumbs or what?'

'I thought I was dumped.'

'Call me sentimental.'

'One for old times' sake?'

'That kind of thing.'

'There's one problem: I've had a few and, as you said, we both know what that means.'

She sits up straight, all business. 'Come here,' she says. 'Challenges bring out the best in me.'

And this is how I'll remember Tania, hunched over my groin for no reason that makes sense, just living up to her lurid self-image. She might think there'll be something in it for her but there won't — I'll only get one shot at this and it'll happen quickly or not at all. Well, what do you know, there's a train a-comin'. I could alert her, I suppose, but where's the fun in that?

four

Tania's a sport about it mainly, I think, because she sees it as quite an achievement on her part and further evidence that she is indeed a sexual virtuoso. Everything is viewed through the soft-focus lens of her self-regard; everything is assessed and either taken on board or discarded, depending on whether or not it fuels her gas-guzzling ego.

I'm sitting at the table with my trousers back on, smoking a cigarette, unmistakably a spent force. Despite that and the fact that we no longer have a relationship to speak of — we both know we won't be café buddies catching up every other week and I know I won't even stay in tenuous touch — Tania's in no hurry to be on her way. She gets more mineral water and perches on the edge of the sofa with her knees together and an expectant air, as if she's waiting for me to entertain her.

Instead I say, 'What's your agent like?'

'Celia? She's okay — pretty eager to please but who wouldn't be in her position? Why do you ask?'

I shrug. 'I feel like a change.'

'I thought you liked Shelley.'

'Yeah, but I've been with her for nineteen years. It's the longest continuous relationship of my adult life.'

'You need to make some changes, that's for sure, but I'd suggest you start a little closer to home. Anyway, Celia's not looking to grow her client list; she'd actually like to get rid of the lightweights and just have, you know, the *crème de la crème*.'

'Well, that's that, then.'

'I guess I could mention your name.'

'Up to you — if you can be bothered . . .' I shrug again, but my diffidence doesn't throw her off the scent.

'Oh, I can be bothered,' she says with leaden emphasis. 'The question is, can you? What exactly would I tell her? I mean, when can she expect to see something?'

'When I'm ready.'

She shakes her head. 'No, Max, it doesn't work that way any more. You're going to have to sell yourself.'

'I'll leave that to those who've got nothing else to sell.' I stand up. 'And on that uplifting note . . . You want me to call a cab?'

Tania's indifferent shrug closes a tiresome chapter. She orders a cab on her mobile. 'It'll be a few minutes,' she says, 'so what are we going to talk about?'

'Who said we have to talk?'

'I'm really curious, Max: why do you find it so difficult to talk to me about your work?'

'Why bring my work into it?' I snap. 'For that matter, why bring yourself into it? It's almost two in the morning and I've had a long, trying day. I'd just as soon not talk to anyone about anything.'

'Suit yourself.' She goes over to the window to look out for the taxi through the chink in the curtains. I wait, certain that this disengagement won't go the distance. After a couple of minutes she turns to me. 'You know what I'd do if I was you? A serial killer book.'

'Really?'

'Yeah, because people have this craving to be scared. We know there's no creature from the Black Lagoon, right? We don't believe in ghosts or vampires any more and we've pretty much wiped out every species that could threaten us. Okay, space is the last frontier and all that but we've been sending out probes and radio signals for fifty years and it kind of looks like there's nothing out there. Which just leaves other people. Well, despite what the politicians say come election time, we know the vast majority of other people, even the scumbags, won't actually go out of their way to do us harm. We've got to be in their orbit, you know, fucking them or buying drugs from them or working in a bank or whatever. But serial killers kill when the opportunity presents itself and because it gets them off, so we're all potentially at risk. They're the last monsters — and the scariest because they're real and they live among us but we can't see them.'

'You've obviously given it a lot of thought — why don't you do it?'

She gives me a get-with-it look. 'In case you hadn't noticed, I already have a rather large subject of which I've barely scraped the surface. I've also got a publisher and a fan base who want me to go way deeper.'

'A dirty job but you're happy to do it, eh?' She's back-lit by a headlight beam. 'Your taxi's here.'

'Think about it, Max. See you around, I guess.'

'See you on the cover of the *Literary Review*.'

She glows and I could kick myself. I could tell her she makes Shakespeare look like Mickey Spillane and she wouldn't suspect irony.

'Before that, I hope.' And with a coy smile and a little wave, Tania walks out of my life.

There's nothing like your lover walking out at two in the morning after one for old times' sake to make a chap nostalgic. And when the severance follows hard on the heels of a doom-laden professional setback and many hours of steady, at times high-tempo, drinking, the urge to look over one's shoulder is irresistible.

These photographs have accompanied me on my twenty-five-year gypsy progress, going from one bottom drawer to another, concealing cigarettes or drugs or, in weak moments, pornography, only let loose from their envelopes on nights like this. Some were taken on all-but-forgotten holidays and barely ruffle the pool of emotional recall. There are snaps of me nursing an espresso or a beer or a late-night drink at writers' hangouts like Deux Magots, Elaine's and Harry's Bar. There are beach scenes from Portugal, Morocco and Barbados in which some women draw attention to their breasts via full and defiant disclosure, while others favour the traditional method of approximate concealment. There are familiar landmark shots from New York and Rome and touristy vistas from the Greek Islands and New England in the fall.

Some date from my spells in London and Paris, where I stayed long enough to pick up their relentless metropolitan rhythm. And though I contemplated calling these colossal and demanding city-states home, the images now seem suffused with a haze of impermanence. They record hasty arrangements in short-term accommodation, base camps, places to replenish and rest up, even hibernate. The glazed smiles on those soft young faces, the matey arms around the shoulders, the goofy expressions and slapstick poses, the inevitable raised glasses convey a sense of fun being had at all costs, of purposeful gaiety. These are scenes from a protracted wake. We got together to mark the passing of our youth and ended up having a hell of a party because our youth would have wanted it that way. And what kept us at it night after night was the knowledge that when we stopped, that would be the end of it. The party would be over; we wouldn't reconvene at someone else's place next week. When the hangovers lifted, it would be goodbye to all that — the pubbing, the clubbing, the all-night parties, the romantic merry-go-round — and time to make some hard, permanent choices: where to live, what to do, who to marry.

Even as these free spirits cleaned up afterwards, letting in a glacial wind off the river to disperse the fallout from a thousand cigarettes and blocking the footpath with an unholy stack of empties, their thoughts were turning to home. Home: the best place on earth to bring up children, the only place on earth where you could be downtown at five and have a perfect beach to yourself at six. Home: Mum and Dad and the friends for life who knew you inside out and loved you anyway. Home: where you belonged. Not me, of course. Bohemians don't settle down with a wife and kids and a dog and a company car and start building up security. Bohemians believe that if you travel light and live for today, you'll never grow old.

There's a photo of five Kiwi lads on the footpath outside a London pub. We're in T-shirts — mine has the Solidarity logo — so it was probably one of those long, beguiling, velvet twilights when anything could happen and sometimes did. There's me, heart-wrenchingly young, before the thickening and the greying and the moulting and the coarsening set in and the optimism started to drain away. The cheerful yeoman on my right went back to the family clothing business in Christchurch and the wide-open spaces and, I suspect, never looked back. I have an idea the spiv on my left is a solicitor in Hamilton. He may look back but selectively, skipping over his arrest for shoplifting and the time his drunken striptease on a flight to Majorca earned him a night in a Spanish prison and a lifetime ban from British Airways.

He hovers anonymously on the edge of the frame, uncertain of where he stands. I forget his name — he was that kind of guy — but he worked in the money markets, which weren't yet the Aladdin's Cave they later became. He still had more money than the rest of us, and spread it around. I don't remember anyone turning down his largesse but behind his back he was disparaged as a square peg trying to buy himself a round hole. Apparently he went to New York and made a fortune. These days, I imagine, people make a point of remembering his name.

Johnny's also on the outer, but he's just taking a break from being the centre of attention. Johnny was adamant that he was never going home. Home was too small, too slow, too far away. It had nothing he wanted. His father was dead, his mother had entered a dubious remarriage and his siblings were small-minded dullards. Of all the people I met on my travels, Johnny was the one I was determined not to lose touch with. He was a wheeler-dealer who fizzed with energy and had a brainwave every day and I was sure he was going to make a fortune.

Johnny would have given rich people a good name. He was stylish, unconventional, generous to a fault. He would have had a fabulous pad in Chelsea and a villa on the Med where I'd always be welcome. But Johnny went down to Nairobi to check out the safari holiday business. He liked exotic women and there are plenty in Nairobi as a result of the influx of Indian labour early last century. Johnny got Aids and shrivelled up and died in a London hospice. The guy whose name I can't remember paid for his body to be flown back to New Zealand. Everyone comes home eventually.

There's a photo taken by my first wife, towards the end. I'd recognised a semi-famous writer sitting by himself in the corner of a Soho pub. He'd been an angry young man in the fifties; now he was an angry old man. What made him angry now was the encompassing liberal orthodoxy that was starting to flex its politically correct muscles. His targets responded by calling him a reactionary and deeming his work irrelevant.

I hesitated before approaching him because the *Guardian* had dubbed him 'the rudest man in Britain' and he professed to find everyone under fifty appalling, but my wife egged me on, perhaps in the hope that I'd be hurtfully snubbed.

He looked up from his *Telegraph* when I halted on the perimeter of his personal space. 'Friend or foe?'

'Friend.'

'Jolly good. Mine's a large Laphroaig.'

I bought him a drink to prove that I came in peace and was invited to take a seat. He was genial, forthcoming and knew how to take a compliment — with a raise of the eyebrows and 'Do you really think so? Well, that's most gratifying.' But when I let slip that my first novel was about to come out he frowned into his glass. If he was in my shoes, he said, he wouldn't waste his time writing fiction, he'd do something in the city. A young man could do very well for himself in this high-finance racket.

'There's more to life than money, isn't there?' I said.

'Well, there certainly used to be,' he said mildly. 'I'm not sure that's still the case and I very much doubt it'll be the case in twenty years' time.'

The semi-famous writer smiled benignly when my wife took the photo and held his smile while I took one of them, both rosy-cheeked and bespectacled. My wife, however, isn't smiling. The writer was charming but held unspeakable opinions and while she was prepared to humour me, she was damned if she was going to look happy about it. That wouldn't have been true to herself.

He insisted that I send him a copy of my novel, care of his publishers, which he promised to read, provide feedback on (my idea) and wittily endorse when it came out in paperback.

I duly sent it off but never heard back, which didn't surprise me. He probably never received it or, if he did, probably never got around to reading it or, if he read it, probably didn't think much of it. The old-school approach to such a dilemma is that if you can't say anything nice, don't say anything at all.

He's dead now and twenty years have gone by.

Last I heard, my first wife was married to a property developer and living in Taupo. It just goes to show: when I first met Jill, she'd no more have given the time of day to a property developer than drunk South African wine. Her parents were prominent members of Auckland's left-wing intelligentsia; in fact, their house on Takapuna beach seemed to be its unofficial summer headquarters. Father was a professor of French and something of an authority on Camus, Sartre and the existentialist scene; mother was a lawyer always on the lookout for a good cause. They were active in the Labour Party but drew the line at standing for Parliament, no doubt put off by the indignities — some self-inflicted — suffered by their MP friends during the long years of Opposition. At first I took Jill to be a compulsive name-dropper and it wasn't until summer arrived that I realised the writers and intellectuals and political figures whose familiar names rolled so easily off her tongue were in fact family friends.

Jill's parents kept an open house, so on any given weekend there'd be up to two dozen visitors, most of them engaged in the life of the mind or attached to someone who was. For a would-be writer and self-styled bohemian it was as close to the ideal environment as I could find without emigrating. Everyone I met seemed to be some sort of writer or someone who slept with writers. The combination of boozy parties — which often began as boozy lunches — and tangled, overlapping love lives guaranteed regular eruptions of drama and bad behaviour. It quickly became apparent that infidelity, jealousy and declarations of suicidal or violent intent were part and parcel of the literary life. On some sweaty-palmed nights the atmosphere was more saloon than salon and the air crackled with impending violence.

I was to witness a number of physical confrontations, not all of them all-male affairs. Once I had to make a tackle to prevent one of our leading poets stabbing one of our leading historians. When a semblance of order was restored and the poet had been banished — I think a woman might have got away with using a knife but men were expected to settle things with their bare hands, in the New Zealand way — I accompanied the shaken historian on a walk along the beach. Seeing I'd saved him from a flesh wound — the poet was far too drunk to have nailed a vital organ — I felt entitled to ask what the story was.

The historian produced cigarettes and matches and asked me to help out because his trembling hands were incapable of the fast and accurate work needed in the whippy on-shore breeze. After he'd filled his lungs he said, 'I screwed his wife.'

I knew the poet and his wife were living apart because the poet's mistress had told me so only minutes before I was called upon to halt his popeyed charge across the living room.

'Why should he care? He walked out on her, didn't he?'

'Ah, but you see he loves her.'

This was said with such solemn authority that it was obviously meant to answer all possible questions and thus put the matter to rest. My inability to grasp what was straightforward, even self-explanatory, reminded me of my bewildered response to higher maths and basic science.

'So why did he leave her?'

The historian's wheezy exhalation may have concealed a sigh. 'I suppose he was cunt-struck. That's usually why men leave their wives, isn't it?'

'Then why the hell doesn't he just go back to her?'

'Too late — she's decided she doesn't want him.' He smiled grimly. 'There's a lesson there somewhere.'

These were people in their forties and fifties with grown-up or teenage children and not blessed with evident or even subtle sex appeal. For all my bohemian pretensions I found it absurd that these wrinklies couldn't keep their hands off one anothers' wives and husbands. I see it differently now, of course. The clock was ticking. They were running out of time.

Jill's view was that the fashionable open-mindedness that encouraged all this illicit humping was a male con-trick. Men claimed to want only an inch, a little leeway, but they took a mile on the basis that they'd been given a licence to stray. (Personal experience was at work here, as I later realised when she revealed hair-raising information about her father.) She warned me at the outset that I'd get zero tolerance and was true to her word. After several years of occasional adultery I felt obliged to own up to an affair that was threatening to get serious. Jill packed her bags and went home.

I wasn't sad to see her go because I didn't love her and was finding it increasingly hard to like her. She'd always been politically strident but we were living in Britain in the Thatcher years and people like Jill managed to convince themselves that they were an endangered species. Now she woke up strident and got more vociferous as the day wore on. I found Thatcher a bizarre human being but what was one to make of her great adversaries, Comrade Scargill and General Galtieri? Try as I might, I couldn't see that Thatcher posed a serious threat to me or anyone else who stuck to the rules and minded their own business. Scargill, though, was Willie Smaile with a Bonaparte complex, while Galtieri and his colonels had waged war on their own people with the toll running into many thousands of disappeared ones. I couldn't see any reason not to welcome their downfall. Jill, however, was belligerently for the miners and against the Falklands campaign, even though previously she'd passed up sleep-ins on sleet-lashed Sunday mornings to demonstrate against the junta.

So Jill went home to Mum and Dad and, so I heard (for there are always people keen to update you on your ex, whether the news is sensational, unremarkable or the last thing you wanted to hear), to an experiment or two before settling down with her property developer. He, no doubt, cast a professional eye over that beachfront property and did the maths. I can honestly say the thought had never occurred to me. It was only years later, when I eventually came home, that I realised I'd effectively shown the door to an only child who was sitting on a goldmine.

And me and my girl went to Paris. Patricia was an aspiring writer and I had indeed got the ball rolling by praising an article of hers that appeared in the *Times Literary Supplement*. I probably wouldn't have made the move to France if I hadn't teamed up with her. She spoke fluent French — her family had a restored farmhouse near Toulouse — and received a tidy allowance from her parents that survived her doing a flit to Paris with a near-penniless writer she'd known for little more than a month.

I dwell on two photos from my time with Patricia. The first is a blurred shot of an unknown man of unknown nationality, although if I had to guess I'd go for Belgian. His toupee is askew and his face is a riot of emotion led by scalding embarrassment. The photo was taken on the Rock of Gibraltar shortly after one of the Rock's celebrated apes dropped out of a tree onto the man's shoulder and whipped off his toupee. The snatch was witnessed by perhaps thirty people, including half a dozen off-duty British soldiers whose lager-boosted mirth was a thing to behold. On the trip back to our Moroccan resort Patricia and I debated whether the ape had known instinctively that there was something not quite right about the man's hair or whether it had got as much of a surprise as the rest of us.

The second photo is more germane to the big picture. Four people sit around a table in a Toulouse restaurant: me, older and hairier than outside the London pub; Patricia, a slim brunette with startling green eyes and a dreamy smile; Serge, a Frenchman in his mid-twenties; and his American girlfriend, Samantha. Serge's is not a face you'd forget in a hurry — there's a wide crocodile mouth, a beak of a nose and hooded eyes that gleam with private amusement. You could argue all day over this face: is it ugly or attractive? Does he look like a nice fellow or someone to be avoided? He smokes a Gauloise from his second packet of the day and his partially unbuttoned shirt reveals a flat, hard, hairless chest. Samantha has long blonde hair and honey-coloured skin, and whereas Serge's features are unruly, hers are quietly flawless, although a contrary view might be that the whole amounts to less than the sum of the parts. If she was giving the camera a golly-gosh smile, she'd look like the sort of girl who appeared in *Playboy* before Hugh Hefner began to demand a lot more of his playmates.

Patricia had known Serge since they were kids — when her parents acquired their farmhouse they'd leased the attached land to his father. She laughed it off when I asked just how close they'd become, but after we'd broken up Serge revealed that he'd deflowered her and been her summertime lover throughout their teenage years. He had no reason to lie and I had no reason to disbelieve him.

Serge and Samantha's story wasn't your usual boy-meets-girl. She was on holiday in Tahiti with her mother. He was doing his national service, cruising the South Pacific measuring radiation levels and keeping an eye out for mutant dolphins. They met in a bar and spent one night together, making low-key love to avoid waking her mother, who was snoring through a six Mai Tai stupor in the next room. The following morning Serge put to sea.

They corresponded for a couple of years before Serge took the plunge. The reunion in San Diego was a mixed success: Samantha was the same All-American dream girl he remembered, but Southern California was a long way from the Haute-Garonne. Language as such wasn't the problem — he'd learned English in the navy and had a good ear — but it enraged him that Americans made such a big deal of his accent. He'd taken the trouble to learn the fucking language, probably spoke it better than half of them, but still struggled to make himself understood. Once in a restaurant he asked for a bottle of rosé. The waitress talked louder and louder, as if volume was the essence of communication. Finally, a breakthrough: 'Oh, honey,' she crooned, 'you mean blush. We don't drink too much of that around here.'

When it was just the two of them, it was fine; the rest of the time he felt like an alien. When he broke it to Samantha that he was going home she floored him by declaring she'd go with him.

Samantha was as displaced in Toulouse as Serge had been in San Diego, the difference being that she was prepared to bite the bullet. Love involved sacrifice: true lovers were prepared to follow each other to the ends of the earth. She'd had two years of her friends telling her she was crazy to burn a candle over a one-night stand — with a French guy yet — but they just didn't get it. So she put up with the thumping foreign language conversation headaches and the patronising shop staff and the Mickey Mouse appliances and the shoebox flat, the sort of place only illegal immigrants lived in back home. She put up with Serge's friends, who seemed to regard her as a notch on the bedpost of French manhood. She put up with Serge's reliance on her remittances from her mother and his male chauvinism, which she wouldn't have stood from an

American, and his occasional unexplained disappearances, which stirred up troublesome thoughts and the chronic anti-Americanism he seemed to share with every goddamn one of his countrymen and women. And she did all this without making a martyr of herself. I thought Serge was the luckiest man I knew.

That night in the restaurant would have been the third or fourth time I'd met Serge and Samantha. By then I was sure he didn't love her and afraid that I did.

But not afraid enough to run away.

I suggested to Patricia that we relocate to Toulouse. Samantha had given me no reason to believe she felt the same way about me or could be persuaded to do so, nor did I have a grand plan for extricating myself from my relationship and her from hers. I just knew that none of it could be achieved from Paris. I put up a case: the weather, the cost of living, the farmhouse, proximity to the Basque coast, the Mediterranean, the Dordogne, Provence, Spain . . . Everything was in there but the kitchen sink and the truth.

Patricia listened incredulously. 'I might consider leaving Paris for New York or Rome or even Berlin,' she said, 'but Toulouse? That's like swapping London for Birmingham.' I tried to point out that, on most counts, Toulouse was more agreeable than Birmingham but she wasn't interested. As far as she was concerned, leaving the metropolis for the provinces was, well, provincial.

Patricia went back to London for a relative's funeral and to drum up interest in her collection of what she called short stories. They were certainly short and quite nicely written; they just weren't stories. I invited myself to stay with Serge and Samantha in their apartment in the old quarter. It was tiny and, despite Samantha's best efforts, shabby. Her remittance only went so far, especially as Serge didn't let his lack of income cramp his style.

With none of us having a job to go to, we spent a lot of time hanging around the apartment. Samantha was no exhibitionist but she wasn't shy either, and the scale and layout of their place meant that I saw quite a lot of her out of the corner of my eye. The second night we ran out of wine so I went out for another bottle. When I returned they were in the bedroom and Samantha was in full cry. I wasn't sure whether she hadn't heard me come in or couldn't contain herself or simply didn't care. Her fiery embarrassment when they emerged eliminated the latter possibility.

The next morning Serge took off in a flurry of evasions. Whether Samantha was distracted by his absence or discomforted by my presence, the result was a gathering awkwardness. I spent the day walking the streets and sitting in cafés, trying to work out what the hell I was doing there. By dusk I'd acknowledged the insanity of the whole enterprise and returned to the apartment with a clear conscience to find Samantha down in the dumps. Serge was in Marseille, visiting friends from his national service days; he wasn't sure when he'd be back — there was talk of a hunting trip to Corsica. He'd left a number and wanted me to give him a call, presumably to say *au revoir*.

When Samantha went out to get something for dinner I rang the number. Serge answered as if he'd been waiting by the phone. I asked him what the hell he was doing in Marseille; he asked me what I was doing in Toulouse. When I hesitated, he said, 'What a strange pair we are, Max, asking questions when we already know the answers.'

'What are you talking about?'

'I'm sure Sam's told you why I'm here and I know why you're in Toulouse — because that's where Sam is. If she was somewhere else, that's where you'd be.'

Serge had black eyes — I thought of them as cut-throat — and military training, and while he affected a drop-out nonchalance, the southern French are not unemotional people. I was relieved that he was several hundred kilometres away.

I forced a laugh. 'Am I hearing things or are you pissed out of your mind?'

'I didn't see this in the bottom of a glass, Max.' He was as laid back as ever; we could have been discussing France's prospects in the Five Nations. 'It was right there in front of my eyes.'

I thanked God that I'd abandoned this folly before walking into Serge's ambush. 'Listen, Serge, I don't know what put this idea in your head but if it was something I said or did, then I'm sorry. But you can set your mind at rest: I'm heading back to Paris in the morning . . .'

'No, don't do that.' Finally, and confusingly, some animation. 'Think about it, Max: would I be here if I was worried?'

'You're telling the story, Serge, and most of it's going over my head.'

'Oh, come on, Max, you don't have to put up this pretence. I'm not going to challenge you to a duel.'

'Well, that's a relief.' It was the first honest thing I'd said.

'You know, Max, you remind me of Jimmy Stewart in *Rear Window*, except you watch from close range. You've observed that Sam and I see our relationship differently. You know there's an imbalance.' I said nothing, happy to let him do the talking. 'Sam wants us to get married; I don't. When I'm ready, I'll marry a French woman who understands what it means to be married to a French man. It's time I explained this to Samantha, don't you think?'

'Well,' I said, still wary of talking myself into trouble, 'if she believes in a fairytale, then maybe you'd be doing her a favour.'

'How do you think she'll react?'

'She'll be devastated, Serge — as you know very well — and she'll try to change your mind.'

'Exactly. She'll say, "Let's just carry on as we are and see how you feel in a year's time." She'll tell herself that this will pass, as if I woke up in a certain mood. But, you know, the possibility of marrying Sam had never occurred to me until she raised it. For me, Samantha has always been an adventure and when the adventurer has had enough excitement, he goes home to his own kind. He doesn't marry a head-hunter's daughter.'

'Nice analogy, Serge. Very romantic.'

'I didn't create this situation, Max: Sam did. Marriage, by definition, is the end of adventure.'

'So it's bye-bye Samantha, just like that?'

'You know a nice way to do it?'

'When are you going to tell her?'

'I've written a letter. When she comes back, tell her to look under the mattress on her side of the bed.'

'Jesus Christ, Serge, this is going to break her heart.'

'Perhaps. At least she'll have a shoulder to cry on.'

'How fucking convenient. And how long do you expect me to play Florence Nightingale?'

He laughed. 'Really, Max, you're very ungrateful and, I must say, somewhat hypocritical. You'll be Florence Nightingale for as long as it serves your purpose.'

'You seem to be forgetting something.'

'What's that?'

'She's madly in love with you.'

Serge laughed again, a hard, ironic sound. 'Tell me, Max, if you were so sure of that, why did you come to Toulouse? What was the point?'

'I don't honestly know,' I said. 'I hadn't thought it through.'

'You just had to be near her, was that it?'

'Something like that.'

'Just as well I think for both of us. The field is yours, my friend. I wish you luck.'

'She loves you, Serge. That's not going to change overnight.'

'She's a woman, Max, and women respond to tenderness, which I'm sure you have plenty of. Give my love to Patricia next time you're speaking to her.'

He was still laughing when I hung up.

That night I lay curled up on the two-seater sofa listening to Samantha sob, and in the morning she looked through me when I asked if she was all right. She showed no interest when I offered to go out for pastries so I went to a café and wrestled my way through it: Serge was the most cold-blooded bastard I'd ever met and I was fucked if I was going to clean up his mess. I'd advise Samantha to go back to the States; I'd offer to help her pack up and accompany her to Paris; I'd even chip in for the airfare if that was an issue. What I wouldn't do was hang around in that apartment putting her back together every time she fell apart.

These scenarios unfold in an orderly, logical fashion when you rehearse them in your head, but when I made my suggestion Samantha stared at me as if I was mad. Why on earth would she want to do that? Everything was going to be okay; Serge would be back in a few days and they'd work it out. She had the raw, flayed look of the trauma victim, but once I'd adjusted to that I couldn't help but refocus on the rest of her — the doll's face and high breasts and long, immaculate legs. But she was also bright — she had an economics degree from Berkeley — and managed to be perky without coming across as if she was auditioning to host a game show. She could have gone back to a good job and a plush apartment and her pick of any number of presentable, well-heeled men who'd treat her like a princess. Instead here she was in this oppressive flat in a noisy, crumbling building in a town where they spoke a language she couldn't really get the hang of and the few people she knew looked upon her as either a figure of curiosity or a figure of fun, waiting for a cynical layabout to have his fill of the whores of Marseille. This, I told myself with weary resignation, was the real thing. This was mad love.

I asked, 'What did the letter say?'

'That he doesn't love me in the happily-ever-after sense. That when he does get married, it'll be to a French girl.' Her voice got stronger. 'Just like his daddy did, and his daddy before him. And so forth and so on, all the way back to the cave.'

'That doesn't sound like much of a basis for sticking around.'

'Do you believe him?'

'Yes, I do.'

'Why?'

'Serge is very French,' I said. 'He's one generation off the land, a peasant at heart. They're conservative when it comes to that stuff.'

'I meant the part about not loving me in the happily-ever-after sense.'

'I'm sorry, Samantha, but yes, I believe that too.'

'Are you really sorry? Something else he said was that if I wanted love, I wouldn't have far to look.' I coped with this treacherous bombshell as best I could, with a red-faced stammer that she gently interrupted. 'There's no need to apologise, Max — in fact I'm kind of flattered — but I think you and Patricia have some issues to work through. Go back to Paris.'

'What about you?'

'I'll get by. I need to get my head straight so a bit of time on my own won't do me any harm.'

'I think Patricia and I have had it.'

She nodded. 'That would seem to follow. Has she got any idea?' I shook my head miserably. 'Well, if it works out that way, Max, do it properly. Don't run away leaving a letter under the mattress.'

After another night of audible heartbreak, Samantha walked me to the station. Frenchmen don't ogle surreptitiously, even when they're with their wives or mistresses. They stop and stare; they cross the road for a closer look. I felt like Roger Vadim stepping out with Jane Fonda.

On the platform I told Samantha I wouldn't be staying in Paris.

'Where will you go?'

'I don't know. Maybe here.' Her face was quite still and I couldn't see her eyes through the sunglasses she wore to conceal the ravages of that flood of tears. 'How would you feel about that?'

She took a long time to answer. 'Max, you should do what you want to do. As I said last night, I'm not going anywhere.'

We didn't say goodbye as if we thought we'd never see each other again. I watched her walk away, me and every other man on the platform.

Patricia came back from London and life went on. I didn't know what to do so I did nothing. We were on borrowed time but, rather than force the issue, I waited for something to happen. I tried ringing Samantha a couple of times but there was no reply. The third time Serge answered and I hung up without a word.

five

I was in the final, slow-breathing, heavy-headed phase of pre-sleep when Patricia slipped across the border into my side of the bed and began stirring up trouble: 'Do you realise we haven't made love since the day after I got back from London?'

Her tone was whimsical rather than accusatory, as if she was passing on some factoid scavenged from the multimedia info-dump. It was the sort of tone in which children alert their peers to the weird shit out there — 'Did you know that in some parts of the world people eat tarantulas?' One doesn't expect much reaction to these titbits, beyond a muted appreciation of their outlandishness.

'Is that right?' I said with moronic laboriousness, hoping to convey that even the most basic exchange was beyond me.

Thirty seconds passed. 'Uh-huh.' Another pause. 'The question is what, if anything, I should make of it.'

Her tone was still casual but I knew now that the casualness was tactical, enabling her to raise a fraught subject while leaving both of us some room for manoeuvre.

I stirred impatiently and tried to make my voice even dozier. 'What's that?'

Patricia snuggled up to my back. 'We used to do it practically every night,' she said with kittenish nostalgia.

'Jesus,' I growled, 'what's got into you?'

An ironic chuckle floated over my shoulder. 'Well, I certainly know what hasn't.'

And because I knew what was on her mind and didn't want the discussion to reach the point where I was forced into a drastic lie — the indignant boilover that asserts that the other party can't trust the evidence of their own senses and takes offence rather than addresses the issue — I rolled on top of her and demanded, with a pantomime leer, 'If you want a good seeing-to, why don't you just come out and say so?'

She started to split hairs but I swooped down and smeared her mouth all over her face. When her lips and tongue had been wrestled to a standstill, I squirmed to the bottom of the bed and opened another front.

I devoted the next week to sex, dragging Patricia away from her desk and nudging her awake in the small hours. As she wondered aloud what had happened to the happy medium, my lips locked onto her neck and my fingers flew to her buttons. On the eighth day she told me to go away when I barged in on her like Lord Foulheart cornering the new chambermaid. She hadn't had much of a say in the matter recently and hadn't seemed to mind so I carried on regardless until she whacked me on the side of the head with the *Shorter Oxford Dictionary* shrieking, 'Get away from me, you fucking sex maniac.'

So we fell back into the old routine and I revived my Samantha fantasies.

Patricia's parents came over for a weekend and took us out to a restaurant near Place du Chatelet that they'd been going to since the Liberation. From the outside it looked derelict, awaiting the arsonist's torch, but her father confidently pushed the door open and beckoned us in. We followed him up a perilous spiral staircase to two plainly furnished connecting rooms where sleek bureaucrats and their exquisite wives looked us up and down. They were obliged to revise their opinion when a leathery old bird, a near-midget in a chef's uniform, scuttled out from the kitchen to lionise us. This remains the only occasion on which I've been accorded respect in a Parisian restaurant. Madame was a national treasure, an esteemed exponent of traditional provincial cuisine and a canny operator who announced each January that this would be her last year in the kitchen, thus ensuring the restaurant was immediately booked out for months to come.

Patricia's father was a senior civil servant in the Home Office, a keeper of secrets. Being a well-bred, well-educated Englishman, he was scrupulously polite and effortlessly patronising. Her mother was a countrywoman and, I felt, had spent rather too much time talking to the animals to qualify as stimulating company. We worked our way through stuffed cabbage and foie gras and beef and carrot daube in near silence, taking our lead from Patricia's father, who ate and drank with the reverence of a communicant. After an array of sublime cheeses, Madame reappeared with a juggernaut of a dessert trolley.

I suspect that over the years Patricia, who was loquacious by nature, had grown impatient with the solemnity that attended this ritual. There was a certain amount of eye-rolling and she drank more than usual. The moment her father pushed back his chair and removed the napkin from his collar, she intruded brashly on his replete introspection: 'So, Papa, what's happening in the real world?'

And he, for his part, was obviously experienced at deflecting these darts. He gave his mouth a fastidious once-over with the napkin. 'Oh, I think you could say it's business as usual.'

'Father's a decorated veteran of the Cold War,' said Patricia who, while nowhere near as doctrinaire as Jill, took the modish left-wing line on most issues. 'Combating the red menace has been his life's work.'

Ronald Reagan was in the White House, working the airwaves like the old hand he was, dispensing one-liners about the Evil Empire and hard-selling a missile defence system that would have driven a laser-guided bus through the Anti-Ballistic Missile Treaty.

Surely any bona fide bohemian, any serious artist, would join the chorus condemning this terrifying simpleton and those who fuelled his Armageddon complex? But if all sane people agreed that the doctrine of Mutually Assured Destruction was, in fact, mad, why did we regard as sacrosanct the ABM Treaty under which the contending superpowers undertook not to devise and deploy defence systems against nuclear missiles and which was, therefore, a sine qua non of MAD? And if the Soviet Union, with its centrally planned famines and Gulag Archipelago and twenty million and counting exterminated enemies of the state and social engineering through the barrel of a gun blueprint for the Maoists and the Khmer Rouge wasn't evil, then hadn't we might as well retire the word?

Perhaps wanting to get it over with, her father said, 'I imagine that strikes you as the height of futility, Max?'

Whether she sensed my quandary or feared I was crass enough to agree with this proposition, his wife interceded. 'You're putting the poor boy on the spot, Charles. He's probably not the least bit interested in all that carry-on.'

'Well, that's where you're mistaken, Mummy,' said Patricia, who was beginning to enjoy herself. 'Max is something of a student of world affairs.'

'Absolutely,' I said. 'I read *Time* from cover to cover.'

Mother looked impressed; Father's nose twitched enigmatically.

'Actually I'm not sure he would see it as the height of futility,' said Patricia. 'In his own bob-each-way way, our Max is a bit of a cold warrior himself.'

'Well, he's a writer, isn't he?' said her father. 'Perhaps he's noticed how the communists treat their writers.'

'Is that it, Max?' asked Patricia.

'Exactly,' I said. 'Writers of the world unite; you have nothing to lose but your one-way tickets to Siberia.'

Patricia said, 'Seriously . . .'

'In the real world,' said her father, the conviction in his voice all but obscured by his upper-crust drawl, 'and there is such a place, even if you two are keeping it at arm's length, it boils down to whether you believe there's nothing much to choose between us and them or you don't. And if you do, you obviously don't give much of a fig for freedom and democracy.'

'Well, Max?' said Patricia.

'I don't believe in moral equivalence.'

'There,' said Patricia with a tinkle in her voice. 'I knew you two would get along.'

'Well, keep it quiet,' said her father. 'We've got reputations to protect.'

Thankful that a scene had been averted, her mother asked what our plans were.

'Max would like to live in Toulouse,' said Patricia, giving me a curious sideways glance.

'Nothing wrong with Toulouse,' said her father.

'It was just a thought,' I said.

'So you don't want to now?' said Patricia.

'You don't,' I replied. 'You made that very clear.'

'What does that mean?'

'It means I know a lost cause when I see one.'

She reached for my hand. 'Well, there you are, Mummy — it looks like we'll be staying right where we are.'

That night Patricia went to bed happy, as if the cloud that had been hanging over her had been whisked away.

Three months had gone by since I'd been in Toulouse and I'd had no contact with Samantha. I thought about her less and less; the yearning was waning and in another month would simply peter out. Little by little, I'd recommitted to Paris and Patricia. It wasn't that hard: we liked the same things and spoke the same language. We wrote, we exchanged, we praised each other's work. We sat out on our tiny balcony above Boulevard Saint Germain and watched *la vie Parisienne* go by. We wandered the Left Bank, window-shopping in the boutiques and antique shops. We took our books to smoky student cafés. We dined out in reasonably grand style when her allowance arrived. I was earning some good reviews but precious little money so it kept us afloat.

I was still in bed when she got back with the pastries — plain croissant for her, chocolate brioche for me — and a day-old copy of the *Guardian*. She made coffee and came in with a tray and sat on the end of the bed with the paper spread out in front of her.

'I was trying to think when we last used the farmhouse,' she said, without lifting her eyes from the page. 'Seems like ages ago.' Now she raised her head. 'Shall we go down next week?'

I shrugged. 'Fine by me.'

Her smile seemed like an afterthought. 'Serge and Sam could come out for a night.' When I didn't respond she added, 'We don't have to do that.'

'I don't mind.'

'I thought you quite liked them.'

I shrugged again. 'I do quite like them.'

'Okay,' she nodded, 'I'll give them a ring.' She finished her coffee, dropped the paper on the floor and began to undress. 'But first things first.'

There was a third person in our bed. It was as if she'd never gone away.

It was overcoat time in Paris but down south an Indian summer held benign sway. Patricia and I were poolside in our swimming togs — or half of them in her case — with our books and a jug of *kir* when our guests came bouncing up the drive in a 2CV. I shook hands with Serge, who grinned like a pirate, and kissed Samantha's cheeks with middle-aged formality.

They hadn't brought swimming gear but Serge didn't have to be persuaded to strip down to his briefs. Samantha followed suit with some diffidence, perhaps because her stylish lingerie was never intended for public display. She made herself comfortable on a recliner, looking more than ever like a pin-up girl from the age of comparative innocence, before spread legs and clinical close-ups became the way to a wanker's wallet. When Serge used the when-in-Rome argument to try to talk her out of her bra she poked her tongue out at him and rolled onto her stomach.

I awoke from a doze to the sound of Patricia fretting about dinner. Serge was quick to volunteer to drive her to the nearest hypermarket, an hour's round trip, and quick to dissuade Samantha from going along for the ride.

As soon as the 2CV was out of earshot I walked around to the other side of the pool and sat on the recliner Serge had vacated. Samantha looked up with a restrained smile. Thus far, our communication had been limited to a few snatches of half-hearted small-talk. When I was observing her from under the cover of my sunglasses I'd noticed Serge smirking at me, signalling that he knew what I was up to even if she didn't. She'd abandoned herself to the sun, regularly changing positions to give it access to every patch and pocket of her sumptuous flesh.

I said, 'So he came back and you worked it out?'

She shrugged. 'What did I say?'

'What changed his mind?'

'You should be able to figure that out, Max,' she said with a lazy smile. 'You of all people.'

Her complacency disappointed me. Did she really believe it was that cut and dried? One of the things I'd liked most about her was that she didn't seem to revel in her sex appeal or use it calculatingly, but perhaps she'd concluded that the lesson in all of this was that if you act like you're nothing special, you'll get treated that way.

'Ditto you and Patricia, huh?'

I nodded.

'What changed your mind?'

'The same as Serge, I suppose,' I said. 'I went back to appreciating what I already had.'

'So we're all back to square one.'

For me, square one meant being with Patricia but wanting to be with Samantha, whereas there was no place for me in her brimming status quo. She lay back, closing her eyes. Now that the boys had got over their brainstorms, everything was back on track.

'Happily ever after,' I said.

'Oh, come on, Max, put some expression into it,' she said, and rolled onto her front.

It hadn't taken long to run out of things to say. I went back to my book and was still there when the others returned. Serge brought out a couple of beers. 'Oh, I beg your pardon,' he said. 'Didn't I introduce you?'

Patricia appeared. 'What's that?'

'Look at these two,' he said. 'Like perfect strangers around a hotel pool.'

Samantha put down her magazine. 'How close would you like us to be, Serge?'

'The same side of the pool would be normal.'

'We're within shouting range,' I said. 'I'm sure Samantha would've saved me if I'd got into difficulties.'

Serge guffawed. 'So this is the New Zealand mentality: a Frenchman would see a beautiful woman in her lingerie; he sees a lifeguard.'

Patricia draped an arm around my shoulders. 'I think he sees your girlfriend, Serge.'

I looked up at her, feeling the others' eyes on me. Serge would have been fighting back the urge to laugh his head off and surely Samantha would have seen the funny side of it too. The only one who didn't get the joke was Patricia, but then the fall-guy never does.

The women went inside to shower and nap and do things in the kitchen. Serge fetched a bowl of ice, a jug of water and a bottle of Pastis 51. He sat on the next recliner, one eye closed to shut out the smoke curling from the cigarette in the corner of his mouth, mixing the drinks. After we'd clicked glasses he said, 'So you and Patricia . . . ?'

'I've already had this conversation.'

'No doubt — and no doubt you didn't shout across the pool — but I was doing the shopping, remember?'

'Did you push the trolley like a good little fellow?'

'Of course. Patricia was saying her parents are very fond of you.'

'I wouldn't go that far; I'd say I managed to exceed their low expectations.'

'You know what this means, don't you? The fact that she even mentioned it?'

I sat up to help myself to his cigarettes. 'You know her

parents, Serge — do you really think they're delighted that she's shacked up with me?'

'I'm not talking about her parents, I'm talking about her. To me, she looks and sounds like a woman who can hear wedding bells.'

I laughed at him. 'You've got us mixed up, Serge. It's your girlfriend who wants to get married, not mine. Mine doesn't even believe in it.'

He gestured dismissively. 'People say those things. They don't mean anything.'

'What about Samantha? Where does she stand on the subject now?'

'She doesn't talk about it — for the time being. It's as I said.'

'And as Sam said,' I said. 'She predicted that you'd come back and the two of you would work things out.'

'I came back and she was still there. She was in pain and I was the only person who could make it go away.' He shrugged. 'I didn't have the heart not to.'

'In other words nothing's changed?'

'I'm not sure. I think Sam's changed a little.'

'How?'

'You said she was madly in love with me; well, maybe not madly any more.'

'You could hardly blame her.'

'I don't, not at all,' he said. 'In fact it's better this way.'

'Why, because it makes it easier next time?'

He nodded.

'You're a fucking charmer, you are. And by the way, I don't think I ever thanked you for telling Samantha I was in love with her.'

He shook his head. 'No, you didn't.'

Serge did a good line in straight-faced irony but not that good. 'You're serious, aren't you?'

'Of course.'

'What exactly should I have been grateful for?'

'Because, my friend, if you want to grow something, first you must plant a seed.'

'Oh, I see, you were playing Cupid? Well, I have to tell you it backfired. The reason I was on this side of the pool was that Sam pretty much gave me the cold shoulder.'

'And whose fault is that?'

'What?'

'What did Sam tell you?'

I stared at him, fog-brained.

'When you talked about it in Toulouse, what did she tell you to do?'

'She told me to go back to Paris,' I said, 'and sort things out with Patricia.'

'And four months later you're still there, and still with Patricia. How's she meant to interpret that?'

He got up to go to the toilet. 'I know you Anglo-Saxons find women mysterious,' he said with a cruel grin, 'but when they spell it out for you and you still don't get it, *merde alors*.'

I sat there, staring into my glass, listening to him laugh all the way inside.

When it came to entertaining, Patricia preferred to err on the side of overkill. There was melon and Bayonne ham, onion tart, langoustines, duck breasts with cherries, salad, cheese, crème caramel and fruit. The secret to feasting is to pace yourself and it was well past midnight before we were done. Another half hour or so, another splash of Armagnac and a last cigarette, and we would have congratulated the hostess, cleared the table and waddled off to bed. In the course of the drawn-out leave-taking the next day we would have vowed to do it again soon but soon was a matter of months and by then I would have gone cold turkey on Samantha.

That's how close we were. This is how quickly it can all unravel.

We got onto the subject of racism. Not heavily; in fact it began as one of those giddy late-night riffs, half the fun of which comes from not taking a serious subject too seriously. There was some raucous dispute over who were the most racist — the English, the Americans or the French. (New Zealanders were yellow-carded for their obsession with playing rugby with South Africa but the panel accepted my plea that it reflected unworldly priorities rather than ideological kinship.)

Patricia had the French in the dock, citing the recent police shooting in Marseille of an unarmed and apparently blameless Arab youth, which had inspired some lively rioting. Serge was having none of it: the whole affair was a media beat-up; the dead guy belonged to a street gang that ran a protection racket in the Arab quarter and moved a lot of dope; and, as for the riot, that was just a cover for some well-organised looting. When Patricia chastised him for recycling right-wing misinformation, Serge said he'd actually seen the so-called rioters back vans up to shop windows and clean them out.

Patricia raised her eyebrows. 'Really? You make a great witness for a man who wasn't there.'

'Why do you say that?' Serge was puzzled — understandably so, since he obviously wasn't making it up.

She plonked her elbows on the table. 'Because I happen to know you weren't in Marseille at the time, that's why.' The booze was talking and it came across as childish point-scoring.

Serge gave her a look of studied bemusement, which he then directed at Samantha and me. 'She knows where I was better than I do?'

'It happened when I was in London,' said Patricia, reverting to a near-normal voice. 'I remember because I was watching the news with my father and he said much the same as you. I believe it's called racial stereotyping.'

Perhaps if I hadn't been stupefied by food and wine and mentally halfway to the bedroom, I might have seen the danger in this little joust and tried to change the subject. Whether I would have succeeded is another matter.

Serge shrugged. 'So you were in London, so what? I thought we were discussing where I was.'

'Oh, but we are,' said Patricia. 'You see, Serge, when I was in London, Max was in Toulouse. And where did Max stay in Toulouse? With you.'

She'd got under his skin so he didn't pause to consider the ramifications. 'That's right, it was the weekend Max came down. I went to Marseille to see some friends.'

Patricia's expression changed like a traffic light. She said to me, 'So when you said you stayed with Serge and Samantha, you actually stayed with Sam?'

I looked blank, as if I couldn't see why we were having this conversation. 'I stayed with both of them until one of them went to Marseille.'

'You never told me that.'

'What was there to tell?'

We tend to associate alcoholic shedding of inhibitions with sex, particularly of the fools-rush-in variety that batters our self-esteem the next morning, but it can find other outlets. It can, for instance, loosen tongues and deprive us of that invaluable capacity to think one thing and say another, which enables us to rub along with people we don't particularly care for in order to keep our jobs or keep the peace or keep the social circle intact. In hindsight, I see an element of that in Samantha's intervention, which might otherwise have been less direct and her tone less chilly (although a degree of huffiness was understandable seeing she'd behaved impeccably while Serge pimped and I lusted).

'What are you trying to say, Patricia?' she demanded. 'That I can't be trusted?'

And why else would Patricia have responded with this offhand provocation? 'Well, since you ask . . .'

Samantha's face froze. 'Excuse me?'

Suddenly I was back in my former in-laws' house on Takapuna beach, waiting for the final intolerable goad to sound the bell on an outbreak of slapstick fisticuffs. Serge was selecting a cigarette with elaborate care, thereby avoiding the risk of eye contact.

Patricia held Samantha's frozen stare. Going by the bitter tilt of her mouth, her first instinct was to up the ante but she thought better of it. 'Forget it,' she said sullenly, ending the staring match with a toss of her head. 'Forget I ever raised the subject.'

'The hell you say,' said Samantha. 'You can't come out with that, then just tell me to forget it as if . . .'

Serge interrupted quietly. 'Sam.'

She turned her head almost in slow motion, her lips a thin white line. Serge didn't meet her eye. I thought she was going to tell him to go to hell but instead she stood up, picked up some plates and took them out to the kitchen.

Serge downed his Armagnac. 'I think it's time we all went to bed.'

Patricia's face was a gathering storm and the darkness in her eyes showed she was still spoiling for a fight. 'You go to bed,' she told him. 'Max and I have some things to talk about. Don't we, Max? Like you out of the blue wanting to go and live in Toulouse. It's all starting to make sense.'

'I agree with Serge,' I said. 'We should go to bed.'

I stood up. Patricia pushed back her chair but stayed seated. Wine and high emotion had turned her face a painful shade of red, the colour of inflammation, and I knew that she was going to take this thing all the way, no matter what got lost or broken in the process.

'Just answer me one question, Max, then I'll go to bed like a good little girl. You've got to give me an honest answer, though.'

'What?'

'The question is, why was it that after you'd been in Toulouse, just you and her in that tiny little apartment, why was it that after that I practically had to beg you to fuck me?'

Serge groaned and put his head in his hands. Out of the corner of my eye I saw Samantha appear in the doorway.

'I don't know, Patricia,' I said. 'Maybe I was just off sex; maybe my biorhythms were out of sync. But what I do know is this: nothing happened between me and Samantha. You owe her an apology.'

Samantha advanced cautiously. 'Actually, I'd prefer an explanation: you obviously think I'm some kind of slut — I mean, where do you get that from? What's the basis for it?'

Patricia got to her feet. She swayed and dropped a hand on the table to steady herself, and the fire in her eyes dwindled, damped down by fatigue. 'Oh, you're both so fucking innocent, aren't you? Pure as the driven snow. Butter wouldn't melt in your mouths. Well, you don't fool me for one fucking minute.'

She stomped past Samantha, who backed off as if she feared a clawing, and we followed her progress through the house via bumps and thuds and slammed doors. Samantha sat down at the table and the three of us exchanged the silent, shaken looks of people who have walked away from a car crash.

'Where does she get off with that shit?' said Samantha, more confused than indignant. 'Jesus, what did I ever do to her?'

Serge leaned back, closing his eyes against the smoke from his cigarette. 'She's jealous,' he said, 'but at the same time, she feels superior because she's a writer and you're — what? My girlfriend. It's a fact of life, isn't it, that beautiful women are stupid and shallow? She also senses that Max finds you desirable and blames you as much as she blames him, as women often do. They convince themselves that the man's just a silly fly who's been lured into the evil spider's web.'

'Or maybe she's just pissed,' I said. 'She's never had a problem with Sam before.'

'Maybe you just didn't notice, Max,' he said. 'Maybe you had other things on your mind.'

'Or maybe someone put the idea in her head,' said Samantha flatly. 'What did you two talk about this afternoon?'

Serge's wide mouth stretched sardonically. 'Oh, so it's my fault now, is it? Nobody had to tell me what was going on so why is it so hard to believe that Patricia could find her own way to the same conclusion?'

'She doesn't have your sort of mind,' said Samantha. 'It just seems like one hell of a coincidence.'

'I don't think so,' said Serge calmly. 'You heard what she said about the sex and Max wanting to come to Toulouse — it's obviously been ticking away at the back of her mind and tonight the bomb went off.'

They'd slipped so easily into talking about me as if I wasn't there that I wondered if they made a habit of it. 'You've changed your tune,' I told Serge. 'This afternoon you reckoned she was acting like a woman who could hear wedding bells.'

'But where's the contradiction, Max? The more one dreams of something, the more one fears anything that might prevent the dream coming true.'

Assuming Serge was right — and by now I was ready to believe he possessed the rare and dangerous gift of being able to see into the human heart — then all I could promise

Patricia was unhappiness. How could I promise anything else, with Samantha standing in the shadows? Patricia was my favourite companion and my best friend but there was an imbalance, to use Serge's term. Even if Samantha put herself out of reach, sooner or later that part of me that Patricia, for all her qualities and all our compatibility, could not fulfil would seek out another dream lover. I was saddened by my flaws and the trouble and pain they caused, and sadness is deeply wearying. Suddenly I was spent; the journey to the bedroom loomed like a hellish endurance course.

I hauled myself upright, muttering, 'You're probably right, Serge; you seem to have us both sussed. Maybe you should sort out this mess.'

'Leave it to me,' he said with an elusive smile. 'Sleep well, my friend.'

I must have woken up during the night because I remembered hearing a car start. Either side of that bleary hiatus, though, I was shut down, deactivated, brain-dead. When I came back to life the bedroom was stuffy from the sun spearing in through the sloppily drawn curtains. It was after midday. I pulled on some shorts and went to see what was happening but there was no one around. There was just the note on the kitchen bench.

Patricia had written:

Max, I had a long talk with Serge this morning which, among other things, vindicated everything I said last night. You're an absolute shit and I'll never forgive you. I'm going back to Paris to move my stuff out of the apartment. That will take a few days so don't come up before the end of the week — I don't wish to set eyes on you ever again. When you leave, make sure all the doors and windows are locked and everything is switched off and leave the key with the patron of the bar in the village square.

I went for a swim, scraped together some breakfast and rang Serge. Samantha answered. Having awoken at six with a raging headache and no stomach for going another round with Patricia, she'd commandeered the 2CV and driven back to Toulouse.

'How did Serge feel about that?'

'You tell me — he was dead to the world when I left.'

'Well, he was alive and kicking later on.' I passed on the news. 'What the fuck does he think he's playing at?'

'God.'

I asked her to get Serge to give me a ring when he showed up but he still hadn't when I rang from the station on my way back to Paris. Samantha was stoic, as if reconciled to the fact that it went with the territory.

Our apartment had been stripped. Either Patricia had worked on the principle that what's ours is mine or the removalists were members of a Marseille street gang. After some dithering I decided not to go back to London, at least until I'd finished the novel I was working on. The reasons were essentially negative: moving was a pain, the old London crowd had scattered, and being down and out in Paris, the traditional home of the starving writer, was a marginally less forbidding prospect. I didn't bother putting Toulouse into the equation.

Serge rang a month or so later. He'd understand, he said, if I was still angry but it was for the best. He knew Patricia inside out — it was then that he told me, in what seemed like unnecessary detail, of their youthful sex education project — and didn't want to see her get hurt.

'Well, that's very noble of you, Serge, but it wasn't your life you were fucking around with.'

'Do you miss her?'

'Of course I do.'

'As one misses a dear friend?'

'Well . . .'

'She didn't want to be your friend, Max. She wanted to be your lover and one day your wife.'

He was right but that didn't alter the fact that he was a manipulative swine whose real motivation I could only guess at. 'How can I ever thank you?'

He laughed. 'I haven't finished yet: at 4.30 this afternoon the Toulouse train arrives at Gare du Lyon. Samantha's on it.'

'Why's she coming here?'

'To catch a plane back to America.' He gave me a few seconds to digest this. 'But I'm sure she'd postpone her flight if she had somewhere to stay and someone to show her the sights. And after what she's had to put up with here, I imagine she'll find your apartment the height of luxury.'

It was so casual I almost missed it. 'What would you know about my apartment?'

'I stayed there while I was helping Patricia to move out. She was very upset, Max, very emotional. I didn't think she should be alone.'

Once again I had to hang up to silence that biting laugh.

The splendours of my apartment notwithstanding, I seriously doubted that Samantha would be interested in hanging around; once she'd made that momentous decision, she'd just want to be gone. But I went to Gare du Lyon anyway. I wanted one last look, even if it left an ache that lasted for weeks.

Everything she couldn't leave behind had fitted into one medium-sized suitcase. I lugged it to the station café, where we eyed each other warily. 'I'm taking your advice, Max; I'm going home.'

'I doubt my advice had much to do with it.'

'It got me thinking.'

'What clinched it?'

'When Serge told Patricia, "This guy doesn't love you like you love him and that ain't going to change," she listened to him. He told me the same thing but I didn't listen and I had more reason than her.' There wasn't a trace of Californian feel-good in her expression. 'Damned if I was going to go through life knowing she's smarter than me.' She paused. 'What else did Serge have to say?'

'That I should talk you into sticking around for a while and show you the sights.'

'Stick around where?'

'He recommended my apartment.'

'On what basis?'

'That's what I wondered. When he went AWOL after that night, do you know where he went?'

'Carcassonne,' she said, drawing it out. 'So he said.'

I shook my head. 'He was here, holding Patricia's hand.'

She nodded as if she should have worked it out for herself. 'You know the history?'

'Yeah, he slipped that in too. I guess he figured he mightn't get another chance.'

'Well, I don't suppose I can go home without doing Paris properly,' she said, glancing around the café as if it was worth committing to memory, 'and I sure as shit can't afford even a halfway-decent hotel.' Her roaming eyes settled on mine. 'So let's go take a look at this apartment of yours, Mr Max.'

six

It was cold in Paris that winter. Not Chicago cold — the stupefying flash-freeze of the interior — but cold enough. It stung your ears and numbed your toes. It came up through the soles of your shoes and tore through your clothes like shrapnel.

Serge had over-sold my apartment but Samantha confined herself to observing that I'd taken minimalism about as far as it could go short of eating off the floor. It was true that bare necessity had been my guiding principle when I'd refurnished after Patricia's loser-takes-all exit, but there was somewhere to sit and somewhere to lay her pretty head. Besides, she only had a few more days of subsisting on this reduced old-world scale. Soon she'd be back in the land of plenty, inspecting duplexes with three toilets and a water-cannon shower with love-seat. I wondered if she'd pine for a bidet.

We were like cousins meeting for the first time, scratching around for something to talk about despite all we had in common. I opened a bottle of wine and proposed a toast: 'Life's rich tapestry.'

She didn't join in. 'Right now that doesn't do a whole lot for me.'

'Absent friends?'

'Fuck them. Let's just drink to us — us and those like us.'

'Who would they be?'

'I hate to disappoint you, Max, but there's plenty more like me where I come from.'

'I thought Americans were brought up to believe they were one of a kind.'

'I was brought up to believe in God,' she said. 'I don't do that either.'

She slouched on the sofa, long denimed legs crossed at the ankle. Two hours in her company and I still hadn't seen her smile. Her disengagement made me feel like a cold-calling telemarketer: *Good evening, madam, could I take just a little of your valuable time to ask you about your preferences in household cleaning products?*

'So,' I said, floundering, 'how will you look back on your time in France?'

'Well, you know what they say: what doesn't kill you makes you stronger.'

'That bad, eh?'

She finally smiled but only to signal irony. 'France might be saving its best till last.' The smile stretched. Those who insist that Americans don't get irony should spend more time in their own provinces. 'Now there's a challenge for you.'

It had taken some doing but Serge had made Samantha a woman of the world: wary, mobile, realistic. Like a boxer who's been knocked out for the first time, she would never again go out there and ad lib it, just react to what was in front of her, confident that her talent and instincts would keep her out of trouble. From now on she'd stay on the move and out of range. It wasn't about winning any more, it was about not losing. It was about damage limitation.

When I'd first met her and Serge, there was something almost childlike in the purity, the heedless generosity of her love. But, as those who operate at a lower emotional intensity than their lovers often do, Serge had come to see her devotion as a web, sticky with sentimentality. The more of herself she gave, the less he wanted.

He, on the other hand, was determinedly unromantic and lacked those middle-class values that can be lumped under the heading of integrity. He was amoral, perhaps to the point of being a bad man. Even in her infatuation, Samantha must have seen or sensed that, so did she turn a blind eye or was it, in fact, part of his allure? Back home she would have been trailed by a posse of young men with impeccable teeth and Hollywood looks and scrupulous hygiene. What drew her to Serge was his otherness: the neglected teeth advertising his disdain for conventional notions of attractiveness (would Samantha herself have fared better if her beauty had been less obvious, more a matter of taste, if she'd been what the French call *belle-laide* — like, for instance, a young Mick Jagger?), the mysterious scars, the casual depravity, perhaps even the gamy, peasant taste of his cock.

So where did that leave me with my prissy version of otherness — book talk and dull routine and cooked-up dramas — and my daily shower and shampoo? Neither one thing nor the other. But she was different now. Perhaps she was ready for in between.

She was watching me over the rim of her glass. 'What's the matter, Max? You don't seem too thrilled about it.'

'I'm still getting used to the idea. A few hours ago, seeing *Touch of Evil* in the original was shaping up as the highlight of my week.'

'I'm sure it's terrific but we should be able to do better than that, shouldn't we?'

'I've seen it before.'

'Well, shit, if we can't do better than that, I'm not the girl I think I am.'

She'd made a conscious decision to warm up. I wasn't exotic or a little bit dangerous but I wasn't a Californian beach boy either. And I couldn't break her heart.

We ate bread, paté, fruit and cheese, and started a second bottle of wine. She'd miss France, she said, but not the French; she'd overdosed on the French.

'You should try a New Zealander,' I said.

'Why?'

'We have more romantics per capita.'

She raised her eyebrows. 'Really? Do you think Patricia would agree with that?'

'She should. She just happened to be on the wrong end of it.'

'Well, that's the thing,' said Samantha with another ironic smile. 'Someone always is.'

As we were doing the dishes, I asked Samantha what she was most looking forward to. Surfing, she said. Also shop assistants who treated people as potential customers as opposed to a pain in the ass, Mexican food, milkshakes, spa baths, cable TV and household appliances designed in the twentieth century.

'I sure as hell won't miss washing up. We may be ignorant, we may be greedy but one thing we Americans are good at is labour-saving devices.'

'The slave, for instance.'

'Don't you start, Max. I've never considered myself particularly patriotic but after two years of Serge and his buddies I feel like John Wayne. Why do the French hate America?'

'It's a love-hate thing,' I said. 'Love the movies, the jazz, the wild west; hate the wealth and power and predominance.'

'And the people.'

'I'm not sure that Serge and co are representative of the entire French nation.'

'Oh, come on, you have to admit they think they're superior to us.'

'They think they're superior to everyone. Look around: they've got a reasonably strong case.'

Americans are bewildered by their unpopularity. Understandably, since what others often despise most about them is the very thing Americans regard as their greatest virtue (and the wellspring of their plenitude): their ardent optimism. Europe has embraced pessimism as a rational response to history so when America insists that anything is possible and refuses to contemplate or be restrained by the possibility of failure, Europeans hear the thunder of guns and the rumble of cattle trucks. To add to their gall, their impotence is a rubbed-in fact of life since this infantile giant, this nation of sunny simpletons and righteous killers, seems impervious to outside influence.

But Samantha hadn't evangelised for the American way or tried to change Serge, wean him off his earthy rituals and dubious pastimes. On the contrary, she'd embraced him and France, warts and all. And still they'd patronised her and used her and, eventually, pushed her away. In the end she might as well have been an ugly American because being beautiful hadn't stopped them telling her she didn't belong there.

'What do you want from me, Max?'

We were drinking cognac, about to call it a night. It had been a strange and disheartening few hours and we were back to where we'd started: friends of friends reduced to each other's company in a foreign land.

What we had in common above all else was Serge, her ex-lover, my ex-friend, our perverse and persistent Cupid. This was the last arrow in his quiver. He'd thrown us together once before but that had been a crude manoeuvre, based on the flimsy assumption that Samantha would be a sucker for a shoulder to cry on. But he'd learnt from that mistake and this was the culmination of a long, subtle and ruthless campaign. He'd embarked on a reverse courtship, an anti-romance, to force Samantha out of love, and he'd ushered Patricia out of the picture. So here we were, sharing another apartment, but this time with empty hearts and nothing to lose.

'What do you mean?'

'Let me re-phrase that: what do you expect from me?'

'When I woke up this morning, as far as I knew you and Serge were going strong and there was no particular reason to think I'd ever set eyes on you again.'

'Well, you know better now and you've been looking right at me for the last . . .' she glanced at her watch '. . . six hours. You've had plenty of time to get used to the idea.'

'Sam, you know how I feel.'

She nodded slowly. 'I'm all out of love, you know.' She was both defensive and defiant, apologetic and self-justifying, like a hostess fallen on hard times serving up an austere meal. 'That's just the way it is. Serge didn't factor that in.'

'Serge is clever,' I said, 'maybe too clever for his own good, but he doesn't understand the meaning of the word.'

'And you do?'

'I think so.'

'Would you follow me?'

'If you wanted me to.'

'What if I was lukewarm?'

'Probably not.'

'Why not?'

'Because that'd be asking for a broken heart.'

'Well, you see, that's the point, Max: if you're really in love with someone, you don't let that put you off. You take the risk.' Now there was warmth in her smile. 'That's okay, I'm not offended.'

'I'm not sure that's the only definition of love.'

'It's the one I use. Okay, we're making some progress here; we've established what you don't expect, right?'

I said yes because there was no point in saying otherwise. She was travelling light, leaving behind everything that didn't have a place in her new life.

'So back to square one,' she said. 'What do you expect of me?'

'A few days of your life.'

'That doesn't seem too much to ask.'

'What would you like to do?'

'You wanted a few days of my life, you got 'em. Now you've got to decide what to do with them.'

She was still asleep when I looked in on her the next morning, her face buried in the crook of her arm and smothered by golden-blonde hair. Her hand was balled into a childish fist, hopelessly inadequate for warding off predators. She defined love as the willingness to follow someone to a strange land, whether they wanted you to or not. Another manifestation, surely, is the terror you feel for them and for yourself when your unquiet imagination puts them in harm's way.

I'd volunteered for the sofa and she was too tired to argue over what she seemed to regard as a temporary arrangement. 'If you insist,' she said. 'I don't suppose it'll be an issue for long.'

She cleaned her teeth, kissed me firmly on the mouth and went to bed, leaving behind the impression that she'd decided to make me a gift of her body in acknowledgement of the love she was, regretfully, unable to reciprocate. And what would it be to her — another bawdy traveller's tale with which to one-up the Cindys and Debbies and Mary-Anns? My days and nights in Paris. With a writer yet. Drunk the entire time and fucked every which way. Another item crossed off the list of things you've got to do once in your life.

I returned from the patisserie with an outline of the day: the Louvre, a long lunch, a walk through the Jardin des Tuileries and along the river, some stocking up from the food stores on Rue de Buci, a long dinner.

She sat up in bed, enviably clear-eyed. There wasn't a trace of the previous night's wine or world-weariness and my suggestion was endorsed with a luminous smile.

As I went to leave her to her breakfast in bed she grabbed my hand. 'You have no idea how much I'm looking forward to this,' she said, already slipping back into overstatement. 'It's going to be so good.'

All she had to do was exert some gentle pressure, like a canny angler testing the fish's will to resist. After a night squirming on the sofa I was ready to abandon my various dissatisfying roles — considerate host, caring friend, love-lorn wretch — and swarm all over her, making a minute comparison with the perfect specimen of my imagination. But she withdrew her hand, replacing it with the empty café au lait bowl, and asked, 'Any more where that came from?'

It took almost three hours for Samantha to confess that she'd exhausted her capacity for appreciating old paintings.

'I've worked out what I feel like,' she said. She sounded relieved, as if she'd no longer have to strive for something that would always be out of her reach. 'I feel like a laboratory rat eating itself to death. You know those experiments where they keep feeding rats to see if they know when enough is enough? Except that to a rat there's no such thing as enough. Even though they've blimped out to twice their normal size, they can't help themselves; if it's there, they'll eat it, and they'll keep on eating until it kills them. You see all these paintings that kind of look the same; then you go into the next room and there's another bunch of paintings that kind of look the same.

Then you go into the next hall and there's a shitload more that look exactly the same as the ones you just saw in the last hall. But because this is the Louvre and you're an airhead from California, you keep on staring at them with that "Oh, wow, isn't that just so fucking amazing" expression, even though deep down you never want to see another painting as long as you live. Is it just me? Please don't answer that if it's a yes.'

'High culture gives you headaches,' I said. 'That's official. They did a study on it.'

'Does it give you a headache?'

'You bet. It kicked in an hour ago.'

'But you're a writer,' she said. 'An artist.'

'In America,' I said, 'you make a TV commercial and you can call yourself an artist; over here they set the bar a little higher.'

'Why shouldn't creative people call themselves artists?'

'Would you call television an art form? How about Hollywood movies or pop music? Or are they in fact industries in which organisations with R and D departments and budget directors and sales and marketing bullshitters generate and hype product with the aim of making lots of money? If it's the latter, you have to ask whether that process can produce works of art. The European view is that it can't — that art and commerce are incompatible for a host of reasons, starting with the fundamental commercial principle that the wider a product's appeal, the better it will sell.'

She pulled her scarf tighter. 'That's got a familiar ring.'

'Familiar as in the sort of thing Serge would say?'

'Familiar as in the sort of thing Serge did say — ad fucking nauseam.'

'I get the message.'

'If you feel an anti-American outburst coming on, just change the subject,' she said. 'I won't take it as an insult to my intelligence.'

'Be nice, in other words?'

'Be nice, Max. Make me happy.'

We had lunch at a little bistro behind the Louvre, packed with Paris municipal workers fuelling up on eaux de vie before going back to their man-holes and safety checks. Thirty-odd heads turned as one when we walked in; thirty-odd Gauloises were momentarily neglected. An old boy raised his glass to me with a goatish smirk.

We sat down; the hubbub resumed. I said, 'Do you ever get used to it?'

'You wouldn't go out much if you didn't.'

'So it doesn't bother you?'

She shrugged, her mouth assuming a Gallic shape. 'I caught on pretty early that being good-looking isn't all it's cracked up to be but you know what? The ones who aren't don't seem real happy about it.'

We ordered and got started on the house red. I was playing the old Paris hand, promising Samantha as much authenticity as she could handle, when she burst out laughing.

'I'm not laughing at you,' she said, sliding a hand across the table. 'I just had the weirdest thought. You know what this reminds me of? Losing my virginity.'

I said, sincerely, 'That's interesting.'

'I was in a coffee shop with this guy. He's talking about I don't what because I'm not really listening. I'm not listening because I'm thinking about what we'll be doing before the afternoon's out.'

I looked at my watch; it was almost 2.30. 'Does that mean we'll have to skip the cheese?'

She laughed again. She still had hold of my hand. 'Hey, if there's one thing I learned from Serge, it's never, ever come between a man and his *fromage*.'

'How old were you?'

'Fifteen. In my circle, if you held out for much longer

than that, you were some kind of freak.'

'Who was the lucky guy?'

'Brett Watts. Brett had perfect hair and a killer tan. I've seen some impressive tans in my time but he was like straight out of a Coppertone commercial. People were always asking him what his secret was.'

'A full head of hair and latent skin cancer: what more could a girl want?'

'For the purpose under discussion, I can only think of one other thing and the word on the grapevine was that he measured up in that department. My friends fell into two groups: those who'd screwed him and a somewhat larger group of those who were ready, willing and able if called upon. That was a big part of the attraction.' She leaned back, letting go of my hand. 'You've got to look at it from the point of view of a fifteen-year-old virgin: he came highly recommended, he was much sought after and I felt it was important not to sell myself short.'

'Did he live up to his reputation?'

'Well, it wasn't seventh heaven but, you know, he got the job done. It was better the second time. And better still the time after that. And so it went.'

'So you became sweethearts?'

She raised her eyebrows. 'Who said anything about sweethearts? It didn't last. I mean, let's face it, hair is hair; it can only take you so far, especially if there's not much underneath it. It wasn't until after I'd dumped him that I realised that San Diego boys were all the same.'

'Hence Serge?'

'Easy on the fast-forward button, Jack — I had some living to do before he came along. Contrary to popular opinion, there's a reasonable amount of variety on offer in California if you look hard enough.'

'Which you did?'

'In every nook and cranny. Down every hole. Under every rock. No man was safe from her all-consuming lust.'

'Who'd want to be?'

'I can tell you've never been to San Francisco. Here's another thing: there was no one before Brett, obviously, and there's been no one else since I met Serge. That's three and a half years.'

'How does that make you feel?'

Her eyes glowed suggestively. 'Like the girl in that song.'

'Which song?'

'"Like a Virgin."'

Madonna was still a novelty act then and it would be a few years before Quentin Tarantino explained that the virgin in the song was, in fact, a nymphomaniac who'd bitten off more than she could chew. You never hear that song any more and I, for one, am not complaining.

I said, 'As you were thinking about what you and Brett would be up to before the afternoon was out — where, as a matter of interest, given that you obviously didn't need the cover of darkness?'

'Both his parents worked. A lot of stuff went down in their house that summer.'

'Who did the laundry?'

She stared. 'I can't think of anyone else I've ever met who'd ask that. The maid did the laundry.'

'I'm a writer,' I said. 'I need that sort of information. It explains how you got away with it. In the movies they skate over that sort of stuff because the audience doesn't have time to think. So what was the maid doing while all these teenage sex maniacs . . .'

'Isn't that what you writers call a tautology?'

'. . . while all these teenagers were running wild in her employers' house?'

'Minding her own business, as she was being paid to do by

Brett and his buddies. She was from El Salvador, an illegal immigrant, needless to say.'

'That's perfect: initiative, opportunism, corruption — America in a nutshell.' She let that one go; she was really starting to unwind. 'Anyway, what I was going to ask was, as you were thinking about what you'd be doing before the afternoon was out, were you already aware, deep down, that you were doing to dump him?'

She frowned. 'Why do you ask?'

'I'm interested in the workings of a woman's mind.'

'I wasn't a woman, Max, and my mind, such as it was, wasn't a sophisticated instrument. I honestly can't remember what I thought but I'm pretty sure it didn't involve us growing old together. I guess you could say I was coming at it primarily from a . . .' — she paused, trying to shake loose the right word — '. . . practical perspective.'

'It was on your to-do list, right? Learn the guitar, get a tattoo, lose my cherry.'

'Exactly.' She mimicked a tick. 'That's that taken care of. Now, let's see, what's next?'

'What was?'

'Drugs, of course.'

Samantha didn't have much to say on the walk back to the apartment. Paris can do that: it can render conversation superfluous and cause the most self-absorbed prattler — which she wasn't — to ponder their place in the grand scheme of things. But I was buzzing with nervous anticipation and couldn't help analysing her reticence. Was she having second thoughts? That seemed unlikely. Over lunch she had, in effect, distinguished between romantic sex, which was a big deal, and recreational sex, which wasn't. The latter was just something you did when you felt like it; not as routine as eating or sleeping but on a par with, say, working out.

That, coupled with my sense that sex was to be my consolation prize, a sweet coating on the bitter pill, raised the prospect of a dutiful physical engagement preceded by quasi-transactional stiltedness: Do you want to use the bathroom? No, no, you go first. Would I return from my ablutions to find her primly abed with the blankets hauled up to her chin, staring stoically at the ceiling, finger poised over the bedside light switch? Would she hustle through it like someone rugging up on a cold morning, as if there was no percentage in dilly-dallying?

We were walking along the embankment, between Pont des Arts and Pont Neuf. A sightseeing boat laden with Japanese tourists came chugging up the river. Some of them waved. We waved back. Camera lights flashed in the murky twilight. Samantha clamped a hand on the back of my neck and tilted her face up. Her mouth was soft and hot and wide open. There was a smattering of applause from the boat but when we drew apart it had ghosted into the shadows of L'Ile de la Cité.

Her eyes were cloudy with arousal. 'Recorded for posterity.'

The first time is the one I revisit on sleepless nights when I ransack my memory for reasons to feel good about myself, as they say. Not that it was all downhill from there. Far from it. It was even better the second time. And better still the time after that. And so it went.

It began with a grapple on the landing, bouncing off thin, ancient walls. How many frantic lovers had they framed over the centuries? We took the last flight of stairs two at a time. As I jabbed at the keyhole she dug into my clothes, snaking cool hands over my skin. We shut ourselves in and went at it again, panting and stumbling. Samantha shucked her jeans and bent over the table, a freeze-frame from the newsreel of our time, that helter-skelter barrage of violence and pornography. Late twentieth century man tossed and turned in anticipation of this moment, but only the lucky ones ever lived the dream.

The days went by in a druggy swirl of wine, bedroom picnics and sexual feasting. There were grateful couplings in the cold dawns and slow, abandoned afternoons threaded with banter that had no meaning outside that time or place. And at night, before we slept, fierce embraces and whispers that she always shushed.

On the second night I asked her to stay. Don't ask me again, she said, so I asked her when she was leaving. She wouldn't tell me. That way, she said, I wouldn't hear the clock ticking.

On the tenth day I woke up to find her dressed and packed for a flight departing in four hours. She didn't want me to see her off; when she walked out the door that would be the end of it. Today was the first day of the rest of her American life.

'What if I came too?'

She shook her head. 'Don't.'

'Why not?'

'Because I can't promise you anything and I wouldn't want it on my conscience.'

'What?'

'You ending up like me.'

When it was time to go, she pulled my head down onto her shoulder. 'Miss me,' she whispered, 'but only for a little while.'

There was a postcard saying she'd arrived safely and France had saved its best for last. There was no return address but then I had nothing new to say.

I had a week and a half in Paris with an all-American beauty, drunk most of the time and fucking her every which way. Everyone should do it once in their life.

seven

How many middle-aged men can claim to be tidier than their mothers?

To be fair, our graphs have gone in opposite directions. When I was a child my mother was as dutiful as the next suburban housewife and I was as slack and careless a little shit as you'd find anywhere. It was only later, when her children left home and her husband's eccentricity ceased to be endearing, that she decided there was more to life than worrying about what the neighbours would say.

I've gone the other way: the older I get, the more anal I become. People who drop in on me out of the blue — a very select group — can enter my kitchen safe in the knowledge that it won't be the usual heterosexual single man hell-pit where helpfulness or self-service risks setting off booby-traps of aged stench.

My bookshelves would pass muster with the most demanding librarian. My household is organised and maintained with the iron discipline of the survivalist who's prepared for every conceivable variation on doomsday.

Whatever the time of the year, I could find appropriate clean clothing in pitch darkness. Not that I'd have to, since I have a powerful torch and a year's supply of candles.

If you think that's depressing, wait until you see the bigger picture: doing chores is much easier than writing. I do all this domestic stuff — including pointless minutiae like assembling this stack of photos in strict chronological order — so that I have something to show for my procrastination.

Samantha was and remains a high point, but I pressed on then as I press on now. I don't spend every night like this, by the way — jacked up on brandy and cigarettes, stumbling down the back streets of my memory looking for a few laughs or a warm glow or something worth shedding tears over. I tire too easily — or perhaps I'm simply not serious-minded enough — to be a tortured, dark-night-of-the-soul insomniac.

The next photo is of a crowd scene in a pub: twenty-odd shiny faces and tipsy grins. We're no longer in *la belle France*. This is middle England at play down at the local, with its pints of Old Peculiar and large G & Ts and fat-titted barmaids — often from the colonies — and alcoholic publicans with actors' smiles and threadbare patter. Seated bottom right is a middle-aged cove in a grey coarse wool pullover brandishing a pewter mug. He has a suspiciously full head of hair, railway clerk spectacles and what appears to be an off-cut from his pullover pasted on his upper lip. He's obviously a lethal bore. Every English pub has one.

I'm in the thick of it on account of being the popular new chum. Village pubs don't attract new regulars, so to speak, every day so they get made a fuss of for a while. Their side of the bargain is to be, or at least appear, mildly interesting, contribute to the staple conversational threads, share the prevailing prejudices and show some talent for gossip.

My arms are around my landlords, Jim and Becky Page, whose granny flat became vacant when Granny Page was run over on the High Street — the village's first recorded pedestrian fatality, according to the bore. He was, of course, writing a history of the village and never let slip an opportunity to 'compare notes with a fellow scribbler'.

Paris was never quite the same after Samantha. Or after Patricia for that matter: without her allowance, the apartment was an essential I couldn't really afford. Anywhere decent in London would've been as much of a squeeze, hence the granny flat in Berkshire. It was forty minutes to Waterloo and now that Thatcher had the unions on the run, the trains only stopped for mechanical problems, leaves on the tracks and winter.

England also offered the prospect of a slightly healthier income. A couple of journalists I knew had gone up in the world while I'd been in Paris and were able to put some freelance work and even the odd junket my way.

Which brings us to this photo of me knee-deep in the waters of the Arabian Gulf. It's not entirely flattering: my tan has gone the way of everything else I acquired in France and I'm not in racing condition. The love handles — all those pints in the Woodlark — are the advance guard of the middle-aged ooze I now struggle to contain.

Not that these lapses from the *beau ideal* seem to trouble my companion, who has a proprietorial arm around my waist. Her eyes are concealed by sunglasses but there's a lip-smacking appreciation to her grin. She's Kate O'Toole, London correspondent of a Sydney newspaper and a co-junketeer.

These press trips always commence with a whiff of adventure, especially when the ice is broken in the first-class cabin. I was sat next to Kate, who signalled her intentions by calling for more champagne before the plane had left the ground. She was the same age as me or, to use the glass half-full approach, at or near her sexual peak. We swapped condensed life stories.

Sydney-born and bred, she'd joined the paper straight from school and clawed her way to the middle. Her reward for five bruising years on the news desk was the much-coveted London posting and the privileged, plagiaristic existence of the foreign correspondent.

Next morning we toured the new airport terminal and the new hotel and the new conference centre, gathering a wheelbarrow load of PR bumf about the go-ahead emirate, this oasis of air-conditioned comfort and agreeable living in a dry expanse. Later we were strapped into jeeps and bounced around the desert, a pointless, jarring exercise intended, presumably, to ram home the message of civilisation imposed on a hostile terrain.

Throughout this ordeal Kate and I consolidated the rapport we'd established in that luxurious bubble eight miles high. That night at the team dinner she seized control of the seating arrangements to ensure that we sat thigh to thigh. There's a school of thought which holds that one shouldn't contemplate marrying a woman who feels you up under the table within twenty-four hours of being introduced, especially when the signs — her adroitness coupled with her ability simultaneously to hold up her end of a conversation with a third party *and* cope with rack of lamb — suggest you're not the first man she's handled during a dinner party.

But I am, after all, a bohemian.

Not that we rushed into the registry office nearest to Heathrow. First we had to cohabitate, like any sensible couple.

A month after the junket I moved out of the granny flat into Kate's smart, employer-subsidised terrace in Barnes, across the road from the Thames. She had a year to go on her posting and, while hopeful of an extension, was determined to make the most of it, so all freebies were gratefully received: restaurant openings, first nights, inaugural flights, Lords,

Wimbledon, Henley, Ascot and the Glorious Twelfth. We weren't the first couple of freeloading — some of Fleet Street's big guns made us look selective — but we did the Antipodes proud.

Kate was easily dispirited by domestic routine and therefore appreciative of my solid and uncomplaining contribution to the running of the household. She felt it more or less balanced out the disparity in our incomes and who was I to disagree? I'd landed on my feet, enjoying a standard of living far beyond my means courtesy of a lover who seemed to think she was the lucky one. Kate was good company, robust and cheerful, albeit with a tendency towards comic self-dramatisation that wasn't always in sync with my state of mind, especially after a less-than-productive day. Socially she was a throwback to the seventies, when women matched men drink for drink in the spirit of anything-you-can-do. (By now we were on the cusp of the neurotic nineties, the health craze was under way and one was starting to come across people who regarded eating as a necessary evil and three glasses of wine as a cry for help.) She was a fine-looking woman fully made up and in a certain light and I liked her. I liked her a lot.

Kate's late-night telephone lobbying was all in vain: Sydney was calling. Down there at head office the politicking surrounding the succession had degenerated into a frenzy of back-stabbing and brown-nosing and her bosses were not prepared to provoke a mutiny by giving her an extension.

She'd adopted a quasi-religious faith in the power of positive thinking that precluded even the sketchiest consideration of what she — we — would do if she didn't get her way. Having failed to prepare herself for the worst, she bore the full impact of it.

After a long day, when she didn't have the energy to put on a brave face, her misery pervaded the house like a musty smell. She blamed her tears on a debilitating period and rows with the editors in Sydney. This was a smokescreen and a pretty wispy one: Kate had sharp elbows, a leathery hide and could throw tactical tantrums with the worst of them; she'd held her own in the never-ending cat-fight of daily newspaper journalism for almost two decades. I was quite touched.

Whereas Samantha, once bitten, twice shy, wouldn't commit to another relationship, Kate could hear the faint, sinister rustle of time slipping away. She'd been around the track more times than she cared to count, picking up a few trophies and walking away from a few pile-ups, but that was a young person's game and she wasn't getting any younger.

Our conversations about Down Under hadn't got past the convict/sheep shagger childishness that passes for trans-Tasman rivalry so she had no particular reason to think I'd want to go with her. What she didn't know — because I hadn't told her — was that I was giving serious thought to tagging along.

Serge's treatment of Samantha (and hers of me, to a lesser extent) had borne out that ugly and depressing truth of human relationships that the less you have to lose, the stronger your position. With Kate, the balance of power and vulnerability was in my favour. This metaphor of competition and conflict didn't do justice to my feelings for her, of course, but if I was going to ride on her coat-tails, I needed to be sure that she would like what she saw when she looked over her shoulder.

Then there were the practical considerations. I'd become accustomed to a lifestyle that would evaporate like a dream when Kate left. Or, to look at it another way, I'd got used to not having to worry about money. The mere thought of going back to penny-counting and rationing and sweating on cheques mysteriously becalmed in the postal system and 'what if?' scenarios culminating in tube-station beggary and sleeping under bridges — 'tramp-dread' to borrow a term coined by a savvy and justly celebrated writer who needn't have worried — made me tremble with nausea.

Finally, there was the professional calculation. After a decade in Europe my career had stalled and I was in danger of drifting into that limbo to which competent tradesmen and unmarketable lady writers are consigned. I'd gained a modest reputation but hadn't taken the next step. Neither the literati nor the trend-watchers nor the proudly philistine bottom-liners thought I was worth keeping an eye on.

I was a little fish in a big pond and that was unlikely to change. Naturally I put this down to the literary establishment's snobbish disregard for colonials. In Australia I'd be a big fish in a little pond. In that respectful environment I would regain momentum and produce big work. Eventually London would be forced to acknowledge my achievements and I'd return in triumph, armed with a blacklist of every talentless hack who'd ever underrated me or placed an obstacle in my path.

This plan contained a major flaw in that if there's anywhere in the world where the creative endeavours of New Zealanders are taken less seriously than they are in London, that place is Sydney, New South Wales, Australia. But I didn't know that then. From my lofty European expatriate perspective I was making the same patronising assumptions about Australia as Australians do about New Zealand.

But there was one Australian who valued this minor novelist from the land of the long flat vowel. Seldom have I caused such joy as the night I took Kate to the local Italian and told her, over a platter of antipasto and a bottle of Sangiovese, that if she wanted me to go with her, I would.

Even as my thoughts turned to a new life in the sun somewhere between the sparkling sea and the burning bush, the old world was limbering up for one last laugh at my expense.

A week before we left, I heard from a friend from my Patricia period. In a roundabout way, via the editor of a literary magazine, because the friend had become an ex-friend soon after Patricia got back to London and began spreading word of my swinishness. The third-hand message was that Patricia had heard on the grapevine that I was leaving and she wanted to meet. This was our first communication since the note saying she never wanted to see me again. Three years had passed but it could have been ten. Samantha aside, I spent my emotional capital carefully and wasn't sentimental about my investments. When they ceased to provide an adequate return, I offloaded them, forgot about them and looked around for my next flutter.

The proposed rendezvous was midday two days hence in one of those enclosed, residents-only street parks in Knightsbridge. It was such an oddball place to meet that my active imagination went hyper: maybe a couple of loping, feral West Indians would be pre-positioned in the shrubbery with a hundred quid in their back pockets, primed to give me a retributive pasting. On second thoughts, perhaps not West Indians: Patricia wouldn't be a party to racial stereotyping. She did, however, have an older brother who'd been in the army. She'd often denounced him as a fascist buffoon but that was when she had no need of his dark skills.

Try as I might, I couldn't quite sell myself on the notion that Patricia was luring me to my comeuppance, whether courtesy of the Brixton Yardies or the Scots Guards. On the other hand, how likely was it that after three years of icy estrangement she wanted one last look before I left the hemisphere? I supposed it was conceivable that the silly little goose still burned a candle: she'd tried burying herself in work, she'd tried running wild with a different man every week, she'd tried drink and she'd tried drugs but she just couldn't get Max Napier out of her system.

It's possible that I looked in the mirror as this train of thought trundled to the end of the line and decided that, when you looked at me from Patricia's point of view, it wasn't so hard to understand.

I was punctual. The gate to the street park was locked, which made sense: how else could it be residents only? It occurred to me, with a spasm of envy, that if Patricia lived in this imposing street deep in the heart of Knightsbridge, she'd made a soft landing on the rebound. And if her principles were now rubbery enough to allow her to move in with some sharky financier, why should she have a problem employing Jamaican muscle?

Patricia was fashionably late. She'd grown her hair and put on weight, enough that an outfit intended to disguise the fact could not do so. Her complexion had lost its girlish softness and she had an interesting fashion accessory: an infant in a stroller.

She stopped a few metres away and tossed me a key. There was nothing in her expression to support the last-lingering-look theory. I opened the gate and stood aside.

The child looked to be female but toddlers were largely a mystery to me; they're thin on the ground in Bohemia. She had blonde curls and blue eyes and examined me even more stonily than her . . . her what?

I pointed. 'Yours?'

'You mean to say you can't see the resemblance?'

The child had pleasantly rounded features but even I knew they were pretty standard. And, as mentioned, Patricia was a green-eyed brunette.

'Well, since you ask, not really.'

'Of course she's mine — why else would I be traipsing around with her? Or did you think that without you as a mentor I'd been reduced to nannying?'

She pushed the stroller over to a park bench and

unbuckled her daughter, who tottered to and fro, plonked her backside down in a puddle and burst into tears. After a couple of minutes of lavish concern the racket ceased as abruptly as if Patricia had found a switch. She sat on the bench dandling her daughter on her knee.

'What's her name?'

'Emily.'

'As in Brontë, I presume?' I'd heard Patricia make claims on behalf of *Wuthering Heights* that members of the Brontë Society would baulk at.

All I got by way of a reply was a terse shrug. There was obviously a very fine line between polite interest and prying.

'How old is she?'

'Almost three.'

'She's a sweet little thing.'

Patricia raised her eyebrows. 'Thanks for pointing that out; I had no idea. I suppose you're wondering what this is in aid of.'

I shrugged. 'Well, we never got to say a proper goodbye.'

She laughed with studied humourlessness. 'We're here for one reason and one reason only, and it's certainly not because I want us to part as friends. When I asked if you could see the resemblance, it was her father I had in mind. That's right, Daddy,' she said, mistaking my clueless expression for incipient comprehension. 'Take a good, long look at your little girl because it's the only one you'll ever get.'

I stood and stared. Patricia's tight little smile unfurled into a malicious grin. When we were together I'd had — or been ceded — the intellectual upper hand. Seeing me struck dumb and disoriented, like a refugee from famine in Harrods' food hall, must have been a sweet moment.

At times like this one desperately wants to be coolly ironic or, failing that, flippant; I would've settled for glibly inconsequential. But the stylish or insouciant comeback requires unflappability and clarity and I was flabbergasted and only capable of suspicion.

'How can you be sure?'

'Because I don't believe in the stork.'

'What about Serge?'

'What in God's name has Serge got to do with it?'

'He told me . . . well, actually, he told me quite a lot, starting with the fact that you two used to screw each other all summer long. Strange you never mentioned that when you were on your high horse about me and Samantha.'

'Oh yeah, the Barbie Doll. I heard she finally cottoned on that she wasn't wanted.'

'Let's stick to you and Serge.'

'You brought her up. As for me and Serge, well, that's easy: it was a long time ago and none of your business. And I repeat: what the hell's he got to do with anything?'

'He said he went to Paris to help you move out.'

'So what?'

'And that to take your mind off things, you and he turned the clock back.'

It was her turn to gawk. 'He said what?'

'I'm sure it was wonderful therapy but it does raise the question, how can you be sure I'm the father?'

She took the matter up with Emily. 'Oh, Uncle Serge is a naughty old uncle, isn't he, darling, messing with Daddy's head like that? On the other hand, Daddy must be very, very stupid to believe it. You'll have to work really hard at school to make up for having a dolt for a father.'

'That's your idea of an answer?' I said testily. 'In case you've forgotten, I'm moving to the other side of the world next week and I've got better things to do than . . .'

'It beats me why I ever thought you were clever. Look at her, for God's sake. I'm dark and Serge is darker still; explain to me how we could've produced a child with blonde hair, blue eyes and a fair complexion.'

All I could come up with was, 'These things happen.'

'Once in a blue moon maybe. Let me spell it out in terms that even you should be able to understand: the resemblance aside, you were the only man I slept with in the relevant period. Serge did come to Paris and, now that you mention it, in the course of one of his twisted little dissertations, he might've said something to the effect that the best way to get over you was to take a lover and he was available on a stop-gap basis. I assumed it was intended as a joke; I certainly took it as one. What you're conveniently forgetting is that I loved you and I believed — because you kept telling me so — that you loved me. But you didn't love me, did you? If you'd loved me you wouldn't have been sniffing around that bitch like some sex-starved schoolboy . . . Although one can understand a sex-starved schoolboy drooling over a Barbie Doll but a supposedly intelligent adult, a supposedly serious writer in a serious relationship with a like-minded, grown-up woman? Soulmates — wasn't that how you described us? My world falls apart, the life I had planned collapses before my eyes and how, according to you, did I react? By jumping into bed with Serge. Something we're taught as children, Max, is not to judge others by ourselves, but that lesson obviously went over your head.'

It was quite a speech and gave me a chance to pull myself together. 'As long as you're not bitter, Patricia, that's the main thing. So if I'm Emily's father, why wasn't I consulted in advance? That's your idea of being a soulmate?'

'How much are you drinking these days?'

'What?'

'You seem to have gone completely soft in the head. I didn't discuss it with you because there was nothing to discuss. I had no idea I was pregnant until the symptoms started and I went for a test. Remember when I changed from the pill to a diaphragm? No, of course you don't. I did try to discuss it but you showed no interest whatsoever. Obviously something went wrong in the transition.' She didn't look or sound as if she was making it up.

'I guess that's one way of putting it. So how did you feel when you found out?'

'How do you think I felt?'

'Like having an abortion?'

'Exactly.'

'What stopped you?'

Apart from the carry-on following her three-point landing in the puddle, our daughter had been remarkably unobtrusive. There'd been the odd wriggle and squawk and a half-hearted attempt to swallow her hand but otherwise she'd been content to observe proceedings from the comfort of her mother's lap.

Patricia gazed at Emily, her expression a template for maternal adoration. 'I thought it would give me a focus, help me put the whole wretched business behind me, and I'd have someone to love who's worth loving. I also thought it would make me a better person and a better writer. I was right on all counts.'

'What was it Cyril Connolly said?'

'"There is no more sombre enemy of good art than the pram in the hall." But he was a man, Max, so he found it awfully difficult to think of anyone but himself.'

'So the work's going well?'

This placatory inquiry was unsmilingly dead-batted. 'Watch this space.'

'I'm going to Australia, remember.'

'How could I forget? It's the best news I've had for ages. You'll hear about me — but not, I think, vice versa.'

'Well, on that generous-spirited note . . .'

'Yes, time to say goodbye. Goodbye and good riddance.'

And that seemed to be that. Patricia turned her back on me to buckle Emily into the stroller. As she straightened up she flicked an indifferent glance over her shoulder. 'Still here?'

'What about Emily?'

Patricia, hands on hips, inspected me sourly. 'You don't listen, do you? That was it, the first and last time. From here on, as far as Emily's concerned, you don't exist. And don't bother claiming you feel all paternal towards her because we both know that'd be a fraud.'

'I have rights.'

'My father's as determined as I am that you won't have a damn thing to do with Emily and, as you'd expect, he has some high-powered friends in the legal fraternity. Feel free to fight for your rights — it'll get you nowhere and cost you a fortune.' She beamed me another malicious grin. 'So you'd better hurry up and write that bestseller.'

'I take it, then, that you don't expect any financial support from me?'

'All I want you to do is disappear.'

Well, that was a relief. 'No support, no entitlements, eh?'

She pushed the stroller past me. 'Call it whatever you like. Fuck off to Australia, Max. I'm sure you'll fit right in.'

'One day she'll want to know who her father is.'

'I'm a writer; I'll make something up.'

And I'd thought her earlier grins were malicious.

Patricia walked and Emily rolled out of my life without a backward glance between them. I haven't seen either of them since and I haven't heard anything much of Patricia. Then again, she wouldn't have heard anything much of me.

eight

We left England in spring. It was nine degrees and a sooty sky hung over west London like a sagging ceiling. We arrived in Sydney in autumn. It was twenty-seven degrees and the light pricked my eyes. I could feel the ocean, hear its whisper on the breeze calling to my long-suppressed Antipodean instincts.

It was April Fools' Day, my birthday. I was thirty-six years old and without assets, savings or insurance. Work-wise I was treading water and, as we know, you can't do that indefinitely. I had a daughter but only in the biological sense. My ex-wife and ex-partner hated me for falling out of love with them and Samantha, wherever she was and whenever I crossed her mind, pitied me for falling in love with her. I hadn't particularly set out to make a mess of my life but if you choose to entertain romantic notions and a raffish self-image, it's always on the cards.

Apart from the odd head-flopping, dribbling doze, Kate and I stayed awake and took our punishment as the jumbo tracked south towards the day after tomorrow. I went easy on the booze at first, not wanting to get off on the wrong foot with her family, but Kate persuaded me that meeting the O'Tooles wasn't an operation to be undergone sans anaesthetic. I knew they were pretty down to earth but as the big moment in the arrivals hall drew closer, Kate started to get twitchy. It wasn't that her family had a problem with writers or New Zealanders (spongers were probably another matter, but I was relying on her to nip that one in the bud). No, she was more worried about how I'd react to them, fearing that I'd take one look at these simple working folk — Dad was a bus driver, Mum did part-time clerical work for the local council, big brother was a copper and little sister a solo mum — and decide that this wasn't my scene.

'I've been accused of a lot of things,' I said, 'but that's a new one: so now I'm a snob, am I?'

'Come on, Max, you get the picture: they just aren't your cup of tea.'

'So what? It takes all sorts.'

'Does it now?' she said. 'Tolerance is a piece of cake until you actually have to put it into practice. It's like those sanctimonious Swedes lecturing the world about race relations; I mean, how many blacks are there in Sweden?'

'There's probably a few in the porno industry.'

'Right, and if that's not racial stereotyping, what is? Anyway, I'm not saying you're a snob, I'm just saying you've got bugger all in common. They don't read books, they don't travel, they're not interested in ideas or abstractions . . . Their idea of a night out is steak and chips and a few beers down at the footy club.'

'Do they vote?'

'Oh, shit yeah, true-blue Labour. But it's that old working-class, Catholic, trade union thing; it doesn't extend to being liberal-minded on social issues — especially not the old man.'

'A touch of the redneck, perhaps?'

'Let me put it this way: whatever you do, don't get him

started on the Asians. Fuck, you'd honestly think Pearl Harbor happened last week.'

'True blue, red neck and yellow peril,' I said. 'The man's a walking, talking colour chart.'

'A walking, talking paranoid bigot, that's what he is.'

'Let me guess: the little yellow monkeys are itching to get their filthy little yellow hands on Australia's wide-open spaces and fair-skinned womenfolk.'

'You forgot our vast, untapped mineral resources,' said Kate. 'I'm telling you, when he gets the bit between his teeth it's not a pretty sight. I strongly recommend that you avoid the subject altogether.'

'So what's safe ground?'

'Rugby league.'

'I don't know the first thing about rugby league. Only criminals play league in New Zealand.'

'That's my whole fucking point, Max: you're poles apart. And you'd have to admit, you're pretty choosy about the company you keep, especially if you suspect there's a risk of being bored. Well, there is a risk. In fact I confidently predict you'll be bored shitless, and we're going to have to spend a fair bit of time with them until we find somewhere to live.'

She wasn't giving me much credit for adaptability or diplomacy but I could see where she was coming from. I was detached — as opposed to estranged — from my family and had spent more than a decade knocking around Europe with people who lived and thought and behaved much as I did and who had also loosened or severed their family ties. I was used to being stimulated and entertained; I hadn't had to pull my head in or play a part in order to co-exist with people who weren't on my wavelength. Bohemia's a bit like Switzerland — small, self-contained, keeping the rest of the world at arm's length. (In other respects Bohemia's the complete opposite of Switzerland — messy, chaotic, impractical, financially illiterate.) I was going to have to engage with ordinary people and Kate feared that I couldn't — or wouldn't — do that.

I told her I understood the situation and would do my bit. I didn't tell her I knew which side my bread was buttered on.

The gang was all there. Kate's father was known to one and all as Ginge because he'd once had red hair; the hair had gone but the freckles remained. He was wearing jandals, a Manly rugby league jersey and dramatically short, tight shorts that if I hadn't known better I would've interpreted as a militant statement of his sexual orientation. (I later discovered they were a working-class fashion icon known as stubbies.) He shook my hand as if I'd saved his life, and called me 'mate'.

Mother Lynne was slim and sun-dried. Her breezy chat and hustle-bustle suggested she was a livewire and proud of it; some people — me, for instance — would probably have picked her as one of those hectic busybodies who lack self-awareness and an off-button. She hugged me as if I'd saved her daughter's life, and called me 'darling'.

Brother Brad was a constable in Dubbo, a place name no writer of fiction could improve on. He was a slab of a man with deep-set eyes and hunched shoulders that caused his strangler's hands to hover over his groin as if he anticipated a threat to his testicles or an irresistible venereal itch. He shook my hand as if he was always hearing that he didn't know his own strength, and called me 'mate'.

Adele looked more like Lynne's younger sister than Kate's. I'd been briefed on her chequered past, beginning with the child she'd conceived while still at school and given birth to after she was expelled. The state took that one off her but she'd had a couple more by different men, neither of whom had hung around to help out. She shook my hand as if I was the Pope, and called me 'Mark'.

I can't imagine what they made of me. Having never

experienced jetlag themselves, they could have been excused for thinking their daughter had had the extreme bad taste to bring home a druggie. We piled into Ginge's Holden and drove for what seemed like three hours but was probably half that to an area known as the northern beaches. Although fading fast by the time we arrived at the O'Tooles' brick bungalow, I was sufficiently aware of my surroundings to realise that 'northern beaches', like 'retirement village', was not a term to be taken too literally.

The guest bedroom had two kiddie beds with pink duvets. The wallpaper had peppermint-green vertical stripes. A black plastic Jesus on the cross hung on one wall: Jesus looked Filipino. A calendar promoting a local butcher was nailed to the opposite wall. The artwork for the month of April two years prior featured a dusky beauty with porn-star breasts. She also looked Filipino.

I thanked Jesus for a safe flight and slid between clean sheets. I dreamt I was in the Garden of Gethsemane waiting for Jesus to rise from the dead. To fill in time Mary Magdalene, whom I hadn't realised was Filipino, showed me her tits. They weren't a patch on the Calendar Girl's.

I got up at sundown for a birthday barbecue. The womenfolk remained indoors making potato salad and coleslaw and remembering absent friends. Being an acquaintance, neighbour or relative of the O'Tooles seemed like a high-risk gig; if the disease didn't get you, the invasive surgery did. The blokes stood around the barbie, drinking beer from cans encased in Styrofoam holders. These were entirely superfluous since Ginge and Brad didn't give their beers a chance to defrost and my first careless gulp triggered a stunning mini-migraine.

'Brain-freeze,' pronounced Brad as I reeled back clutching my forehead. 'Cunt of a thing.'

'If you'd prefer a cup of tea,' said Ginge with a snaky grin, 'fuckin get it yourself.'

As Kate had warned, the conversation revolved around the Manly rugby league club, the Sea Eagles. It seemed to work this way: the Sea Eagles were 'dead-set champions' to a man, while opposing teams consisted of 'fuckin low mongrels', 'fuckin bludgers', 'fuckin sheilas' and 'fuckin poofters'.

Inevitably it fell to me to explain why I didn't share their love of league and burning — and somewhat paradoxical — hatred of all league players who weren't Sea Eagles. I'd barely uttered the words rugby union before Ginge set off on a mad rant about 'rah-rahs' and 'silvertails'. I later learned that these were derisive characterisations of, respectively, people who played and followed rugby union and the preening, parasitic middle-upper class to which they invariably belonged.

Brad came to my aid. 'Geez, Ginge, give the bloke a chance. It's not his fuckin fault he grew up in a place where union's the go.'

'Yeah, those All Blacks,' said Ginge. 'What a bunch of fuckin dirty bastards they are.'

Ginge's diatribes were delivered with great vehemence but, the yellow peril aside, I came to realise that none of it should be taken personally and hardly any of it was worth taking seriously. What Ginge and his mates regarded as a little light banter would, in other, less robust cultures, have caused vendettas that would rage for several generations.

Patricia was right about one thing: as a child, I was instructed not to judge others by myself, a trick that requires more imagination and less ego than many of us possess. The message drummed into little Aussies, I decided, was that sticks and stones can break your bones but names will never hurt you.

Keen for us to settle on their side of the harbour, Ginge and Lynne lobbied hard for the inner north — the likes of Neutral Bay, Crow's Nest and Cremorne. Kate finally broke it to them in language Ginge could understand: 'There's no fuckin way we're living on the North Shore, okay? I'm not going to cross that fuckin bridge twice a day and I don't want Max to have to go to a fuckin shopping mall to feel part of the human race. So can we please drop the fuckin subject once and for all?'

We chose Darlinghurst for its centrality, Italian cafés, cheap restaurants and louche street life. Same city, different world.

I'd never been to Australia before, never had any interest in doing so. Growing up in New Zealand, I cast longing glances towards Europe, the land of antiquity and a millennium of momentous history, the centre of the civilisation of which we were the last, loneliest outpost. Australia, I assumed, was just a family-sized version of New Zealand. What did it have that we didn't, apart from poisonous snakes, marsupials and continental vastness, mile upon soul-crushing mile of uninhabitable moonscape? And what was Sydney if not Auckland with a trailer-trash accent and one piece of zany, postcard-friendly architecture? Both had a harbour, a harbour bridge and rather too many philistines per capita.

It took a month to turn those preconceptions on their head and make me burn with embarrassment when I recalled the times I'd held forth on this theme. Auckland was an overweight, immature teenager of a town, growing out but not up. Sydney was the real thing — a plantation of granite; a humming, restless, new-world metropolis embedded in the edge of the continent like a precious earring. Unlike Auckland, where virtually every structure of any age and distinction had been put to the wrecking ball to create space for the neon-lit façades of merchant capitalism or monuments to foxy property developers, Sydney had preserved at least some of its graceful and ambitious heritage.

Auckland had Karangahape Road, a scruffy stretch of inner-city decay where the vice scene just plugged away, not underground enough to suit the old maids and political Christians nor bold enough to come right out and say, 'Sin is our business: show us the colour of your money.'

Sydney had Kings Cross, a few lurid blocks strategically located among the CBD, Woolloomooloo wharf where the US naval ships disgorged their complements of cashed-up gash-hounds, and the eastern bays where plutocrats luxuriated in glossy-magazine high style, counting their money, old and new, and chuckling over the fact that there were people out there, millions of them, who genuinely believed money couldn't buy happiness.

Like an obscene tattoo, the Cross demanded your attention whether you liked it or not. Teenage junkies and lanky transsexuals jostled for prime position, and pimps lounged in doorways, inviting passers-by into anonymous back rooms for watered-down drinks and other costly disappointments. A block back from the strip, heroin dealers conducted business from their double-parked Mercedes, brown paper bags full of cash under the passenger seats awaiting collection by the drug squad.

When a red-light district becomes a tourist attraction, everyone's a winner. Even Rotarians and their wives can rubber-neck with a clear conscience.

Sure, there was the dross, the endless dormitory suburbs differentiated only by name and post code, where people subordinated their identities to their jobs, their kids and their TV sets. And there was worse: there was first-world poverty, mini-ghettos where the mighty cockroach roamed and social workers checked children for cigarette burns. But all great cities have their dreary swathes and wastelands, where the underclass breeds and bickers and rots. When people who don't live there talk about Paris, they mean the core, a few gorgeous arrondissements. They don't mean the weedy, graffittied suburbs where working-class fascism brews in the tower blocks or whole streets bow towards Mecca.

The Lucky Country lived up to its billing. I found hardcase humour, winter sunshine and the best cheap red wine, but not in the hayseed setting of my uninformed imagination. Auckland was only a two-and-a-half-hour flight away (long enough by European standards but a commuter ride for the global traveller), but that sense of being an extra on the world stage, a spectator to history, always the last to know, was conspicuously absent. Australia was plugged into the global community and the Zeitgeist; Sydney was a jetset city whose residents expected every visitor, no matter who they were or where they came from, to depart in a state of envy.

During this eye-opening familiarisation each day provided a new reason to congratulate myself for making the move. I was so busy congratulating myself that I failed to draw the obvious conclusion: I'd been wrong about Sydney in every other respect so it followed that I was wrong to assume I'd take it by storm.

The penny would drop eventually.

Kate and I were resigned to some belt-tightening now that we had to pay our own way. We'd almost talked ourselves around to the view that self-denial and the quiet life would be good for us. In our sillier moments we even discussed, with due solemnity, going on a full-blown health kick. This fantasy came complete with home-made muesli, alcohol-free weeks, gym membership and crack-of-dawn canters around Rushcutters Bay. But I didn't realise — and after two years in all-expenses-paid exile Kate had forgotten — that money went a lot further in Sydney. And after months of ominous shiftiness and equivocation in head office over whose shoes she'd step into on her return, Kate was put in charge of an about-town column that recorded the extravagances and vulgarities of the rich, famous and notorious. It came with a no-questions-asked expense account, so before you could say 'It's on the company,' the gravy train was rolling again.

Her friends were mostly journalists, as merry a bunch of cynics and self-promoters as ever sexed up a CV. Our non-columnar social life revolved around journos' pubs and raucous dinner parties, which either went swimmingly or horribly wrong. But the dramas were short-lived. The propositions welcome and unwelcome, the reckless insults and blistering denunciations, even the invitations to settle things outside floated away on the warm west wind or evaporated in the morning sun. Names didn't hurt them.

Like many Australians, Kate was both hard-bitten and sentimental. She'd kept in touch with her childhood friends, who still lived out in the northern beaches and were married to men called Wayne or Shane or Duane who had heavy-metal hair, wore stubbies to work and supported the Sea Eagles. And while I felt obliged to make an effort with Kate's family (although, to be fair, Ginge's demented soliloquies on the issues of the day and Brad's laconic accounts of crime-fighting in Dubbo — whose underworld was handicapped by quite phenomenal stupidity — had a certain entertainment value), I regarded anything more than cursory contact with these bleached-blonde sheilas and their bodgie husbands and semi-housetrained children as above and beyond the call of duty. And Kate, sensible woman that she was, concurred.

Shelley (remember her? — my agent) secured a reasonable advance on a two-book deal with the Australian arm of my UK publisher. Kate and I celebrated at a voguish restaurant. As I was flipping through the winelist in search of a dessert wine, she suggested that we get married.

Her laugh had a self-conscious rattle. 'You didn't see that coming, did you?'

I shook my head, realising — too late — how she'd interpret my silence and demeanour of prick-eared alertness.

'Listen, forget it,' she said, swivelling her eyes as if there was a mosquito in her airspace. 'Forget I ever mentioned it. I don't know why I brought it up. You tried marriage and didn't like it; I know that. I also know that if it ain't broke, don't fuckin fix it.'

It had come out of the blue, in the sense that there had been no softening-up process, but not as a complete surprise. I knew she fretted that time was picking up speed and life was getting away from her. If by saying nothing I encouraged her to retract, what would her fall-back be: the 'if it ain't broke' mantra or gnawing insecurity? Or would her thoughts turn to a pre-emptive strike to forestall heartbreak down the track and give herself one last shot at finding Mr Right before she hit forty and all bets were off?

There was nowhere else I wanted to be; there were no particular cons and some persuasive pros. It would make her happy and I very much wanted to do that, partly because she deserved happiness and partly to relieve the faint, slow throb of guilt I felt for not loving her back — and, of course, for the lie I told every time she said, 'I love you.' All I can say in my defence is that I lied out of tenderness rather than calculation.

I said, 'If you want to get married, it's fine by me.'

Her smile was uncertain and short-lived. 'That implies you don't.'

'No, it means I'm relaxed either way. So if you want to do it, fine, let's do it.'

'Seriously?'

'Absolutely.'

'You realise what you're getting yourself into?'

'I think so: me husband, you wife, happily ever after.'

That night as I lay in bed listening to the ceiling fan creak, I pondered the implications of marrying a woman I didn't love. It meant I'd given up on romance and where did that leave me? At the end of the line, that's where. Then I thought, what's so wonderful about romance? What the fuck has romance ever done for me? It's not the end of the line at all; it's the end of adolescence, the end of illusion. Congratulations, mate, you've finally grown up.

We kept it simple — a terse exchange with a celebrant and a piss-up at Ginge and Lynne's — preferring to splash out on the honeymoon, a lavish fortnight on a Fijian island. My mother and sister came over from New Zealand. By that stage my mother was herself exhibiting an eccentricity that wasn't always endearing. She could be roguish or she could put on airs and graces. Predictably this homely occasion brought out the grande dame.

Late in the evening Ginge pulled me aside. 'Mate, your old sheila — what's the fuckin story?'

'Beats me, Ginge. She's a farmer's daughter from the back of beyond but you'd swear she's third in line to the throne.'

'No offence, mate, but it's no fuckin wonder your old man's putting in time at the loony bin.'

'None taken. You've just got to hope it doesn't run in the family, eh?'

'Don't worry, mate, if you go troppo, we won't let them bung you in the bin. Me and Brad'll take you out into the bush and put a fuckin bullet in you.'

I never met Myra. She'd been the head librarian when Kate started at the paper. She had nothing much in the way of family and friends so she'd dreaded retirement and postponed it for as long as she could. Although my wife wasn't in the habit of bringing home strays or doing good works, she didn't let Myra shuffle into a lonely twilight, ringing her every second day and dropping in on her at least once a week.

Kate wasn't holier-than-thou about it. Myra could be hard work and once or twice Kate was moved to say that if she'd known what she was letting herself in for, she would have put a few more bucks in the kitty for Myra's farewell present and left it at that. But she did it and did it selflessly, expecting nothing in return, and when Myra died she was distraught.

Myra left Kate her mortgage-free two-bedroom apartment in a landmark Art Deco building in Potts Point. Having arrived in Australia with practically nothing, I was now the joint owner of a property that, as Kate's pal who covered real estate repeatedly and enviously told us, with a coat of paint and a renovated kitchen would fetch upwards of half a million dollars.

Just when my life was on as even a keel as it had ever been, I met the pornographer.

nine

There's one at every party: the needy misfit who interprets pro forma pleasantry as an invitation to make himself at home in your life, the social burden you try to offload, the killjoy those in the know steer well clear of.

He stood in the corner, alone and ignored, blinking behind his spectacles. Everything about him said fish out of water. This was a jeans and T-shirt scene; he wore chinos with a knife-edge crease and a long-sleeved Oxford-weave white shirt with a button-down collar. He was the only person at the party who had used both an iron and a hairbrush.

I felt a bit sorry for him. Ten minutes, I told myself; it'll be your good deed for the week.

I walked over and stuck out my hand. 'G'day, I'm Max Napier.'

He smiled uncertainly, as if he couldn't — and didn't — believe his luck. 'Walter. Walter Cribb.'

He had a spongy handshake and an American accent and looked overfed, under-exercised and unworldly, like many of the white US navy guys who filed past our apartment building in search of stuffed koalas, plastic boomerangs and the mythical whore with a heart of gold. They were probably the techno-geeks, the remote-control killers who programmed cruise missiles to fly through a certain window in a certain building in downtown Khartoum and take out a terrorist mastermind and his cleaning lady.

'You wouldn't be a naval man by any chance?'

'Do I look like a cornholer?' he asked mildly.

'A what?'

'You don't know what a cornholer is? Here's a clue: Sydney's full of them; Sydney's Cornhole City.'

'I guess I shouldn't overlook the obvious,' I said. 'By cornholer I presume you mean a member of the gay community?'

'You call them gay; I call them cornholers; my father calls them spawn of the devil and my brother, who I used to share a bath with, calls them girlfriend.'

I took a closer look at Walter Cribb because it seemed I'd missed something the first time around. He looked back at me with polite expectation, like an airline steward waiting for me to choose between the rosemary lamb with gratin potatoes and the chicken with pilaf rice.

'So you're not in the navy . . .'

'No, sir.'

I waited for him to tell me what he did for a living but he just smiled his I-can-do-this-all-night-if-I-have-to smile. Most people don't need much encouragement to talk about their work and the more limited their outlook, the more eagerly they seize the opportunity. The fact that Walter passed on it suggested he wasn't a bore or unduly bothered about being alone in a crowded room, which in turn suggested he wasn't the social cripple I'd taken him for.

I was moderately intrigued. 'What's your connection to the hosts?'

The hosts were a media couple. She nattered inconsequentially on the radio and was, by all accounts, adored by her audience, mainly middle-class women with empty nests and a belated interest in broadening their minds. He was a columnist on Kate's paper, a bottomless pit of moral outrage which he vented in prose that clanked and droned like a battletank in bottom gear.

'Who are the hosts?'

'I get it,' I said. 'You crashed the party.'

He made a slow 180-degree sweep of the room, as if he was looking for someone to cadge a cigarette from. 'Who the fuck would want to crash this party?'

I mimicked his survey. 'You know what? I'm pretty sure that if you decided to leave, no one would try to stop you. At least not physically.'

His smile broadened. 'You're probably right, Max, but I figure why take the chance?'

'Well,' I said, 'it's been nice trying to talk to you.'

'Whoa there,' he said. 'What's the rush? We're just getting to know each other.'

'No we're not. Getting to know each other would involve exchanging a certain amount of low-grade personal information, which you seem disinclined to do.'

I wasn't sure how or why I came to be prodding Walter Cribb into telling me about himself, especially as I had the feeling he was having private fun at my expense, paying me back for my patronising assumptions by playing hard to get to know. If so, he hadn't finished with me.

'Okay, let's start over,' he said. 'And let's do it properly this time.' He produced a silver flask from his hip pocket. 'Care to join me in a taste of Kentucky's finest? Let me tell you, they don't serve this at your local titty bar.'

'Why not?' Why not indeed? By now I was reasonably sure that meeting Walter Cribb would be the high point of my evening.

He had a bottle of Evian stashed in the corner. He rinsed out an abandoned wine glass, emptied it into a pot plant, poured some whiskey and added a splash of water. I took a sip. I wasn't a big fan of bourbon but this wasn't bourbon as I knew it.

'You like that?'

I nodded. 'I do.'

'Lovingly made by some courtly old southern gentleman who probably bankrolled the hit on Martin Luther King.' He shrugged. 'Still, as I always say, we can't let politics and such get in the way of a good time. Now, you were interested in knowing how I weaselled my way into this fabulous soirée. Well, I'm here as the guest of Lorraine, whose second name escapes me; she's a journalist, like most everyone else here as far as I can tell. A year or two back she got a scholarship to Columbia University in New York City. My kid sister Joelene was on the same course and when she heard I was going to be in Sydney, she asked me to give Lorraine a call. I made the mistake of telling her the truth — that my plans for the evening amounted to a room-service meal and whatever's on TV — and she insisted I come along here to meet her interesting friends and update her on where Joelene's at. Well, as it happened we ran out of conversation within five minutes, at which point Lorraine developed a powerful need to go to the can. I haven't seen her since.'

'That's women for you.'

'Ain't that the truth? So what brings you here, Max? I don't pick you for a journalist.'

'Why's that?'

'Well, you're talking to me, for a start.'

'My wife's the journalist,' I said. 'They're fine one on one but I've got a low tolerance threshold for other people's shop talk.'

'Amen to that. Everyone does it, though. What do you talk shop about?'

'Books, writing. I write novels.'

Walter raised his eyebrows. 'Is that so? I've come across a few novelists in my line of work.'

'Oh?'

'I'm on the product development side of the entertainment industry.' He paused. 'The X-rated part of it.'

'You mean you're in the pornography business?'

'That term has negative connotations for some people — Lorraine, for example.'

'That's what killed the conversation?'

He nodded. 'I could've skated over it or pure and simple lied — sure as hell wouldn't have been the first time — but every now and again I like to test my first impressions, just to make sure I'm not getting ahead of myself. I picked Lorraine as a witch-burner. And I was right.'

'And me?'

'I don't see you as a witch-burner, Max. I see you as a witch-fucker.'

'Well, that would depend on the witch.'

'There's a fine line between being particular and being picky. It's a line you don't want to cross.'

I wanted to hear more about the novelists.

'We've got a paperback division,' said Walter. 'Pretty old-fashioned but some people like that: easy to hide and you don't need instructions. You'd probably recognise the names of some of the guys — and gals — who do stuff for us. These aren't hacks we're talking about; these are some well-respected folk in literary circles.'

'Try me.'

He shook his head. 'Uh-uh. If they wanted the world to know they were writing porn, they wouldn't be using pseudonyms, now would they?'

'Why do they do it?' I knew the answer but I was curious about the going rate.

'Money. What else would it be?'

'What sort of money?'

Walter cocked his head. 'Do I detect a spark of interest?'

'Just plain old curiosity.'

'Two, maybe two-and-a-half grand. Per book.'

'Shit, is that all? Why would a serious writer want to waste their time doing smut for that kind of money?'

Walter looked sceptical, as well he might have. 'Well, I don't know how many books you sell, buddy, but one thing I've learned about the writing game is that being the talk of Greenwich Village doesn't necessarily translate into an income that's going to have them sharpening their pencils down at the tax department. Something else I learned is that being able to look into the human soul and set it down in three or four hundred pages of flowery language ain't the most marketable talent under the sun. I mean, what are the other options? There's teaching and journalism, I guess, but the third thing I learned about writers is that some of you don't function too well in the real world. You seem to have a problem with basic stuff like being at a given place at a given time and working with other people and dealing with the public. Let's face it, all you really want to do is sit in a room by yourself and make shit up. So if someone's prepared to pay you twenty-five hundred bucks a week to do that . . .' — he shrugged — '. . . well, if you can afford to shine them on, good luck to you.'

'When you put it like that . . .'

'You know what's kind of interesting? My boss had a hell of a job persuading the company that we should pay writers that kind of money. Their attitude was that any degenerate with a typewriter can crank out a dirty book; it's not like the sick fucks who buy the goddamn things are looking for a zinger of a plot and a way with words. So what would happen was, we'd pay these creeps a few hundred and get pure skank, as you'd expect. Then we had a choice: either cut our losses and kiss off the few hundred, or publish the skank as is and more than likely kiss off the few hundred and the cost of publication, or pay another writer to rewrite the skank and give ourselves a shot at recovering our costs and maybe making some cream. My boss eventually managed to convince them that if we paid enough to get decent writers, it wouldn't cost any more in the long run, plus we'd stand a better chance of having a product that the great jerk-off community — or at least the part that can read — would actually buy.'

'How long do these books have to be?'

'Thirty-five thousand words.'

'And they write them in a week?'

'Five thousand words a day for seven days. It's porn, okay? We're not talking about the great American novel, half-a-dozen drafts and changing some fucking adjective twenty times to get the only word in the entire language that says it exactly right and doesn't fuck up the rhythm of the sentence. Besides, there are some, let's say, conventions of the genre that the porn novelist ignores at his peril.'

'Like what?'

'Well, first and foremost the action should come thick and fast and get progressively juicier.' He narrowed his eyes theatrically. 'You know, Max, if I didn't know better, I'd be getting the impression that you mightn't be averse to doing a little moonlighting down in Fucktown.'

Well, I was between projects.

Kate had seen me buddying up to Walter and was impressed by this show of compassion. I didn't tell her what we'd talked about and I didn't show her the sample material Walter sent me. If your partner trusts you, it's not that hard to hide something in a two-bedroom flat.

I kept it from her because she wouldn't have understood why I'd even contemplate writing pornography. My income wasn't an issue. Like many people, Kate had an exaggerated respect for writers based on a highly romanticised conception of the creative process. In her eyes I was every bit as much an artist as some olden-day tubercular poet wasting for his art in picturesque poverty. Like the poet, I had no choice but to follow my dream, and the little I had to show for it was society's fault, not mine.

I wasn't sure I understood it myself, although money did come into it. I hadn't absorbed many of my parents' petit-bourgeois anxieties and cautionary tales but a side of me — which I kept well-hidden and which comprised equal parts cynicism, pessimism and solitariness — foresaw me ending up on my own and could therefore see some merit in establishing a contingency fund.

I also rationalised that there were writers more self-consciously serious and better off than I who happily and lucratively demeaned themselves by spinning candyfloss for glossy magazines and weekend supplements. Leaving aside the mass-market junk merchants, the weavers of Walter Mitty fantasies for an unheroic generation or love-conquers-all melodramas for women on the domestic treadmill, how many writers earned a decent living solely from fiction? Most did something on the side — like teaching creative writing to people who, in the main, were born to read — or else had their gums clamped to the public tit. If those were the alternatives, why not write porn? Compared with soliciting for government patronage or putting one's name to calculatedly cosy profiles of other writers or destination pieces for the travel pages, the spiritual home of advertorial, it was a radical, even subversive, thing to do. Fuck it, it was bohemian.

Reading the sample material with what was now an alert apprentice's eye, I saw pornography's arc more clearly and firmed up my hazy take on its raison d'etre.

Pornography, I realised, was militantly anti-love. Where

love intruded, it caused terrible suffering, in the form of sexual frustration, through its monstrous insistence that you must give your loved one exclusive access to your body. And given that in Fucktown sex with one person at a time is the equivalent of driving with an L-plate, sex with the same person day in, day out (not for long: you're already on the slippery slope to separate bedrooms) is a form of living death, like zombiism.

The porno novel's basic narrative is a woman's journey of sexual self-discovery. When we meet our heroine she may be alone — widowed, divorced or spinsterish out of conviction or a broken heart — or trapped in marital fidelity. She may think she's happy and fulfilled but that's just the socio-religious brainwashing.

Our heroine doesn't realise or won't acknowledge that she's brought this on herself by denying her true nature: she wasn't put on this earth to be celibate or monogamous. So now she's a ticking sex bomb; it just needs someone to get their finger on the button. The detonation may be foreshadowed by a guilty bout of masturbation which, for plot purposes, may be covertly witnessed by an admirer — or, for that matter, a passing able-bodied male — who's thus encouraged not to take no for an answer.

He doesn't. Neither does her bisexual best friend or her bisexual best friend's husband or the muscular lads who clean her pool or their friends who decide they'd like a piece of the action or the basketball team whose bus is the first vehicle on the scene when her car breaks down on a lonely stretch of road . . . And of course they're right not to take no for an answer because once our heroine gets over her socio-religiously programmed resistance to being simultaneously vaginally, anally and orally penetrated by brusque if not abusive strangers, she discovers that SHE LOVES IT. JESUS FUCKING CHRIST, DOES SHE LOVE IT!!!! (Her various epiphanies are often accompanied by orgasmic vocalising that has more impact — a little trick of the trade here — when rendered in capital letters.)

What this means, in stuffy legal terms, is that our heroine gets raped rather a lot.

(Things have changed a little since those days, if my casual research is any guide. What's coyly referred to as the 'non-consent' motif was one area where the feminist critics had an obvious point. Aware that their *sine qua non* is unbridled female lust, some pornographers have toned down the coercion or simply cut to the chase: when we meet our heroine in this thoroughly modern manifestation, she's already ready for anything.

Technology has also played a part. If the paperback was low-tech back then, it's positively primitive in the internet age. An old-time Hollywood mogul was fond of saying that there's really only one story: the delayed fuck. Well, delayed gratification is a hard sell these days. Hunched over his laptop or sprawled in front of TV with his trousers around his ankles, the contemporary consumer may feel, for various reasons, that there's a limit to how long he can and should drag this exercise out. Character development and context, therefore, take a back seat to action. Furthermore, the marquee stars of the adult film industry are the leading ladies, and stars must always be seen to be in control. These tawny lionesses with their state-of-the-art tits don't need their buttons pushed by some meat-sack pumped up on steroids and Viagra. They are huntresses like Tania's Louise, but without the pseudo-intellectual song-and-dance.)

When Walter rang to see if I was coming on board, I expressed reservations about the 'non-consent' motif.

There was a long silence. 'Is that a yes or a no?'

'Well, that's up to you, Walt. I'm prepared to have a crack but not if the women have to be forced into it.'

'Why not?'

'I just told you: I have a problem with that stuff.'

'You do realise it's not rape,' he said.

'Oh, really?'

'How the fuck can it be rape if they enjoy it?'

'It's rape if it's against their will. And the fact they end up enjoying it implies — make that asserts — that there's no such thing as rape. There's just a lot of screwed-up women who haven't caught up with the fact that happiness is eighteen hard yards of cock.'

'Max...'

'And we know that's bullshit, don't we, Walt, we know that's vile and dangerous crap. We know that, in real life, pathologically promiscuous women who allow themselves to be used and abused need help. Don't we, Walt?'

'Max...'

'How would you feel if your sister carried on like that, Walt?'

'Max, shut the fuck up. It's pornography, it's for guys to jerk off over, it's a way to make a buck.' There was another bemused silence. 'So if you won't do non-consent, what's it going to be?'

'I haven't given it much thought but I guess, you know, one thing leads to another.'

He grunted unenthusiastically. 'You could do a slut wife.'

'A what?'

'Slut wives; it's a real growth area. Basic storyline: a guy sees his prim and proper — so he thinks — wife being porked by another guy and finds it a colossal turn-on. He spies on her, hoping for a replay, and guess what? Mrs Homemaker turns out to be a screaming slut: getting nailed by the TV repairman is just the tip of the iceberg. Cue the usual menu: oral, anal, lezzies, threesomes, big-buck negroes with unfeasibly big...'

'There's a market for that?'

'There's a market for anything and everything; some

markets are just a little more niche than others. You know what's the hottest ticket in books right now? Incest.'

'Incest?'

'Check.'

'Well, frankly, Walt, I wouldn't know where to start . . .'

'I wasn't suggesting it, Max; you've got to walk before you can run. Maybe down the track.'

'I don't think so.'

'Well, you know, the thing about incest, there's less need for non-consent.'

'Why's that?'

'It's contrary to the laws of God and man, Max. It's dirty enough as it is so why gild the lily?'

I didn't have strong views on pornography, one way or the other. I'd consumed a certain amount of it without becoming a misogynist or an abuser of women. On the other hand, I could see there would be men who'd take porn's core anti-women message to heart. Banning porn was pointless and probably counter-productive — as Walter's company was in the process of demonstrating to the Australian authorities — but it didn't leave a hole in my life.

I understand now what the attraction was then. The discrepancy between expectations and recognition/reward (the jury was still out on actual achievement) had sapped my self-belief and appetite for lonely toil. Seeing my work on bookshop shelves was no longer a buzz. There I was, me and a thousand others: all those titles, all those authors, all that choice. Why should anyone choose Max Napier? I wasn't that good or that different and certainly not that lucky.

This was where it really began — the loss of momentum, the running out of steam that Shelley talked about and that has brought me to where I am tonight: contemplating life as a failure.

ten

A book a week, said Walter: five thousand words a day for seven days.

We're not talking about the Great American Novel, said Walter. Or, for that matter, the Great New Zealand Novel. In fact, we were hardly talking about a Novel. We were talking about writing Crap for Money. Do it once, do it quick, bank the cheque. That's how it works. That's the only way it makes sense.

The first one took me seven months. It was respectfully derivative of the Terry Southern/Mason Hoffenburg romp *Candy*, a seminal text among my little circle at university. My pal Chas Harley, who went on to a career in English lit, reckoned *Candy* was the ultimate novel because it made you laugh out loud *and* gave you a hard-on. Simultaneously. Eventually he conceded that this made *Candy* unusual if not unique, but not necessarily the last word.

Chas and I bought all the copies of *Candy* that the university bookshop had in stock with a view to using them to grease the social wheels. Working on the theory that any girl who enjoyed the book — or, even better, 'related' to it — would be a prize catch on several grounds, we forced it on every likely lass we came across. Sadly, for all their loose talk and liberated attitudes, they generally failed to get the joke and dismissed it as smut, pure and simple. The passage in which the eponymous heroine is aroused by a hunchback ('Give me your hump!') was deemed particularly repellent.

Candy was itself a parody of Voltaire's *Candide*. I reverted to a male protagonist: Randy is a naïve sixteen-year-old, the only child of suffocatingly protective parents. When they're wiped out in that ever-reliable *deus ex machina* the car crash, he goes to live with his depraved Aunt Claudia, becoming a plaything for her and her like-minded friends. Torn between shame and guilty pleasure he runs away, taking refuge in a nunnery. But beneath its ascetic façade the Order of Saint Lavinia the Chaste is — you guessed it — the proverbial seething hotbed of debauchery. And so it went.

I made every mistake you can think of: I created characters rather than lavishly endowed ciphers; I constructed a story with a beginning, a middle and a conclusion; I introduced humour, bawdy and satiric; I inserted the odd moment of tenderness among all the heaving and writhing; I had Randy fall in love. I forgot I was writing Crap for Money.

I also wasted many hours dithering over a suitable pseudonym. At first I favoured something suavely man-about-townish, suggestive of the sort of swinger who would hang out at the Playboy Mansion and wake up in his rotating circular bed with a sumptuous breast in each ear: Brad Lance, Nero Blake, Drew Cheyney, Felix de Mille.

But that wasn't really me or what this was about. What was needed, I decided, was a name that distanced the writer from the material and infused the whole enterprise with postmodern irony: Rod Gripper, Aldo Tripod, Augie Nadir, Dirk Firkin, Strobe Riggle, Humbert Kinkade, Benny Pagan,

Jolyon Slot, Chester Swill, Lex Raby, Lew Goatman. I even toyed with the idea of a sex change: Greeba Bint, Kitty Hornhardt, Patsy Frothmader, Juanita Dank, Poppy Clamm, Pandora Boxx. In the end I settled on Woody Bleek, which I felt had a foot in both camps.

I sent the manuscript off. A week or so later Walter called from LA.

'Max, I'd pretty much given up on you.'

'I don't blame you.'

'It's good, Max, damn good. In fact, if I'm ever tempted to read porn in a non-professional capacity, this'll be my benchmark. Shit, it's almost respectable.'

I said, 'Thanks,' although I suspected it wasn't entirely meant as a compliment.

'But we have a problem, Houston: the average strokebook buyer won't appreciate the care and attention that's gone into it. That added quality, Max, that extra mile — there's no percentage in it.'

'You mean you can't use it?'

'Oh, we can use it all right, but at the going rate. Would you feel exploited, Max? Would you feel like a wetback picking oranges for chump change?'

'What's new? I can't say you didn't warn me.'

'No, you can't. So we have a deal?'

'Well, fuck, I've got to have something to show for it.'

'You have, Max — twenty-five hundred US and a harsh but valuable lesson. And, by the way, what the fuck sort of name is Woody Bleek?'

By the fourth one I was down to fifteen working days and feeling as if I was getting the hang of it. Then my mad dad died.

Jerome Maxwell Napier died, aged seventy-three, in the institution for the deluded and despairing into which he'd disappeared at ever-shorter intervals during the last eight years of his life.

Since we'd been in Sydney I'd been over to Auckland for a couple of visits. Outwardly he didn't look too bad, apart from the deepening grooves in his face that made him look like Samuel Beckett's melancholic little brother. But talking to him was hard work and sometimes a waste of time because he either couldn't — or chose not to — keep up his side of the conversation, or wandered off the subject down a private path that no one else could follow.

My father was a lower-middle-class Englishman, bright enough to get into a grammar school and thence a red-brick university. He was invited to join the staff of an Auckland private school that really preferred Oxbridge men but, failing that, red-brick was better than home-grown. He sailed away from postwar rationing and didn't return until his post-retirement European tour. He and my mother caught the tail-end of my time in Paris, then spent six months 'doing' France, Italy and the UK. Whatever memories it stirred up, he was never quite the same afterwards. Within months of getting home he was institutionalised for the first time.

He was a wry, diffident man but when the mood took him he could send me and my sister into laughing jags with his repertoire of funny voices and nonsense stories which, I later discovered, owed much to *The Goon Show*. He seemed more easy-going and slower to censoriousness or anger than my friends' fathers and, perhaps because I didn't fear him, I didn't put him on a pedestal.

Even during my moody teenage years we boxed along well enough, something he put down to the fact that I didn't attend the school at which he taught. Those of his colleagues whose sons did inevitably had spiky relationships with them. Said sons' attitudes were shaped by peer pressure and the gradual realisation that, far from being a worthy object of hero worship, one's father was actually a mediocrity and perhaps a blowhard or weakling or clown to boot.

And as I learned when he wrote to me in Paris to tell me that he was retiring, despite spending his entire working life — thirty-seven years — teaching at the same school, he didn't believe in private education. For all that time he'd kept his socialism — among other things — to himself.

Flying over for his funeral, numbed by a bottomless glass of vodka and a detached sense of loss, I found myself reliving his fiftieth birthday party. Our birthdays were a month apart (I'd just turned nineteen) and in a fey moment he'd floated the idea of a joint party with the quixotic aim of reducing the generation gap. I ruthlessly scotched the idea, pointing out that my do was already doubling as a celebration of America's defeat in Vietnam.

The communists believed in the tide of history and for a time it seemed as if the red tide was going to roll around the world. The decline of the West was there for all to see in a grainy news photo of an overloaded US chopper heaving itself off the roof of the Saigon embassy, like a weary old pheasant flushed from the undergrowth for the last time. Uncle Sam had turned tail, his will broken by haemorrhage on the ground and dissent at home, his high-tech war machine bogged down in paddyfields and nullified by the implacable jungle, his imperial mission routed by Third World revolutionaries.

We know now that the fall of Saigon was the red tide's high-water mark. But for my parents' friends, greying suburbanites with their Cold War mindsets, absolute belief in the domino theory and active memories of those panic-ridden months following Pearl Harbor when the dominoes tumbled — Guam, Wake Island, Hong Kong, Singapore, the Philippines — it unleashed their deepest insecurities, evoking the history that, deep down, they had always feared would repeat itself.

And while they fretted for their children's future, imagining New Zealand under the heel of some inhuman Oriental in a Mao jacket, said children mocked their anxieties and raised their glasses to posters of Ho Chi Minh.

I arrived at my father's fiftieth just before midnight with a few beers under my belt. Everyone drank and drove in those days. How else were you meant to get around at that hour of night?

Most of the guests had more on board than I did. They were social drinkers, instinctively suspicious of alcohol and inclined to blame France's military fiascos and Italy's perpetual political crisis on the Latins' wine habit. But it was okay to let one's hair down on special occasions, and let it down they did.

In the hall I met a woman of my parents' generation whom I'd known since primary school. She emerged unsteadily from the toilet, still trying to hoist her slacks over her paunch. She enveloped me in a smothering embrace and asked me personal questions, emphasising each interrogative with a nudge of her breasts. This was a woman whose son had once been my best friend, at whose house I'd often slept over, who'd sent me home in disgrace when I sullenly baulked at macaroni cheese, who gave me a four-piece test-standard cricket ball for my thirteenth birthday.

In the lounge my mother, a harmless party flirt, was executing bobbysoxer twirls with the next-door neighbour. Some of the other dance-floor moves bordered on the spastic. The deputy headmaster of my father's school, a lay preacher renowned for his savage virtuosity with the cane, had his shirt open to the navel and was circling his partner as if trying to decide where to bite her. The Dave Clark Five were on the turntable. Piss-weak first-generation Britpop — the Searchers, the Hollies, Gerry and the Pacemakers, early

Beatles — was the appropriate soundtrack for this bourgeois bacchanal.

Some of my father's colleagues were in a huddle, roaring like morons over a dirty joke, but the man himself was nowhere to be seen. Looking for a beer, I found sister Felicity, sweet little sixteen, backed into a corner of the kitchen by Bob, my father's bridge partner and a recent grandfather. It was a replay of the mammary attack in the hall: the same age difference, the same salacious interrogation, the same invasive proximity bordering on frottage. Both adults were only a bacardi and Coke away from a shameful bit of history that would have to be rewritten in the morning.

As sisters went, Felicity was acceptably middle of the road: neither plain Jane nor knockout, neither Miss Goody Two Shoes nor town bike. Unlike some guys I knew, I'd been spared the unsettling pub urinal experience of noticing among the obscene and psychotic graffiti the claim that one's sister rooted like a rattlesnake or took it up the arse. Occasionally a friend would declare an interest but I discouraged it. Felicity's tastes were mainstream; she favoured sports stars, wiry, blond, spoilt, supercilious airheads. She thought my friends were freaks who'd take her to movies with subtitles and ply her with dope, and she was right.

Bob helped himself to a few squirts of Chateau Cardboard Muller-Thurgau as he asked how my studies were going. Without waiting for an answer, he cast a final hot-eyed, dry-lipped glance at Felicity and faded away.

I put it to her that there was safety in numbers.

She screwed up her nose as if something stank. 'You've got a one-track mind.'

'I'm obviously not the only one. What was he suggesting — one-on-one bridge lessons the night his wife goes to cooking class?'

She smirked, playing along. 'Actually, he's just taken up

photography; he wants me to pose for him.'

'All in the best possible taste, no doubt?'

'Of course.'

'Who gets to keep the lingerie?'

That made her shudder. 'Do you seriously think he's a dirty old man?'

'He's pissed,' I said. 'It amounts to the same thing.'

'Does that go for Dad as well?'

'Come on. Can you imagine him carrying on like that?'

'No, but I don't suppose Bob's kids could either,' she said. 'Have you seen Dad?'

'I've just got here. Where is he?'

'Last I saw him he was out the back.'

'That's a strange place to be while your fiftieth birthday party's in full swing.'

She shrugged. 'That's our Papa.'

An uncle came into the kitchen arm in arm with a woman who wasn't an aunt. They didn't hurriedly disentangle so it was either entirely innocent or they were too drunk to care. Felicity and I exchanged raised eyebrows. I went out to the back veranda, where the birthday boy was sitting on the swing seat, smoking his pipe.

'The son and heir,' he said. 'Nice of you to drop in.'

I sat down beside him. He was undemonstrative in the English way, so he wouldn't have expected a handshake and would have been alarmed by a hug.

'What are you doing out here?'

'Enjoying a contemplative pipe and a breath of fresh air,' he said. 'And don't bother pointing out the contradiction.'

'A bit bloody anti-social, isn't it? The gang's all here to celebrate your fiftieth and you're skiving off for a smoke.'

'My little milestone was duly acknowledged several hours ago. Since then the evening's taken on a life of its own.'

There was a tremendous uproar inside, as if a couple of

men had squared off or a woman had started removing her clothes. My father expelled smoke through a sardonic smile.

'It's still your party.'

'Your mother likes dancing and she's good at it,' he said. 'I don't and I'm not. Besides, I can't abide that music. I thought it was rubbish when you and Felicity started listening to it years ago and it'll take more than a few glasses of sparkling wine to change my mind. Ah, there you are.' This was addressed to a couple who had emerged from the darkness of the back yard. 'You know my son Max? Max, this is Peter and Doreen. Peter's the young lion of the Auckland bridge scene. He's taught me a thing or two, I can tell you.'

Peter was a sleek shortarse who looked a decade younger than most of the guests, including Doreen, whom I didn't know. Depending on your taste and vocabulary she was either plump or Rubenesque, and had probably once been pretty. Now she looked like she'd come straight from a torrid session in the back row of the local cinema. Her hair and lipstick were in disarray and the buttons up the front of her dress were in the wrong buttonholes.

As they approached, she stumbled and had to grab Peter's arm to avoid a spill.

'Damn these heels,' she muttered.

Doreen bent down to take off her shoes, giving us an eyeful of her breasts that had the same well-exercised flush as her cheeks. She straightened up, giggling at herself and at us. 'God, I need to pee. I'll see you boys inside.'

She came up the steps with her head down, struggling to keep a straight face, but couldn't resist a swift sideways glance to make sure she had our undivided attention. I don't know about Dad but whatever she saw on my face triggered another spacey giggle.

Peter cleared his throat. 'I've just been showing Doreen your hideaway, Jerry,' he said. 'Nice little set-up you've got there.'

My parents lived in Epsom, on the Cornwall Park side of Manukau Road. The house was at the front of the section, creating a deep back yard with flower beds, a vegetable garden, a few grapefruit trees and, at the very bottom, a converted garden shed that was, increasingly, my father's home away from home. He spent a couple of hours a night and entire weekends down there, listening to classical music, re-reading his favourite authors and his bridge and chess books, and attending to schoolmasterly duties that, like a woman's work, were never quite done.

Dad stood up to tap his pipe out on the railing. 'Well, Pierre, as I always say: every man needs a bolt-hole. I suppose we should rejoin the happy throng.' As Peter went past, my father dropped an avuncular hand on his shoulder. 'A quick trip to the bathroom might be in order,' he murmured. 'I'm no expert in the cosmetics department but it looks to me as if your lady friend and Doreen use different shades of lipstick.'

Peter turned pinker and scuttled inside. My father looked at me inquiringly. 'Well, my boy, what do you make of that?'

'A bit bloody cheeky apart from anything else.'

He nodded. 'Nip down and open the window, there's a good lad. I've got a pile of marking to do tomorrow and I'd rather the place didn't reek of minge.'

When it was all over, when the drunks and sleepyheads had been flushed out of the bedrooms and the die-hards had downed their three or four for the road, Felicity and I sent my parents off to bed and cleaned up.

As we were doing the dishes I threw Doreen into the conversational mix.

'Dor the Whore.'

'What?'

'That's what Mum calls her,' she said. 'Who'd she pounce on tonight?'

'The bridge midget — Peter Someone.'

'Peter Quinn. He's not a midget. In fact, if I had to sleep with one man who was here tonight . . .'

'Which you don't. Let's get that perfectly clear.'

'No, but let's say Mum and Dad were kidnapped by a satanic cult who threatened that unless we . . .'

'Jesus,' I said, 'how much piss did you put away tonight?'

'A lot less than you, that's for sure. And don't be such a hypocrite; I bet you and your filthy friends play this game all the time. If it meant saving our dear parents from becoming human sacrifices, I'd do it with Peter Quinn. What about you?'

'I'd ring the cops.'

'Gosh, a hypocrite and a spoilsport.'

'Why Dor the Whore?'

Her face lit up. 'You would choose her, wouldn't you? You're so predictable — go for the trollop every time.'

'Well, this is the thing, Felicity: you keep calling her names without anything to back it up.'

'I've heard of short-term memory loss but that's ridiculous,' she said. 'You saw her at it with your own eyes a couple of hours ago.'

'One swallow doesn't make a summer. Besides, for all you know, she might be in love with Shorty.'

'Yeah, and Shorty might be Piggy Muldoon's love-child. Anything's possible.' She shook her head, signalling that this silliness had gone far enough. 'Mum won't go into the sordid details. Actually, she puts on the sourpuss face and changes the subject.' Felicity raised her eyebrows at me for the second time that night. 'Makes you wonder, doesn't it?'

It was almost afternoon when I woke up in my old bed. There was a note on the kitchen table saying my mother and Felicity had gone for a walk in Cornwall Park. I had something to eat and went down to the shed. Strictly speaking the shed was a no-go area but I considered myself exempt now that I was flatting and my father, I suppose, felt he had to show willing.

He was lanky, with placid grey eyes and a beaky nose, hence his longstanding school nickname 'Birdface'. His weekend wear was felt slippers, corduroy trousers that had once been dark green and a sleeveless cricket jersey of unknown origin over a flannel shirt. Chas Harley, who dabbled in the theatre, had expressed an ambition to cast him as Sherlock Holmes. To my mind he looked the part of an otherworldly scion of a once posh, now downwardly mobile family who'd been bilked out of his inheritance and reduced to a shabby genteel existence in the colonies.

The walls were covered with scenes of Britannia ruling the waves, the bookshelves untidily crammed with the works of his favourite authors — Wodehouse, Waugh, Greene, De Maupassant, Forester, Simenon, Saki, Kipling. A chessboard was set up in the corner; a thermos of tea was at his elbow; tobacco smoke and Concert Programme violin music hung in the air. As he'd said, this was his bolt-hole, the last retreat of a solitary man who'd begun to withdraw from the world and from his nearest and dearest.

I asked, 'What was the atmosphere like first thing?'

He frowned. 'Sorry, not with you.'

'The minge factor.'

'Oh, that. Mercifully subdued.'

'So that's Doreen's party trick, is it?'

Realising that this wasn't the hi and bye leave-taking he would have preferred, he took off his glasses and swung around in his swivel chair. 'It would be fair to say her reputation precedes her.'

'Dor the Whore?'

'You've been talking to your mother.'

'Felicity.'

'Same thing.'

'What's the story?'

'Why this sudden interest in middle-aged foolishness?'

'Call it prurience.'

He smiled quizzically. 'Given that you aspire to being a writer, Max, I thought you might be starting to grapple with the eternal mystery of women.'

'No, just plain old prurience, I'm afraid.'

'There's a lot of it about,' he said. 'Well, the story, such as it is, is hardly original. Two people persuade themselves that they're in love; they get married. Some time later — it might take two years, it might take ten — it dawns on them that they no longer have the feelings they mistook for love. The marriage deteriorates into a rather grim practical arrangement that doesn't satisfy their emotional and physical needs so every now and again they go a bit haywire.'

'By going a bit haywire you mean slipping out the back for a quick screw with someone they met half an hour earlier?'

'Are you sure you haven't been talking to your mother?'

'I take it she's a bit more judgemental than you?' I said.

'She's heard about a husband who's got no head for drink and tends to peg out in the spare bedroom and a wife who takes the opportunity for a bit of slap and tickle. Last night Quinn was the beneficiary but if it wasn't for the presence of forewarned and therefore eagle-eyed wives, I'm sure Doreen would've been spoilt for choice.'

'How spoilt?'

This was new territory for us. We'd never really discussed the facts of life, to use his generation's euphemism. When I was twelve he took me to a fathers and sons night at the local church hall to watch a film apparently produced by Ministry of Agriculture veterinarians in the days before Technicolor. Apart from clearing up a few murky anatomical issues, it didn't tell me anything I didn't already know.

Questions were encouraged but not forthcoming. On the

way home my father repeated the invitation. I gave him the answer he craved and we hadn't as much as skirted around the whole fraught subject since.

And now here I was, nineteen years old and thinking myself worldly on the basis of having watched a few French new-wave films and persuaded a few girls that sexual licence was the in thing, grilling this fastidious and reticent man on a subject he probably avoided with his closest friends.

'Well, I can only speak for myself.'

'So you and Mum are the exceptions?'

He took his time refilling his teacup. 'You know, I don't hugely mind answering these questions as long as you answer a couple of mine first. Do you have any reason to think otherwise?'

'No.'

'Then what's prompted all this?'

'Last night's carry-on. As Felicity pointed out, their kids couldn't imagine them behaving like that.'

'Doreen and her husband don't have children,' he said. 'Perhaps that's part of the problem.'

'In what way?'

'Tell me, Max, how do you see yourself at my age?'

That was easy. 'As a writer, living in Europe, in a relationship but not necessarily married.'

'Children?'

I shrugged. 'Don't know. Probably not. Not really my cup of tea, domesticity.'

'And you think you'll be completely fulfilled by writing?'

'That's how it works, Dad.'

'Well, it sounds a little selfish but the object of the exercise is happiness and fulfilment and making a contribution, so if writing books does all that, good for you. But you'd be one of the lucky ones. For most people, even those with a real sense of vocation, their work eventually becomes the thing they do because they have to, in order to have the wherewithal to live in a modicum of comfort. If your job becomes a grind and a bore and your relationship doesn't stand the test of time and you have no focus for your finer feelings — assuming you have any — then where does that leave you? Apart from very much looking forward to the weekend?'

'What if your children turn out to be shitheads? Wouldn't that make it worse?'

He smiled thinly. 'Well, we'll keep our fingers crossed. Anyway, to answer your question and close this discussion, your mother and I get along quite well enough to make me immune to Doreen's charms, evident and abundant though they are.'

'Felicity reckons Mum's got a bit of a thing about Doreen.'

'You're like a dog with a bone, aren't you? I suppose I should be flattered, but on the other hand there's an unmistakable implication that I'm not telling the truth.'

'I don't think that for one minute. I'm just wondering why Mum's got this bee in her bonnet about Doreen. I mean, if it's no skin off her nose . . .'

'It doesn't occur to you that she might disapprove of Doreen's behaviour on moral grounds? Your mother's a little more conservative in these matters than she likes to let on. It might also have something to do with the fact that we had one of our very occasional rows over this Dor the Whore business.'

'Let she who's without sin cast the first stone?'

'Really, Max, I hope for your sake this cynicism is either a pose or a passing phase. Cynicism is the enemy of art, you know.'

'That's debatable.'

'Everything's debatable as far as your generation's concerned. That's because you don't believe in anything.'

'What are you talking about? We believe in lots of things.'

'Well, you've got lots of slogans; I'm not sure that's quite the same thing.'

Under normal circumstances I wouldn't have let him get away with that but I suspected he was trying to change the subject. 'One thing at a time, eh? You were saying?'

'Such single-mindedness,' he said. 'A pity it's not in a worthier cause. I objected because I happen to believe one should know all the facts before one starts pinning nasty labels on people. I don't know all the facts but I've picked up enough to know it's not black and white.'

'Well, all I can say is, you're very tolerant for a man whose study was commandeered for a sly root.'

'You're jumping to conclusions.'

'Look who's talking. Who sent me down here last night to get rid of the minge odour?'

'You surprise me, Max; I would've thought a young blade like you was intimately acquainted with the workings of the female nether regions.' He produced another quizzical smile. 'You look baffled. Surely you're aware that female sexual arousal and its physical manifestations can occur without intercourse taking place — or indeed without the minge coming into play, as it were. I used the term "slap and tickle" and I used it advisedly. As I understand it, Doreen goes so far and no further.' He paused to savour having bested me at my own game. 'The eternal mystery of women — now there's a subject for a young writer to get his teeth into.'

eleven

I'm studying the expressions in a family photo taken at my father's wake. What's the appropriate expression for a wake? After all, the solemnities marking his death and our loss are out of the way. This shindig is to 'celebrate' the dear departed's life, to swap fond memories with that happy band who also knew and loved him and to demonstrate through our wit, conviviality and, yes, bravery that we're better people for having followed, in our different ways, his inspiring example. There will always be time to cry: all the time in the world. Right now, though, it's time to put our best foot forward and eat, drink and be merry — because he would have wanted it that way.

Can we be sure of that? Was there an empty, lucid afternoon when he realised his time had come?

This old body's like a besieged city, out of arrows and boiling oil and the will to resist. The enemy's at the gates, battering away. Hit something hard enough, often enough, it's going to give. And then? Well, this enemy's different from the ones we've tangled with in the past; this enemy gives no quarter. It will put me to the sword and to the torch and that will be that.

And, having got that far, did he give any thought to the hymns he'd like sung at his funeral or the budget for the wake? Was there any solace in visualising family and friends enjoying this event at which his non-appearance would be the major talking point? I doubt it somehow. My father wasn't exactly a party animal and most of the guests — the retired schoolmasters and bridge-playing pensioners and their fragile or all-too-robust wives — looked all partied out.

My mother's putting on a brave face but the camera always has that effect on her. My eyes are hidden behind dark glasses secret-service style and there's a moody cast to my mouth. Felicity, who now prefers to be called 'Flick', the dismal pet name conferred by her dismal husband, has a half-hearted, artificial smile, but she's in sales and marketing so that might be her default expression. Husband Murray — he insists on 'Muz' or 'Muzza' but I'm a refusenik — looks aggrieved, as if the photographer didn't give him time to fix his hair.

The only person putting on a funeral face is, paradoxically, the professional: the presiding cleric. You'd think he'd be used to it. He must spend half his working life in death's shadow, visiting old folks' homes and keeping sickbed vigils. He probably does one of these gigs a week. Professionals are meant to be immune to stuff that would make the rest of us puke or faint or go to pieces. Surgeons can banter as they fossick among glistening, pulsing innards; cops can debate All Black selection oblivious to the eviscerated corpse nailed to the floor; paramedics can swap holiday plans while cutting teenage joy-riders out of the concertinaed wreckage of a stolen car. It's not that they don't care, but experience has taught them that shit happens and will continue to happen whether they care or not. Experience has also taught them that the only things worth a damn they can give those poor bastards sliced and sandwiched in the sheet metal are drugs and cool professionalism. Pity is neither here nor there.

But even though he's an old pro, a veteran of the bereavement caper, Reverend Bert Logan looks the saddest of all.

I took a bottle of red wine down to the study. The stacks of essays and exercise books had gone and a layer of dust had settled; otherwise it was just as I remembered. There were no more books in the bookshelves because all my father's favourite writers were long dead and he wasn't interested in extending his range. He believed that being widely read was overrated. Which was better, he would ask: to have read thousands of books once or a few hundred several times? You didn't buy a painting to look at it once. If it was any good it revealed itself, layer by layer, over time. Books were the same: the first read was just to find out what happens, which was often the least important aspect.

I was sitting in the swivel chair thinking that one more glass of wine would probably have me in tears when there was a knock on the partly opened door.

'Pardon the intrusion,' said Reverend Logan, 'but I've got to be on my way.'

I stood up. 'Oh, right. Well, look, thanks for everything. Mum's been telling me you were a very good friend to Dad towards the end there.'

Logan was about sixty, a fatty and a baldy. He'd been a bit hangdog since the service but that seemed to cheer him up. 'Nice of her to say so,' he said, cheeks dimpling, 'but it went both ways — Jerry was a very good friend to me. He was terribly proud of you, you know; recommended your books to everyone he came across. Wasted on me, I'm afraid. I'm not a fiction man — history and biography are more my style.'

I'd heard this statement before (despite the wording — 'I'm afraid' — it's not an admission, let alone an apology) and, as always, it bugged me. Why not keep quiet about it? Why advertise the fact that you're a philistine?

'Well,' I said starchily, 'as they say, there's no accounting for taste.'

'Exactly,' he said complacently. (And, yes, I admit it, I find complacency all the more unattractive in a fatso.) 'I suppose that just makes your job more difficult: you spend all that time writing something without knowing whether it's what the public's after or not.'

'I don't write for the mass market so I don't have that problem.'

'Oh? I seem to remember your father saying you were writing a whodunit. I must've got the wrong end of the stick.'

This bloated God-botherer was getting on my nerves but I held my tongue. Telling him to piss off before my father's ashes were cold was definitely not what the dear departed would have wanted. Besides, Logan had just poked his nose in to say goodbye, hadn't he?

Instead I said, 'Well, whodunit's a bit of a misnomer. Okay, it's a mystery on one level but just because a writer employs some elements of genre, that doesn't mean the novel has to conform to all its conventions and formulae or should automatically be classified as genre.' He clearly had no idea what I was talking about. 'I mean, just because there's a murder and a narrative culminating in the identification of the murderer, that doesn't necessarily make it an escapist yarn. There are plenty of murders in Shakespeare, for instance.'

'Well, you're the expert,' he said with a smug half-smile; perhaps he'd picked up the tremor of desperation in the Shakespeare reference. 'As I say, I stick to the stuff I enjoy — rather like your father did.'

This bogus comparison also grated but I didn't respond, in the hope that my sullen silence would encourage Reverend Lard to shove off as promised. But he hovered in the doorway. Nothing, it seemed, would be left unsaid.

'Yes, Jerry was very pleased that you'd done what you set

out to do. And a bit concerned, it would be fair to say.'

'What about?'

'I think he sometimes got the feeling that being a writer perhaps wasn't quite as fulfilling as you'd expected it to be.'

'What gave him that idea?'

'Seeing you and talking to you. And reading your books, I suppose.'

'Yeah? The last couple of times we saw each other I got the strong impression he wasn't taking a hell of a lot in.'

Logan decided he had some time up his sleeve after all. He lowered himself into the old armchair in the corner where my father used to replay famous chess matches or pursue his futile quest for an opening gambit that would send the chess world into a tizzy.

'Your father,' he said with stagy emphasis, 'was less . . . detached from reality than you — and others — seem to think.'

'Maybe you should enlarge on that.'

'It wasn't depression that killed him so much as general wear and tear. What got him down, in the main, was not being very well. Add the fact that being chronically below par is a tiring business and it's hardly surprising he wasn't always a box of birds. If you don't see much of someone and those odd occasions coincide with him being down in the dumps, it's easy to assume he's like that all the time. But he wasn't. And even when he wasn't particularly responsive, the brain was still working.' He tapped his forehead. 'It was all filed away up here.'

'How do you know?'

'He told me. As you know, I saw quite a lot of him.'

'Is it my imagination or do I detect a hint of reproach?'

'You were overseas,' said Logan. 'You had your own life to lead. Your father understood that. As for me, well, it's not my place to judge.'

I'd had enough of this sanctimonious puffball, who'd obviously been itching to lay a guilt trip on me from the moment my father was pronounced dead. 'You could've fooled me.'

That pinged off the armour-plating of his self-righteousness. 'Jerry accepted that he'd reaped what he'd sowed. If he didn't blame you, why should I?'

'Reverend, you've obviously got something you want to say so why don't you just get on with it?' I had an unnerving role-reversal flashback to the Doreen joust, my father trying to hustle it to a conclusion and me wanting to spin it out. 'As you can imagine, it's been a pretty draining few days. I came down here to have a few minutes to myself to remember Dad as he was to me. Not to you, or the others up there or anyone else. But I can't do that because I'm stuck in this conversation which, frankly, I'm having trouble seeing the point of.'

Logan rose with much heaving and huffing, like a lorry tackling a steep hill. 'I'm sorry if I've upset you; that certainly wasn't the intention. All I really wanted to say — because your father fretted that perhaps he hadn't communicated this as well or as often as he should've — was that he loved you and was proud of you.' He paused. That was the good news. 'I've wrestled with this a good deal and come to the conclusion that I owe it to him to also convey that he worried about you.' He paused again. 'He saw a lot of himself in you.'

I took my time digesting this. Logan held my smouldering gaze. 'Come on, Reverend, spit it out.'

'He thought you shared certain traits and characteristics which, in his case, contributed to his state of mind. He felt that he'd let things creep up on him so that by the time he realised he had a problem, it was too late. Hopefully in your case, forewarned is forearmed.'

'Can you be more specific?'

He shook his head. 'I think the process of thinking it

through and working it out for yourself is really the key. It's a matter of self-knowledge and having the will to act on it. Goodbye, Max, and good luck.'

'So apart from being unwell,' I said when he was halfway out the door, 'what else made him unhappy?'

Logan turned and gave me a long, expressionless look. 'I can't reveal what was said to me in confidence.'

'He's dead, for Christ's sake.'

'And the world's a lesser place.'

He left me to my own devices, which boiled down to half a bottle of Hawke's Bay cabernet merlot. I was right: it only took one more glass.

Logan was the last straw. I'd endured my mother emoting like some soap opera matriarch hell-bent on testing the limits of her dramatic range. Lamentation ('How will I get by without him?') gave way to martyred resentment ('It hasn't been easy, you know. I could tell you things that would make your hair stand on end'). Hard on the heels of tender selflessness — 'He's at peace now' — would come a self-pitying riff on the unalloyed bleakness of widowhood in a coupled-up world.

Hysteria was never far from the quavering surface of these monologues. One minute she could be listing — and not without a faint buzz of anticipation — potential or even actual admirers (apparently a few old dogs had sniffed around during my father's incarcerations); the next she'd be vapouring at the prospect of being paired off with every decrepit bore who'd managed to outlive his wife.

And there was guilt, enough for all the family. She felt guilty about collaborating in my father's solitariness because it suited her or she couldn't be bothered nagging him back into circulation. She felt guilty about not doing more to alleviate his dark moods and her lack of resistance when they drove him to commit himself. She felt guilty about not looking forward to visiting him and then arriving late and leaving early when she did.

Just when it seemed nothing could get her off the subject, I asked if, with the benefit of hindsight, she had a theory on what had tipped my father into his downward spiral. She said she didn't want to talk about it any more and went to bed.

I could take my mother in limited doses but Felicity and Murray constituted a far less palatable brew. He was a real estate agent. The attributes that make an effective salesperson are not those you'd look for in a desert island companion but, even so, it was impossible to believe that Murray's personality was an asset, professionally speaking. But he'd seen the Ponsonby/Herne Bay property boom coming so while he was a fuckwit who'd had only one idea in his life, it was a good idea and had made him a well-off fuckwit.

They lived in a beautifully restored villa overlooking Westhaven Marina with their expensively educated kiddies and his-and-hers BMWs. The trappings weren't the issue: I knew and liked others who lived in similar style. What made Murray tiresome and ultimately repulsive was his noisy certainty that there was nothing more to life than more of the same — more money, more property, better lifestyle — and his noisy contempt for those who didn't have the acquisitive urge or simply weren't very good at making money.

To Murray, society was a meaningless concept. People fell into three categories: the demi-gods with helicopters and ocean-going pleasure boats and a home on every continent; the ordinary rich; and the burdensome rest. Everyone in the third category, from the salaried white-collar brigade all the way down to the feckless underclass, was despised. He resented every cent of tax he paid, and gloried in every scam and shortcut that enriched him at the expense of the state or the sucker on the other end of the deal. And all of it — the nouveau riche vulgarity, the fascist instincts, the dog-eat-dog rorts and rip-offs, the lack of any sense of national identity (apart from skinhead jingoism on sporting occasions) — was justified by one thing: the fact that he'd worked fucking hard to get where he was today.

Those villas didn't restore themselves, you know. I used to put in a full day's work, then go home, get changed and strip and sand and paint till midnight. Same with Flick. Fifteen years of holding down day jobs and spending our nights and weekends making old dumps look good enough to double our money.

Do it once, do it quick, bank the cheque.

So don't come to me for a hand-out. I don't collect a pay cheque for doing fuck all all week. I'm on commission: sell or starve. Flick and I didn't work our arses off all those years for other people's benefit. We did it for us and our kids.

The worst part of it was that he'd converted Felicity to this miserable set of attitudes. She looked good; she and Murray brought their ferocious self-enhancement ethic to bear on their physical appearances via the gym, Pilates and annual half-marathons. Below the surface, though, there was nothing left of the person she used to be.

I had dinner with them and two other couples, their closest friends. I felt like I'd infiltrated a cult. A cargo cult that worshipped the Lear jet.

Then there was the funeral. Imagine it backstage at Miss World, the contestants checking each other out: *Christ, get a load of Miss Ukraine — if she was any more butch, she'd have to shave twice a day. And don't tell me Miss Brazil's tits are for real; that slut's had more surgery than a Siamese twin.*

The old-timers ran the rule over one another as minutely as their eyesight would permit, trying to work out who would outlive whom. *Old George isn't too steady on his pins; he'll be lucky to make the millennium. Crikey, what's Jack trying to do — drink himself to death? He looks like a marinated plum. And as for Bill . . . I tell you what, I saw faster-moving snails in the garden this morning. We should do this more often, dear.*

At Felicity and Murray's it was all about money: how to make it, how to keep it, how to spend it. You were defined by how much you had and how badly you wanted more. At the funeral it was all about death and how long it could be kept waiting. When my father's contemporaries pawed me with their mottled mitts and peered into my face, they weren't searching for a trace of their dead friend. They were trying to remember what it was like to be unafraid of time.

There were eulogies from a bridge pal and a former colleague portraying my father as a one-dimensional figure with no existence worth recording outside the bridge club or the college grounds. They evoked a dusty anachronism: courtly, particular, stuck in his ways. Despite having known him for decades, they apparently hadn't noticed that he had a keen sense of humour and the absurd. On the other hand, there was no mention of the fog of despair into which — Logan notwithstanding — he'd receded, so perhaps they felt on safer ground with the sensible public individual than the sad clown.

Felicity made an effort to splash a little colour onto this study in grey but while she provided a few snapshots of a happy family under a benign paternal regime, the years of righteous overtime and upward mobility and absorbing Murray's crude and spiteful Social Darwinism had cooled her heart and deprived her of the capacity to treasure human foibles and fallibilities. And when all was said and done, my father was a wage slave, a worker bee — dangerously close, in fact, to being a loser. He'd given his working life to one employer; he'd been an acting head of department any number of times but hadn't lobbied for bigger things or sought a fast track. He'd collected the weekly pay cheque. He hadn't sincerely wanted to be rich.

To top it all off, I'd had Reverend Logan popping up like

Banquo's ghost and passing on a cryptic warning from beyond the urn. If ever a man was entitled to make a beast of himself, I was that man. And there was no better guide and companion in that cathartic exercise than my old friend and partner in crime, Associate Professor Chas Harley.

He was talking to Felicity. I could tell it wasn't going quite as he'd expected.

I butted in. 'Ready when you are, Chas.'

'You're not leaving?' Felicity demanded.

'Watch me.'

'What's the rush?' she said. 'For crying out loud, Max, it's Dad's wake.'

'I wondered what all these people were doing here.'

'Well, you're certainly behaving as if it's slipped your mind.'

'By all means, Felicity, be the last to leave. You're more than welcome to the kudos attached to that. I happen to have reached saturation point. You right, Chas?'

He shrugged. 'It's your call.'

'Well, then, let's get the fuck out of here.'

Felicity's jaw snapped up and she dragged in air through flared nostrils. 'I don't bloody well believe it,' she hissed. 'Today of all days, it's still all about you. You really are a fucking selfish prick, aren't you?'

Over the years I've tended to fight fire with fire but I didn't want to prolong this spat or embarrass our mother by escalating it to a full-on sibling brawl of the sort that can end in blood libels and bitter tears. Not today of all days. So I said, 'Whatever,' and walked away.

My mother pouted when I told her I'd had enough. 'You think you're the only one?'

'I do, as a matter of fact,' I said. 'You can handle it, Felicity can handle it, I can't. I'm not proud of it but that's just the way it is.'

Her expression softened and she laid a hand on my forearm. 'It's all right, dear; off you go. It's mostly sentimental waffle anyway.'

I kissed her on the cheek. 'Thanks, Mum. I'll stay at Chas's tonight so I'll see you tomorrow.'

'Don't forget, Max: you're a married man these days.'

I stared. 'I beg your pardon?'

'I remember what you two used to get up to,' she said equably, 'and when I was speaking to Chas a little while ago I was left in no doubt that he's still very much the bachelor gay. I'm just saying, don't you let him lead you astray.'

'It's not going to be that sort of night,' I said.

'Well, I'm sure you'll start out with the best of intentions but boys will be boys.'

'Except we're not boys.'

'Maybe not but you haven't exactly settled down, have you?'

'Shall we talk about this some other time?'

Chas had the motor running.

'Fuck me,' I said as I got into his car. 'I've copped the lot today, up to and including Mum telling me it's high time you and I started acting our age.'

'Eh?'

'What the fuck did you do: give her a blow-by-blow account of your sex life?'

'No, but now that you mention it, I did get the impression she wouldn't mind a vicarious thrill. Meanwhile Felicity, who used to guest-star in my fantasy life, has turned into a redneck bitch from hell.'

'That's what happens when you marry a real estate agent. Did you meet brother-in-law?'

'Briefly. He struck me as a complete cunt.'

'I'm pretty sure he strikes most people that way. So what does that make Felicity?'

'Shit, she's not the first to fall into that trap,' said Chas. 'Many perfectly fine people marry their exact opposite, then shed every attribute that made them worth knowing and adopt every attribute that makes their spouses unbearable. Fucked if I know why. Yet another reason not to get married.'

'I don't know that marriage per se is the issue. I didn't turn into a clone and neither did my wives.'

'Yeah, but you're different,' he said. 'Not everyone has your sense of self, ego if you like . . .'

'Not everyone's a fucking selfish prick, in other words?'

'Correct. It's a well-known scientific fact that people who aren't fucking selfish pricks are fifty times more likely to surrender their individuality upon entering the state of matrimony. The other thing in your favour is that, philosophically and temperamentally, you're not the marrying kind. I know you keep doing it but it's not your natural state.'

'Is that why you didn't come over for the wedding?'

'Come on, mate, you know I'll go anywhere for a piss-up and a few laughs. It was just bad timing.'

'Clashed with a Queer Theory conference, did it?'

He shook his head. 'This chick got up the duff. It was all pretty loose but I figured I ought to be around when she had the scrape.'

As we went down the ramp into the carpark beneath Chas's apartment building he said, 'So, are you committed this time? I mean really committed?'

'I'm older and wiser.'

'Is that a yes?'

'You're an intellectual,' I said. 'You work it out.'

Chas had a nifty little pad at the bottom of Parnell Rise. We got out of our funeral kit and into a bottle of Moët and a few fat lines of cocaine. Coke was like dessert wine and other people's cigarettes: I never turned them down if they were on offer but didn't miss them when they weren't. Drugs are one thing I'm relatively sensible about.

That set us up nicely for the evening, which began in a raucous Italian restaurant halfway up the rise. Chas wanted to hear about my work in progress. Rather than lie, I changed the subject.

'Do you reckon I take after my father?'

'Are you serious?'

'It's a theory. I don't go along with it but maybe I can't see the wood for the trees.'

'Well, let's consider this proposition,' said Chas. 'Your old man was a solid citizen, a devoted husband and family man . . .'

'As far as we know.'

He raised his eyebrows. 'Do you know something I don't?'

I shook my head. 'No. Neither of us knows fuck all, if the truth be told. We're just assuming he was all of the above.'

'On pretty good grounds, I'd have to say. Your track record, on the other hand, is an appalling litany of exploitation, infidelity and betrayal. He was a gentleman, you're a cad; he held down a proper job for however many fucking years, you've never done an honest day's work in your life. Need I go on?'

'He spent a lot of time on his own — as I do.'

Chas sighed and nodded but not because he thought I had a point. 'He probably spent too much time on his own doing stuff he didn't enjoy. You're doing exactly what you want to do. There's no fucking comparison.'

Coked up and carbo-loaded, we were on our second margarita in a nearby bar when a young woman walked up to Chas and kissed him, at great length, on the mouth. Far from being taken aback, he gave as good as he got.

Eventually he remembered me. 'Max, this is Emma, my special friend. Emma, say hi to my old pal Max Napier, the distinguished novelist.'

Emma epitomised aggressive post-feminist sexiness: pretty but not innocent, with brazen cleavage, a flat, tanned, bejewelled stomach and a sublime backside showcased in fiercely tight trousers. Little was left to chance or the imagination but she was relaxed in the hot glare of strange men's desire because this was her time and place.

None of this came as a surprise. Men and women often part company over what constitutes an attractive heterosexual male but Chas was one they could agree on. For as long as I'd known him, this self-perpetuating consensus had clung to him like a mysterious past. Early on he cultivated a persona modelled on the late rock star, delinquent and poet *manqué* Jim Morrison. Twenty years on he still had his looks, his figure (thanks to a devotion to jogging that his hero would surely have scorned) and the ability to blur the line between charm and manipulation.

I was wondering where Emma's materialisation left the boys' night out when we were joined by her friend Christine. They were the classic Friday night double act: the hot chick who has to beat them off with a stick and her parasitic friend who feeds on the beat-offs. Under different circumstances we would have been a one-night stand made in heaven: she lacked Emma's chiselled glamour and taut sexuality while I came a long way second to Chas in looks, patter and, crucially, cool.

The girls and I were making small-talk of such creaking awkwardness that I sensed they were on the verge of cutting out the middle man when Chas returned from the bar with a fresh round of drinks and an icebreaker: 'By the way, Max, Christine is doing our creative writing course.'

'Really?' We locked eyes as the penny dropped. Reluctantly I cut to Christine: 'How's it going?'

I half-listened to her answer, which took the form of an exposition jam-packed with unsubstantiated assertions and inexact superlatives, darting hostile glances at Chas, who was understandably giving Emma his undivided attention. By the time she and Christine left on their inevitable pilgrimage to the bathroom, I'd built up a powerful head of steam generated by the ambush and Christine's pulverising critique of the late twentieth century novel.

'Nice work, arsehole,' I snarled.

Chas opted for wide-eyed bemusement. 'What?'

'The double date. I don't recall putting in a request for female company.'

'I don't recall you being averse to it.'

'She's into magic realism, for fuck's sake. Don't tell me you had no idea how profoundly averse I am to discussing magic realism with a creative writing student.'

'Fuck, Max, give the poor bitch a break; it's not every day she gets to meet a real live published novelist. She's excited; her little head's bursting with things she wants to talk to you about. Once she's got it all out . . .'

I mimicked his shrug. 'What does that mean?'

'It means normal service will be resumed; we'll be four people having a drink on a Friday night.'

'Four people or two couples?'

He grinned crookedly. 'You do the maths.'

After another round of cocktails in another bar we drifted back to Chas's place to hoover up the rest of the cocaine. Despite the hedonism, the conversation was relatively elevated. Emma turned out to be another literature head, recently embarked on a doctoral thesis on Ronald Hugh Morrieson under the supervision of none other than Associate Professor Chas Harley. Unfortunately there wasn't an opportunity to interrogate him on the ethical implications of this overlap.

I was sharing a sofa with Christine, who couldn't sit still. Each shift and squirm brought her closer until our thighs came into contact. I could have moved or gone to bed but I was curious. I wanted to see how this set-up would unfold.

Unsubtly, as it turned out. Chas and Emma were on the opposite sofa. She was lying back with her legs across his lap and during a lull in the conversation their horseplay segued into foreplay. Christine giggled, exerting unmistakable pressure on my thigh. It had been a big night but I wasn't drunk or high enough for whatever they had in mind. I announced I was off to bed.

No one tried to talk me out of it. I began a parting speech but Christine said she'd crash on the couch so we'd see each other in the morning. I brushed my teeth and retired to the spare bedroom. There was movement and murmured conversations followed by traffic in and out of the bathroom, as if everyone was calling it a night. Seven minutes after the other bedroom door closed (my watch had a luminous dial), mine opened. Christine came and sat on the edge of the bed; she was down to her camisole and knickers. She understood I didn't want to do anything and that was cool but would I mind sharing the bed? The couch was uncomfortable and she wasn't used to the street noise.

I said okay. She slid in. I lay on my side facing the wall; she followed suit, cautiously fitting herself against my back. It was a single bed and that arrangement was probably the most efficient use of space. We stayed like that for quite a while. Eventually I rolled over and one thing led to another.

This is how it unravelled:

I'd made a courtesy call to my publisher's New Zealand arm. Another of their overseas authors had pulled out of a writers' festival in Christchurch at the last minute so they arranged for me to take his place. I didn't mention this to Christine; I thought it would only complicate things. I actually told her I was heading straight back to Sydney.

Kate had been badgering me to let her see my work in progress. I'd fobbed her off, not wanting to admit that I'd spent a year writing pornography and not having come up with a credible cover story. My absence was too great a temptation and her rummage through my computer files turned up the manuscripts of four pornographic novels as opposed to the budding masterpiece she was expecting. Her subsequent search unearthed the porn that Walter had provided for research purposes and the cheque book and bank statements relating to my secret contingency fund, which contained $9613.

At this point, when I was already in reasonably deep shit, things took a serious turn for the worse.

I hadn't bothered to inform Christine that I was married. Doubtless all you amateur psychologists will have an explanation for this; all I can say is that by the time it seemed pertinent, it was already too late. As I found out in the debrief, Chas had given Emma the impression that while there was a woman in my life, it was all pretty loose. And I was, after all, a bohemian.

Christine had mentioned that she had friends in Sydney but I hadn't attached any significance to it. Most Kiwis do.

Christine had a pile of air points. On a whim she decided to visit her friends in Sydney. She persuaded Emma to extract my phone number from Chas's address book.

I was still in Christchurch when Christine rang our apartment. She got Kate instead. By this stage Kate's opinion of me as a husband and all-round human being was undergoing radical revision. Showing a deviousness I didn't know she possessed, Kate pretended to be my sister, thereby extracting further damaging information.

Kate said she was meeting me for a drink that evening, why didn't Christine join us? They connected at the pub, Kate saying I was running late. She got a couple of drinks into Christine and probed for the smoking gun. Not content with the bare facts, as damning as they were, Christine flexed the imagination that had got her into the creative writing course and transformed a brief spark into a towering inferno.

Kate revealed herself. Christine fled weeping into the night. By the time I arrived home twenty-four hours later, Kate had changed the locks.

twelve

The rest, as they say, is history.

We went through the process of seeing what, if anything, could be salvaged but our hearts weren't in it. Kate was implacable — another revelation — and, as I realised on emerging, saliva-splattered, from another counter-productive face-to-face, I wasn't prepared to fight — or grovel — for our marriage. If I did and Kate relented, I'd be sentenced to a life of impeccable conduct. To beg for a second chance and then abuse it would be monstrous, and while I had a conscience it wasn't busy enough to sustain a long-distance moral obligation. Perhaps my premonition of ending up alone became self-fulfilling; in any event I came to believe that Kate would be better off without me.

As much to my surprise as hers, Kate's family didn't rally to her cause. When the news broke, Ginge vowed to hunt me down and administer the Aussie equivalent of a horse-whipping, which provided some welcome light relief. He'd often been sprung with his freckled mitt up a neighbour's skirt or doggied over some tragic old footy groupie he'd plied with piss down at the league club. And he'd always got away with it.

Lynne would ring me after getting no change out of Kate. 'Believe me, Max, me and Ginge have had our ups and downs. Talk about rocky patches. There've been times when I've been this close. I've had the suitcase out; I've rung my sister to say this is it. Didn't have to say any more, she knew exactly what I meant. But I'm a positive person, Max.' Short, mirthless laugh. 'Some people would call me a saint. I see the good in people, not the bad. I know what Ginge can be like, especially when he's had a few. Doesn't make it any easier, mind you. I know exactly how Kate feels. You men have no idea what it's like to find out your husband's been playing up. And then to find out that half the blinking suburb knows about it. And you know what they say? "Oh, things can't be too good in the O'Toole household; Ginge wouldn't be chasing skirt if everything was sweet on the home front." I'm not a gossip, Max. I live by the golden rule. I put myself in the other person's shoes and ask myself how I'd feel. But I've found out the hard way that not everyone's like me. They'd never admit it, of course, but a lot of people enjoy the misfortunes of others. And if they were jealous of you to begin with, well, look out. Who knows why? It beats me. Maybe it's because I'm a warm, positive person and, deep down, they wish they could be more like me. But at the end of the day, Max, you've got to be bigger than them; you've got to rise above it. Compared to forty years of marriage and everything we've been through and the lovely children we've brought up and the life we've built, what does it amount to? I mean, really? I know why you did it, Max. Same reason they all do. You did it because you could. That's all there is to it. So some scrubber drops her panties in an alley, so what? She's the one with the problem, not me. If Ginge tripped over her the next morning he wouldn't recognise her.' Long-suffering nasal exhalation. 'I've just finished telling

Kate this, and not for the first time. I tell her, Max, but she won't listen.'

Who could blame her? I'd hang up from these confessions of a serial martyr praying that Kate didn't change her mind. One thing I surely didn't need was a mother-in-law who saw me as a captive audience, to be endlessly confided in.

Sister Adele was on my side too. Any man who was prepared to stick around was okay in her book.

But Kate didn't change her mind. 'Fucked if I know, mate,' lamented Ginge late one night, his voice clogged with booze and exasperation. 'You'd swear to Christ you were the first bloke in history to have a poke on the sly. Either that or she thinks she's so fuckin special no bastard's going to root around on her.'

We tried mediation, one last shot at settling out of court. As we were waiting to start she said, 'How come I've got all these shitheads in my ear telling me I should take you back but you're not saying a word?'

Kate's fervent belief — to have downplayed it as a negotiating position would have been the height of wishful thinking — was that I'd entered our relationship empty-handed and done little to address the imbalance, therefore it was only right and proper that I should leave with not much more than I could wear and carry. The apartment was non-negotiable: Myra hadn't left it to us, she'd left it to her, bequeathing her worldly goods to the daughter she never had, whose care and companionship had illuminated what would otherwise have been a grim twilight. I'd never met the woman, despite having plenty of opportunities, not to mention invitations.

Fortunately for me, matrimonial property settlements are no longer exercises in establishing fault and measuring contributions. Kate and I were a married couple of more than three years' standing so it was just a matter of adding up and dividing by two. I was a twenty-first century house-husband reaping the benefit of changes driven by women for women, to the delight of my lawyer, who was ecstatic at getting one back for the boys.

So in the end Kate had to divvy up. She could have taken her share and traded down to something more manageable but the apartment had become her anchor and refuge. I'd failed her, her family had failed her and her column had been watered down to a sickly blend of PR froth and celebrity worship. The highlight of her day was getting back to the apartment and shutting the door on all of it and all of us. The mortgage was like a physical weight. She felt like one of those around-the-world-on-$5-a-day backpackers bowed under their brutal swags. She cut down on everything from coffee to makeup and did the sums five times a day, searching for a set of numbers and assumptions that would make it look like a smart move.

I had no such problems. For the first time in my life I was a man of substance, cashed up, debt free, unencumbered — quite a catch, in fact. Blessed with the means and freedom to go anywhere in the world, I went home.

My first instinct was to stay put. Weather is weather — you adjust to it, wherever you are — but I've never struck a better climate than Sydney's. Especially the winters, if you can call them that — one mild, blue day after another with just enough of a chill first thing and after sundown to maintain the rhythm of the seasons. And while summer could be too much of a good thing, there was always the possibility of an epic storm: biblical rain sheeting from purple-black thunderclouds a thousand storeys high, and wild electricity prancing across the horizon, colouring the night like the first air raid of an American war. All in all, a far cry from New Zealand summers that arrive late and leave with the job half done, like cowboy tradesmen.

But while Australia had filled my saddlebags, it had done nothing for my career. I'd imagined I'd make those Aussies sit up and take notice but the ex-colony was growing up and not disposed to fuss over minor-league blow-ins. Quality lit heavies and authorial brand names with global reach were a different matter. When they dropped in, the fawning was as unbecoming as ever but with a pushy familiarity and less sense of gratitude now that Australia was so much more than a comfort stop on the international circuit.

When the stars jetted out, the flag-waving resumed. Australia was embracing its home-grown writers, tellers of Aussie tales who embraced the vernacular, revisited the history, placed iconic figures and national archetypes in a unique landscape and explained — for those who couldn't work it out for themselves — what it meant to be Australian.

The little pond had turned out to be a reasonable-sized body of water, a bigger-than-you'd-think pond. I'd left the big pond because I couldn't make enough of a splash, but had created hardly a ripple in the little pond. That left the tiny pond. (For a while, in emails to friends and acquaintances elsewhere, I referred to New Zealand as 'Tinpon'. The joke soon wore thin.)

The Tinpon strategy — Kate preferred 'Chicken Run' — also had its flaws. (Does that surprise you or do you see a pattern emerging?) I'd assumed nothing much would have changed in New Zealand but in fact there'd been a cultural flowering similar to Australia's, driven by and reflecting the burgeoning of a post-colonial national identity. Back in the seventies there'd been a handful of novelists grafting away in semi-obscurity but now I was greeted by a cacophony of fictional voices.

They say that in Hollywood there are a hundred film scripts for every movie made. The New Zealand literary scene hummed with similar frantic, frustrated ambition. Whenever

I went to a bookish event or party I'd be bailed up by three or four would-be writers. Some, not all of them male, were steely-eyed, impatient and occasionally chippy, seeing me as yet more competition for publishing slots and grant money. Others, not all of them female, stroked my ego and fluttered their eyelashes as they sought my views on all manner of things in the hope of panning a nugget or two of inside information from the flow of dross.

When not disarmed by fluttering eyelashes, I opened fire on those who whined about the plight of aspiring writers and the craven reluctance of publishers to support Generation Next. Been in a bookshop lately? I'd growl. The novel isn't dying because publishers don't put out enough new fiction; it's being crushed to death by a vast accumulation of crap that should never have been published in the first place. Easy for me to say, as more than one young Turk riposted.

Although I had a reputation in Tinpon, it was out of sync with the new mood. None of my books were set in New Zealand. In fact, a skim of my oeuvre would leave the impression that my working premise location-wise was Anywhere But Here. And I'd given other hostages to fortune in the form of interviews with various Tinpon publications in which I'd rather belaboured the point that you wouldn't find pohutukawas and Maori place names in a Max Napier novel anytime soon.

This sort of thing: 'I draw a distinction between being a New Zealander — which, by the way, is how I see myself; quite a proud one in my own quiet, non-jingoistic way — and a New Zealand writer, i.e. someone whose work is inspired by a New Zealand setting or a New Zealand experience or who sets out to explore subjects and themes that are unique to New Zealand or have a particular resonance for New Zealanders. As Bob Dylan put it, that ain't me, babe. New Zealand was — and no doubt still is — a great place to grow up, and my upbringing obviously had quite a lot to do with the sort of person I am today but not, I think, the sort of writer I am today. Right from my earliest woolly daydreams I looked to Europe and America. They supplied the events and settings and ideas — and, of course, the books — that inspired those daydreams and stimulated my imagination and eventually drove me to a typewriter. I think it's a generational thing and maybe my generation will be the last to look outwards rather than inwards. But who knows? One day I might ransack the old memory vault — assuming those brain cells are still up to the job — and fashion a novel out of all the weird shit that was floating around Auckland in the seventies. Then again, maybe not.'

Bullshit, of course. Pure manure. As with most of the guff I've spouted in interviews and question and answer sessions over the years — and I'm certainly not the only one — there's very little substance here, very little deliberation. What happens is that you pick up the phone to do an interview or show up for a signing session or an appearance at a writers' festival expecting the standard questions: 'What's your book about?' 'Is it based on personal experience?' 'Who are your favourite writers?' 'Where do you get your ideas from?' 'How many books have you sold?' You come prepared — you might even have jotted down a few notes — so that you'll have something to say. It probably won't be intelligent or original but it will fill in time and reduce the risk of embarrassment.

But sometimes these questions don't get asked. (Thankfully, in the case of the last one, because that blunt impertinence must be deflected without being too obvious and without sending any writers or book-trade folk who happen to be present into sniggering fits.) Instead I get asked: 'Were you a lonely child?' 'Why do you hate women?' 'Which characters represent your mother and father?' 'What do you dream about?' 'Who do you want to win the election?' The natural-born performers lap this stuff up. A little striptease is all part of putting on a good show for the pushover audiences of the festival circuit.

When asked about something I haven't really thought about, I tend to say the first thing that comes into my head, but I ran into a few NZ lit types who not only remembered those interviews but could parrot them, sometimes with damaging embellishments. They were letting me know that it was too late to ditch that snooty expat act and rediscover my roots. They had a nice little scene going in Aotearoa but it was a closed shop with no room for Johnny-Come-Latelies.

At least I had money. Most of it went on a flat. It was a step down from Casa Myra but it was mine and it was mortgage free. I put some in the bank and the balance into banking shares on the advice of a sharebroker Felicity put me onto. My occasional daydreams of winning literary lotto now had a tacked-on scene in which I shouted Kate the renovation she couldn't afford. I guess we all process guilt in our own way.

I quit writing porn. Writing fiction, as Hemingway said, is hard work. ('It's hell. It takes it all out of you ... So I do it.') Porn was easy once I'd got the hang of it so I'd kept doing it. Ten or twelve days on auto-pilot, zap it off to Walter and wait for the cheque, trying not to think about what I was doing and what was happening to me. But if journalism blunts the pen, as Hemingway apparently also said, then pornography snaps off the nib and upends the ink-pot.

I knuckled down. I wrote a book of short stories that was respectfully reviewed but didn't sell. I wasted the best part of a year adapting one of my novels for the screen and participating in the daily round of futility and deceit that accompanies any film project, however pie-in-the-sky. Nothing came of it and the bandits who'd inveigled me into it simply welshed, not even covering their option. I wrote a crime novel that I can't, in all conscience, dress up as a genre-buster, and you know what Shelley thought of that.

This is where we came in: the middle-aged writer — I turn fifty in a few weeks — alone in his little flat, strung out on alcohol and buffeted by rejection, reliving the past through a stack of faded photographs because the future doesn't bear thinking about.

part two

thirteen

Dinner at Felicity and Murray's isn't the ordeal it used to be. No thanks to Murray: once a fuckwit, always a fuckwit is the moral of that life story.

I have to say, though, these days there's something to be said for the sight of Murray, as opposed to the total Murray experience. Middle age hasn't been kind to our Muz. Up until a year or so ago you'd have said he wasn't that bad-looking, if you didn't mind a touch of the primate. And some women don't because it reassures them there's not much going on beneath the surface. They like knowing there isn't an interior world where their status is uncertain. With Murray, what you saw was what you got. On meeting him for the first time, a physiognomist would have assumed the following: this man owns a jet-ski; he has a personalised number plate; if one were to relate an anecdote with wry understatement and irony, he'd laugh in the wrong places or not at all; he has no sense of shame or capacity for self-doubt.

Murray's torso is much the same but his head has put on weight. Usually it's the other way round. You often see men whose faces have retained definition long after they've succumbed, sometimes alarmingly, to middle-age spread. From across a table they appear to be ageing quite elegantly but when they stand up, you're confronted by a spinnaker-like expanse of billowing shirtfront. And many a man, his head turned by a pretty face, has altered course for a closer look only to find that all hell has broken loose south of the breastbone. There's a theory that people who dote on their pets eventually come to resemble them. Murray has become the incarnation of his opinions. He's become a fat-head. If I could be bothered, I'd check it out on Google in case it's a symptom of something sinister as opposed to an odd twist on the ageing process. Perhaps I should encourage Felicity to have a word with their GP. I mean, it can't go on like this. If his head continues to beef up, there'll come a time when his neck simply won't be able to support it.

Professional rugby players — or at least those who frequent the bars and cafés of Ponsonby — have extraordinarily big heads but they're to scale. These are enormous young men with necks so thick their bison heads can seem undersized. It's tempting to see evolution — or maybe counter-evolution — at work here: a head like a boulder might be a drawback in some walks of life but it's probably a useful attribute for a rugby player.

I digress. Dinner at Felicity and Murray's isn't the ordeal it used to be because Felicity isn't the person she used to be. Or, to take the big-picture view, she's reverting to the old, pre-Murray Felicity. I wouldn't go as far as to say she's back to her old self but there's no doubt that Murray's mysterious hold over her is weakening. Even six months ago I wouldn't have contemplated sharing my thoughts on Murray's head. But then six months ago she didn't have a mind of her own.

'Your pal must be moving in any day now.'

Felicity says this *a propos* of nothing, without looking up from her chicken in garlic and white wine, as if she's not really expecting a response. Murray doesn't raise his head either; it's been a long day and perhaps his neck muscles are feeling the pinch. Instead he gives Felicity a drawn-out look from beneath bunched eyebrows. His face sags. His mouth hangs open for a few seconds, then snaps shut.

I don't normally play the straight man but this seems promising. 'What's this?' I ask Felicity.

'The new place down the road,' she says. 'They were moving stuff in there today.'

Her smile, which is aimed at Murray, is lopsided and full of private amusement. I remember this smile. Our parents often mistook it for sardonic affection, Felicity being renowned in our house for her roundabout ways. Having been on the wrong end of it many times, I know better. It's the smile of a wind-up artist who has zeroed in on a raw nerve.

'And?' I say.

She shrugs. 'Well, it's not your average home, that's for sure. If you believe the gossip, it's the most expensive private residence in Auckland. That's all up, when you add the building costs to what the guy paid for the land. There were two perfectly nice houses on decent-sized sections. This guy bought both and bulldozed them to create one huge section, then proceeded to build a mini-palace. It's caused quite a ruckus.'

'Why's that?'

'Well, some people think it's over the top; it makes most other places around here look a bit pokey. Our problem with it is more . . . quantifiable.' She sends Murray another goading smile. 'Isn't that right, Muz?'

Murray slaps his napkin down on the table. 'You're telling the story,' he says, making it sound like a warning.

'Muz was hoping for a piece of the action but it didn't

happen,' says Felicity, clearing away the dinner plates. '*C'est la vie.*'

As she disappears into the kitchen Murray pretends to notice my empty glass. 'By Christ, Max, you can put this stuff away. You'd think I'd be onto it by now but you always catch me out.' He pours me another glass of a middling pinot noir, more expensive but inferior to the Australian shiraz I supplied and largely accounted for.

'Well, Murray,' I say, 'not all of us count our drinks.'

'No shit?'

'So what happened?' I ask. 'To your piece of the action, I mean.'

'I know what the fuck you mean.'

This is unusual. Away from home and in male company Murray's inclined to over-swear, trying to show, I suppose, that making it hasn't turned him into a softie. Never mind the designer shades and the $200 Italian silk ties: beneath this slick exterior there's a farting, sweating, hard-arsed Kiwi bloke who can fuck and cunt like any public-bar Neanderthal. But here, with his children within shouting range — they've had home-delivered gourmet pizzas and slouched off to their no-go areas — he normally restricts himself to profanity-lite, the stuff that barely registers any more.

'Look, if it's a painful subject . . .'

'Of course it's a fucking painful subject.' This comes out in a rush of ugly scorn. He's giving up on everything: me, the evening, any pretence at hospitality. 'Deals like that don't grow on fucking trees.'

'Okay, I get the message. Forget I ever raised the subject.'

He stands up abruptly, scraping his chair on the burnished floorboards. 'I've tried to fucking forget about it,' he snarls, 'but certain people seem to get a kick out of reminding me. And I've had a fucking gutsful of it.' He sloshes wine into his glass and stomps off and that's the last I see of him.

Felicity brings in dessert. 'Where's Muz?'

'Don't know,' I say. 'He just took off.'

She puts down a bowl of pears poached in red wine. 'In what frame of mind, would you say?'

'Troubled.'

She exits on Murray's trail, closing the door behind her. I think about helping myself but decide against. From a far-flung corner of the house comes the muffled boom of a cranked-up male voice. I'm refilling my glass when Felicity reappears, unflustered.

'Drink it all, why don't you?' I pour her some as she dishes up dessert. 'You should've helped yourself.'

'Manners.'

'Oh, really? Your impeccable manners don't seem to have stopped you hogging the wine.'

'I've already been rapped over the knuckles for that.'

She raises her eyebrows. 'I apologise for Muz. Catastrophic sense of humour failure.'

'Will he be rejoining us?'

'I think not.'

'Would I be right in thinking this thing didn't happen yesterday?'

'Try fourteen months ago,' she says.

'Isn't it time he, as they say, moved on?'

'You'd think so, wouldn't you?'

'What happened? I tried to get it from the horse's mouth but he bolted.'

'Actually he mentioned just now that tonight's the first time in however many years that you've shown the slightest interest in his work. He has a theory about that.'

'I just followed your lead,' I say. 'Isn't that what I was meant to do?'

'You're imagining things,' she says, straight-faced. 'I suppose it's an occupational hazard. Muz had been cultivating one of the vendors, a pair of empty-nesters rattling around a five-bedroom villa. They'd decided in principle to move but hadn't worked out where to. One week they're all set to retire to Pauanui, the next they're looking at apartments in the Viaduct Basin, the week after that they're on the net checking out Noosa. So Muz is on the case, brown-nosing away as all good real estate agents do, and eventually they promise him that when they've sorted themselves out, it'll be his sale. But . . .'

'There's always a but.'

'This was a biggie. A senior partner from one of the big law firms knocks on their door and makes the proverbial offer they can't refuse — high end of the price range, cash, full and final settlement in fourteen days. With a couple of conditions. One, that their next-door neighbours come to the party, because if his client can't get both properties, the deal's off. Two, that it's a private sale — no publicity, no agents.'

'And no agent's commission?'

'Apparently the buyer despises real estate agents.'

'How perverse of him. So who is he?'

'Muz did tell me his name but I've forgotten — not that it meant anything to me. Apparently he's an expat money-markets wizard who's made his fortune and wants to come home.'

'They all come home eventually.'

I'm sitting at my desk looking out the window when the phone rings. It's the call I've been waiting for — and hotly hypothesising around — since that lunch with Sally and Brigit.

'Hi Max, it's me,' says Sally. 'How are you bearing up?'

'I'm okay. How are you?'

'I've just heard about Tania. I'm really sorry, Max.'

I'm prepared for this. 'Don't be. It's a bit like bungyjumping, I suspect. You're quite proud of yourself for actually going through with it, you buy the T-shirt and for a while you drop it into every conversation but, just quietly, you wouldn't do it again for all the tea in China.'

'Oh? Well, I'm glad to hear it. I'd have to say, though, that's not the impression you gave last time we had lunch.'

'Poetic licence,' I say. 'All in a good cause.'

'Which was?'

'Giving you and Brigit your money's worth.'

'So you're not sitting around feeling sorry for yourself?'

'Hell, no. I'm feeling tip-top; tanned, rested and ready.'

'Ready for what?' she says.

'The next big adventure. Life's next ambush.'

'Can't keep a good man down, eh?' she says. 'I was going to offer you lunch and a shoulder to cry on but sounds like there's no need.'

'Can't I have one without the other?'

'I can't see why not. I'm driving though, so I can't drink. That needn't stop you, of course.'

'Not me. I've got work to do.'

Sally's obviously got something on her mind because she lets that pass without comment. 'I'll pick you up in an hour.'

Sally's had her hair cut in that Audrey Hepburn gamine style. It suits her. So do the white-framed sunglasses, the yellow sundress with spaghetti straps, the spike-heeled cherry-red shoes, the bold makeup and the heavy fragrance. Call me smug but I suspect a lot of thought went into this ensemble.

While pondering Brigit's theory that Sally's working herself up to a fling, with yours truly the prime candidate, I've visualised her taking various approaches and me making various responses, some of them appropriate. Now as we curb-crawl down Ponsonby Road looking for a park, studious detachment gives way to steamy anticipation.

We get an outdoor table at a generic Ponsonby eatery, one of those places where the management, staff, cuisine, atmosphere and standards change every eighteen months, as if by edict. If the chefs are any good, they're poached. If not, they pop up in the suburbs grilling eggplant for ladies of leisure or in tourist traps like Queenstown and Taupo where people are either too unworldly to realise they're being ripped off or too rich to care.

Sally animatedly recounts piddling domestic dramas. She knows I'm not interested in this stuff; she's gabbling to cover her nervousness. I offer a nod here, a raised eyebrow there and the occasional banal interpolation. I'm not the most patient person in the world but compared to her I'm a Zen master. She won't spin this out.

Our meals arrive, along with the glass of wine she's talked me into.

She leans towards me. 'I can trust you, can't I, Max?' she says as if it really matters. 'I mean, if I was to confide in you, it wouldn't go any further?'

'If that was the deal, of course.'

'Brigit won't be in on it. She's my best friend and we tell each other most things but this would be our secret.'

'I think I get the picture.'

'And needless to say — but I'm going to say it anyway — under no circumstances to be hinted at in one of your cryptic little asides when you're on the piss with the boys.' I can't help smiling. 'You're not taking this seriously, are you?' she says crossly. 'Okay, look, just forget I ever mentioned it.'

'I am taking it seriously,' I say. 'I was a little amused by the extent of the preamble, that's all. I know what a secret is, Sally. If you tell me something on the basis that it mustn't go any further, then it won't. You can rest assured of that. One thing I've never been accused of is betraying a confidence.'

Given that I've been accused of practically everything that

doesn't involve violence or hard-core criminality, it seems unlikely that betraying confidences hasn't cropped up somewhere along the line. But I certainly can't remember being accused of it lately.

'Cross your heart and hope to die?'

'Sally!'

'Okay.' She downs her mineral water in one gulp and takes a deep breath. She fixes me with a hypnotist's stare, then goes pink and looks away. 'God, this so embarrassing. I don't think I can go through with it.'

It occurs to me that I never actually resolved how I'm going to handle this. I've tried often enough but what starts out as a careful weighing of the pros and cons always dissolves into a fantasy in which the decision is taken for granted. What does that tell me — that I'm kidding myself?

'Okay,' she says. 'Now or never. I'm having an affair.'

We stare at each other like it's a contest. Sally starts nibbling her lower lip. I've always assumed we men were meant to find this lip-nibbling routine erotic but perhaps I've been barking up the wrong tree. Meanwhile, Sally's getting anxious because she's mistaking deflation for disapproval. It's comical, really; she thinks I'm in shock because she's confessed to something I saw coming a mile away. As always, the devil is in the detail.

'Who with?'

She tosses her snazzily coiffed head. 'I have to know where we stand first. I need someone to talk to, Max, and I chose you because I thought, of all my friends, you'd be the last to get on your high horse.'

Is that a compliment? 'Don't jump to conclusions,' I say. 'I haven't.'

'Well, you certainly don't look too impressed.'

I take a steadying sip of wine. 'Rick's a good mate of mine.' A pointless statement if ever there was one. 'I'm not sure I should be patting you on the back.'

Her hands fly to her face. 'I knew it,' she says, her voice wobbling. 'I shouldn't have said a word to anyone.'

The pricked-balloon sensation is already fading, replaced by relief that I don't have to choose between dutiful self-denial and a potentially ruinous intrigue. I gently prise her hands off her face.

'Come on, Sally, I'm not going to tell on you or turn my back on you. You should know that.'

She tries not to smile, like a child who's succeeded in getting off lightly by turning on the pathos. 'Thank you so much, Max,' she gushes. 'I really need someone to lean on right now. If you weren't there for me, I wouldn't know where to turn.'

'Lean away, my dear.' I hope to Christ her conduct hasn't been completely beyond the pale because I haven't left myself much room for manoeuvre. 'Why don't you tell me all about it?'

She giggles. 'All?'

'Well, as much as you think my delicate ears can cope with.'

It's a very Remuera affair. Their daughters go to the same private school, their eyes meet across a netball court, they exchange tentative smiles at a parent-teacher evening and then that first, electric, skin-on-skin moment at a fundraising sausage sizzle when they both reach for the tomato sauce. She casually asks around: he's divorced but has been seen with the mandatory bimbo. Part of her thinks he couldn't possibly be interested in her; the other part goes with her instincts.

As far as she and Rick go, it's not like the wheels have fallen off but the signs are beginning to point that way. If she had to put her finger on it, it started when Rick sold the business (and, by the way, she'd be the first to admit that she was all for it at the time and it was a brilliant move for them financially). But it had got to the stage where the business was more or less running itself so he had lots of time for her and the kids. Next thing, he's locked into a management contract, the new owners want to take over the world and he's working harder than when they were first married and he was trying to get the business off the ground. Plus, head office and the board he reports to are in Sydney so he's either over there or working all hours to get things done before his next trip or putting together his next report and presentation to the board or just back from a trip and completely exhausted. And you start to wonder; you wouldn't be human otherwise. All those nights away from home; all those times she got no answer when she rang his hotel room. She doesn't want to make too much of it because it'll sound like she's trying to say he pushed her into it but, honestly, it would explain an awful lot. So many little things that might mean something or might not. You can put them down to coincidence or you can see a pattern.

With that simmering away in the background she bumps into the other guy in Mission Bay. They have a coffee and get on really well. In the course of the conversation it comes up that Rick's in Sydney for a week and both the kids have sleepovers on Friday night. She asks if he's seen any good movies lately because she'll have an evening to herself. He suggests dinner. She ums and ahs, wanting to say yes but a bit freaked out by the suddenness of it. Half an hour ago she was a good little wife with a harmless little fantasy. Now it's like take your marks, get set . . . Because we all know that when a man of the world asks a woman out for dinner, it doesn't end with the after-dinner mints. On the other hand, if she knocks him back, he probably won't ask again. But she's got forty-eight hours to change her mind and even then, what's to stop her saying thank you for a lovely meal, see you in the netball season, as he's paying the bill?

So she has dinner with him and gets home as the paper's being delivered.

'When was this?' I ask.

'Three months ago.'

Brigit was almost right. She just underestimated Sally's ability to keep a secret.

'Still going strong, I take it.'

'We see each other once a week.' Another giggle. 'Well, at least once a week.'

'Where do you see it going?'

That doesn't make her giggle. 'Jesus, Max! Don't go there, okay?'

'Fair enough. So how much longer are you going to keep me in suspense?'

'Would you like to meet him?'

'What, right now?'

She looks at her watch. 'You've got time to finish your pasta.'

fourteen

Sally drives towards the sea. We pass Felicity and Murray's place, crossing into exclusivity, a real estate concept marked by sea air, tennis courts and surveillance cameras.

'Where are we going?' I ask.

'Patience is a virtue we don't all possess, as my mother often says.'

'I wasn't asking her.'

'Hold your water,' she says. 'We're almost there.'

'So what does the great lover do for a crust? Clean swimming pools?'

'Here we are.'

She pulls up in front of a high, whitewashed wall, something you'd expect to see in the plush parts of Johannesburg or Buenos Aires, but not in egalitarian NZ where there's no tradition of the mob and we like to know how often our neighbours change their tea-towels.

'Is this his place?'

'You could say that.'

We squeeze through massive wooden gates. A drive of

crushed white shells lined with mature palm trees leads to a whopping example of twenty-first century designer grandiosity, an archipelago of creamy stucco in a sea of glass. Imposing houses abound on this patch of the isthmus, where a million dollars buys a letterbox and a birdbath, but this makes most of them seem dourly understated. I remember a bus trip to the dusty edge of Cairo. We came around a corner expecting another tract of Third World urban sprawl and found ourselves in the shadow of the pyramids. This has to be the house Felicity was talking about; there can't be two of them.

'Well, what do you think?' says Sally, enjoying my reaction. 'Could you be happy here?'

'More to the point, could you?'

Before she can reply, two men come out of the house. They observe us from the portico.

'Christ almighty,' barks the shorter one, 'I haven't finished unpacking and I've already got trespassers.'

There's an anxious tremor in Sally's smile, as if things are not going entirely according to plan. I hope this giddy gesture isn't going to backfire on her.

Both men are of my era. The taller one looks enviably fit and has a sailor's tan. He wears an open-necked white shirt outside his jeans and seems pleased to see us. His sidekick has on shin-length khaki trousers with pockets for every eventuality and a Hawaiian shirt decorated with near-naked hula girls. He could do with a shave but the hobo stubble may be intended to offset a dainty little teen princess mouth. His eyes are out of sight behind the sort of impenetrable dark glasses favoured by celebrities who like being recognised but not approached.

The taller one extends a hand. 'Hi there, I'm Gavin and you must be . . .'

'Well, I'll be fucked,' says the other one. 'Max Napier, as I live and breathe.'

'You two know each other?' says Gavin.

'I know Max,' says the other one, grinning like a lunatic, 'but it doesn't look like he remembers me. These arty-farty types, they've got so many big ideas clogging up their heads there's no room for names and faces.'

My brain churns but fails to spark, like a clapped-out engine on a cold morning. He watches me, chuckling, disinclined to let me off the hook.

I play for time. 'You looked a bit different then?'

'We all did.'

'All being . . . ?'

'You. Me. Other guys.'

Here's something. It's not the answer but it's a clue: London.

'It was long ago and far away, right?'

His head bobs. 'Now we're cooking. Dig for it, Max, it's in there somewhere — unless you took too many drugs and fried that big brain.'

'There's nothing wrong with Max's brain,' says Sally stoutly.

He gives her a wink. 'I hope not, darling, I really do.'

Then suddenly it's sitting there in the forefront of my mind, alongside this morning's shopping list and the usual preoccupations. I feel as if I could pinpoint the exact spot on my forehead where the knowledge resides. He's the guy in the photo who worked in the money markets and didn't quite fit in, the guy who paid for Johnny's body to be flown home. And his name is . . . .

'Long time, no see, Stanley.' Stanley's grin goes supernova and he claps explosively. 'Nice place you got here, even if it is a bit on the small side.'

'Don't blame me,' he says, 'blame the architects.' He turns to Gavin. 'I fucking told you, Gav: my friends aren't easily impressed.'

'I don't know what you and your friends plan to do in there, Stanley,' says Gavin, 'but if it can't be done in seven hundred square metres you probably won't get it past the city council.'

'I was just thinking of the odd Roman orgy,' says Stanley. 'You still on the orgy circuit, Max?'

'I'm semi-retired,' I say. 'Cameo appearances only.'

'One word,' says Stanley. 'Viagra.'

Stanley, who's obviously become a take-charge kind of guy, decides he and I will have a coffee while Gavin gives Sally the guided tour. The espresso machine is the houseguest's department but she's not around so we'll have to go up the road. Everyone seems happy with this arrangement.

Stanley stops at the gates. 'Hey, Gav,' he yells, 'remind me again: how many bedrooms are there?'

'Five,' says Gavin with the patient smile of a man who's well paid to put up with his client's idiosyncrasies. 'All with harbour views and ensuites.'

'Right,' says Stanley. 'So if you and Sal get the urge to take a load off, maybe even kick off your shoes and stretch out, you'll be spoilt for choice.' He waits for a reaction, which isn't forthcoming; Sally's non-plussed while Gavin appears to be holding his breath. 'What I mean is, you won't have to use my bed because, you know, I'm a bit anal about that kind of thing. Not that I have any reason to believe your personal hygiene isn't impeccable.'

Sally blushes vividly. Gavin doesn't like it but has to pretend otherwise. He forces a laugh. 'Okay, Stanley. We'll stay out of the wine cellar too.'

Stanley gives them a wave. 'Have fun, you crazy kids.' I follow him through the gates. 'One of these days,' he says, 'I'll answer the doorbell and Gavin will be standing there with a gun.'

'Given him a hard time, have you?'

'He'd probably say I've made his life a fucking misery.'

'Just for the hell of it?'

'Partly that. Partly because he lets me. Mostly because he's an architect.'

We get into a Porsche SUV.

'What have you got against architects?'

'Are you serious?' he asks. I shrug. 'Let me ask you this: have you ever met an architect who doesn't think he's some sort of superior being? They're a smug, preening bunch of supercilious fucks who, generally speaking, don't even have the excuse of being gay. But that's not the worst part. The worst part is they think they're fucking artists. He's humping her, right?'

'I wouldn't think so.'

He laughs and starts the car. 'Swore you to secrecy, did she? Lighten up, Max. That just means she doesn't want you to tell her friends. She takes it for granted you'll tell your friends.'

'One of whom happens to be her husband.'

'Not for long — her husband or your friend.'

'You're way ahead of me, Stanley.'

'I've got very sensitive antennae, Max, and I've spent twenty-five years in an industry in which the aim of the game is to fuck other people up the ass without them being aware of it until it's too late. Warn her, Max — assuming, of course, you give a fuck. Gavin's a single guy; he's got nothing to lose. And he's got an image to live up to.'

We're driving west on Jervois Road. Up ahead a car pulls out of a park right outside a café.

'Just like in the movies,' I say.

Stanley slots the Porsche into a tight space. 'I'm lucky that way. Always have been.'

We order. Stanley says, 'Last thing I remember hearing about you, you'd dumped your wife and run off to Paris with a lady writer. It seemed like exactly the sort of thing a young artist should do.'

'It didn't last.'

'Those things aren't built to last, Max; that's part of their charm. Then what?'

'Well, after a while I got married again. That didn't last either.'

Our coffees arrive. Stanley decides he's had worse. 'Well, our generation might be good at a few things but staying married isn't one of them. So where does that leave you: free as a bird?'

I nod. 'And you?'

'Ditto. It's a bit late for this old leopard to be changing his spots.'

'You mentioned a houseguest.'

'My little Argie-bargy. We have fun. Well, at least I do.'

'Looking at your new pad, Stanley, I guess I'd be right in thinking you've done pretty well for yourself?'

'That I have, Max. If you'd said to me back in London that in twenty years' time I'd be worth what I am now, I would've said you were blowing bubbles out your ass. It would've been inconceivable to me that I, Stanley Muir, born and bred in Timaru, bright but certainly no genius, diligent but no workaholic, ambitious but not driven, a brown-noser, sure, but only up to a point . . . The idea that someone from my background and with my limitations could become wealthy on that scale would've seemed the height of fantasy. And when I look back, three things occur to me. The first is that my self-assessment was pretty much on the mark. The second is that it wasn't actually that hard. And third, getting rich is like most human endeavours: to achieve your goal, you need a few things to go your way and, as I said before, I was born lucky. Some people, they just seem to get one bad break after another. Not me; I'm a lucky son of a bitch.'

'If it's that easy,' I say, 'how come there aren't lots of people as rich as you?'

'You'd be surprised how many there are, especially in the States. I wouldn't say it's all that easy to get seriously rich in this country but over there . . . You a boxing fan, Max?'

'No.'

'Nor me, particularly. But the guys I worked with in New York belonged to the work hard, play hard school. Every couple of months we'd charter a private jet and fly off to somewhere like Las Vegas for a wild weekend. You know, you hear a lot of shit about the real America. Most of the time they try to tell you the real America is a bunch of inbred retards out in the boondocks who really, truly believe there were such people as Adam and Eve. I wouldn't know; I never went to those places. Personally, I'm not sure that's any more typically American than a bunch of faggots in a Manhattan salon discussing ballet. But if I had to make the call, I'd say the real America is Vegas on fight night. Sex and money and violence; rich guys going nuts watching a couple of beasts from the projects beating each other's brains out, then going up to their suites and getting a thousand-buck blowjob from a six-foot-tall showgirl with plastic tits. Anyway, that's by the by. The point is, the ring announcements are made by this guy, he looks like a fucking tailor's dummy, who's got this line, "Let's get ready to rumble." Having made a meal of that, he tells you something about the fighters, you know, Calvin over there weighs two hundred and forty-five and comes out of Dogdick, Mississippi, as if you give a fuck, and at the end of the fight he tells you the result, which you can usually deduce from the fact that one guy's in a coma. And that's it; that's his night's work. Anyway, about fifteen years ago this tailor's dummy slapped a trademark on "Let's get ready to rumble" and according to what I read the other day he's earned four hundred million US in the last seven years.' Stanley stares at me as if he's said something incredibly profound. 'You see what I'm saying?'

'America's the land of opportunity?'

'Well, that and the fact no one ever went broke underestimating the taste of the American public. During my working life the finance and investment industry has generated a truly staggering amount of wealth. By one means or another and with a fair amount of luck on my side I managed to scam a tiny fraction of it and, as a result, got rich beyond my wildest dreams. But in seven years this blow-dried prick's earned more than twice as much as I made in my whole fucking career. And while I had a lot of luck and a lot of help, both in terms of benefiting from other people's brilliant ideas and capitalising on other people's idiotic decisions, I also had to work hours that no human being should have to work, under pressure that fucked up my sleep patterns for all time. All this asshole had to do was holler, "Let's get ready to rumble."'

'How the fuck,' I say, 'do you earn that much money from one brainless catch-phrase?'

Stanley shrugs. 'Commercials, video games, dolls . . .'

'Dolls?'

'You bet. You pull a string or squeeze it and the fucking doll goes "Let's get ready to rumble". I dare say you can have it as the alarm that wakes you up in the morning or as the ring on your cellphone. For all I know you can have a microchip implanted in your wang so whenever you get a boner the object of your desire hears "Let's get ready to rumble". The point is, every time that brainless catch-phrase is uttered anywhere in America, and probably the world, the cash register goes bing! He has two ideas in his life: one, the brainless catch-phrase; two, slapping a trademark on the brainless catch-phrase. Hey presto, the cunt's got more money than Ethiopia. That's critical mass for you, Max; two hundred and seventy-five million Americans with disposable income. If you asked them what's the meaning of life, most of them would say, "To shop, to spend money, to buy shit." The rich people, by and large, are the ones who dream up new shit for them to spend their money on.' He pauses. 'How many words would you say you've written?'

'I hate to think.'

'But I imagine you'd like to think you've come up with a line or two that bears comparison with "Let's get ready to rumble"?'

'Yes, I would.'

'And would I also be right in thinking you're yet to chalk up your first million?'

'Well, I'd need to consult my accountant . . . You keep mentioning luck: how did luck come into it?'

'I was in the right place at the right time when the IT sector took off. I got in on the ground floor and I got out of the elevator before it ran out of juice and the law of gravity took over. The only reason I got out in time was that I ran into this guy who warned me what was going to happen. The difference between me and the people who lost their shirts was that I didn't have a problem accepting the fact that this guy was brighter than me and knew a fucking sight more about the tech sector and Wall Street and the American economy than I did. And if this expert, as I perceived him to be but others thought was just a dipshit trying to make a name for himself, turned out to be right, I could come back from lunch one day and find myself in the same tax bracket as the shoeshine boys on Fifth Avenue.

'I rang my broker and told him to sell everything as soon as the markets opened. Six weeks later the bubble burst. I know guys who were worth as much if not more than me who now can't afford to live in Manhattan. I know of guys who cleaned out the family trust and fucked off without a trace, leaving their wives and kids to fend for themselves. There was one flame-out I heard of who actually whacked his parents to get his hands on their life savings. I, on the other hand, have more money than a bear can shit. Leaving aside what I've got parked in hedge funds and tied up in property, the interest I earn off what's in the bank gives me an extremely healthy income by New Zealand standards.'

Stanley leans back in his chair. I'm not the first person he's given this speech to and I won't be the last; I suspect he'll never get tired of it.

'There you have it, Max: How to Get Rich and Stay that Way, by Stanley P. Muir, B. Com. Twenty-five years at the cutting edge of market capitalism distilled into a ten-minute rant.'

'That's it?'

'Have I missed something?'

'Well, for instance, will I need a calculator?'

Stanley chuckles. 'It might come in handy. But like all tools, Max, it's only as effective as the user.'

'So what now? You can't tell me you'll be happy doing nothing for the rest of your life. How old are you, for Christ's sake?'

'Forty-eight. How old are you?'

'I turn fifty on April the first. That's right, Stanley; I was born on April Fools' Day.'

'What's happening?'

'What do you mean?'

'I mean what the fuck are you doing to mark the occasion?'

'What is there to celebrate?'

'Don't be an asshole, Max. You're sane, able-bodied, reasonably presentable. I've no doubt that if you really put your mind to it, you could get laid tonight. I assume you're still writing?' I nod. 'Which is what you want to do? Shit, that's all you've ever wanted to do, isn't it?'

I shrug. 'Yeah.'

'Jesus Christ, man, you've got every fucking reason to celebrate. Not that it matters, because as of this moment your opinion is irrelevant. Your fiftieth birthday party will be held at my place on the night of April the first. You provide a guest-list; I'll do the rest.'

'Don't take this the wrong way, Stanley, but that's the craziest fucking thing I've ever heard.'

He frowns. 'What's the right way to take it?'

'Look, Stanley, an hour ago, by pure chance, we clapped eyes on each other for the first time in twenty-odd years. And even back then we weren't exactly inseparable so why should you . . .'

'With the greatest respect, Max,' he says, and for the first time I sense that I'm meant to take him absolutely seriously, 'my reasons — or lack of them — aren't the issue. I'm offering to throw a party for your fiftieth. If you don't like the idea, fine; if you don't like me, fine. By all means, tell me to fuck off. But please, don't give me this lame shit about us not being blood brothers.'

I have the strong feeling that if I say thank you for the kind offer but I can't in all conscience accept, he'll take it in his stride but this will be the last I'll ever see of him. I don't want that to happen. I sense possibilities around Stanley Muir.

I attempt a graceful shrug. 'Well, when you put it like that . . .'

'Let's drink to it.' He beckons a waiter and orders a bottle of Veuve Cliquot. 'We mightn't have been best buddies, Max, but you didn't treat me like shit and I wouldn't say that about everyone in your circle.'

I squirm in my seat, discomforted by the prospect of self-pitying reminiscences courtesy of an elephantine memory that noted and filed every slight. I was hardly a Good Samaritan so there must have been times when I was as offhand as the worst of them.

'I knew what they thought of me: who is this deadshit? He's not one of us. Why doesn't he take the hint instead of hanging around like a bad smell?' I start to protest but he hushes me. 'I'm not including you in that, Max. You never froze me out or used me as an audience or talked down to me. You thanked me when I bought you a drink and you returned the favour. Little things, Max; you probably weren't even aware of them. Little things that meant a lot to someone who half the time was thinking, they're right, I don't belong here.'

He shrugs as if he's already regretting giving me this glimpse of himself from the time before we entered the Age of Money and those who grasped its mysteries became the new elite. (What about me: was I a Good Samaritan after all? Was I a better person than I am now?) But seeing he's raised the subject, I ask the question I've been wanting to ask ever since I placed him.

'Are you a different person now, Stanley, or were we too far up ourselves to see the real you?'

'A bit of both, I suppose. There were times when I thought someone was talking shit on a subject I knew a bit about but I didn't have the confidence to put my two cents' worth in. I was always worried that it wouldn't come out right and people wouldn't laugh when they were meant to or wouldn't think twice before they tried to put me down. Money gives you freedom but it also gives you confidence. Money's how we keep the score in the game of life so if the arithmetic says you're a winner, why not act like one?'

Stanley offers to drop me home but I choose to walk, saying I could use the exercise.

'Does walking count as exercise?' he says. 'Fuck me, I've got a roomful of exercise machines for muscles I never otherwise use and you're telling me you just walk around the block?'

'All by myself. You don't even need a personal trainer.'

'Speaking of which. You asked me what I'm doing with myself. Well, one thing I'm doing is making up for all the sex I missed out on. I was a complete suckback, sex-wise. I wasn't cool or good-looking, I didn't possess conventional panty-dampening skills like water-skiing or playing the guitar at parties and I couldn't chat up a girl to save myself. My brain would only allow me to grunt at two-minute intervals or talk non-stop about exciting new developments in accountancy. As you can imagine, I shattered masturbation records that had stood for generations. But money fixes that like it fixes everything. My personal trainer is the proverbial gym-goddess. At our first session she looked me up and down like I was the most abject physical specimen she'd ever set eyes on.'

'And?'

'I got her to make a house call. That's all it took.'

fifteen

The exercise is a smokescreen: I want to walk because I want to think. As you know, I spend much of my working life staring out the window but, increasingly, my mind is as inactive as the rest of me during these glazed time-outs. Sometimes, though, walking seems to trigger sunbursts of mental energy. Who knows why? Maybe tiny shockwaves from my feet hitting the pavement swarm up my spine to stir my brain into action. Or maybe it's just the fresh air.

From the moment I recognised Stanley and placed him in that monument to himself he calls home, a thought has buzzed fitfully in my head, like a dying fly. This is that Stanley personifies the great historical shift of our times: the triumph of money.

There are various ways of coming at this. You could, for instance, argue that when we stopped believing in God, and Marx couldn't fill the void, we reverted to every man for himself. Without religion there is no morality, there's only the law, and greed isn't against the law. Okay, insider trading is illegal but how many bureaucrats does it take to catch a shadow?

When I was a child the worst name you could be called was 'skite'. You don't hear that word now because there's no longer such a thing as skiting. What used to be skiting is now confidence, self-belief, being positive, feeling good about yourself, having attitude, and adopting this mindset is the key to everything we desire. The self-improvement gurus earn fortunes by pushing the line that every one of us has what it takes to be a glittering star. All we have to do is believe. Not in a Higher Being or Big Brother or a Little Red Book; in ourselves.

When Marxism was revealed as the economic equivalent of the emperor with no clothes (nowadays the spectral, weed-eating North Koreans are history's witnesses that the theory of permanent revolution delivers the reality of permanent famine) and social democracy ran out of steam, that only left man's exploitation of man, AKA capitalism. Western governments loosened their grip on the economic levers and the dark, acquisitive side of human nature was back in business. We know the rest: the entrepreneur worship that ended in tears as it was bound to do, the weird-outs on Wall Street, the tidal movements of money — nine-figure sums vanishing into a decimal point. And while the emperors of the new age, the Murdochs and the Gates, colonised our consciousness, their shadowy courtiers made hay.

Men like Stanley Muir.

Back in the days of wage/price controls and import licences and devaluations, a man like Stanley stayed in Timaru and became a bank manager or loaded up his Humber and trundled the hundred flat, straight miles across the plains to try his luck in the Big Smoke. If things worked out for him in Christchurch he might have become a partner in a firm of accountants or kept the books for a sturdy family business.

He would have made a placid home with his typing-pool bride and sent his sons to Boys' High, Christ's College being a bridge too far for someone with no ties to the ruddy-cheeked squattocracy and who couldn't trace a convincing line back to the first four ships. He would have beavered his way to where all decent Kiwi folk aspired to be: deep in the pale, bland heart of the middle class.

But in the age of money Stanley goes to Christchurch to catch a plane to the other side of the world and comes back twenty-five years later with more money than a bear can shit. And wealth on that scale makes an old school tie and a family tree and the very concept of respectability seem like the relics of a vanished civilisation, an Inca bracelet or an amphora unearthed in the excavation of a Roman emperor's holiday villa.

Stanley's both more and less than a Kiwi made good in the big, wide world, those expatriate success stories that the media get off on and the rest of us can't get away from: the scientist who beefed up the kill ratio on a generation of missiles; the executive sitting at Bill Gates' right hand; the diva and the character actor and the ex-rock star's ex-wife and the bloke who's famous for carrying someone else's golf bag.

Stanley isn't a celebrity or a role-model or a distinguished person or a human headline. He did his thing out of the spotlight, unnoticed and unacknowledged except for the odd mention in investors' tip-sheets. Like one of those fabled Hollywood writers who are fabulously paid for scripts that never make it to the screen, there's nothing to show for his career except the rewards. It's the wealth that's remarkable, rather than the achievement or the man himself.

There will be no second act in Stanley's life. Despite having money to burn and time on his hands, he won't turn a hobby into a second career and produce a movie or set up a political party or go eccentrically green, buying an island to create a safe haven for some ugly little lizard that no one in the real world gives a shit about. He won't become a visiting professor at a business school or seek a footnote in the history books by chairing weighty government commissions. He won't become a patron of the arts. He won't even buy a super-yacht and keep trying to win the Sydney to Hobart.

His role is to be a frontman for the new elite, a wised-up, filthy-rich hedonist inhabiting that plane where character, achievement, contribution, celebrity and even power don't count for much because money has all those bases covered. Money doesn't go in and out of fashion. It can't be deconstructed, disgraced or thrown out of office.

Stanley's a man from nowhere living the dream of the scratch-card society: quick, effortless wealth that frees us from irksome routine and three o'clock in the morning anxiety. In his pure, narrow, mysterious talent and his unthinkable fortune, he personifies the triumph of money.

He's my Jay Gatsby.

Here we are, a few days later, in another Ponsonby eatery, waiting for our steak frites. Stanley's been an Aucklander for all of a month and he's already fuming over the traffic. It took him that long to get to the airport, his little Argy almost missed her flight.

'Do you have any idea,' he says, squinting at me as if the choked motorways are somehow my fault, 'what that would've meant?'

'I wouldn't even hazard a guess.'

'Another fucking night of hysterics. They don't believe in bottling it up, your Latins.'

'How long has she gone for?'

'She's gone for good,' he says. 'Hence the hysterics.'

'Past her use-by, eh?'

'Jesus, Max, she's only twenty-four; even by my exacting standards she's got a few more miles on the clock. No, she made the fatal error of lobbying for us to go back to New York. I fucking told her Auckland wouldn't be her cup of tea.

Here's this hot little wannabe, right? Where's she going to feel more at home: here, where I'm her entire social circle, or there, where's she's in with the fucking in-crowd? I even offered her a more-than-generous kiss-off but she insisted on coming with me. So I spelt it out for her: any overt pining and her pert little ass would be in a sardine-class seat on an outbound 747 quicker than she could say Los Malvinas belong to Argentina. But did she fucking listen?'

'That's pretty bloody harsh, isn't it? Maybe she didn't quite get the message, English being her second language and all.'

'She speaks English a damn sight better than most people in this town,' he says, 'and I was very clear. I didn't say, "Don't harp on about it"; I said, "Don't go there, period."'

'You drew a line in the sand.'

'Dead fucking right.'

'And she crossed it so you had to act or join the swelling ranks of the chronically pussy-whipped?'

'You may laugh,' he says, 'but that's how it works: you're either serious or full of shit. And I was serious and she obviously couldn't get New York out of her system so we were on a collision course. That being the case . . .' — he shrugs — '. . . why delay the inevitable?'

'Well, you'd still have her pert little ass to go home to.'

Stanley chuckles and pours the wine. He's matching me glass for glass, which not many people can do — or want to do. 'My personal trainer's ass is, if anything, even perter so, regrettable as this development may be in some respects, it hasn't left a void ass-wise.'

'What about heart-wise?'

He gives me a pitying look. 'I can see I got here just in time. Rule number one, Max: men our age do not become emotionally involved with drop-dead gorgeous babes young enough to be our daughters. That way lies humiliation, poverty and despair. You feast on them, and the moment they start getting on your nerves you usher them off the premises and audition for a replacement.'

'Which is where the pad and the Porsche and the platinum card come in handy?'

'Look at me, Max. If I was a schoolteacher, how many gorgeous twenty-four-year-olds would give me the time of day? Fortunately for me, most gorgeous twenty-four-year-olds have the moral compass of a cash register.'

'You believe every woman has her price?'

He shrugs. 'It's a fact, like the sun rising in the east. Not only does every woman have her price, these days it's a buyer's market.'

'Well, I beg to differ,' I say. 'I know at least one woman who's not for sale.'

'Who?' Stanley points like a retriever. 'Who is this paragon of virtue? I bet she's just a figment of your perverse imagination.'

I tell him about Brigit Cole.

He cocks his head thoughtfully. 'I have to confess, your fortyish, happily married mum is a niche I haven't really explored. And why would I when the world's full of gorgeous twenty-four-year-olds?'

'Oh, so we're just talking about eye candy, are we? Human blow-up dolls who'd go down on a complete stranger for a line of coke and a backstage pass? In your own words, Stanley, the moral compass of a cash register. I thought you were making a broad philosophical statement about the nature of women.'

He smiles thinly. 'Do my ears deceive me or did I just hear a gauntlet being thrown down? Okay, lead me to this saint and we'll see what she's made of.'

'Forget it.'

'Why?'

'Because she's a close friend of mine, as is her husband. For that matter, I'm rather fond of their kids . . .'

'So what? If she's such a fucking saint, I'll just be wasting my time, won't I? Your turn to put up or shut up, my fine friend. If you're not prepared to introduce us, then I can only assume that, deep down, you suspect she's like all the rest. You've put her on a pedestal, haven't you, Max, and now you're scared I'll expose you for the great romantic ninny you are.'

I shake my head. 'I just happen to think it's not the sort of thing you do to your friends.'

'What sort of thing is it?'

'Make them a pawn in your private games.'

'Well, that's a pity,' he says. 'Challenges bring out the best in me.'

'You want a challenge? Swim Cook Strait — you could do with a cold bath.'

A cutie-pie waitress brings our meals. Her jeans are so low-slung that it's hard to conceive how they can accommodate underwear or even pubic hair but maybe I'm just behind the times.

Stanley appraises her with a carnivore grin. 'Do you mind if I ask you a personal question?'

She's used to feeling the hot breath of middle-aged men who lose their bearings and their dignity after bolting a few drinks. 'That depends,' she says. 'How personal is personal?'

'Let's say personal but not intimate.'

She nods warily. 'If I take offence, you won't go running to the manager?'

'Shit, no,' says Stanley. 'I wouldn't dream of it.'

'And if he does,' I say, 'I'll back you up.'

That earns me a blank stare; she's not interested in me or my support. 'Okay.'

'In terms of a steady but not serious relationship,' says

Stanley, 'i.e. you're more than just fuck-buddies but you don't expect it to last till Christmas, if you had a choice between a young, good-looking guy without a brass razoo or a chap our age who's nothing special looks-wise but is absolutely loaded and keen to show you a good time, who would you choose?'

'That's easy,' she says with a cool smile. 'I wouldn't touch either of them with a barge-pole.' She waits for Stanley's frown. 'I'm a dyke.'

Stanley and I have a routine. I won't hear from him for a few days, then he'll ring to say he's been looking at property in Wanaka or watching cricket in Adelaide or cruising the Whitsundays. He certainly gets around but one thing he doesn't do is visit; other people have to come to him. That's what the overpowering house with the four guest bedrooms with harbour views is for — to rub it in.

I'll go around for dinner, which he orders in from a restaurant. At first I offered to pay my way but he told me not to be so fucking stupid so now I don't bother. The booze, needless to say, is exquisite. The house wine is an Italian red, Brunello di Montalcino, which starts at around seventy bucks a throw. Later on he brings out the sort of cognac that duty-free shops keep under lock and key.

He likes the sound of his own voice but that suits me. This is, after all, research; this is the writer at work. By and large, his world view is what you'd expect from someone for whom the American Way delivered in spades. I can only take so much of it but it makes a change from the Land Rover liberal consensus with its faux-worldly conspiracy theories that never have to be substantiated because to challenge them is to expose yourself as unspeakable or naïve to the point of fuckwittedness. Many's the time Alan Cole has dropped his head and wearily dragged his fingers through his hair, groaning something like, 'Oh, for fuck's sake, Max, it's about oil. You must be the only person I know who doesn't get that.'

I haven't mentioned Project Gatsby. I'm thinking of a father and son tale, father being a career teacher and pillar of the community, son a buccaneering tycoon of the devil-take-the-hindmost persuasion. Both will be fleshed out and equipped with a full set of idiosyncrasies, contradictions and sexual tics courtesy of their real-life models. Then it's just a matter of shoe-horning them into a narrative in which the son and his ilk hack away at the father's generation's legacy until all that's left are the empty churches.

Now if I can just shake off this paralysing first-draft funk.

Sally rings in distress. Gavin has ended the affair.

With some style. He went back to her place for one last romp then took the high road out of there, saying he didn't want a marriage break-up and a divided family on his conscience. He had to be 'upfront', he said: for him it was just a passing fling. When Sally was unavailable due to wife/mother commitments he didn't curl up with a good book, he kept his hand in with other women who meant as much — or as little — to him as she did.

This is related in a traumatised monotone. The wretched silence that follows should be filled with sympathetic crooning but I'm crass enough to say what I'm thinking.

'Well, I guess he's got a point.'

Sally howls and the line goes dead. I ring back but get the answerphone.

When we finally reconnect a couple of hours later her misery has turned to cold anger, with guess who in the firing line.

'Well, I've got to the bottom of it.'

'Of what, Sally?'

'Gavin's hundred-and-eighty-degree turn. You must be

feeling very pleased with yourself, Max. Your little scheme worked to perfection.'

'Sally . . .'

'Don't try to lie your way out of it. I know you talked to Gavin. What did you say, as a matter of interest? "Think about what it would do to the kids?" As if you care. Or did you threaten to put in a bad word with your new best friend?'

'Sally, I haven't breathed a word to anyone and I haven't seen or spoken to Gavin since the day we met.'

'The giveaway was saying Gavin had a point. Once I realised where you stood, it all fell into place. Everything was fine until I told you — in fact, I was having to cool him down. But after that he was always in meetings or having to spend time with his daughter. And now he's dumped me.'

'Look, Sally, I understand this has come as a shock and you're trying to make sense of it but . . .'

'I've just seen him. I asked him point blank. He wouldn't give me a straight answer but he didn't have to — it was written all over his face. I trusted you, Max. I came to you because I needed someone to confide in and you betrayed me. Thanks a million, you fucking hypocrite.'

Stanley's in Hawke's Bay inspecting wineries. I offer to ring back but he's done for the day and heading out to Waimarama Beach for a dip.

'Never swim alone, Stanley.'

'Don't worry, I like an audience.'

'Do you remember the circumstances of our reunion?'

'How could I forget?'

'You were with your architect and I was with my friend Sally.'

'That's right,' he says. 'We went one way, they went the other.'

'Yeah, and as I recall you engaged in some speculation as

to the precise nature of their relationship.'

'Did I? You're probably right. I have that tendency.'

'Stanley, did you tell Gavin to pull the plug? The reason I ask is that I've just been hissed at by Sally who's convinced that I persuaded or bullied Gavin into giving her the arse. Which I didn't. A, it would never have occurred to me; B, if it had, I'm sure he would've told me to fuck off. But I can imagine that if you signalled your disapproval, he'd drop her like a hot potato. Which he did.'

'It's all coming back to me,' he says. 'I didn't tell him to drop her and I certainly didn't express disapproval. What I did do was ask him if she understood the rules of the game. If not, he had a responsibility to get her up to speed pretty damn quick.'

'That's it?'

'Oh, I might've added something to the effect that if it ended in a cluster-fuck, I'd hold him responsible. I did her a favour, Max. She had a one-way ticket to a broken heart or a broken marriage. Or both.'

'She thinks she's got a broken heart.'

'Thinks being the operative word. It'll heal a hell of a lot quicker than if he flicked her in six months' time. She's had some fun, Max. Now she can get back to the yoga.'

'That might be easier said than done. But then I suppose if you'd entertained the possibility of doing more harm than good, you wouldn't have played God in the first place.'

Stanley laughs. 'Well, it's like everything: practice makes perfect and there's bound to be the odd fuck-up along the way.'

'And tough shit for Sally if this happens to be one of them?'

'But it's not. You know that as well as I do. Right?'

'Probably.'

'Well, there you go.'

The difference is that I would have been inhibited by the fear that things wouldn't go according to plan and the patient might suffer a violent reaction to the surgery. That scenario wouldn't have crossed Stanley's mind. Like most successful people, he believes in the power of positive thinking; to contemplate, however fleetingly, the possibility of failure is to invite it. Besides, if Sally goes off the deep end, it won't be his problem. Like Gavin, he's got nothing to lose.

'How about you, Max — have you ever had a broken heart?'

I mention Samantha. He demands details and I end up telling him most of the story. He calls me a lucky bastard.

sixteen

I don't get apologised to. Oh, people might say sorry about that, as you do when you turn up a quarter of an hour late or take a few days to get around to replying to an email, but it's just an expression. The aim is to disarm, to acknowledge that the other party has been mildly inconvenienced and pre-empt any attempt to make a fuss about it.

Some might say I don't attract apologies for the simple reason that I'm more sinning than sinned against. I suppose I could argue that if love means never having to say sorry, I must be a much-loved fellow but I don't buy either proposition.

I don't win raffles either. Given the good causes I've modestly supported, all the Girl Guide biscuits I've bought and chucked in the bin, you'd think my number would have come up at least once. It's a sickening thought that one of these days Stanley will find himself in a dairy with a book of raffle tickets on the counter, will be persuaded to contribute a few bucks towards sending a local hero to the World Human Cannonball Championships and will win the Ford Fiesta he wouldn't be seen dead in or the family holiday in Disneyland.

But I don't win raffles, I always get the booby prize in a lucky dip and I don't get apologised to. Until today. This being the first day of the rest of my life, I've had two apologies and it's not even lunchtime. At this stage I'm putting it down to coincidence rather than a seismic shift in the sinned against/sinning ratio but watch this space.

First into the hair-shirt is Sally, who catches me as I'm heading out for breakfast. Stanley has been in touch to advise that she blamed the wrong guy and, boy, is she ever ashamed of herself.

No big deal, I say; don't give it another thought. So what does she do? She goes through the whole routine all over again. Why do people think repetition is the essence of sincerity? I ask how she's bearing up. My attention wanders during her in-depth answer but she closes by saying she and Rick are really looking forward to my fiftieth birthday party, which I assume is code for a resumption of normal service. I tell her the party is nothing to do with me but she thinks I'm being facetious.

An hour later I'm still at the café, debating the pros and cons of a third espresso, when the brother-in-law sits down at my table and bores his great blunt head into my personal space.

'I thought I'd find you here,' he says. His tone is cagily neutral. 'You like your routine, don't you, Max?'

'Don't most people?'

'Most people don't have a choice; you do. I mean, it's not like you have to be at a given place at a given time.'

I could deliver a spiel about self-discipline and the writer, the importance of establishing a routine and sticking to it. It seems to resonate with the reading public. People are always telling me, 'I could never be a writer; I just don't have the self-discipline.' No one's ever said, 'I could never be a writer; I just don't have the talent.'

But I don't. As they say in America, don't try to bullshit a bullshitter.

'Call it a security blanket.'

'Fair enough,' says Murray. He nods at my empty cup. 'Having another?'

'Why not?'

He returns from the counter with a giant muffin and the revelation that we only live once.

Murray's not a dainty eater. The conversation he presumably wants to have is put on hold while he savages the muffin. Our coffees arrive. I down mine and watch the lower half of his face churn like a concrete mixer.

When it's all over, when his tongue has dislodged the last pockets of resistance, he says, 'Listen, Max, sorry for that carry-on the other night. I made a bit of a dick of myself.'

'Forget it,' I say. 'I have.'

'I wasn't exactly the perfect host, was I?'

'The food and wine were fine. Two out of three ain't bad.'

'It fucked me off no end missing out on that deal but that's no excuse for carrying on like a pork chop.'

There's that second helping of humble pie. Normally I'd be wondering what he's up to but all these apologies are making me benevolent. I'll assume he's sincere until there's reason to think otherwise.

'Murray, I'll accept your apology if that's what it takes to wrap this thing up but I wasn't hanging out for it.'

He nods, smiling ruefully. 'You're a bit of a strange bugger, aren't you, Max?'

'What makes you say that?'

'You want an example? Okay, what's with calling me Murray? Not even my mother does that.'

'Well, since you ask, I associate the double Z nickname and variations thereof with yob culture: westies, page-three girls, cretinous loudmouths on the radio, Australian soap operas, fat skinheads chanting racist slogans at football matches, tracksuits as a fashion statement, queer-bashing, ready-mixed bourbon and Coke, rugby league — specifically the Manly Sea Eagles . . . Need I go on?'

'And you wonder why I think you're a bit strange?'

'It seems perfectly reasonable to me. Strangeness is in the eye of the beholder, Murray — like a lot of things.'

He nods placidly. 'Fair call. We've never really been on each other's wavelength, have we? Is it too late, do you think?'

'Well, they say you mellow with age.'

'I don't see much sign of you mellowing,' he says, 'but I suppose you'd say the same about me.'

Another half-hour of this and we'll be holding hands. Murray, though, glances at his watch. 'Shit, I'd better get moving.'

He gets halfway up, hovers for a few seconds like a defecator sensing there might be more where that come from, sits down again. His face shifts and twitches as if he's unsure of the appropriate expression.

'Flick was saying you see quite a bit of the guy in the new house — what's his name again?'

'Stanley Muir.'

'Right. What's he up to?'

'Not much. He just seems to cruise around looking for things to spend his money on.'

'Well, shit, lead me to him.' He produces a business card with a magician's flourish. 'Next time you're talking to him, tell him I'd love to have a chat about this property project I'm working on. It's a fucking screamer. If he's got some lazy dough he wants to put to work, I'm telling you he couldn't do better.' He reaches across to pat me on the shoulder. 'Good on you, bro.'

He's up and moving before I can quibble or refuse. And people wonder why I'm cynical.

On the way home I make a detour to get some fresh pasta and almost walk right past them. They're having coffee at a sidewalk café, they being Stanley and Brigit.

Stanley's eyes gleam. Brigit's not exactly put out but I've been greeted more warmly.

'Since when do you two know each other?' I ask, trying not to sound like a prosecuting counsel.

'We met at a dinner party the other night,' says Brigit. 'Stanley was talking about bumping into you after . . . how many years?'

'Twenty,' I say. 'That's little old NZ for you — you can't cross the road without risking being run over by a long-lost friend.'

'Another reason why it's good to be back,' says Stanley. 'Pull up a chair, Max. We're not ashamed to be seen with you.'

'Actually, I think I'll leave you to it,' I say. 'I've spent all morning in a café.'

'Don't be anti-social,' says Brigit, standing up. 'You can sit here. Sophie's class is going to the museum and I'm on transport detail.' To Stanley: 'Thanks for hearing me out, Stanley. Promise you'll think about it?'

'Cross my heart,' he says, getting to his feet like the gentleman he isn't. 'See you soon, I hope.'

Brigit's parting smile has lost a little of its sparkle by the time it gets to me. We watch her walk away.

'What a nice person,' says Stanley sitting back down. 'In the best sense of the word.'

'Nice is underrated.'

'I agree,' he says. 'There's not enough of it about. We need more nice.'

'And less cynicism?'

'Exactly. More nice, less cynicism. That's your job, Max, that's what writers are for: to shine a light in this fog of cynicism and self-gratification.'

'Speaking of which, what was that all about?'

'Brigit? She's involved with some child cancer charity. You didn't know that, did you?'

'No.'

Stanley tut-tuts. 'Perhaps you should engage in less speculation about your friends' sexual inclinations and focus on what really makes them tick. There's a vacancy on the committee and she seems to think I'm just the chap. So I said let's get together over a coffee and you can tell me all about it.'

'Why would they want you?'

He shrugs. 'These outfits always need money.'

'Are you going to do it?'

'I shouldn't think so.'

'So why the charade?'

'Gosh, let me see,' says Stanley. 'Why the fuck would I want to spend an hour with an intelligent, attractive, charming woman . . .'

'You forgot nice. I thought we'd agreed we wouldn't make Brigit a pawn in a private game.'

'I didn't agree anything of the sort. That was your reason for not introducing us and I went along with it.' There's a hint of challenge in his smile. 'Now, as it's turned out, we didn't need a go-between. Fate has brought us together.'

'Really?'

'Come on, Max, lighten up — this moral guardian act doesn't suit you. And for what it's worth, I think you're right: I don't think Brigit has her price.'

'Does that mean you're not going to put it to the test?'

'Let's just say I don't believe in fighting losing battles.'

This is said with heavy finality, which I take as a signal that I shouldn't press for an unequivocal undertaking. I wouldn't claim to read Stanley like a book but I can't help wondering whether he'll be reluctant to stop now that I know he's started. If I hadn't stumbled upon them, their tête-à-tête would be like a tree that falls in the forest and he could give up on Brigit without me knowing he'd started.

Perhaps he'll be satisfied with having made the point that he can't be thwarted: if he wants to see Brigit in close-up, he'll find a way, with or without my help. I believe in coincidence but not this coincidence. I don't believe they just happened to be invited to the same dinner party. I think Stanley made it happen.

I hand over Murray's business card. Stanley pockets it without a glance, saying he'll give him a call. I don't believe him but that doesn't matter. I can look Murray in the eye and say I did my bit.

With that out of the way, we move on to my other woman friend into whose life Stanley has insinuated himself.

'I heard from Sally.'

'I had to set her straight, Max. That couldn't be allowed to stand.'

'What did she say when you owned up?'

'She thanked me for my caring and timely intervention.'

'What?'

'I filled her in on Gavin. I might've gilded the lily but the overall thrust was fact-based. So all's well that ends well, eh? Did she say how much she's looking forward to your fiftieth?'

'Yeah.'

'She told me that too.' The challenging smile reappears. 'Women: wouldn't life be a drag without them?'

That's enough socialising for one day. Now I want to shut myself away in my little flat and please myself. Some work: half a dozen pages of busy notes and perhaps even a few hundred hesitant words on the computer. Some reading: for several weeks the new Dellasandro has sat menacingly on my bedside table, like a suitcase bomb. Poised as I am, or hope I am, on the verge of a new book, should I tamper with it or would it be wiser to dispose of it? Dellasandro requires careful handling at the best of times and I'm not exactly on a winning streak. Then again, Dellasandro's a giant. So he makes me look like a hack; he makes most writers look like hacks. Better to measure myself against certain successful and celebrated writers who, when you get past the pack-mentality reviews and mythologising profiles and bestsellerdom based on assiduous networking and a hefty marketing spend to the work itself, don't make me look like a hack.

Perhaps a sensible balance would be an awestruck hour with Dellasandro and an hour grimacing at the utilitarian prose of some mid-table operator who clearly believes fiction is no laughing matter. And I'll endeavour to look on the bright side, reminding myself that literature isn't a zero-sum game and other people's success isn't at my expense. Good luck to them because if they can do it, then it's not out of the question for me. Not if I give it my best.

I have a programme: a sandwich; a cyber-scan of the English broadsheets; a couple of hours work on Project Gatsby; an hour (devoid of lacerating comparisons with self) of Dellasandro; another hour's work; a well-earned beer while deciding I can't be bothered with the evening news; a second beer, also well-earned, while preparing dinner, spaghetti bolognese served with baguette, green salad and unassuming Argentinean malbec; an hour of mixed feelings with a critics' darling who doesn't make me feel like a hack; a pointless channel-surf; bed with an old favourite that takes me back to the time when I read for the pure, uncluttered, unselfconscious pleasure; lights out.

I have a programme but other people won't leave me to it.

Chas's Volkswagen Golf is parked in front of my flat. He gets out, flinging the door shut.

'About fucking time,' he says.

I don't know why. I can't have kept him waiting because

we didn't have a rendezvous. I'd take it for the juvenile trash-talk we've always traded but that usually comes with a grin or a pantomime sneer. Something's definitely amiss. Chas prides himself on his hipster nonchalance but today he scowls and smoulders like a hormonal teenager.

'What's up?' I say.

'How long have you got?'

This is evidently a serious question.

'Well, I could reschedule my dominatrix.'

My little joke dies messily on the footpath, like a trodden-on snail.

'Are we going in or what?' asks Chas.

We go in. I offer plunger coffee or tea. He wants beer.

'Finished for the day, are we?'

'You could say that.'

So it's to do with work. Another surprise, since Chas has always breezed through the academic year without anxiety or visible effort. Having a rapport with the students helps, of course, as does his ability to charm or brazen his way through whenever his short-cuts or minor negligences come to light.

'Had lunch?'

'No.'

He inspects my bookshelves like a first-time visitor when in fact he's a regular and I've long since kicked the compulsive book-buying habit.

'You want a sandwich?'

'Whatever.'

I put a sandwich and a beer on the table and retreat to the kitchen side of the bench. Whatever it is, it might be contagious. He sits down, muttering thanks.

'All right, Chas, let's hear it.'

He sighs and stares at the ceiling. 'Have you ever told me that my cock would be my downfall?'

'I shouldn't think so,' I say. 'That doesn't sound like me.'

'Have you ever thought it?'

'It might've crossed my mind.'

'In what context?'

'Oh, you know, the old staff-student sexual interface. But then I'm hazy on exactly what you can and can't get away with. I took it for granted you'd know where to draw the line.'

'I might be cavalier,' he says, 'but I'm not stupid. If it was that fucking simple, I wouldn't be in this mess.'

I've heard Chas likened to a fox in a hen-house. Not a pretty comparison nor, in my opinion, entirely fair. A fox will kill every hen in the hen-house; that's its nature. Chas takes his womanising too seriously to be indiscriminate.

Each year he takes his pick of the crop, trading on his looks, position, reputation and showy, theatrical lectures, a head-turning package for the dreamers, bookworms, groupies and opportunists who pour into university wanting, above all, to be dazzled.

He has a few rules. He never asks twice. If they don't come running, he backs right off and thereafter keeps his distance to avoid any suggestion of pressure or harassment. Subsequent contact is conducted in an atmosphere of cool formality and if he's in two minds over a grade, he errs on the side of generosity.

He favours young women who are either exceptional, and therefore not in need of patronage, or just going through the motions and therefore not looking for a leg-up. He warns them that they're not the first and won't be the last. At the first hint of instability, neediness, excessive ambition, doctrinaire feminism or familiarity with the machinery of grievance, he cuts and runs.

Chas thought he had it all under control. Then Emma happened.

Emma was the drug he couldn't take or leave. But she wasn't the only post-graduate whose doctorate he was supervising; there was also Jane. Plain Jane as he thought of her, although she wasn't unsightly, she was just older. With her kids at high school, Jane had decided to pick up where she'd left off and get some use out of the perfectly good brain that had spent fifteen years in mothballs.

With Emma, the heat was always on. They sparked off each other intellectually and every exchange was charged with an electric sub-current of desire. Jane, though, was making up for lost time and earnest to a fault. She was a suburban mother who coached her daughter's netball team and went bush-walking with her husband, who worked in human resources. Time crawled whenever she updated Chas on her thesis, a revisionist study of a trio of forgotten women writers of the 1950s. He didn't consciously short-change Jane but he never made an effort to correct the inevitable imbalance. Emma's doctorate ran smoothly and was deemed sufficiently heavyweight to land her a junior lecturer's job at Victoria University. Jane's never really picked up steam. When the assessor sent it back for salvage work she lost heart, abandoned it and dropped out of sight.

That was five years ago. Yesterday Chas was summoned to the dean's office and shown a dossier chronicling his personal relationships with female students going back a decade. There was a statement from the woman whose abortion had taken precedence over my wedding. Another contributor dwelt on her suicide attempt triggered by an abrupt severance after which no correspondence was entered into. (Chas informs me that she spectacularly failed the stability test.)

The dossier was compiled by Naomi, a student with whom Chas briefly dallied last year, under the auspices of a campus feminist group which, it transpires, has had him in its sights for some time. Naomi meticulously recorded pillow talk in which Chas discussed previous relationships and how, despite his best efforts, the personal/professional line sometimes got blurred. Emma and Jane came up in this context.

Naomi, the compiler of the damning dossier, the pretty second-year who laid the honey trap into which he obligingly sauntered, is Jane's daughter.

This is Chas as I've never seen him: self-pitying, diminished, defeated.

'What now?' I ask.

'I have a choice,' he says. 'Grovel to every woman I've ever made eye contact with, take a demotion and a pay cut, put out a statement expressing deep shame and undertaking to change my evil ways. That's the attractive option. The alternative comes under "or else".'

'Have you actually committed a sackable offence?'

'We're way past that. If I fight it, I'll be on my own — no one's going to go into bat for me. The femmos would love me to fight it; they want my head on a stick. They'd turn it into a great moment in feminism, the media would be all over it, and there's no fucking way the university's going to swim against that tide.'

'What about negotiating an exit — agree to go quietly if they throw money at you and bury the whole thing, then get a job somewhere else.'

Chas rolls his eyes. 'Get real, Max. It wouldn't matter a fuck what the university agreed to, these bitches aren't going to let it fade away. And how would you rate my chances of getting another job after they've sent their shame file to every women's organisation at every university in Australasia? I could probably squeeze some fuck-off money out of them but what do I do when that runs out? Anyway, it's all hypothetical. I don't want to move and I'm way past starting over as a junior lecturer at somewhere like Adelaide or Otago, even if they'd have me which, as I say, is highly fucking unlikely.'

There's the saying that we always kill the thing we love but, as has been pointed out, that works both ways. And we've all heard, more often than we'd like, of that phoney ancient Chinese curse about getting what you wish for.

We follow our impulses and desires despite the risks. That's sometimes called living life to the hilt. Chas thought he had it made: he was a big man on campus, a rock star. He could have found his girlfriends somewhere else but that would have taken considerable self-denial, walking away from all those sweet things who didn't have to be pursued or persuaded. All he had to do was notice them.

He was having too good a time to realise that the seventies were long gone and the world had changed. The university, once an enchanted place of pliant minds and bodies where no one grew old, had become a battleground in an attritional war to make the world unsafe for men like him. But the infatuation, the constant, grateful submission, blinded him to the danger. He wasn't even aware that he was dancing in a minefield.

Poor, dumb Chas.

Both of us have done what we want, without compromise. And look where it's got us.

seventeen

Stanley rings to present me with a *fait accompli*: the party — my party — is now fancy dress.

'Otherwise it's just another fucking party,' he says. 'Same little cliques, same old conversations. Fancy dress breaks the ice. Trust me; I'm experienced in these matters.'

'Why would we need an ice-breaker? My friends all know one another.'

'I was getting to that: I've taken the liberty of whistling up a few ring-ins. You don't mind, do you?'

'You're the host,' I say. 'You can invite whoever you like. Just as a matter of interest, though, how many's a few?'

'Who's counting? It just seems sensible to do the house-warming and meet-the-neighbours thing while I'm at it. They're probably killer bores but if they're drinking my piss, they won't be calling the cops to complain about being woken up by Led Zeppelin at three in the morning. Parties need critical mass, Max. I'm sure your friends are hell-raisers from way back but there's not that many of them.'

'Is that my fault?'

'Let's not get into the blame game,' he says. 'The point is, quality rather than quantity is a perfectly sound strategy for a dinner party but your full-on knees-up needs a good turnout.'

'You've left it a bit late, haven't you?'

'It's all under control — I've got a party organiser on the case.'

'A what?'

'A party organiser. I would've thought the term speaks for itself.'

'How did you find this person?' I ask. 'I mean, are party organisers listed in the yellow pages?'

'How the fuck would I know? It must be fifteen years since I looked in the yellow pages. I did what I always do: I asked around. By the way, I spoke to your brother-in-law.'

'Shit, did you?'

'Wasn't that the idea?'

'Not really. He ambushed me. Even then I only agreed to it because I assumed you'd have a rubbish bin full of unsolicited business cards.'

'Yeah, but this one came from you, Max, not some bozo whose name I didn't catch.'

'Well, I appreciate it, Stanley, but don't take it any further on my account. For all I know, he might try to sell you the harbour bridge.'

'I think I can handle it, Max. I'll do what I always do: I'll ask around, I'll talk to people in the know and I won't be parting with a cent until I know exactly whose pocket it's going into and what it's buying. And I told him that. So what's he like?'

'What can I say? He's my brother-in-law; I wasn't consulted.'

'And if you had been?'

'He wouldn't have got my vote. But that's a personal view. As far as I know he's pretty good at what he does.'

Stanley snorts. 'He's a fucking real estate agent.'

'Yeah, well...'

'It could be worse, right? He could be a crack dealer or a gay escort. Which reminds me: the fancy dress has a theme — Bring Back the Seventies.'

'Any particular reason?'

'I wasn't ready for them at the time. I sure as hell am now.'

It's April Fools' Day. I'm fifty years old.

I check my look in the mirror: peroxide fright wig, red-framed glasses, Mao jacket, glazed idiot-savant stare. The face is all wrong but then I'd have to live on steamed vegetables and mineral water for a year to have Andy Warhol's sinkhole cheeks. Still, it's more of an effort than I was going to make, having started out in the spoilsport spirit of doing the bare minimum. I'd rather not be laughed at but with any luck there'll be sillier sights — perhaps someone with his cheeks stuffed with cotton wool making constipated noises about offers that can't be refused. With any luck there'll be a Star Wars mutant or a Bay City Roller or a varicose-veined bag of bones who thinks she's a perfect 10.

The intercom buzzes. My ride's here.

Chas lounges in the back seat of the cab. He's got on brown leather trousers, a loose, collarless white shirt, cowboy boots and aviator sunglasses. There's a dark rinse through his hair and he must have stopped shaving as soon as he heard from the party organiser. He looks a lot more like Jim Morrison than I look like Andy Warhol.

'Jimbo, *quelle surprise*. Why, it seems like only yesterday that I visited your grave.'

'I faked it,' he says. 'Things were out of control. I had to break the spiral and disappearing seemed to be the only way. For the last twenty-five years Elvis and I have been sharing a bungalow in Mount Roskill. When I say "sharing", I mean in the sense of co-occupying, although I have to admit that late at night, when the demons come and the loneliness kicks in, I sometimes find myself thinking, "You know, if you just lost some weight..."'

'What, thirty or forty kilos?'

'Well, that'd be a start. Of course, Andy, you realise that we — I'm speaking as the real me here — have something in common: rabid feminist bitches tried to destroy us.'

'That's right. I'd forgotten Andy stopped a bullet.'

'Fired by the woman from SCUM — the Society for Cutting Up Men.'

'Well, let's hope she's not there tonight. Speaking of the fairer sex, I can't help but notice you're flying solo.'

Chas stares as if he can't believe I'd raise that subject. 'Given the events of the past few weeks I think it's prudent to pull my horns in, as it were, on the boy-meets-girl front. But every cloud has a silver lining — that opens up the option of getting methodically and piggishly drunk, which I fully intend to do.'

'A noble ambition, young Harley. However, I see a flaw in your plan.'

'Which is?'

'Once you've got a couple of drinks into you, you won't be able to help yourself.'

'There won't be any unattached women there, will there?'

'I'd say there's every chance. Stanley's beefed up the guest-list. He felt my friends were too few, too staid and possibly too poor to make the party go with a swing.'

'Well, well,' says Chas. 'No harm in checking out the lie of the land, I suppose.' He tosses a gift-wrapped hardback book onto my lap. 'Happy fucking birthday. First-edition early Dellasandro. I spent an entire fucking day on the net tracking the bastard down.'

'Good for you. Which one is it?'

'*Dead Air*,' he says. 'I'm reliably informed it's unreadable.'

'Does the term postmodernism mean anything to you? Readability's an outdated concept.'

'Call me old-fashioned but I prefer novels that have a narrative and don't give you a headache.'

'I bet you like happy endings too.'

Chas turns his sunglasses on me. 'The odd one wouldn't go amiss.'

Brazier fires blaze along the sea-shell drive. The house looms through the smoke, lit up like a cruise ship. Two penguin-suited Samoans of the brick shithouse persuasion guard the door. They want to see our invitations. Chas produces his but I have to confess that mine is otherwise employed (marking my place — page thirty-something — in the new Dellasandro, as it happens).

The Samoans exchange a fatalistic raised-eyebrows shrug, like surgeons who have carved someone open only to discover it's hardly worth sewing him back up.

'I'm sorry, sir,' says one. 'This function is strictly invitation only. Our instructions were very clear.'

'For Christ's sake,' yelps Chas, 'he's the guest of honour. It's his fucking birthday party.'

'We'd appreciate you minding your language,' says the other Samoan, stone-faced. 'We're Christians.'

Chas is about to give them the free-speech speech but I head him off, suggesting it wouldn't be helpful or particularly germane. When I turn back to the gatekeepers, they're consulting a clipboard. 'Mr Napier?'

'That's me.'

'Mr Muir thought you might forget your invitation. He said we could make an exception for you.' They stand aside, all smiles now. 'Happy birthday, sir. Have a great evening.'

I feel like I've gate-crashed an impersonators' convention.

There's a late-period Elvis with what I hope is a cushion down the front of his spangled jumpsuit; a John Lennon–Yoko Ono couple (in white suits, thankfully, rather than their Amsterdam love-in skin); a Mick Jagger with his Bianca, who has baulked at the see-through wedding outfit; a Stevie Nicks peering through a riot of frizzy hair; a couple of zany Split Enzers; some cavemen heavy metallers; and a he and she David Bowie: she's dolled up like Ziggy Stardust, he's the Thin White Duke.

Hollywood provides a white-tuxedoed James Bond, a Dirty Harry who can't be persuaded to put away his gun, a Luke Skywalker, two Sally Bowles, Jane Fonda in both her Klute hooker persona — shaggy hair, long overcoat, microskirt — and as Hanoi Jane with red bandana and Ho Chi Minh T-shirt, a Kojak whose freshly shaved head is coming out in a rash, and a man in drag whom I take to be Myra Breckinridge although that might be fanciful. I tentatively ID Norman Kirk (another stripped sofa), Germaine Greer and Jackie O, but there's no mistaking Fred Dagg or Billy T. James.

Some I can't place, either because of obscurity or poor execution. I feel better for knowing I won't be the only John Doe.

A Playboy bunny, one of those young women who look pretty from the other side of a crowded room, materialises with a tray of champagne flutes.

'Bubbly, gents?' she asks brightly. 'It's Dom Perignon.'

Chas tells her he's not fussy. She giggles and moves on. I wonder if she can feel his gaze crawling up the seams of her stockings to the blob of white fluff on her backside. Abstinence, I sense, is very much an hour-by-hour proposition.

The action — rock 'n' roll music (the Rolling Stones' 'Tumbling Dice'), bull-elephant trumpeting, girly shrieks — is coming from the rear of the house, the pool area. At the mention of the pool, Chas's expression freezes.

'Tipsy women in bikinis,' he says reverently.

On the way we run into Stanley, who's attired in black silk pyjamas, a red smoking jacket and embroidered purple slippers. An unlit pipe protrudes from the corner of his mouth and there's a leggy, underdressed blonde on his arm.

'Hey, swingers,' he says, accepting a glass of champagne from a passing bunny, 'welcome to the Playboy Mansion.' He checks a leaf-thin gold watch. 'Topless bathing starts in half an hour.'

The blonde kisses me on the cheek. 'Happy birthday, dear Max.'

On closer examination she turns out to be Brigit. As I've never seen her. She's wearing a long blonde wig, a man-size, tantalisingly unbuttoned paisley shirt that just makes it to her tanned thighs, hippy sandals, rings on every finger, a collection of pendants and necklaces and a loose belt of silver hoops.

Chas processes this information before I do. 'It's BB, the original sex kitten, my all-time fantasy girl.'

'Join the club, pal,' says Stanley. To me: 'And who the fuck might you be?'

'Andy Warhol,' I say. 'Cultural impresario and interpreter of the Zeitgeist, at your service.'

'Speak English.'

'Campbell's Soup? Mao? The guy who said in the future everyone will be famous for fifteen minutes?'

'He was right,' says Stanley. 'Look around.'

I ask after Alan.

'He's out by the pool,' says Brigit, 'having a perv.' That's Chas's cue. She tells him, 'Look out for Bjorn Borg. You should see him, Max — he's in a wig, not that different from mine actually, with a headband and tight little shorts. I'd almost forgotten how skinny his legs are. All in all, a truly comical sight.'

'The racquet cracks me up,' says Stanley. 'That old wooden piece of shit. And he's stuck with it; it's like the key to his identity.'

'He should've thought of that, shouldn't he?' says Brigit.

'So, Brigit,' I say, 'were you able to persuade Stanley to join your committee?'

'I was.' She glows at him, re-linking arms. 'It's fantastic. We're so lucky to have him.'

Stanley wiggles his pipe jauntily. I excuse myself to go to the toilet.

Stanley and Brigit are where I left them, still arm in arm, talking to my mother and sister. My mother's wearing a floor-length gown, a tiara and a dead fox. Felicity, whose hair is dramatically short, is in a multi-coloured mini-dress with white stockings and buckled shoes.

Stanley says, 'Sorry, Mrs Napier, did you say you were the Queen Mother or the queen's mother?'

My mother, bless her doughty old heart, doesn't join in the chortling. She kisses me, wishes me happy birthday and asks who I'm meant to be. The explanation takes some time.

'I associate Twiggy with the sixties,' I tell Felicity. 'Carnaby Street, Swinging London and all that.'

'She overlapped,' she says. 'Just. I checked.'

'Where's Murray?'

'Good question,' says Felicity. 'He's been at work all day. He said he'd be a bit late but I thought he'd be here by now.'

'Who's he tonight?'

'Guess.'

'Frank Sinatra.' Late at night and under the influence, Murray performs a murderous rendition of 'My Way'.

'Close,' says Felicity. 'The Godfather.'

'No shit?' I say. 'Complete with mouthful of cotton wool?'

'The whole nine yards,' she says. 'He's even been practising the voice — I'll make him an offer he can't refuse.'

'Well, that's something to look forward to,' I say. 'Let's hope he gets here soon.'

I look around. Jim Morrison has the Queen Mother in stitches. Hef and BB are nowhere to be seen.

I'm with Sally and Rick, who've come — and this can be read a number of ways — as Elizabeth Taylor and Richard Burton. In front of us the dance-floor crush heaves and sways and sings along to Bachman Turner Overdrive's 'You Ain't Seen Nothin' Yet'. Stanley's dancing with Felicity, Alan's dancing with Brigit (a virtually statuesque Brigit, perhaps conscious that exuberance might expose her underwear; I can't be the only man in the room keeping an eye on developments), and Chas has hooked up with a bunny.

The song ends. Brigit and Alan decide to sit out Bowie's 'Rebel, Rebel' and thread their way to the sidelines, passing Sally and Rick. Alan, who's ditched his racquet, volunteers to fetch a couple of cold beers, a sensible move at this point in the evening — the pause that refreshes between the champagne and the serious business.

Brigit stands on tiptoe to shout in my ear. 'Sally's putting up a good front, don't you think?' My expression amuses her. 'Don't tell me you thought you were the only one she confided in.'

'That's what she told me.'

'Ditto, but it never occurred to me to believe her.'

'Why lie?'

She shrugs. 'All part of the intrigue, I suppose. And compared to the whoppers she must've told Rick, it's just a wee white one.'

'That's a point.'

'It was quite weird, really. Even when she was telling me it was out of this world and how she felt really alive for the first time in years, blah, blah, blah, I had the feeling she wanted me to disapprove, to haul her back into line. Of course, like you, I was far too sophisticated to do that.'

'I don't know,' I say. 'She was hugely fucked off with me when she thought I'd sent lover boy packing.'

That also amuses her. 'Stanley's quite something, isn't he?'

'He sure is. You two seem to have got very chummy very quickly.'

'Meaning?'

'What I said. Just making an observation.'

She gives me a cool smile. 'In that way people do when they're having a little dig. Is there a problem with me being chummy, as you put it, with Stanley?'

I see Alan coming. 'Well, if there is, it won't be my problem. Be careful, Brigit.'

Her smile disappears into itself, like a computer screen shutting down. 'Be careful yourself. You're giving a very good impression of someone whose nose is out of joint.'

Alan shoves a beer into my hand and plunges into a rave about his latest TV ad.

Brigit says, 'I'm just going to freshen up.'

'Okey-doke,' says Alan, barely missing a beat.

I watch Brigit over his shoulder. She exits without looking left or right. I glance over my shoulder: Stanley's yelling in Felicity's ear. She smiles and nods. They negotiate their way through the crush, Felicity to join us, Stanley to follow in Brigit's footsteps.

I ask Felicity where Murray is.

'I wouldn't want you to take this the wrong way,' she says, 'but who gives a rat's arse?'

It seems everyone's a party person except the birthday boy.

Bunny-girls circulate, encouraging the friends of Max Napier to gather in the library.

The library's modelled on the reading room of a

gentlemen's club. This is where Stanley comes when he feels like resting on his laurels. There's a full-size snooker table, leather armchairs, a baronial fireplace and a sideboard stacked with airmail editions of British and American broadsheets and recent issues of *Fortune*, *New Yorker* and *Vanity Fair*.

The floor-to-ceiling bookshelves are a paperback-free zone. There's lots of Churchill — a good half-dozen slabs of biography plus the four volumes of the great man's *History of the English Speaking Peoples*. Churchill is the man of destiny's man of destiny: the meteoric rise, the headstrong behaviour, the calamitous fall, the voice in the wilderness, the resounding vindication, the date with destiny. He's a role-model for all those driven men, unhinged by ambition, who are convinced they're different from (read: superior to) the rest of us and for the greater good should be given their head rather than being hamstrung by pygmies, like Gulliver in Lilliput. De Gaulle is another favourite. Napoleon and perhaps Bismarck will get a look-in but today's man of destiny tends to stick to the modern era. To the Self-Made Man, secure in his utilitarian ignorance ('History is bunk'), everything before the invention of the steam locomotive seems like a fairytale.

One whole wall is dedicated to money. There's also brand-name journalism — the likes of Theodore White, Alistair Cooke and Bernard Levin — and a surprisingly contemporary selection of fiction, although Dellasandro's breakthrough book is in pristine condition and opens stiffly, as if for the first time.

Stanley stands with his back to the fireplace, waiting for quiet.

'Evening, all. For those who don't know me, my name's Stanley Muir and you're drinking my piss. I hope it's hitting the spot. We're here tonight to celebrate the fiftieth birthday of your friend and mine, Max Napier. Where the hell is he? Show yourself, man.'

There's a murmur of agreement. Someone yells, 'Yeah, Max, front and centre.'

It can't be avoided. I join Stanley by the fireplace.

'Now when I first put the idea of a party to Max,' he says, 'he was lukewarm. What's that? That doesn't sound like the Max Napier you know?' There's a collective scream of laughter; God help us if Stanley says something funny. 'Eventually he agreed, on three conditions: he wouldn't organise it, he wouldn't pay for it and there wouldn't be any speeches. Well, Max, two out of three ain't bad and, anyway, talk is cheap. Or, to put it another way, fuck you and the horse you rode in on.'

Stanley grins wildly. You'd swear he's having the time of his life. He reminisces about London, making it sound like a non-stop bohemian carnival in which I was the most daring performer. The Queen Mother looks on anxiously, fearing he'll dredge up filth in the worst tradition of best-man speeches: the indecency arrest, the phone-booth shag, the lost weekend with a transvestite. But with a few surprisingly deft brushstrokes he creates a flattering portrait of the artist as a youngish man, then fast forwards twenty years to freeze on a secure and worldly figure approaching the height of his powers: 'Max took a hard road but he's still on it, still moving forward and the best is yet to come. And through it all, through the ups and downs of a writer's life and some pretty tough times, he's stayed true to himself.'

'Steady on, Stanley,' I say, 'these people know me.'

'They don't know the half of you,' he says. 'I was proud to call Max a friend twenty years ago and I'm even prouder to call him a friend tonight. Okay, bunnies, let's have you.'

After the bunnies have dispensed champagne, Stanley presses on: 'I've been to fiftieths where there've been toasts to the next fifty years, as if the aim of the game is to live as long as possible. Well, I've seen too much bad shit come out of nowhere to take anything for granted and just lately I've visited a few relatives in old folks' homes and if that's longevity, you can shove it up your ass. So let's just drink a toast to Max at fifty and wish him all the success and happiness he deserves.'

They drink. Someone starts up 'For he's a jolly good fellow.' 'Why was he born so beautiful?' inevitably follows. My cheeks burn and there's a rainforest under the wig. I'd rather be in the pool.

I'm about to respond but Stanley's not finished. 'Hang on, Max, one more thing before you bore the crap out of us: your presents are in the dining room but I can tell you there's booze, booze and more booze. Like you said, these people know you. I'll have it delivered on Monday.' He takes an envelope from the breast pocket of his smoking jacket. 'When I was thinking about what to give Max, I asked myself, what do you give the man who has nothing? I suppose I could give him everything I've got but where would that leave me?' He hands me the envelope. 'Besides, some things you can't put a price on, right?'

The envelope contains an open return first-class air ticket to Paris. I thank Stanley but can't resist adding, 'Anyone would think you're trying to get rid of me.' His eyes narrow; he knows what I'm talking about.

The crowd bays, wanting in on it. When I tell them, they ooh and aah and applaud Stanley's largesse.

He says, 'There should be something else in there.'

It's a folded, A4 sheet of what the Queen Mother would call quality writing paper on which someone — not Stanley, whose handwriting is a ludicrous scrawl — has written a Parisian street address and a name: Samantha Marchand.

'I hired some people in the States to track her down,' he murmurs. 'It would've been a lot easier if she'd reverted to her maiden name after her marriage broke up.'

eighteen

The security men have emptied the pool and herded the die-hards down the sea-shell drive back out into the real world. The caterers are cleaning up. The married couples have taken each other home and Chas has disappeared into the night panting after a bunny.

Felicity left as she arrived — alone — having woven a narrative around Murray's no-show: 'You score a commission on a Saturday, you want to celebrate. A few of you score commissions, it's party time. Muz would've thought one drink, half an hour of telling each other how wonderful we are, then do a quiet fade. The obvious flaw in this plan is that, like most men, without his wife there to tug on his sleeve, he's incapable of having just the one. And when he finally managed to tear himself away, he had to go home to get dressed up, which is where he made his second mistake: the old I'll just lie down and rest my eyes for a few minutes trick. Well, all I can say is he'd better get a good night's sleep because tomorrow he'll have some serious grovelling to do. You've got one more thing to look forward to, Max: an abject apology from your dear brother-in-law.'

The host and I are deep in leather armchairs, sipping single malt scotch, not saying much. Tomorrow, as always, I'll berate myself for adding an oily layer of hard liquor to the pond of beer and wine but right now, as always, it would seem perverse not to.

Stanley breaks the silence, insisting I stay the night. 'There are four guest bedrooms up there. You should find one of them to your satisfaction.'

'What's the difference? They've all got harbour views and ensuites, haven't they?'

'True,' he says, 'but only one of them's got a bunny.'

'A bunny, you say?'

He nods. 'I would've put a voucher in the envelope — this entitles the bearer to a night of consensual activity with a bunny — but someone was bound to take offence.'

'You can't be too careful these days. I'm interested in the consensual part: that means neither party has to be coerced, bribed or otherwise inveigled into it, correct?'

Stanley dismisses my qualm with a seigneurial chuckle. 'Not an issue, Max. I wouldn't say these chicks are working girls but they ain't debutantes, if you get my drift. As a matter of fact, I've got a tag-team upstairs waiting for me.'

'Do you think you'll do justice to them?'

'Maybe not tonight,' he says, 'but tomorrow's another day. I might even take on the water-jump.'

'The what?'

'It's like this: morning has broken; shafts of golden sunlight filter through the curtains; birds twitter. As you emerge from a drunken stupor, you become conscious of three things. Your bladder feels like Krakatoa; you're not alone, the other party in the bed being a near-naked young woman whose name escapes you; and you have the mother of all boners. But there's something not quite right about it — if anything, it's too hard. It's so fucking hard that it's lost all feeling. It's like it's been injected with rhino tranquilliser. You could drop the *Oxford Dictionary* on it or zap it with a cattle prod and you wouldn't feel a goddamn thing. You assume this state of affairs is related to the fact that you should've had a leak four hours ago but now there's a decision to be made: do you slip out of bed, make your way to the john, contort yourself into a position where you can unload without hosing down the shaving mirror and then watch that mighty boner shrivel up and die? Or do you decide to strike while the iron's hot, holler "Incoming" in your young companion's ear and go for the doctor? The latter option, my friend, is the water-jump.'

'If you've got no feeling in your dork, what's the point?'

Stanley shakes his head. 'Fifty years old and it's still all about me. Didn't your vicar ever tell you it's better to give than to receive?'

'No, but then I was never an altar boy. Tell me, in the course of your frequent one-on-one moments with Brigit tonight, did you happen to mention the tag-team?'

'I don't think the subject came up.' Stanley puts his drink down on the side-table and leans forward, putting his elbows on his knees and softly clapping his hands. His laugh-lines melt away. It looks like the party's over. 'I really hope you're not going to be a pain in the ass about this, Max. That's not what friends are for.'

'What exactly is "this", Stanley?'

'You know fucking well. I'm not asking for your blessing; I'm just asking you to stay the fuck out of the way and let nature take its course.'

There's a knock on the door. It half opens and a caterer hovers in the doorway. 'Excuse me, Mr Muir, one of your guests is here . . .'

He steps aside for Felicity. She's changed out of the

Twiggy kit. It looks like the party's over for her too.

'I tried your place first, Max,' she says, as if that explains everything. 'Sorry about this, Stanley, but I'm a bit worried about my husband. You know he didn't make it here tonight? Well, he didn't make it home either.'

The house was as she'd left it. The kids had checked in as requested, leaving cryptic messages that left plenty of room for manoeuvre. On nights like this she wished she could believe in a guardian angel but there were no short-cuts to peace of mind and nothing she could put her faith in except their sense of self-preservation.

Halfway up the stairs she thought, why am I doing this? Muz wasn't going anywhere. The dark three-piece suit he'd borrowed from his churchgoing older brother would still be wrapped in dry-cleaner's plastic and he'd be flopped out on the bed in his socks and boxers snoring like a pig. It occurred to her that the pig comparison had cropped up a few times lately but she was in no mood to beat herself up about it.

Muz could wait. Whatever issues he'd — they'd — had with me over the years and however much I rubbed him the wrong way, I was family and fiftieth birthday parties were a big deal. And what was almost as infuriating was that if he'd rung her early on to say he wasn't coming because he was buggered or pissed or simply couldn't be stuffed, she would have been furious and embarrassed but at least she would have known where she stood: on her own for the night. But he didn't even have the consideration to do that so she'd spent the whole night expecting him to turn up at any moment, which was a distraction she could have done without. It was a long time since she'd been able to go with the flow and please herself, as opposed to being an extension of her husband.

Lying there listening to him snore held no appeal, nor did

the guest bedroom, so she ran a scented bath in the downstairs bathroom, mixed a gin and tonic in a tall glass with lots of ice and fresh lime and soaked for half an hour thinking about the party. Even with Don Corleone's ghost floating in her wake, it was more fun than she'd had for too long.

After that, she was ready for bed — snorting, vexatious husband and all. But he wasn't there.

I ask, 'When was the last time you tried his cellphone?'

'On the way over,' she says. 'It's been turned off all night, which isn't like him at all.'

'Have you spoken to anyone from his work?'

'Do you know what time it is?'

'It's past the point of worrying about waking people up,' says Stanley crisply, causing Felicity to gulp. 'If they can't shed any light on it, you'll have to bring in the cops.'

They go in search of a phone book. I apply more whiskey and my pickled mind to Murray's vanishing act. Car accident? Unless he and the car were reduced to charred skeletons, you'd think the authorities would have contacted Felicity by now. Fallen down drunk and banged his head? It's Saturday night; if it happened in the vicinity of a pub or bar, you'd think someone would have tripped over him. Mugged and left for dead in an alley? When real estate agents go out on the town, that usually means Ponsonby or Parnell or the Viaduct Basin, hardly mean streets prowled by a predatory underclass. Passed out in a K Road massage parlour under a human pyramid of underage Thai hookers? I wouldn't discount the possibility that Murray has a secret life but whorehouses are not hotels. They operate on emergency ward rules: someone needs your bed. When his time was up, they'd slap him awake and send him on his way.

Stanley returns, closing the door behind him. 'I thought this could wait,' he says, 'but it can't. I got a call yesterday from a big-time property investor. He said this thing Murray tried to get me into is a black hole that's sucked money out of everyone who's gone near it.'

'Would that include Murray?'

'When someone wants me to invest in something, the first questions I ask is, have you put your money where your mouth is? Murray said he was in for a couple of hundred grand.'

Felicity reappears. This will probably turn out to be one of those high-anxiety non-events caused by crossed wires and Murphy's Law but now she's starting to entertain the possibility that it could be for real. After all, shit happens — mostly to other people, but it happens. It's like Lotto in reverse: you don't expect to win but someone has to.

'This gets more bizarre by the minute,' she says. 'He was in the office this morning, I mean yesterday morning, went out to an open home around lunchtime and didn't come back.'

'Were they expecting him?' asks Stanley.

'It was pretty vague,' she says. 'Put it this way, they didn't think anything of it, the fact he didn't come back.'

The party's definitely over. Hef and the bunnies might have a pillow fight and a sex sandwich and drink tequila sunrises watching the sun come up but my sister needs looking after. On the way out Stanley drops a hand on my shoulder. If we find Murray sleeping it off in a broom cupboard, he murmurs, I should double back; my bunny will still be there. I tell him to release her into the wild; I'm saving myself.

'Samantha might've changed,' he says. 'I don't mean the normal ageing process, I mean ruinously gone to seed.'

'She might be a whole different person. She might be a mystic or a bomb-maker. She might be off men, like that little waitress you wasted your charm on.'

Stanley screws up his face. 'Oh, man.'

'Anything's possible.'

'You'll be able to handle it, though?' It's only now occurring to Stanley that, having bankrolled this sentimental mini-drama, he can't stage-manage a happy ending. 'If it doesn't work out, for whatever reason.'

'If it fucks me up, Stanley, rest assured I'll sue the arse off you.'

Felicity rings the police. Rock in a crisis that I am, I make a cup of tea.

She hangs up feeling better. 'The duty sergeant said nineteen times out of twenty these things turn out to be false alarms. He thinks Muz probably got sidetracked over a few drinks. When he realised he was going to be in the dog-box, he figured he might as well be hung for a sheep as a lamb. Apparently it happens all the time: people get themselves in the poo but instead of doing something about it, they freeze. When reality finally bites, they can't face whoever they've let down so they go AWOL.'

'Does that seem likely to you?'

She shrugs. 'More likely than anything we've come up with.'

'I don't know,' I say. 'Murray paralysed by shame? I find that hard to believe.'

Felicity sighs. 'Not now, Max. When he turns up it's open season but until then, lay off him, okay?'

'I'm actually trying to be dispassionate. The Murray I know doesn't fit into that scenario; it'd take a bit more than that to make him flip out, wouldn't it?'

She holds up her hands to indicate that she'd rather not have to listen to me being dispassionate. She just wants Murray to walk, stumble, crawl or be carried in the door so she can stop worrying about him and start tongue-lashing him.

She goes upstairs to email the police a photo. I hear her calling and go out into the hall.

'What?'

'Can you come up here?' There's a shake in her voice but I can't tell if it's panic or relief.

I trudge up the stairs. She sits on the edge of the bed, hands trapped between knock knees. She doesn't look panicked or relieved, she looks at a loss.

'What is it?'

'The sergeant told me to check his clothes. Some of them are gone.'

I was sceptical when Stanley passed on Murray's claim that he'd tipped a pile of his own money into the black hole. If I'd been in Stanley's shoes, I'd have assumed Murray was bullshitting, just telling me what he thought I wanted to hear. I also thought that if he had squandered two hundred grand, Felicity would have had plenty to say about it. It didn't occur to me that she mightn't know.

'Do you do internet banking?' I ask.

Felicity stares at me.

'If you do, you should check that everything's in order.'

'Oh, I get it.' The stare hardens, becomes a glare. 'You think he's emptied our bank accounts and run off to South America?'

'It's a way of tracking people's movements,' I say, avoiding the question. 'He might've used his eftpos card or an ATM.'

She'd like to shoot me down but hasn't got the energy or the ammunition. 'I suppose what you think of him isn't really the issue.'

I don't hang around. If he's gone, I don't want to be looking over her shoulder when she finds out from a computer.

She comes into the kitchen a few minutes later with a bottle of wine, a hundred-dollar Waiheke Island red. I know Murray has a stash of fine wine reserved for special occasions and special people because he's often said so in my hearing.

'Happy birthday for the last time,' she says. We click

glasses and drink. She thinks the wine is overrated.

'It's probably not at its best at four in the morning.'

'Tell me about it. We bought this place for two hundred and fifty thousand in 1983 and cleared the mortgage in five years. I remember it well: we had an Out of Debt party and I made myself sick on strawberry daiquiris. I haven't had one since. According to the bank, though, we're mortgaged to the tune of one million dollars. What are the chances of that being a computer error?'

'Not great, I wouldn't think. He didn't tell you about his get-rich-quick scheme, did he?'

She shakes her head. I repeat what Stanley said.

There are no dramatics. She's either going into shock or she's tougher than I thought. 'That doesn't particularly surprise me. He's always had this dream of getting into property development and making a killing. I wouldn't let him so he did it behind my back. Meet the new me: a forty-six-year-old solo mother with two children at university, a job I was hoping to give up soon and a colossal mortgage. What do I do now? Start by selling this place, I suppose. So much for the dream home.'

'You've got other assets, haven't you? I seem to remember him banging on about some flats.'

'There's a couple of apartments and some shares.' She pours herself another glass; I'm not even halfway through mine. 'What's the bet he's sold them?'

'The money aside, how do you feel?'

'Fuck, Max, that's right up there with "Apart from that, Mrs Lincoln, how did you like the play?" How can I forget about the money, for Christ's sake? That's food on the table and a roof over our heads and you're treating it as some kind of optional extra, like a third movie channel. How do I feel? Betrayed, I suppose. We made promises to each other, we created something. He's just washed his hands of all that and put us out on the street. To tell the truth, what I really feel is very fucking scared.'

She puts her head in the crook of her arm and weeps. I try to comfort her with hugs and caring words as our father did whenever the capricious world found a new way to make her cry but I don't have the gift: I can't transmit love via my voice and fingertips, I can't make her feel safe. All I can do is help her upstairs, suggest she take a couple of pills and leave her to her visions of lonely struggle.

Murray isn't sleeping it off on a mate's couch or in the back seat of his car. He isn't on the operating table or waiting to get patched up by an exhausted junior doctor. He's not face down in some side-street with empty pockets and a caved-in skull. He's not in the morgue. He's eight miles high in business class, drinking Jack Daniel's and Coke, not sure whether to laugh or cry.

In the morning there's a note on the kitchen table. Felicity has gone to see our mother. What a doleful get-together that will be: two generations of Napier women keening for their men. I'm guiltily grateful to Felicity for not asking me to attend a family crisis meeting.

I walk over to Stanley's place in the hope of a swim and of finding someone who feels worse than I do. He's poolside, still in the Hefner outfit except for the pipe, which has gone the way of Alan's tennis racquet. From across the pool the huge orange-tinted sunglasses make him look like a mutant, an insect from the neck up, a Kafkaesque metamorphosis in progress. Up close and without the sunglasses he looks worse. The lank, unwashed hair, lifeless eyes and air of joyless depravity bring to mind those grey nonentities with weak chins and soft hands who haunt suburban parks and sit in third-hand hatchbacks with the window down listening to playground noise.

A stainless steel cocktail shaker and an empty glass are at his elbow.

I ask how he's feeling.

'A damn sight better for having put away three of these babies. There's another batch in the fridge, if you'd be so kind. Get yourself a glass while you're at it.'

About once a year I feel like a Bellini. Today isn't the day but it seems churlish to prefer something else. As Stanley pours, I give him a Murray update. He seems more interested in his fourth cocktail.

Eventually he says, 'If I'd asked you yesterday, would you have said he was a good husband and father?'

'I suppose so.'

'Did he treat Felicity like shit in public?'

'No.'

'Was he domineering? Did she have to walk on eggshells and avoid contradicting him at all costs?'

'No.'

'Was he affectionate towards his kids?'

'Yes.'

'Was he proud of them?'

'Shit, yeah. You'd swear they were the greatest prodigies since Mozart.'

'Did they do much family stuff together?'

'Yes.'

'Did he have any expensive bad habits? Coke, horses and whores are the usual suspects.'

'Not that I'm aware of.'

'Okay. Anyone's theoretically capable of walking out on his wife and kids. Your average Joe, from the moment he wakes up his wife's nagging him about money and standing up to his boss and demanding a level of recognition and reward he might deserve but is never going to get. He thinks about the day ahead and it's more of the same — tedium, frustration, shit-fights with people he despises. When he says hi to his kids, they don't even look up from their cornflakes. To the outside world he's a good family man with a steady job but you can see why he might want to be somewhere else.'

'The mass of men lead lives of quiet desperation.'

Stanley sits up, jabbing his finger at me. 'Exactly. I couldn't have put it better myself. The point is, though, fuck all of them ever do anything about it. They might fantasise about it in the shower, then they have breakfast, try to get a few grunts out of the kids, kiss the wife, pat the dog, go to work, do their job. And they'll do it all over again tomorrow and the day after that and so on and so forth until they retire or drop dead. Guys like that need a catalyst.'

'Such as?'

'It begins with P and ends with Y.'

'Penury?'

Stanley slumps back on the recliner. 'Not penury, you fucking dunce, pussy. The French have got a phrase for it.' He clicks his fingers impatiently.

'*Cherchez la femme?*'

'That's the bugger: *cherchez la femme*. Take it from me, there's a woman involved.'

'Hold on,' I say. 'You're the one who found out that he's blown a fortune. If that's not a fucking catalyst, what is?'

'Do the math, pal. He blew a couple of hundred grand. That's a setback, a kick in the teeth even, but a two hundred K mortgage is hardly the end of the world. But he made it an even mill. What's that money for? I'll tell you what it's for: it's to underwrite his new life. I reckon he got into this property venture with the idea of making a quick bundle so he could split without leaving Felicity and the kids in the shit. But it went tits-up and he had his girlfriend whispering in his ear — "It's now or never, baby, let's take the money and run."'

'Jesus,' I say. 'That would be adding insult to injury.'

'I'll tell you something else,' says Stanley, warming to his work. 'When you *cherchez la femme*, start in his office. I bet you anything you like they worked together. Simple physical proximity — it's fucked more marriages than stretch marks and mothers-in-law put together.'

nineteen

Stanley's right, of course. There is another woman — the client relations manager at a printing outfit used by Murray's agency. While she and Murray didn't work under the same roof, they *interfaced* on a regular basis.

All is revealed in a letter posted at the airport shortly before Murray went airside, passing the point of no return. He regrets the upheaval and upset but insists his weasel run — which he characterises as a 'clean break' — is for the best. He undertakes to help with the children's running costs and hopes they'll treat his new abode (in Noosa or on the Gold Coast, depending on value for money and professional opportunities) as a home away from home.

Their son Josh is reluctant to take sides and enthused at the prospect of an alternative residence in subtropical Queensland. Daughter Bella is vowing never to speak to Murray again. While appreciating her daughter's stance, Felicity frets that Murray will use it as an excuse to backslide on his studiously unspecific promise of financial support.

On the wider money front, Murray is unapologetic. As he

sees it, he has simply divided the spoils, unilaterally but fairly, thereby avoiding the expensive viciousness of a protracted, lawyer-driven negotiation. The house is worth two million so Felicity has effectively bought him out. If she can't handle the mortgage, she can trade down to something more manageable, a sensible option seeing the children aren't too far off quitting the nest. He has pocketed the proceeds from the sale of one apartment, leaving her the other, and sold their shares to cover his losses on the property venture which is only fair since, naturally, he would have split the profits if it had proved a winner. So they're all square and, far from being hard up, Felicity has a net worth of more than a million. This ignores her looming budget crisis: she has a part-time job and limited prospects, having put family ahead of career for most of her married life.

As for Felicity, she insists that the emotional storm blew itself out in forty-eight hours. Now as she steels herself to break the news that they'll have to sell the house and settle for less in a less desirable part of town, she's consumed with anxiety over the children's reaction to the imminent decline in their standard of living. Mother offered to put them up indefinitely and at no cost but Felicity turned her down on the spot. Josh and Bella supposedly adore their grandmother but would regard moving in with her as an unbearable humiliation.

I wonder if it should be up to them but that battle was fought and lost some time ago. If push came to shove, Felicity thinks Josh would be on the first plane to Brisbane and, notwithstanding Bella's vehement solidarity, she probably wouldn't be far behind.

What about the other woman? I ask. Even for spoilt, insensitive, pathologically status-conscious teenagers, it's one thing to like the idea of kicking back on the Sunshine Coast, quite another to live *en famille* with Dad's new, home-wrecking squeeze.

Felicity's shoulders slump. Josh has spoken to the new squeeze on the phone and thinks she sounds 'cool'. Josh is a little turd but saying so won't help matters. Felicity would find a reason why it's all her fault.

As usual, I seem to be the only person with a bad word to say about anyone. Mum is endorsing Murray's spin that skipping out on his family was 'for the best'. She approves of the avoidance of bad blood, lawyers at ten paces, mutual friends lining up behind one or the other like pick-up teams, and the ongoing guerrilla war in which the children play various roles: hostages, peacekeepers, innocents in the firing line. When I complain that she's lapped up Murray's bullshit and banged her plate on the table demanding a second helping, she snaps back that she would have expected a little more tolerance from someone who has scuttled away from two marriages in similar circumstances. Having got that off her chest — how long has she been bottling it up? — she goes on to accuse me of hypocrisy in that, if I was honest, I'd admit I'm glad to see the back of him.

I don't argue with her. That's guaranteed to make me feel ashamed of myself. Neither of us is inclined to hold back but she can't go the distance and would end up taking a brow-beating. And, of course, she has a point.

But not *the* point. It would be hypocritical of me to be scandalised by Murray falling in love — for the sake of argument, let's give him the benefit of the doubt — with another woman or to claim that I'm diminished by his leaving. But this isn't about me, it's about Felicity. And about Murray. He's the hypocrite here; he's the one who bullfrogged on about the joy and fulfilment and importance of family life.

I feel I ought to be outraged on Felicity's behalf but perhaps there's no need. Her heart appears to be intact. If there ever was love, it wasn't the sort that poets harp on about. This was, at bottom, a marriage of convenience, appearances, convention. Now she contemplates the wreckage with an insurance assessor's fishy eye, calculating the social and financial damage.

Josh and, to a lesser extent, Bella are at that age and stage where it's uncool to make moral judgements because only God-botherers see things in black and white. And Felicity and Murray are essentially irrelevant to them now. They'll take whatever's on offer because they know their parents would be bereft if they refused. Lavishing love and treasure on their children is what parents do, that's how they define themselves. But no matter how much Josh and Bella take, they'll reserve the right to disengage. Because, when all's said and done, they didn't ask to be born.

Felicity drops by. A new Felicity: this isn't Felicity Abandoned, or Felicity Domesticus whom I had to get used to when she became Mrs Murray, or the little sister I don't expect to see again. This is Felicity Unbound, giddy with excitement, unable to believe her luck.

My immediate thought is that after years of paying tribute at the corner dairy, she's been smiled upon by the Lotto God. That would make Murray choke on his Bundy 'n' Coke. Benign fate has intervened but not in the form of little coloured balls. The local sugar daddy is at it again.

'That man's a saint,' she gushes. 'No two ways about it. You're probably not surprised because you see this side of him all the time but I can't believe he'd do this for someone he hardly knows. Okay, I know it's because I'm your sister but even so. I always thought that thing about having to pinch yourself to make sure you're not dreaming was just an expression but if I don't keep doing it I start thinking, Oh my God, I'm going to wake up and it'll all be just a dream.'

Stanley has had her around for a glass of wine and a chat about the financial predicament that, as Murray alluded to, many people would be only too happy to have.

This is what he proposes. The house is mortgaged for half its value. He'll take over the mortgage, thereby becoming the joint owner. Felicity will receive a guarantee, with full legal trimmings, of sole occupancy for five years. If at any time within that period she decides she wants full ownership, she can buy Stanley out at the market rate as determined by an independent valuation. When the five years are up, Felicity will either buy Stanley out or the house will be sold, with the proceeds split fifty-fifty.

Having delivered her glad tidings, Felicity clasps her hands to her chest and awaits my hugs and hallelujahs.

'So is it signed and sealed?'

'God, no,' she says. 'I've just come from Stanley's. He insisted that before I did anything else, I had to make sure you were okay with it.'

'Why wouldn't I be?'

'That's what I said but he's adamant he won't do anything involving your family that you aren't a hundred per cent happy with. I told him, look, I know Max is my only sibling and I love him to bits and all that and I know he's a really good friend of yours but if I had to make a list of people I wouldn't dream of asking for financial advice, he'd come in just behind that friend of Mum's who's gone bankrupt two or three times.'

'Close but no cigar, eh? What did Stanley say to that?'

'That it wasn't a matter of getting advice from you — I should get that from my lawyer and my accountant. He's doing this because of his friendship with you so if you've got a problem with it, for whatever reason, it kind of defeats the purpose. What it boils down to, Max, is that you've got the power of veto.' She cocks her head, frowning. 'And seeing you don't look exactly overjoyed, I'm beginning to get nervous.'

I pull her into a hug. 'Of course I don't have a problem

with it. Stanley's dead right though — you need to get professional advice and make sure the agreement's crystal clear. You don't want to get down the track and find that you and he have very different ideas about what you actually agreed to.'

She rests her head on my shoulder. 'It's pretty straightforward. There's really nothing that's open to interpretation.'

'Then it shouldn't be hard to nail it down in black and white. And seeing you seem to need it, you have my blessing.'

Stanley didn't want my blessing but he's going to great lengths to stop me running interference on his Brigit play. Is it a case of a man who always gets his own way wanting to rub in the fact that what Stanley wants, Stanley gets, or is he getting a kick out of pulling the strings and watching us fall into line?

Or is just possible he's fallen for her? Is Brigit his Daisy Buchanan?

Ah yes, Project Gatsby. You must be wondering how it's travelling. Well, at this stage Project Gatsby resembles an aeroplane still bumping along the runway a hundred metres past the point at which it should have taken off. One of three things will happen. The plane may take off, better late than never, and climb smoothly to cruising altitude where any lingering white-knuckle anxiety can be treated with a little something from the drinks trolley. The pilot may abort the take-off. The plane may run out of runway, plough through a fence into a field and go up in a fireball, to the great misfortune of all on board and the herd of cows who happen to be grazing there. One doesn't envy the pilot, who knows that if the third scenario comes to pass, he'll be among the first obliterated or flash-fried in jet fuel.

Perhaps what it needs is a passionate but doomed love affair. Here I am mulishly opposed to a Stanley–Brigit liaison when it might in fact provide the surge of juice needed to get the thing off the ground. I'd just have to watch and listen and write it all down.

But while that could lend a documentary quality that might appeal to the critics ('A bleakly gritty, all-too-convincing depiction of love gone wrong'), reportage has never been my MO. I prefer to make things up. Besides, I wouldn't want my friends to suffer for my art. Gatsby, of course, is the victim; Daisy goes back to her odious husband, leaving Jay adrift on his pneumatic mattress. I can't see the equivalent happening here. Stanley would walk away without a scratch, like the driver of some precision-engineered Nordic tank involved in a head-on with a motorised shopping basket. It would be Brigit and/or Alan who'd have to be cut from the wreckage and put back together.

Unless he's fallen for her. Unless she's his Daisy.

Even though I can visualise my friends as casualties, I can do nothing to prevent it. Stanley has sidelined me. He's bought my detachment.

A curious call from the books editor of our daily newspaper, who has forgiven my tantrum and readmitted me to the reviewers' stable.

Assuming I must have seriously overshot a deadline for her to be ringing this early in the day, I tell her it's practically in the mail: 'I just have to tidy up a couple of things and hit send.'

When it comes to stalling for time, I find shifty evasions and half-truths are more trouble than they're worth. Better to brazen it out. The bare-faced lie gets them off your back and puts you under pressure to deliver. This one should buy me twenty-four hours, enough to skim-read any novel ever written and crank out the generic on-the-one-hand, on-the-other-hand review.

'No hurry,' she says. 'It's not due for another week.'

'So is this a social call?'

'More or less,' she says. 'I like to keep in touch with the literati, see what everyone's up to. So what are you working on?'

I waffle about Project Gatsby in such vague terms that it could be an east meets west cookbook or a self-help manual for vertigo sufferers. She expresses feverish anticipation, although the tone doesn't quite match the sentiments. The whole conversation, in fact, creaks with the gritted-teeth bonhomie of a school reunion.

Then: 'How's your partner-in-crime Chas Harley?'

As mentioned, I like to ease my way into the day but I'm sufficiently with it to hear an alarm bell when a journalist casually drops that name into the conversation.

'He's okay. Why do you ask?'

'His name came up the other day,' she says. 'I thought, gosh, it's ages since I clapped eyes on the handsome Dr Harley. How about you?'

'How about me what?'

'Have you seen him lately?'

'We were at the same party last Saturday night. Is that a recent enough sighting for you?'

'How was he?'

Maybe I've read this wrong; maybe she hankers after becoming a notch on Chas's heavily scarred bedpost. Notoriety has that effect on some people.

'He seemed to be enjoying himself,' I say. 'I wouldn't say it was a vintage performance but there was still much to admire.'

'Well, next time you see him give him my regards.'

'Will do. Is there a message I can pass on?'

There's a pause. 'Just tell him life goes on in the real world,' she says. 'Nobody died; nobody went to El Paso.'

'Now there was a writer. No one loaded up a simile like Ray Chandler.'

'Yeah, but does anyone read him any more — apart from you and me?'

'Of course not. He doesn't do serial killers.'

I think about giving Chas a call to see what he makes of it but that can wait; coffee can't. The phone rings as I lock the door. I let it ring.

Speak of the devil. What brings Dr Chas Harley, senior lecturer, to my café this bright morning? He looks out of sorts, as he often does these days. Humiliation, demotion and a pay-cut can do that to a man.

'The last time I saw the runaway brother-in-law was right here,' I say, 'at this very table. He also showed up unannounced. Should I regard that as an omen?'

'I tried to ring you,' he says glumly.

'What's up?'

'You know my recent troubles were meant to remain strictly confidential? Well, we didn't factor in the feminazis who helped Naomi stitch me up. They narked me to a journalist.'

That explains the curious phone call from the literary editor. I pass on her message, prompting an equally curious response: 'I think it was meant for both of us.'

'How do you mean?'

'It's actually not that big a deal for me,' he says, either too preoccupied or just plain unwilling to answer a simple question. 'The university will stick to their side of the bargain and publicity's the last thing Naomi wants — understandably, given that she'd emerge as a vindictive, conniving little slut. It hasn't got legs, as they say.'

'But?'

He looks down, looks up, looks away. 'I'm really fucking sorry about this, Max: I told Naomi about your dabble in porn; she told the feminazis; they told the journalist. Two birds with one stone.'

His face crumples into that blur of shame you see under shriek headlines: the father who left a toddler in a locked car in the casino carpark on the hottest day of the year while he gambled away his wife's inheritance. I refrain from laughing out loud out of respect for the effort that has gone into his wretchedness.

'Okay,' I say. 'Let's see what we've got here. A few years ago a writer that hardly anyone's heard of wrote a few porn novels that no one in this country's ever read. Now that's what I call a scoop. Hold the front page and double the print run. You reckon your story hasn't got legs — that fucker's a double amputee.'

'It's all in the timing,' he says stonily. 'They're doing a bloody great feature on porn and see this as a spicy companion piece. They want to look at what differentiates erotica from porn, with you and Tania giving the two sides of the argument.'

'Well, they don't need me; Tania will give them enough pseudo-intellectual wank to fill the paper twice over. Seriously, Chas, there's nothing to worry about. They got the thing third hand; if I won't talk to them, what are they going to do?'

Chas plumbs new depths of misery. 'They got in touch with your ex-wife. She was only too happy to confirm it.'

'How the fuck did they . . .'

'From the same source: me, via the conniving little slut.'

I push my chair back. 'I'll say this for you, Chas: when you decide to be indiscreet, you don't fuck around.'

He lowers his head and rubs his face as if trying to ease pain deep in the bones. 'I'm sorry, Max.'

'Ah, well, it's not the end of the world. So I wrote porn, so what? Who cares?'

'Lots of people,' he says. 'That's the problem.'

'You're looking on the dark side because of what you've

been though,' I say. 'This is different. It'll be a complete non-event.'

Chas shakes his head. He seems almost miffed by my disinclination to shit myself. 'You don't get it, Max. You're in your own little cocoon, you don't realise what it's like now. All these fucking people, they make out they're so hip and broad-minded, but when the PC heat comes on they fall over themselves to join the lynch-mob. You know the feminist line on pornography. When this comes out, you'll go on their shit-list, mate, and those bitches have long memories. They never fucking forget.'

'I don't know that it's quite that bad,' I say, 'but even if it is, what are they going to do — picket every bookshop that sells my stuff?'

'It's way more subtle and sinister than that. You apply for a grant, someone will bring up the fact that you wrote porn; you apply for a residency, someone will bring it up. When arts festival committees are deciding who to invite, someone will bring it up. Every review, it'll be there in the first few paragraphs. Is that how you want to be remembered: Max Napier, the novelist who wrote dirty books on the side?'

'To be honest, I don't spend a lot of time thinking about how — or, for that matter, if — I'll be remembered. And as for this shit: I've made my bed, I'll lie in it.'

'Well, I'm pleased you're so relaxed about it,' says Chas. Actually, he's not; he's sore because I don't share his apocalyptic vision. 'Anyway, last word on the subject: when I drove past your place on the way over, a photographer and what I assume was a reporter were hanging around outside, so be prepared.'

The photographer is a tracksuited greybeard whose demeanour suggests he's getting too old to be ambushing sex fiends. The reporter is an attractive young woman, Julie

Something, whose cynical, almost certainly male boss obviously believes a pretty face and svelte figure are the way to a pornographer's heart.

I adopt what I hope is an expression of amused, unflappable worldliness as Greybeard lurches around, snapping me from every angle. Julie asks if we could have a chat.

'What about?'

'Your porn career.'

This comes with a pleasingly ironic smile, presumably intended to convey that she, for one, isn't taking it too seriously.

'Well,' I say, 'it was a while ago now and hardly a career. More a busman's holiday, really.'

'Just to give you the background, we're doing a major feature on the sort of creeping respectability of porn, how it's becoming more and more mainstream . . .'

'So I assume I'll be portrayed as a visionary — as opposed to a creep?'

She smiles again. 'You'll be in a sidebar looking at the difference between pornography and erotica. We've already talked to Tania Sterling.'

'I'm sure she said all there is to say. After all, it's her pet subject.'

'Yes, but she's only written one book' says Julie, polite but firm. 'You . . .' — she leafs through her notebook in search of information it doesn't contain — '. . . wrote how many on your busman's holiday?'

'I couldn't tell you off the top of my head,' I say, 'but I haven't got into double figures.'

'So,' she says, 'are you okay to do this?'

I guess I am. We go inside. Greybeard shoots another roll of film (Max relaxed, Max studious, Max brooding, Max sincerely hoping he doesn't come across as a poster boy for the dirty raincoat brigade) before heading off to another job. Julie presses record and asks me to begin at the beginning. I give a breezy, unembarrassed account, starting with Candy and embellished only by having Walter bet me that I couldn't write a publishable porn novel in eighty days.

Julie laughs in all the right places. When I finish she asks what differentiates erotica from pornography.

'A certain sickly style,' I say. 'Some pretentious navel-gazing on the theme of self-discovery and liberation from the constraints of bourgeois morality. The writer's conviction that the work has literary merit.'

'Tania reckoned you really rated *Submission*. "Completely blown away" were her exact words.'

'What else did she say?'

Julie hesitates.

'Come on, if she slagged me off, it's only fair that I have the right of reply. Besides, you might have a good old book-scene bitch-fight on your hands.'

She turns off the tape recorder. 'Her basic take is that she's creating art; you churned out jerk-off fantasies for sickos. Writing porn was a symptom of your creative decline, which she tried to help you out of but you wouldn't help yourself. She canned the relationship because she didn't want to get dragged down by your negative energy. Not that it will appear in print but she doesn't see your story having a happy ending. I was talking about it with our books editor and, for what it's worth, she thinks Tania's full of shit.'

I take Julie into the study and turn on the computer. After showing her the last modified date on my review of *Submission*, I print it off.

'Feel free to check the dates with Tania,' I say, 'but I wrote this before I met her, not after we broke up.'

twenty

BATTLE OF THE EXES
When writers who once were lovers lock horns over sex in fiction, little is left to the imagination. JULIE ASHFORD *reports.*

They made an odd couple but for a few months their relationship was the talk of the local literary scene.

After two decades as one of New Zealand literature's least homesick expatriates, Max Napier came home to a muted welcome. The author of twelve novels, including *In the Midst of Life*, *Road to Nowhere* and *The First Casualty*, he's built up a solid rather than stellar reputation. However, his recent output has left the critics noticeably underwhelmed and the former Young Turk, who recently turned 50, seems at risk of becoming the Nearly Man.

Tania Sterling, 29, is the hottest item in New

Zealand literature in more ways than one. Her debut novel, *Submission*, has reportedly sold almost 20,000 copies in less than a year, an unheard-of figure for local fiction, and is into its fourth reprint. Given the similarities between the main character and the author, this steamy story of a young woman's sexual odyssey is widely assumed to be semi-autobiographical.

Sterling hasn't exactly gone out of her way to discourage this speculation. Her interviews read like a script conference for *Sex and the City*, and she has loved and left a number of well-known men, most recently model-about-town Marcus Grey.

Whether or not Sterling really is as uninhibited as her heroine, there's no doubt she's a shrewd and energetic self-promoter.

'Right from the get-go, Tania understood that writing the book is only half the battle,' says her agent, Celia Sheridan. 'Once it's written, you've then got to sell it. Fiction's a hard sell because, as a society, we're increasingly focused on so-called reality and you can't market a novel under a convenient, unambiguous label like sport or cooking or travel.

'But the public and media need something they can get their teeth into and that pretty much has to be the author. Tania's a publisher's dream: she's beautiful, raunchy and outrageous, she understands that she's got to sell herself and she goes about it with the same single-mindedness and perfectionism that she brings to her writing.'

The two writers met last December at a publisher's Christmas party and embarked on what was, by all accounts, a passionate affair. According to a fellow writer who prefers to remain nameless, 'Whenever you saw them, they were all over each other. It was a bit much really.'

Despite Sterling's avowed preference for short, intense affairs, some observers got the impression that this was serious.

'To hear her tell it, it was Soul Mate City,' says another fixture on the literary scene. 'You got the feeling she saw herself and Max as like the first couple of NZ lit.'

But within three months it was all over. While Napier declined to discuss the circumstances of their split, Sterling is typically candid. She puts it down to them being in very different phases of their career.

'I get up in the morning, have breakfast and go to the computer,' she says. 'Once I'm at it, I resent any and every interruption or distraction. With Max, it was like he only got down to work when he'd exhausted all other possibilities.

'I wouldn't go as far as to say he was jealous of my success but he must've been uncomfortably aware that I'm much more passionate about writing and being a writer than he is. I probably reminded him of what he was like twenty years ago, which must've been a bitter-sweet thought.'

The pair haven't exchanged a word since their break-up, and things went from bad to worse this week when it emerged that in the late 1990s Napier virtually abandoned his calling to churn out pornographic novels for an American adult entertainment company.

Despite *Submission*'s X-rated content, Sterling

professes to be outraged: 'Pornography's the absolute antithesis of what I'm about. It's the polar opposite of literature.'

If she'd known about it, she 'wouldn't have had a bar of him. It's completely offensive to me, both as a woman and a serious writer.'

And even though she was 'gobsmacked' by the revelation, with the benefit of hindsight she sees 'a certain twisted logic'.

'Quite clearly Max lost confidence in himself and his work some time ago,' she says. 'I could speculate on the reasons for that but it's probably best not to. Let's just say you don't produce masterpieces with a hangover. When you're in that place, writing porn makes sense in a horrible kind of way because it's a denial of art and therefore an acknowledgement that you haven't got what it takes, in terms of talent or sensitivity or dedication, to be an artist.'

Not surprisingly, Napier sees it in less dramatic — and damning — terms. 'When I was living in Sydney, I met this American guy at a party. He was in the porn business and, after a certain amount of bourbon-fuelled banter, he bet me that I couldn't write a publishable porn novel in 80 days.

'I won the bet. He was so taken with my effort that he prevailed on me to do more. I was between projects, as they say. I wouldn't call it my finest hour but I don't propose to lock myself in the library with a revolver.'

Typically disarming, but not the whole story. Napier concealed his sideline — and the earnings it generated — from his then wife, Sydney journalist Kate O'Toole. His explanation: 'It just never seemed to be the right time.'

'I found out I was married to a sleaze,' said O'Toole from Sydney this week. 'It's an unpleasant discovery and I wouldn't wish it on any woman. What you do is immediately change the locks and call a lawyer.'

Once again, Napier declines to comment. 'Publicly airing the soiled sheets of a failed relationship is a bit like suicide bombing,' he says. 'You tend to come out of it as badly as your target.'

The manner in which Napier's secret life as a porn writer came to light is a story in itself and a sign of the changing times — changes that haven't necessarily been for the better for men of Napier's generation, products of the swinging sixties and seventies.

Napier's closest friend is Dr Chas Harley, an academic in the University of Auckland's English Department. Until a few weeks ago Harley was an associate professor; now he's a senior lecturer.

Neither Harley nor the university authorities will comment on the reasons for this apparent demotion but according to informed sources, Harley's well-earned reputation as a campus Casanova and his blithe disregard for protocols governing staff–student relationships came back to haunt him.

It's understood that last year Harley admitted to a student with whom he was having an affair that his romantic liaisons have often spilled over into his work and impacted on his professional conduct. He allegedly gave examples of instances when he'd aided and promoted his girlfriends at the expense of other students.

The student concerned, who's a party to Harley's confidentiality agreement with the university, sought advice from a campus women's group. They urged her to pass on the information to the university authorities, which she did. The loquacious Harley had also revealed his friend's adventures in the pornography trade. That information, along with details of his own murky behaviour, was leaked to this newspaper.

Napier dismisses the suggestion that he and Harley are paying the price for having failed to move with the times.

'I can't speak for Chas but I find it hard to understand why, at a time when young women happily wear T-shirts emblazoned with the legend "porn star" and porn star memoirs are practically a publishing staple, my little dabble should be regarded as beyond the pale. If there's a lesson in this it's that if you're going to do it, be upfront about it. In this age of shamelessness, to be even a little bit ambivalent is just asking for trouble.'

The whole affair raises the questions of whether pornography really is coming in from the cold, as some both inside and outside the industry believe (see accompanying story), and where exactly is the line separating pornography from the graphic treatment of sex in mainstream entertainment or high-brow art?

Sterling's *Submission* is a case in point. Although she damns pornographic fiction as 'misogynistic masturbation fantasies', a casual reader might find it difficult to spot the difference between her self-styled work of art and the dog-eared paperbacks that fill whole shelves in second-hand bookshops and whose titles (*Arlene's Anal Ordeal*) leave the browser in no doubt as to what to expect.

In both cases the female characters have an inexhaustible appetite for sex of any kind except one-on-one in private with the man they love. While *Submission* features a self-consciously literary prose style and a main character who occasionally interrupts her hectic sexual schedule to philosophise about . . . well, basically about sex, both it and the unashamedly pornographic novels sampled by this reporter left the feeling of having had far too much of a good thing.

One critic who was in no doubt that *Submission* erred on the side of pornography was Max Napier. He was commissioned to review it for this newspaper but opted out, citing his romantic involvement with the author.

While Sterling still believes Napier was 'blown away' by her book, his unpublished review, written a matter of days before their relationship began, shows nothing could be further from the truth. The answer to the question, 'So how was it for you, Max?' was, apparently, 'God-awful.'

He derides *Submission* as 'the diary of a nymphomaniac who nevertheless manages to be a crashing bore, as written by someone whose schoolteachers failed in their most basic task — they didn't strangle little Tania's literary pretensions at birth. The reader suffers the consequences of that dereliction of duty, having to wade through the interminable, stinking mangroves of one putrid sex scene after another.'

And that's one of the milder comments in what is a diatribe of spectacular viciousness.

Literary editor Trish Bradley had her own reservations about *Submission* but wouldn't have run Napier's review. 'Max got right off the leash,' she says. 'Leaving aside the harshness of the critical assessment, the commentary is way over the top and unnecessarily personal.'

So what made Napier froth at the mouth?

'I might've been guilty of overreacting to some of the absurd claims that were made on the book's behalf,' he says, 'but seeing the issue's arisen, there are a couple of points worth making. Firstly, the woman's raunchy confessional novel isn't new. Erica Jong's *Fear of Flying* with its celebration of the zipless fuck came out in 1975, and in the last year or so we've had *The Bride Stripped Bare*, *The Sexual Life of Catherine M* and *100 Strokes of the Brush before Bed*, to name but a few. Secondly, extreme subject matter doesn't necessarily make a novel daring or ground-breaking or even very interesting. It may just be a wallow in the gutter.

'There've always been dirty books for men but that hasn't been the case for women, so I can understand why there's a demand for this stuff — women have some catching up to do. I would just urge perspective. Titillation in flowery prose with interludes of mock-profound navel-gazing is still, when all's said and done, titillation.'

Love it or loathe it, there's no denying that by New Zealand standards *Submission* is already a commercial phenomenon. According to Sheridan, the book has been picked up by publishers in every major English-speaking market as well as

France, Italy and Germany. The really big news, though, is that it looks like becoming a Hollywood blockbuster.

'It's been optioned by a major Hollywood producer,' says Sheridan. 'I'm not at liberty to reveal his name but he's not one of those phonies who talk a good film but nothing ever gets made; this guy's got a track record as long as your arm. He's already teed up a top LA scriptwriter and *Submission*'s being read by a number of A-list actresses as we speak.

'If this comes off — and I'm absolutely confident it will — it'll catapult Tania into the super league. She'll be the first New Zealander to become an international brand-name author.'

For her ex-lover, however, the outlook is less promising.

According to poet, academic and critic Dr Noelene King, Napier faces a bigger challenge than living down the revelation of his porno past.

'I guess in some quarters he'll always be tarred with that brush,' she says, 'but the reality is that these days Napier doesn't really loom large enough on the New Zealand literary landscape for it to cause that much of a stir. By living overseas for as long as he did, he missed the boat when local fiction really came into its own.

'He needs to find a way of plugging into the New Zealand experience and contemporary consciousness, otherwise he's in danger of fading off the radar and ending up as one of those writers who promise more than they deliver.'

Employing both strings to his bow, he could write a male version of *Submission* but it probably wouldn't enjoy the same success.

Publishers and pornographers agree that men prefer the no-frills approach. Given the choice between erotica with a literary flourish and mass-market hard core, they'll take the porn every time.

The photograph of Tania is as contrived as a perfume advert in a glossy magazine. She's sitting outside a café wearing a black beret, tortoiseshell sunglasses, blinding lipstick, knee-high boots and a leopardskin print skirt, displaying a sophisticated amount of cleavage and lean, pale thigh. On the table in front of her are a notebook and fountain pen, a folded copy of the *Times Literary Supplement* and a book — *A Spy in the House of Love* by Anaïs Nin.

It's captioned, 'Tania Sterling: tomorrow the world?'

The photograph of me was taken before I'd put on my amused, unflappable, worldly face. I look peevish, seedy, caught in the act. Whatever that was, it was obviously very, very wrong.

It's captioned, 'Max Napier: so yesterday?'

My daughter Emily has started appearing in my dreams — as the teenager I've never seen rather than the infant I remember.

Dreams are phantom experience. Those flurries of electrical activity in the brain during the latter stages of REM sleep can make us believe anything at all. Then we wake up to discover that the experience that was real enough to scare us silly or fill us with joy or make us ejaculate was all in the unconscious mind. Dreams leave nothing behind: no bliss, no scars, no accomplishments, no memories worth clinging to.

These dreams of Emily skirt around the issue of her appearance. Sometimes her face is indistinct, sometimes she's an identikit pretty teenager. Once she looked just like Naomi Watts in *Mulholland Drive*. There have been blonde and brunette versions. It doesn't matter — who else could it be? Who else in this world would call me Dad?

They're all variations on one of two themes. There's what could be called the wishful-thinking dream in which radiant, talented daughter and proud, sheepish father are reunited. I turn up unannounced at her school prizegiving or theatrical production or the all-England horse trials. Patricia is there, revelling in Emily's distinction, so I hide in the crowd. If she spots me, she'll bundle Emily into a car and whisk her away, like a bodyguard panicking over a backfire.

Eventually Patricia goes off to have strawberries and cream with the headmistress and I seize the moment. Emily takes some convincing, firstly that I'm who I say I am and, once that's established, that she should have anything to do with me. I promise not to bug or embarrass her; she only has to say the word and I'll get back in my bottle, like an unwanted genie.

There's no soppy stuff — no tear-streaked, happy-ending money shots. My dreams don't work like that. One minute we're in a will-she-or-won't-she face-off, the next we're in a gondola in Venice and I'm pointing out the bridge where the dwarf slashed Donald Sutherland's throat at the end of *Don't Look Now*. *Res ipsa loquitur*: the thing speaks for itself.

I awoke bewildered and a little shaken from the first of these dreams. It's not that I haven't given Emily a thought these past fifteen years, but without the substance and context provided by up-to-date physical and biographical information they've never got beyond fuzzy sentimentality. I've wondered what sort of person she is, what she looks like, what her interests are; I've hoped she's happy. That far and no further. Even if Patricia has tired of painting me black, there's no reason to suppose Emily would welcome the opportunity to make up her own mind. Plus, there's probably someone who, to all intents and purposes, is her father. Assuming she's aware of my existence, I might pop into her head inconsequentially and with eccentric irregularity, like the idea of becoming a private detective or a vegetarian. When she reached ten I gave up sending her, care of friends of Patricia who'd once been friends of mine, Christmas cards and money. They all came back marked Return to Sender.

Now with each successive dream I come down to earth a little harder.

The others are more difficult to categorise. In these jump-cut narratives, Emily is an enigmatic figure, prepared to acknowledge our blood tie but otherwise detached and unforthcoming. I can be going around in futile circles but she won't intervene, even though she knows I've forgotten to pack my passport or back up my work in progress onto CDs.

Fizzing with malice and eager to fuck me up in any way they can, the women in my life make guest appearances. Emily looks on impassively, occasionally shrugging her shoulders as if to say, 'What did you expect? Forgiveness? Tenderness? *Love?*'

Last night I rendezvoused with Samantha in a restaurant, presumably in Paris. She seemed keen to pick up where we left off but coming back from the toilet I overheard her talking on her cellphone in the corridor. She was calling someone *mon cheri* and laughing about me behind my back, saying I must have a screw loose to make such a big deal of a few sympathy fucks all those years ago.

I went back to the table. Emily was sitting at the bar sipping a cocktail. She shrugged. I tried to read her expression but it kept shifting. After a while I realised she was feeling sorry for me but at the same time trying not to laugh.

Stanley answers his cellphone. He's a little tentative, which I assume means he'd like to laugh his head off but is restraining himself until he's reasonably sure I'm not suicidal. I give him the go-ahead.

'You're telling me you don't give a shit?'

'I can't change the past,' I say, 'and I can't control what people think of me so there's not much point stewing over it.'

'What about that yesterday's man stuff?'

'It's up to me to prove them wrong, isn't it? And if I can't, well, then you'd have to say they got it right.'

'Jesus, we are philosophical this morning. Did you get laid last night?'

'Not that I recall.'

'I'll take that as a maybe,' he says. 'So when are you off to Gay Paree?'

'Now seems a good time.'

'So what are you waiting for?'

'I need one more favour. Could you get your bloodhounds to track down someone else?'

'Who?'

'My daughter.'

'You've got a daughter?'

'I do.'

'Fuck, Max, you never cease to amaze me. Where's she at?'

'Last I saw her — in fact, the only time I saw her — was in London. That was fifteen years ago; she was three at the time.'

'Two birds with one stone, eh?'

Someone else said that recently. That's right, Chas, talking about the feminists narking us to the press.

'That's one way of looking at it.'

'Another way of looking at it is that you're a glutton for punishment.'

'There's an encouraging thought.'

'As you pointed out, Max, people change.'

'I hope so in her case. It'd be a bit of a let-down if she's still being pushed around in a stroller.'

'Tell you what,' he says, 'you email me the details and any useful info and I'll get the boys onto it. I've got to go now — my Eggs Benedict have arrived.'

'Sorry, bad timing.'

'No problemo. Hang on, I'm just trying to decipher what Brigit's written on her napkin; oh, she says hi and keep your chin up.'

Do you ever have that feeling of being watched? It's hard to know what to make of it. If you glance around and someone's looking at you, it's tempting to chalk one up for your sixth sense. But it might just be coincidence: you happened to look up just as the other person's gaze happened to alight on you. Because your eyes meet, their gaze lingers for a moment or two before continuing the search for someone worth looking at. On the other hand, it might appear as if no one in the vicinity is taking the slightest notice of you when in fact until a split second ago the woman in the corner pretending to do the crossword had you in her cross-hairs.

Or not. When you start thinking this way, it's a good idea to ask yourself, am I really that fascinating? If the answer's yes, then your sixth sense is neither here nor there — fascinating people get stared at. I don't have that problem but right now my sixth sense is picking up bad vibes. Either someone's giving me the heavy eye or paranoia's setting in.

I'm at the café, down the back just out of hearing range of the toilet, minding my own business, nose in the Dellasandro. I'm not fascinating but my photo is in today's paper, along with an incriminating article. If I am being stared at, it won't be with fascination or heavy-lidded desire. Kate branded me a sleaze and I imagine most readers would agree. Perhaps Chas was right and I'd better get used to being Max Napier, pervert.

The young man sitting against the opposite wall with his

back to the door doesn't look away; he's not embarrassed or intimidated by my counter-stare. It's hard to tell what he's thinking but I associate bony faces attached to necks you could snap over your knee with the persecution-complex loopiness of the bedsit.

I raise my eyebrows inquiringly. He looks down at the newspaper spread out in front of him, looks back up and raises his eyebrows. I shrug and return to Dellasandro. Chair-legs scrape on the floorboards and I register movement in my peripheral vision. It looks like he's coming over to give me a piece of his mind.

He drops a hand on the unoccupied chair. 'Well, if it isn't the one and only Max Napier.'

'I'm not in the mood.'

'You're an anti-social sod, aren't you?' he says, sitting down. 'Last time I tried to have a chinwag, you buggered off before I had a chance to introduce myself.'

Yes, he looks like one of those threadbare psychotics who hang around writers' festivals, their backpacks sagging under the weight of vast, concussive manuscripts.

'I must've been caught short.'

'You've forgotten, haven't you?' he says. 'It was right here, a couple of months ago.'

Oh, Christ, it's the wanker. 'You've had a haircut.'

'Yeah, ponytails are so yesterday, don't you think?' He grins; the makeover didn't extend to his teeth. 'Not the only thing, eh?'

'So it would seem.'

'You're also a fibber, Max — you said you'd never tried your hand at porn.'

'Well, if you've read the article, you'll understand why I kept it to myself.'

'Yeah, but didn't I tell you I was a porn freak? Shit, I would've asked for your autograph. When was the last time that happened?'

'I can't remember.'

'There you go.' He grins again, this time with such lavish warmth that I'd reciprocate if he wasn't so obviously a disturbed individual. 'So how do I get hold of your books? I can't wait to read them. Man, what a buzz, reading porn when you've met the author.'

'You can't get them here,' I say. 'They were only published in the States.'

'Bummer. Well, how about lending them to me?' He actually places his hand on his heart. 'Promise I'll return them.'

'I used to have a few copies hidden away but I think my ex-wife distributed them among our friends, to show them what a degenerate I was.'

He groans.

'Look, I'll have a hunt at home; if I've got any, they're yours. What's your name?'

'Bevan.'

'Okay, Bevan. If I find any, I'll leave them with Luciana, the manager here, you know who I mean?'

He nods.

'I'm off overseas in a couple of days so check with her at the end of the week.'

'Will you sign them? You know, to Bevan from Max Napier.'

'You bet.' I stand up. 'I'm not walking out on you, I've just go to go.'

'That's okay. How long are you away for?'

'I don't know.'

'But you're coming back, right?'

'Yeah, I'm coming back.'

'So I might see you around?'

'Well, I'm a regular here.'

He treats me to another sunny grin. 'I can't wait to tell my girlfriend I've been hanging out with Max Napier.'

'You've got a girlfriend?'

He nods shyly. 'My first. She wouldn't go out with me until I lost the ponytail.'

'Well, good luck to you both.'

'You too, dude. Keep up the good work.'

In my study there's a carton containing old notebooks and abandoned manuscripts and, I hope, at least one of my porn novels. I'll have to write a covering note explaining that Woody Bleek was my nom de porn. I hope Bevan believes me.

twenty-one

The lunch club meets at a venue of Sally's choosing, a new place in Remuera where young mothers exuding serene indifference to the world outside their antiseptic bubbles discuss birthday parties and renovations over Salade Niçoise and Italian mineral water. As they split the bill and weigh up the tip, the second sitting arrives: older women inclined to overkill in their grooming who eat and drink and gossip robustly to take their minds off creeping obsolescence and futures measured out in meandering rounds of golf and weekends at beach-houses flicking through last year's glossy magazines.

This stainless steel salon where suburban aspiration mingles with middle-aged ennui is an appropriate setting for our last lunch. Rick and Sally are moving to Sydney, joining the great relocation. Although Rick's plan was to work out his management contract and wind down to consultancy work, the people who bought his business offered him a fat package to get hands on Sydneyside.

It's rush-hour in the fast lane: Rick's already there living out of a suitcase and Sally heads over tomorrow to house-hunt. It hasn't taken her long to get used to the idea; suddenly Auckland's shortcomings are barely tolerable and to stay here would be to sell themselves short. They belong in Sydney, that sun-blinded powerhouse of energy and ambition where high achievers and style queens can revel in their success without a placatory nod to the tall-poppy syndrome.

I used to go on about Sydney but there's a limit to how long you can wish you were elsewhere. After a while the place you've left stops tugging at you and the place you're at starts growing on you. In fact, this wanderer is coming to terms with the realisation that his rambling days are done. I won't be hitting the road again. I no longer believe that a change of scene will make a difference and no longer have what it takes to go somewhere new and cobble together an existence of sorts.

What used to bug me about Auckland — mainly that it wasn't London or Paris or Sydney — doesn't bug me any more. I've adjusted to the chilly nights and the fact you can't get magret de canard or kipfler potatoes, and my friends put on as good a dinner party as the people who entertained me in those other places. There were some fine hosts among them but few took me to their hearts. I was always someone's boyfriend or husband or a friend of a friend, an extra who might or might not add value to the evening. Some found me good company, others didn't. Some found me hard to talk to; some didn't like the way I talked to their wives or girlfriends. Some probably wouldn't mind seeing me again and others would look straight through me. Very few have kept in touch and many wouldn't give me a thought from one year to the next.

Old friends don't always age as you expect them to. Some become less interesting. They might become active Rotarians or local body politicians or succumb to new-age silliness, living on green tea and seaweed and worshipping a shard of coloured crystal or believing Republicans are the new Nazis. Some stagnate. Some get bitter because they haven't become notable, as was widely predicted when they were young and tidy and overly respectful of their elders. Some let their children take over their lives. Some become bores who divert all conversation to their pet subjects. And some stay exactly the same, which doesn't necessarily work for them or you.

But old friends stay the course. They hold on to you even when you give them every reason not to. Primitives fear having their photographs taken because they believe their soul is stolen in the process. Old friends file away mental snapshots and assemble a portfolio that shows you in your best light.

Old friends understand, rationalise, make excuses, find a way to forgive. Like these two. If any other writer had been exposed as a secret pornographer they wouldn't have laughed it off. They would have blackballed him at the book club.

So I speak up for those of us who are staying put, pitting Auckland's melting-pot multiculturalism, temperate climate, uncrowded beaches and old friends against Sydney's bushfires, lethal spiders, terrorism jitters and four million strangers.

Sally seems to think this amounts to a betrayal. 'I can't believe what I'm hearing,' she shrills. 'Jesus, Max, when I think of the times I've listened to you crap on about how Sydney pisses all over Auckland . . . Well, I'm just gobsmacked.'

'Much as I like hearing it from you, Max, I have to say Sally's got a point,' says Brigit with the cool smile she's maintained from the outset. 'Have you been converted or are you just being contrary?'

'A bit of both,' I say. 'But then there was always an element of contrariness in my cheerleading for Sydney.'

'Okay, now we've established you're Mr Contrary,' says Sally, 'how about you tell us what you really think.'

'Well, put it this way, if I wanted to, there's nothing to stop me moving back to Sydney tomorrow.'

That's true, insofar as they'd allow me to enter the country.

'So we shouldn't expect a visit,' says Sally. 'I don't know how we'll cope.'

The lunch doesn't spark. God knows I've soured this sort of occasion often enough to know when I should have kept my opinions to myself or expressed them with less flamethrower intensity but I didn't spoil this one because there was nothing to spoil. All Sally wants to talk about is Sydney house prices and family stuff and why should I have to take an interest in which schools her kids will go to? Last time Brigit was rolling her eyes at Sally's salaciousness; now she's suppressing a yawn.

Privately Sally must squirm when she thinks about how she gambled with her emotional savings, perhaps to the point that if her lover had chosen his moment and pushed hard enough, she would have gone for broke. She seems to have concluded that she can't risk even pretending to be a little bit sinful. Like a dry alcoholic who can never be a social drinker, one taste and the craving would come flooding back. So she's gone good with a vengeance, making the rest of us suffer for her sins.

Her cellphone rings as we browse the dessert menu. The real estate agent has a prospective buyer who wants a private viewing. Two minutes later Sally's gone in a flurry of mild regret and fleeting embraces, rushing to catch up with her heart and mind, which have already left the country.

Brigit's in no hurry. In fact, the glass of dessert wine is her idea. So is talking about Stanley.

'I hear he bailed out your sister.'

'That was nice of him, wasn't it?'

'Is that really how you see it?'

'I'm reasonably sure.'

'Well, you know him a lot better than I do . . .'

'I don't know about that,' I say. 'You two must've clocked up a fair amount of face time by now.'

'That's more like it,' she says. 'That's the Max Napier we know and love.'

'A perfectly innocent observation.'

'As my kids would say, yeah, right. Come on, Max, you know perfectly well Stanley doesn't do anything, especially if it involves spending money, unless there's something in it for him.'

Seeing she's raised the subject and I'm leaving the country tonight . . . 'All right, you tell me: where's the angle for Stanley in sinking a million bucks into a house he can't rent out or move into?'

'Felicity owes him, which means you owe him.' She chuckles, shaking her head. 'I don't know why I'm telling you this, Max — you're the expert on the games people play. It must've taken you all of ten seconds to figure out.'

'Bear with me. Why would Stanley want to put me under an obligation?'

Breaking the habits of a lifetime, Brigit decides to finish what's on her plate. She takes her time rounding up the remnants of her tiramisu, applying her napkin to an imaginary speck of cream and having a sip of Noble Riesling followed by a mouthful of mineral water. My scrutiny draws a slow, mysterious smile.

'I'd say there are a few reasons, some of which go back to the London days, which he's always talking about. He's very fond of you, Max, but he knows you're not an uncritical admirer. Part of him quite likes that but there's another part that prefers unflagging esteem. With Stanley it all comes down to control: he likes to control relationships so they wax and wane and inevitably end according to his needs and his timetable.'

'See, I told you,' I say. 'I don't know him as well as you do.'

Brigit laughs, tossing her head back. She's particularly relaxed today — and particularly desirable. Despite the talking to I gave myself on the way here, I can't help envying Stanley his opportunity and his ruthless exploitation of it.

'Oh, Max, I doubt there's anything I could say about Stanley that would surprise you. I mean, you know perfectly well what he's up to with Felicity and you know perfectly well what he's up to with me.'

'I owe him, remember? I have to watch my step.'

'You should take it as a compliment that he sees you as the only obstacle to having his wicked way with me.'

'I didn't think we'd ever get around to having this conversation.'

'Oh, I did,' she says. 'It just took me a while to realise that I'd have to initiate it. You're taking this obligation very seriously, aren't you?'

'As far as Felicity's concerned, if it wasn't for Stanley, she and the children would be sleeping rough under Grafton Bridge. If I piss him off and he reneges on the deal and she has to sell the house, she'll blame me for the consequences — for instance, the kids deciding they'd rather live with Murray. So if you turn Stanley down, I'd appreciate it if you didn't bring my name into it.'

'You sound as if you don't care one way or the other.'

'I guess Stanley doesn't see it that way,' I say, 'otherwise he wouldn't have gone to all this trouble.'

'You must've given him a reason.'

I shrug. 'Perhaps he sensed a certain protectiveness.'

Her mouth twitches. 'Protectiveness or possessiveness?'

'It's a fine line. Sometimes it's hard to know which side you're on.'

'So what's your honest opinion?'

'On whether you should give him what he wants?'

'That is the question,' she says.

'Well, it depends.'

'On what?'

'On whether or not you're in love with him.'

'We seem to have a crossed wire,' she says with a mock frown. 'I thought we were talking about me and Stanley.'

'I'm trying to see it from your point of view. If love doesn't enter into it then we're talking about a casual sexual liaison, right? I wouldn't have thought you were in the market.'

'Really? I would've thought most people in my position — forty-something, monogamous for the best part of two decades — are either in the market or thinking about it.'

'You're not most people,' I say.

'I'll take that as a compliment but I don't see myself as being all that different.'

'If Sally's the benchmark . . .'

'Sally's a textbook case, I'm not. Alan's work set-up hasn't changed for ten years, he works reasonable hours, he's hardly ever away . . .'

'And you still love him.'

'And Sally still loves Rick. That's not the issue, Max. We're talking about married-with-kids love. No matter how hard you work at it, you end up taking it for granted — to the point where it can be a bit boring and inhibiting, like family holidays when you're sixteen. The big difference between me and Sally is that she actually went out and did it. It might cross my mind but I'm too stitched up — or responsible — to take it any further.'

Oh, the relief. 'So Stanley's wasting his time?'

'Even if I was in the market, which I'm not, he'd be wasting his time,' she says. 'He's not my type. I like Stanley, he can be a lot of fun; I like the way he's so hopelessly non-PC. I disagree with ninety per cent of what he believes, or says he believes, but I get so bored listening to people congratulating each other for having the full set of correct opinions. You don't mind going against the tide either but you're not so loud.'

'I can think of a couple of hundred million reasons why Stanley doesn't give a shit what he says or who it offends.'

'So can I, believe it or not. His saving grace is that he's funny with it. Not the most subtle humour, perhaps, but a little raucous vulgarity never hurt anyone. The other endearing thing about Stanley is that for someone who thinks he's so clever and has everyone dancing to his tune without them knowing it, he's actually quite transparent. But anyway, the fact is he doesn't do it for me. I like the creative touch, among other things. I know you think Alan's a bit of an impostor, getting so hyped up over his mobile phone ads and whatnot, but there is an element of creativity in it and he's fulfilled by it. You can say well, so what, it's just another crappy ninety-second ad that the world could easily do without and you'd have a point. But you'd also be missing a point: not everyone can be a Spielberg or a Jane Campion — or direct *Shortland Street*, for that matter.'

'Or be a novelist who promised more than he delivered?'

'You've been a writer as long as Al's been making ads, and in his detached, unstoned moments I'm sure he'd acknowledge that your books amount to more of an achievement. But he enjoys it as much as he ever did; could you honestly say that?'

'Don't believe everything you read in the newspaper,' I say, 'especially when it comes from an ex-lover with a tenuous grip on reality.'

'Is that a yes?'

'When it's going well, it's as satisfying as ever; when it's not, it's as frustrating as ever. You become more self-conscious and self-critical as you get older, so what was a good day's work when you were thirty now has you lunging for the delete button. Tania can't wait to get to her computer because she's convinced she's a genius whose next masterpiece is awaited with bated breath. By the time she's my age she'll know better.'

'Well, she certainly made it sound like you'd hit the wall,' says Brigit.

'I have hit a wall. It's not the first and it won't be the last. It goes with the territory. But I'm not about to drink myself to death — or go out and get a job writing advertising jingles.'

'The money's great if you're any good at it.'

'I believe the same applies to drug-dealing. Getting back to the matter at hand: so Stanley can pull every lever and press every button and throw money around like confetti but it won't get him anywhere?'

'As I said, I'm not in the market.' She shrugs again. 'If and when the kids leave home and Alan replaces his old battleaxe of a secretary with a twenty-year-old exhibitionist who can't spell sincerely, that may change.'

'You obviously haven't told Stanley that.'

'He hasn't asked.'

'And if he did?'

'I'd tell him, in words of two syllables or less if that's what it took.'

'Has it occurred to you that he might feel you've led him on? After all, by your own admission you've known what he was up to from the word go.'

'He doesn't know that,' she says. 'Besides, all I've done is accept a few invitations — does that qualify as leading him on? I mean, why shouldn't I meet him for a coffee? I enjoy his company; I like having him as a friend. After it's come to a head and I've knocked him back, I hope we can still be friends, although I won't be holding my breath.'

'Why not?'

'We're back to where we started: whatever Stanley does, he does for a reason. I'd like to think he quite enjoys my company but the main reason he's paid me all this attention is that he wants to sleep with me. It beats me why he's so keen on the idea — there must be plenty of gorgeous young things out there who wouldn't take much persuading to hop into Stanley Muir's bed.'

'Maybe he sees you as a challenge.'

Her eyebrows arch. 'It sounds like you have inside information.'

She obviously thinks I do, so I might as well tell her. 'Stanley's convinced every woman has her price; I put you forward as exhibit A for the defence. He wanted to put you to the test. I told him he couldn't do that, not because I was worried I'd be proved wrong but because I don't think you should make your friends pawns in a private game.'

'Hence the bail-out. I'm not sure whether to feel flattered or insulted, Max. You made me sound like Snow White. Is that how you see me?'

'No.'

'How, then?'

'I think Alan's a very lucky man.'

That earns me a gorgeous smile and a quick squeeze of the hand. 'Keep writing those novels, Max. One of these days he might forget it.'

'If I was a really good friend, I'd say I hope not.'

'You are a really good friend and you don't have to say anything. As for Stanley, I suggest we enjoy him while he lasts because he won't last long.'

'Eh?'

'Stanley's got a low boredom threshold. I get the distinct impression he's struggling to fill his days and it's only a matter of time before he starts wondering why the hell he's here instead of New York or London or the Riviera. I'll make a prediction: one day in the not-too-distant future you'll go around to his place and there'll be a For Sale sign outside. You'll knock on the door but there'll be no one home; you'll look in the window and won't see a stick of furniture. He will have packed up and gone without a word to anyone. And everything will return to normal.'

Brigit organises a cab for me. As I buckle up the driver says, 'Well, well, Mr Napier, we meet again.'

The accent takes me down terraced streets in dying northern towns. The expression in the rear-vision mirror is as bleak as an abandoned quarry. The hair colour isn't in my vocabulary. It's the Limousine communist.

'How's the revolution progressing?' I ask. 'Should I be making plans to flee the country?'

'I wouldn't leave it to the last minute if I were you. New information has come to light since I last had the dubious pleasure of having you in my car. I had you taped as a decadent bourgeois pseudo-intellectual dilettante but after what was in the paper, I had to re-categorise you. Now you're lumped in with the most parasitic, anti-social elements. Frankly, come the revolution, there'll be no place for your sort.'

'I never thought there would be. Just as a matter of interest, what qualifies you to call me a pseudo-intellectual?'

'I may be an auto-didact, Mr Napier, but I'm a very well-read one. Some of these names mightn't mean much to you: Saint-Simon, Hegel, Nietzsche, Engels . . .'

'Stalin, Mao, Pol Pot . . .'

'Not them,' he says. 'They were unsound.'

'You don't say? I take it you don't read for enjoyment or aesthetic pleasure?'

'Correct. See, everything you lot do, whether it's poetry or pornography, just serves the ruling class's purpose by distracting the masses from the real issues. I'll say one thing for your generation, though: at least you went through a phase of resisting the power structure and aligning with progressive forces before you sold out, which is more than can be said for what's come along since. Pure, unadulterated scum. Mark my words, the excesses of the Vodafone generation, as I call them, will bring about the downfall of capitalism.'

'I also take it you don't have children.'

He glares into the mirror. 'What makes you think that?'

'It might have something to do with you describing everyone under forty as pure, unadulterated scum.'

'It's not about individuals,' he snaps. 'People like you always make that error. It's about classes, societies, economic and historical forces. My kids don't come into it.'

'Don't be so touchy,' I say. 'All those commie bigwigs indulged their kids like crazy. Brezhnev's kids were the biggest party animals east of the Danube, by all accounts. So what do yours do?'

'One's a teacher, the other's an engineer.'

'Christ, what's wrong with that?'

'Did I say there was anything wrong with it? They've done all right, have my two.'

'You're proud of them?'

'Of course I bloody am.'

'Even though they don't share your political views?'

He says something under his breath and shifts in his seat.

'Sorry, I missed that.'

I get another glare via the mirror. 'What would you know about kids?'

'I've got a daughter.'

He looks over his shoulder to make sure I'm not having him on.

'You'd better add that to my file.'

'What does she think of her father writing pornography, then?'

A good question. If Emily Googled Max Napier, that would be the first item up.

'She thinks I'm a parasite.'

We pull up outside my mother's place. Without turning his head he tells me the fare's been taken care of. As I get out of the car he says, 'She'll get over it.'

twenty-two

My mother wants to cook me dinner before I fly out. I decline her offer of rump steak with baked potato and tomato and avocado salad, pleading my three-course lunch, the near-certainty of overeating on the plane and the havoc air travel can play with one's excretory routine.

This doesn't go down well. I don't recall this force-feeding urge but perhaps I took it for granted. Or perhaps it's part of her gentle regression since my father's death.

By the time her children left home, she'd jettisoned much of the conditioning that caused women of her generation to measure their self-worth by the family's reaction to the evening meal: if they wolfed it down and asked for seconds, washing up afterwards was almost a pleasure and the house-wife–mother could enter her bedroom justified. But when even her husband began to treat home like a hotel, she understandably adopted the attitude that if we didn't like it, we could lump it.

These days, though, she's eager to cook for us, as if the ritual re-connects her to the full-time mother she used to be and the home life she used to have. She has revived the extended family Sunday lunch, attendance at which is non-negotiable for our dwindling clan. These are dire occasions, since Josh and Bella make no attempt to hide the fact that they're there on sufferance. Last Sunday, when they were granted early release after repeatedly checking their text messages while picking at their meals like explorers hosted by a tribe suspected of cannibalism, I asked what the point of it was. My mother looked stricken and later I copped a verbal swatting from Felicity, who accused me, not for the first time, of rank insensitivity. I offered a trade-off: I'd be sensitive if she'd do something about her children's behaviour. She still hasn't got back to me.

The other manifestations of Mum's regression are equally harmless. She repeats herself; she listens to talkback radio and recycles gobbets of craziness as if she heard them on the BBC news; she natters about people I can't remember as if I go ballroom dancing with them once a week; she's violently pro or con television personalities and therefore a compulsive channel-hopper; she wishes she was fifty years younger.

And she has regained the sweetness that middle age threatened to squeeze out of her.

Ignoring my protestations, she prepares a sandwich platter — egg and cress, red salmon and Spanish onion, cucumber and tomato — that I couldn't do justice to even if lunch had been a packet of two-minute noodles.

'Have what you can, dear,' she says. 'You can't rely on what you'll get on the plane. There mightn't be anything you like.'

'I'm in first class, Mum. I'll be spoilt for choice.'

'You never know,' she says with the air of someone so well travelled she sleeps through clear-air turbulence and engine-out landings. 'My friend Joyce just got back from visiting her daughter in Brisbane. She said the food on the plane was an absolute disgrace.'

These last two words are broken down into their constituent syllables and spat out like fish bones.

'I bet she was on one of those budget flights where they give you a cup of water and a couple of stale Gingernuts.'

'She didn't go into details. She just said that by the time she got home she was practically fainting from hunger. Next time she's going to take her own food.'

'Can you actually do that?'

'I'm just telling you what she said.' She nudges the platter a couple of centimetres closer. 'Better to be safe than sorry.'

To divert her attention I ask if she'd like a glass of wine. The remnants of my father's stash are in the cupboard under the stairs, in among the swill brought but not consumed by cheapskate guests.

When I've opened and poured the wine and embarked on my second sandwich — I'm working on the assumption that I won't be allowed to leave until I've put away at least four and to hell with the check-in time — she returns to the subject that has exercised her since the birthday party.

'Now this girl you're going to see . . .'

'Samantha.'

'Yes. Give me the background again.'

I do as I'm told, the short-attention-span version.

'And you've been pining for her all these years?'

'I wouldn't say that, Mum. I was married for a fair few of them, remember?'

'I do remember. I also remember what happened to that marriage.'

'What about the one before that?'

'That one too,' she says, maintaining an entirely straight face. 'It's nothing to be proud of, you know. So I'm not likely to be laying an extra place at Sunday lunch?' I shake my head as if I'm limbering up for a fight. 'Just as long as there won't be one less. You are coming back, aren't you?'

'That's the plan.'

'When?'

'I'm not sure. It's a while since I was in Europe so I might as well make the most of it.'

I finish my second sandwich. At least half a minute goes by before she instructs me to help myself.

'So what, a fortnight, a month . . . ?'

'Work on a month.'

'I realise I'm an old fuddy-duddy,' she says, 'but I can't for the life of me see the point of the exercise.'

'It's a free trip to Paris. What's so mysterious about that?'

'To see this Samantha . . .'

'I'll look Samantha up for old times' sake. Chances are we'll have a drink or a meal and fill in the missing years, then go our separate ways vowing to stay in touch but not really meaning it.'

'That's one day; not even that, an evening. It's an awfully long way to go for an evening of Auld Lang Syne. And then what?'

'Well, I might check out some of the places I never got around to seeing, like Lisbon and Prague; I might pop over to London; I might stop off in New York on the way home. Think of it as a holiday.'

'A pretty pricey one, by the sound of it.'

'Mum, I know what I can and can't afford. When I've blown what's in the budget, I'll come straight home like a good little boy.'

'I can remember when you were a good little boy. It seems like another lifetime.'

She withdraws into memories from the age of innocence. I feign an interest in her magazine's cover story, an update on Hollywood anorexia.

Eventually she says, 'Well, I hope it turns out all right,' without sounding as if she'd put money on it.

'Why shouldn't it?'

'I know Paris is a beautiful city and all that and you obviously enjoyed living there but I don't have fond memories of it. That's where your father started to go downhill.'

Jesus, what? 'Go on.'

She holds up her empty glass. I fill it.

'He used to write — stories and such. That's why he spent so much time in that damn shed.' She observes my astonishment, possibly with the slightly cruel satisfaction that people often get from dropping bombshells. 'He kept it from me, too, Max; I found out purely by accident. The deputy headmaster rang up in a state one weekend. There was some sort of drama: grog, probably; this was before the boys took up marijuana. I went down to the shed but he'd gone for a walk without telling me. The desk was littered with pages covered in his handwriting and you know nosey old me. It was a story about a married teacher having an affair with a colleague's wife and for once it was perfectly true: I really couldn't put it down. In fact, I was so absorbed, I didn't hear him come back. Well, did he do his nana. I'd never seen him so worked up, banging his fist on the desk and going purple in the face. I was very silly: instead of calming him down, I got cross and made a fuss — why that particular subject and why the secrecy? Do you know what he did? He grabbed the pages, screwed them up, took them to the incinerator and set them on fire. "Happy now?" he said.

'It took him a couple of days before he could talk about it. He'd been writing on and off for a few years. Occasionally he'd get completely fed up because he couldn't get it quite right, chuck it all in the incinerator and vow never again. Writing didn't do him much good, Max. He'd shut himself away down there so he could write, then he'd get depressed because it didn't come out quite the way he wanted. God knows how much stuff he threw away. Towards the end he made me promise that after he'd gone, I'd go down there and burn everything I could find — without reading it first, needless to say.'

'Why, for Christ's sake?'

'He didn't want anyone else to read it until it was perfect and it never was. Having said that, it wasn't completely desperate. Sometimes he'd stroll in with that little smile of his and, after some prompting, admit to being rather pleased with his day's work. So he got something out of it but when you look at the other side of the ledger, it wasn't enough. Not nearly enough.' She pauses before cutting to the chase. 'Personally, I've always wondered if the real reason he didn't want anyone to see it was that they would've cottoned on pretty quickly that it was about him — what's the term?'

'Autobiographical.' I dread to think where this could end up but I feel I have to try, for both their sakes. 'Leaving aside that story, did Dad give you any reason whatsoever to think he was playing up?'

'No, but if he could keep the writing a secret, it stands to reason he could keep other things secret.'

'No, it doesn't. As you've pointed out, he was slightly batty about the writing.'

'Yes, but how could I be sure?'

'There's no such thing as absolute certainty, Mum. There's only absolute trust.'

'Of course I trusted him,' she says shakily. 'And I never, ever stopped loving him. But there was that tiny nagging doubt I couldn't put out of my mind. Believe me, I tried.' Her eyes leak and her voice cracks. 'And when I finally did manage, it was too late — I'd lost him and I couldn't get him back.'

She balls her little old hands and squeezes them into her

eye sockets. I hug her until the shaking stops and she insists she's fine.

I should let this lie but I need to know the whole story. 'What happened in Paris?'

'He was pleased when you went to live there,' she says. '"That's the place for a young writer," he used to say. He had a book, something like *The Reader's Guide to Paris*, that told you where famous writers had lived and their favourite watering-holes and whatnot. While I was shopping, he'd wander off to have a Campari where Hemingway or whoever used to drink.'

'Why didn't he say so? I would've happily gone along.'

'It was all part of the secret. And knowing your father, he probably thought you, being a real writer, would think that sort of thing was beneath you.'

I let out a groan.

'That's the way he was, Max. But it seemed to tip him off balance, going to these writers' haunts and seeing you in your apartment working away. I think that's when he started to feel as if he'd wasted his life. Bear in mind he really didn't talk about it so some of this is guesswork but I suspect he'd always had an ambition to be a writer. He really admired the fact that you'd just gone ahead and done it, ignoring the people who were telling you to get a steady job and write in your spare time. He often pointed out that you'd gone off to Europe to be a writer at practically the same age he came out from England to be a teacher. "There's my son being published all over the place," he'd say, "while I'm scribbling away in a garden shed writing stuff no one will ever read."'

'Why didn't you tell me this before?'

'Because he wouldn't have wanted me to. He'd be beside himself at the thought, God love him. And I wouldn't have if it wasn't for this Paris thing bringing it all back.' She frowns at her empty glass. 'The wine probably helped.'

I offer a refill.

'Why not?' she says. 'I only have to get myself up the stairs and I can do that on my hands and knees if need be.'

'So a few years down the track what was Dad saying about my brilliant career?'

She looks away. 'Nothing in particular that I can remember.'

'Come on, Mum. That old holy-roller Logan dropped some pretty heavy hints after the funeral.'

'Did he?' she says, flaring with indignation. 'What on earth gave him the right?'

'He sees himself as the keeper of the flame. You've got this far, Mum, you might as well finish the story. I can handle it — I've had a bit of practice lately.'

She grimaces. My porno past is one skeleton we won't be rattling. 'There was nothing specific but I think he worried about how you'd cope if it didn't quite work out for you. You always had to read between the lines with your father: he'd say something about himself and later the penny would drop that he was also talking about you.'

'For example.'

'Well, he used to say there's a lot to be said for only having to please yourself because once a book's published, it's no longer just what the author wrote, it's what other people say about it.'

'But he couldn't please himself.'

Before she can reply, the doorbell rings. That will be my driver. We're out of time. I kiss my mother goodbye and leave her to her memories and her regrets.

Stanley tosses an A4 envelope and a paperback in bookshop plastic onto my lap.

'Guess where they found your sprog.'

'Sydney.'

'Why Sydney?'

I shrug. 'It seems to be popular with middle-class English kids on their gap year.'

'She's not English, she's French.'

'What?'

'All will be explained. Have a look at the book.'

The cover is a cityscape; I'd recognise those pink terracotta walls and roof tiles anywhere. The book is *La Ville en Rose: The Toulousain Way of Life* by someone called Patricia Morville. I've heard of it, indeed briefly contemplated buying it when it came out last year, supposedly breathing fresh life into the *Year in Provence* sub-genre. I'll get to it after the Dellasandro, which I'm coldly determined to overcome before we land at Charles De Gaulle.

Stanley tells me to check out the author bio. It begins:

> Patricia Morville has been coming to the Languedoc region of France since before she could walk. In 1995 she finally surrendered to its seductive charms and moved her family (daughter Emily, black Labrador Smudge, cat Nikolai) over from London, married a local and has never looked back . . .

'I looked her up on the net,' says Stanley. 'She's shifted nearly half a million copies of the fucker.'

'Nothing surprises me any more. So I don't even have to cross the channel?'

'You don't even have to leave Paris,' he says. 'The fruit of your loins is a student at the Sorbonne. There's some photos in there.'

'I'm not opening this envelope until I'm at cruising altitude clutching a glass of champagne.'

'Suit yourself,' he says. 'No offence, Max, but are you absolutely sure she's yours?'

'You can't see a resemblance?'

'There is no fucking resemblance.'

'Now that you mention it, I've only got Patricia's word for it.'

'Did she try to screw some dough out of you?'

'Not a cent. She just wanted me to fuck off.'

'Well, that sure as hell doesn't sound like any woman I've ever heard of,' he says. 'Maybe it was all a mind-fuck.'

Stanley pulls up outside the international terminal. 'Well, mate,' he says as we shake hands, 'I hope everything works out a treat.'

'I suppose I should say the same.'

'Brigit?' He chuckles mirthlessly. 'Speaking of mind-fucks . . . I can't work the bitch out. Can you shed any light on the subject?'

'Which subject?'

'Where she's at.' He flutters his hands like a mime artist. 'Adultery-wise.'

'Remember where this all started? My view hasn't changed.'

'Ah, fuck it,' he says. 'Maybe I'll just forget the whole thing.'

I clap him on the shoulder. 'Plenty more fish in the sea, brother, and most of them are queuing up to take the bait. See you in a month or so.'

'Email me,' he says. 'I might come over. We could do a bit of a tiki-tour, like a couple of old fags on their dream holiday.'

The bloodhounds have been thorough, creepily so. Emily is studying philosophy, politics and literature; she flats with a couple of other students in the thirteenth, near the Mitterrand Library. There's an outline of her routine, right down to the cafés she frequents. There are photographs of her standing in front of a metro station fiddling with her iPod, examining a peach at a market, and getting a light from a young black guy outside a café. The thought of her being tailed and spied on at my behest makes me queasy. I remind myself about omelettes and eggs.

There's no particular resemblance but then she's a pretty eighteen-year-old with punked-up chestnut hair and retro spectacles. I can't tell how tall she is and although it's springtime in Paris she's wearing an overcoat that reaches down to her ankles. I study these photos minutely but they give up no clues as to what reaction I'll get.

Eating and drinking in moderation, I forge through the Dellasandro and make a mental note to track down Tania's review to see if she's still capable of humility. I arrive in Paris feeling faintly virtuous on account of my restraint and application and in that spirit resolve to tell the truth at all times. France opens its doors to me and I emerge into pale sunshine hoping that when I return to Charles De Gaulle Airport, I'll have something to show for my visit.

twenty-three

I'm in a third-floor apartment on Boulevard des Grands Augustins, booked through a boutique travel outfit that Brigit put me onto. It overlooks the river opposite L'Ile de la Cité, a few minutes' walk from the Sorbonne.

Who first? Unless Samantha really has been transformed, she won't be hostile or rudely dismissive but she might find my presence intrusive or discomforting. ('You call that a stalker? Listen, there's this guy I had a ships-that-pass-in-the-night thing with in the late eighties, really a glorified one-night stand. Well, last week I answered the buzzer and there he was, all the way from New Zealand, would you believe, looking at me as if to say "Now, where were we?"')

She might have a tight little circle and a comfortable routine or be in a relationship and resent having to put herself out for this fool from the end of the world. She might even be offended by my unilateral decision to disturb the memory of that interlude whose magic was largely generated by the context: no outside world, no consequences and, above all, no future.

Emily, on the other hand, should be clear-cut: she'll either give me the time of day or she won't. If it's the latter, I'm really no worse off because you can't lose something you never had. With Samantha, though, there's a risk that I'll walk away the poorer, having tarnished a treasured memory.

I'll start with Emily.

Her main daytime hangout is a café on Boulevard St Michel, near the Luxembourg Gardens. On day one I spend four hours there in three separate shifts — coffee, beer and wine. I read Patricia's book, which is an unimaginable divergence from what she used to do. Her writing, never notable for its dense muscularity, is now a sugary froth that threatens to float off the page and evaporate. Her intention, which was often unclear, is now unmistakable: she's out to make middle-class England envious.

I finish it in a tiny restaurant in St Germain where the menu hasn't changed since I last ate there almost twenty years ago. I contemplate hoofing it over to Samantha's place — she lives in the seventh, in the shadow of the Eiffel Tower — but do the sensible thing and go home to my duty-free single malt.

I'm sitting in the café on Boulevard St Michel with a brioche and the *Observer* when Emily blows in with half a dozen others. Her hair is now dirty blonde — natural or not, I can't tell — and she's mothballed the overcoat and squirmed her way into drainpipe jeans. She's Patricia's height — between short and average — but more sinuous than her mother was pre-motherhood. It's hard to get a sense of her personality because the group vibe is high-decibel animation.

She has café au lait and toasted baguette with jam. The others have cordials or tea. Their conversation is a free-for-all. They talk over and around one another, sometimes swirling off into brisk one-on-ones, in rapid-fire, looping sentences that never seem to finish. There are two males: one is coupled up, the other's keeping his options open. Four of them, including Emily, smoke; a fifth snatches the odd drag on her boyfriend's cigarette. None of them look as if they're doing university the hard way — op shop clothes, third-hand textbooks and the smell of an oily rag. What could be finer than being eighteen and a student at the Sorbonne, with Mum the bestselling author 600 kilometres due south?

I've found my daughter but I can't approach her while she's locked into this tight little crew. Apart from the difficulty and potential embarrassment of making my pitch in front of an audience of French teenagers who seem unlikely to hear me out in respectful silence, I need to be sensitive to Emily's situation. Patricia could have told her just about anything or nothing at all. She mightn't know I exist and certainly wouldn't want to find out at the same time as her friends. But if I do nothing, they'll probably leave en masse and I'll be left with the choice of coming back tomorrow or following her, with all the risks that entails.

Emily and another girl stand up, shouldering their backpacks. The others stay put. The two of them head for the door in a crossfire of *ciao*s. They brush past my table but pay me no attention. I have the bill so I leave a handful of coins and follow them out. They set off towards the university arm in arm.

I catch them up. 'Excuse me,' I say. 'Emily.'

She stares at me through her sunglasses.

'Sorry to turn up out of the blue like this but I'm Max Napier. Does that name mean anything?'

She gasps. Her friend starts chattering but Emily cuts her off.

'Max Napier,' she says, as if she's trying to get her tongue around an exotic place-name. Her accent is pure French. 'My old penfriend.'

I nod.

She tells her friend Josette to go on without her but Josette has a powerful need to know. Emily says she'll explain later. Josette looks me up and down, rehearsing the description she'll give the authorities, then goes on her way with a sulky hitch of her backpack.

'So, Mr Napier,' says Emily, 'we meet at last. It's like a line from a Victorian melodrama.'

'Would you mind very much taking off your sunglasses?'

She obliges, the corner of her mouth curling with amusement. 'I have you to thank for my baby blues.'

'But not much else.'

She shrugs. 'So am I as you imagined?'

'You're as I hoped: happy and healthy. Pretty is a bonus. How about me?'

She laughs. 'Well, you don't have these.' She puts her fists to her temples and makes horns with her index fingers. 'You don't look like a shit but I guess if you did Mama wouldn't have fallen for you in the first place.'

'I take it she hasn't let bygones be bygones?'

'I shouldn't think you cross her mind very often,' she says. 'What do they say about the best way to get revenge?'

'Living well is the best revenge?'

'*Voilá*. She has a very nice life.'

'I read her book yesterday. She's done well.'

She shrugs again. 'Yours are more to my taste.' Before I can exploit this opening she says, 'What do you want? My lecture starts in two minutes.'

'A little of your time.'

'When?'

'Whenever,' I say. 'I'm here for a week or two.'

'You came from Australia?'

'New Zealand.'

'Even further.' She puts her sunglasses back on. 'See this café? I'll meet you here at six, okay?' As she walks away she says, 'Have a nice day.' I don't think she's being ironic.

My winning streaks tend to be short-lived so I'm tempted to go for the double but Samantha's probably at work and I've got enough on my emotional plate for the time being. Instead I wander the Left Bank, guided by a fallible and sometimes duplicitous memory which ushers me down half-familiar side-streets in search of a bar or café that isn't there and never was because it's a montage of various half-remembered establishments where I once ordered felicitously or got closer to someone who mattered.

Emily turns up ten minutes late and wary, as if on reflection she thinks she made it too easy for me.

'I rang Mama,' she says.

Uh-oh. 'And?'

'I didn't tell her. She would've tried to talk me out of coming and since that would have had the opposite effect, there didn't seem much point.'

'Well, if she thinks I'm a shit, it would follow that she wouldn't want you to have anything to do with me.'

'But she has no idea what's become of you. You might be a different person, like Paul of Damascus.'

This is said with such solemnity I can't help laughing.

'What's so funny?' she demands. 'Is that the laugh of a cynic who finds it amusing that anyone should think he's capable of redemption?'

'Not at all. Actually, I distrust the Road to Damascus syndrome, the moment of epiphany from which you emerge a whole new person. It happens in cults because they surrender free will and volunteer to be whittled down to a number. True redemption comes from within and takes time. It's a work in progress.'

'Is this part of it?'

I smile but her expression doesn't soften. 'Not consciously.'

'How did you find me?'

I tell her everything, starting with Samantha. Given its role in both our histories, I've been wondering what Emily will make of that convoluted love story.

In fact it brings her to radiant life 'But this is a great romance,' she says, eyes aglow. 'Have you seen her yet?'

'No,' I say. 'I've only been here two days and I spent most of yesterday right here, waiting for you.'

'I had an assignment.'

'I wasn't complaining.'

'I want to be there when you meet her.'

'Forget it. It'll be hard enough without having my daughter, of all people, observing every awkward silence.'

'You think of me as your daughter, do you?'

'I do now. Do you mind?'

'It's not a matter of minding, it's just a big thing to absorb, meeting a stranger who's my flesh and blood. I know you're my biological father but I don't think of you in the Mama and Papa sense.'

'It'd be strange if you did. To be honest, I thought there was every chance you'd tell me to leave you alone.'

'Lucky I found out about the letters.'

'How did that happen?'

'The people you sent them to, Mama's friends, had two children, a boy my age and a girl three years older. Daniel was the first boy I kissed.'

'The first of many?'

'You'd encourage that?'

'I'd encourage you to have a basis for comparison before making a long-term choice.'

She laughs. 'I'm working on it. Anyway, the sister, Louise, wanted to know why her mother was writing Return to Sender on a letter addressed to me. She was told to mind her own business but Louise was very good at getting what she wanted from her father. He said it had to be their big secret but of course she told Daniel and Daniel told me.'

'And you took it up with Patricia?'

She nods. 'I called her a liar because she'd said you had no interest in me. We had an enormous row. But you know what mothers and daughters are like — they hiss at each other and sulk, thinking bad thoughts, but they always kiss and make up. And, besides, it's hard to hold on to someone when all you have is a little black and white photo on the back of a paperback.'

We eat at another student hangout. When we were deciding where to go, Emily asked me if I was rich.

'Phillipe, my stepfather, is rich — he has the franchise for almost thirty service stations. When he and Mama come to Paris, they always take me to expensive restaurants because that's where they want to go.' She shrugs. 'The life of a student is like the life of an athlete: it doesn't last long so you must make the most of it.'

She wants to be a journalist — and a writer. I admit to having been through a lean period and am as upbeat as possible about Project Gatsby.

'Mama says everything fell into place for her when she remembered something she was told when she started writing: stick to what you know.'

'So we can expect more books about Toulouse?'

'Well, variations on the theme.'

'*Service Stations of the Haute-Garonne*, perhaps?'

Emily scribbles on a paper napkin. 'I'll pass that on. With what — your kind regards? Best wishes? Love and kisses?'

'Whatever feels right at the time. So you are going to tell her?'

'I have to. If we're going to stay in touch, I don't want it to be behind her back.'

'I vote we do stay in touch.'

'You could email me chapters of your novel as you go and I could send back helpful comments.'

'Are you serious?'

'Of course,' she says. 'It would be very useful for me to see how a novel evolves.'

'You realise you'd have to go the distance? I mean, your feedback could become a critical part of the process so if you got bored and decided you couldn't be bothered any more, the whole thing might grind to a halt.'

'What do you think I am — a dilettante?' She lights a cigarette. 'Mama hates me smoking. She offers me all sorts of bribes to give up. What about you?'

'I think it's a little early for me to be trying to change your behaviour.'

'Actually,' she says 'I think it's a little late.'

'Well, it looks to me as if Patricia and Philippe have done a pretty good job.'

'Maybe it's a little early for you to reach such a conclusion. You should get to know me better before you pay any more compliments.'

'A very sensible suggestion,' I say, 'and that's the last compliment you're getting tonight.'

'Now the rules of our collaboration must be fair to both: you'll have to work in a disciplined manner so I know when to expect the next chapter. If I become hooked, it would be unfair to make me wait too long.'

'You've got yourself a deal.'

We shake on it.

It's 7.30 am and already humid. I'm loitering opposite Samantha's apartment building, trying not to look like a plain-clothes cop or a public nuisance.

At ten to eight she appears, the all-American beauty in her golden maturity. She's wearing a white shirt, black trousers, sneakers and sunglasses. Once her backpack is sitting comfortably, she sets off towards the river.

I cross the road on an intercept course. For a good-looking woman in the big city she doesn't have great antennae because I don't register with her until I'm within striking distance.

Before she can run, scream or kick me in the balls, I say, 'Hello, Samantha.'

Her mouth falls open and she whips off her sunglasses. A few faint lines spoke out from the corners of her eyes and her jawline is no longer geometrically defined but the rest is largely as I remember, including the transparency of her expression.

'Max? Where the fuck did you spring from?'

'The ends of the earth.' She doesn't get the reference. Why should I have expected otherwise? 'Literally. New Zealand.'

'New Zealand?' she repeats. 'You've come all the way from New Zealand?'

I nod.

'But how did you know where I live?'

I explain about Stanley and the bloodhounds.

'Let me get this straight,' she says. 'You're here to see me?'

'Well, you and one other. And Paris.'

'Jesus, I don't know what to say.'

'You could invite me to join you for coffee and a croissant.'

'I kicked that habit years ago,' she says. 'It's herbal tea and muesli these days.'

'Is that why you look exactly the same?'

'Hey, I appreciate flattery as much as the next girl but let's not go overboard. Time catches up with us all, one way or another.'

'It's barely laid a glove on you. Besides, when a man's come twenty thousand kilometres, he's permitted a little gallantry, isn't he?'

'I can't argue with that.'

We go to a health-food place where I have orange juice and fruit salad. Nine hours ago I was drinking Armagnac and smoking one of Emily's Marlboros but this has a lot going for it too.

'Okay,' she says. 'Let's fill in the missing years. You first.'

'Why me?'

'You can set the groundrules: full disclosure or the *Reader's Digest* version.'

'How will you know?'

'Believe me,' she says, 'I know a highlights package when I hear it.'

'Woman's intuition?'

She shakes her head. 'Logic, common sense and bitter-sweet experience.'

The smile seems friendly enough and the tone is light but there's a message in her still, unblinking eyes: whatever fairy-tale or sob story you might have had in mind, forget it; I'm immune.

I tell it pretty much as it was and is. She shakes her head over the porn episode and asks me what I was thinking.

'Now that's what I call cutting to the chase.'

'And what's with tracking down your daughter after all this time? Are you on some kind of life-begins-at-fifty trip?'

'Maybe I'm just getting sentimental in my middle age.'

'So how's it going?'

'So far, so good,' I say, 'but let's see what happens when the novelty wears off. At the moment we're like a couple of strangers sitting next to each other on a long-haul flight, striking up a friendship courtesy of an airline computer.'

'I always think those airplane hook-ups are the social equivalent of throwaway lighters,' she says. 'They come cheap and they don't last and there's something to be said for that. You promise to keep in touch but you never do. Around the time they start collecting the headsets, you scale it back to polite chit-chat because you know the plug's about to be pulled on what is, let's face, it, an artificial connection. Then you touch down and it's over. So over, in fact, that if you see the other party at the baggage carousel, you avoid making eye contact.'

I shrug. 'Yeah, well, maybe that's all it is — a brief, artificial connection.'

'No, Jesus, that's not what I meant,' Samantha protests. 'I was going on to say that you're not like strangers on a plane because the connection's based on a lot more than a boarding pass.' I suppose I should take her word for it but I'm not entirely convinced. 'I imagine you'll be a regular visitor from here on?'

This is a neutral inquiry rather than a wish. I shake my head. 'Assuming I'm welcome, I'll come as often as I can afford, which won't be often. I'd like to think we'll be email pals, though — me and Emily, I mean.'

'I'm on email, believe it or not.'

'Well, it'd be nice to stay in touch.'

Any moment now she's going to look at her watch and discover she's late for work. My stomach flutters with nausea, a prelude to the heartsickness of rejection.

Again, I might have read her wrong or she might have had second thoughts. Perhaps she saw vulnerability in my expression and it reminded her who she was dealing with.

'How about I tell my story?' she says with a smile that doesn't require interpretation. 'When we've got the past out of the way, we can focus on the here and now.'

She never settled back in California. The people and the things she'd missed didn't live up to the yearning she'd invested in them. Her friends were glad to have her back but couldn't get over what she'd done — as they saw it, wasted some of the best years of her life. And when it finally dawned on them that France wasn't an aberration that she'd got out of her system but an expression of her difference, they became wary, as if she'd been infected with an old-world bug that had hollowed out her American core. The greatest lifestyle in the history of mankind was on offer but she couldn't bring herself to embrace it. Perhaps that was the problem: you didn't embrace it, you succumbed to it.

Surfing was still fun but the beach scene was an illusion of permanent adolescence. The girls obsessed about their tans and the guys were only interested in the next wave. Until the sun went down and their thoughts turned to sex, which, they assumed, any girl still on the beach was up for.

The intensity of the self-obsession shocked her. There was no longer any restraint or attempt to disguise narcissism or naked ambition so that they could be excused or interpreted differently. People claimed to be spiritual and in touch with their feelings but it was just another excuse to talk about themselves. She soon learned the code: self-esteem meant breast implants; achievement meant recognition; a good time meant cocaine; love meant sex.

After two years of it, she had to get away. She got a job with the World Bank in Paris, co-ordinating policy advice for developing countries. On a visit to the Philippines she met a Swiss doctor working for Médicins Sans Frontières. Idealistic francophone Swiss was perfect: French without the superiority complex. They got married on a Mauritian beach.

'It didn't last,' she says. 'But I guess you knew that.'

I nod. 'I wouldn't have got in touch otherwise.'

'Why not?'

'It would've seemed like stirring up your existence for no real purpose.'

'That's a very all-or-nothing attitude, isn't it?'

'No, I just think that when people have got their lives on a nice, even keel they can probably do without that sort of blast from the past. Apart from anything else, who the hell wants to answer all those questions afterwards?'

'Aren't you the thoughtful one?'

'Well, up to a point. I don't imagine you spend every night eating tuna out of a can and watching old Alain Delon films on TV.'

'Oh, I've been there. I married a man who couldn't be in Paris for more than a couple of weeks without getting itchy feet.'

'What was his problem?'

'He just couldn't switch off. You know, I understood he didn't work nine to five but twenty-four seven? Basically, if he wasn't in some hell-hole saving lives, he wasn't happy, which isn't a great recipe for a chill-out vacation in the Canary Islands, let me tell you. So the field trips got longer and the breaks got shorter and, well, being a student of human behaviour, Max, I'm sure you can figure out what happened next.'

'You had an affair?'

'A serious affair.' She sighs. 'With a colleague.'

'What were you thinking?'

'Touché. Anyway, Guillaume found out . . .'

'How, as a matter of interest?'

'Same old Max: still a fiend for the gritty detail. He just knew. I'm not cut out for adultery — can't act and can't lie. Guillaume was typically noble: he forgave me and blamed himself for not being the husband I deserved. By the time he finished I felt like the lowest form of life on the planet.'

'They're ruthless bastards, these saints.'

She nods. 'Tell me about it. Then he pissed off to Darfur.'

'Where is he now?'

'Funny you should ask,' she says. 'He's in Switzerland, at his parents' place. He got sick — so sick the doctors have confined him to the First World for the foreseeable future.'

'Let me guess: he wants to kiss and make up?'

'Damn, Max, you're on a roll. I've been to see him a couple of times and, yes, the suggestion did come up.'

'And you replied . . .'

She looks at me with her head on one side as if she's not sure which version to give me. 'Well, here's this guy I thought was the love of my life but who kind of fucked me up and who I cheated on, propped up in bed looking as weak as a kitten, saying it'd be so different now because all he wants to do is work in a proper hospital and come home to me every night — oh, and by the way, he's never stopped loving me. What would you say?'

'Something along the lines of let's talk about this when you're back on your feet.'

'That's pretty much what I said. But in the meantime the proposal's on the table so I think about it — even when I don't want to.'

'Meanwhile, the colleague with whom you had a serious affair . . .'

'. . . Got posted to head office in Washington DC where, as it happens, I've just been offered a fantastic job.'

'Is it just me or has it suddenly got a little crowded in here?'

'Still glad you came, Max?'

'As I said, I didn't expect there'd be no one else in the picture. I'd have to say, though, the queue's a little longer than I'd hoped.'

'And I don't think you should expect them to be as accommodating as Serge.'

'No, I guess that would be too much to ask.'

She leans towards me, her eyes full of certainty. 'You and Emily aren't those travellers bumping elbows on a 747. That was us.'

'So how come we're still making eye contact?'

The distance between us dissolves in her slow-burning smile. 'Another time, Max; another plane.'

We arrange to have dinner. Emily never let up on meeting Samantha and in the end I gave in. For my sake as much as hers — who knows when or if I'll get another chance to introduce my daughter?

Samantha and I are at the bar waiting for our cocktails when Emily arrives. She kisses me on both cheeks and says, 'Hello, Papa.'